# TO SURRENDER TO A ROGUE

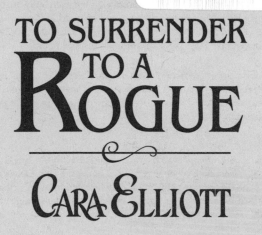

## CARA ELLIOTT

**FOREVER**

NEW YORK   BOSTON

This book is a work of fiction. Names, characters, places, and incidents are the product of the author's imagination or are used fictitiously. Any resemblance to actual events, locales, or persons, living or dead, is coincidental.

Copyright © 2010 by Andrea DaRif
Excerpt from *To Tempt a Rake* copyright © 2010 by Andrea DaRif
All rights reserved. Except as permitted under the U.S. Copyright Act of 1976, no part of this publication may be reproduced, distributed, or transmitted in any form or by any means, or stored in a database or retrieval system, without the prior written permission of the publisher.

*Cover design by Diane Luger*
*Cover art by Alan Ayers*
*Book design by Giorgetta Bell McRee*

Forever
Hachette Book Group
237 Park Avenue
New York, NY 10017
Visit our website at www.HachetteBookGroup.com.

Forever is an imprint of Grand Central Publishing. The Forever name and logo is a trademark of Hachette Book Group, Inc.

Printed in the United States of America

First Printing: June 2010

10 9 8 7 6 5 4 3 2 1

"You are a war hero, so courage comes naturally to you," stammered Alessandra. "But not to me."

Lifting her chin, Jack traced a thumb along her quivering lip. "Trust me, fear is a formidable opponent, even when one is a seasoned soldier."

"You are kind to offer such encouragement," she whispered.

"I'm not being kind, Lady Giamatti." He leaned in closer, the subtle scent of spice and neroli perfuming his nostrils "Far from it."

*Hell.* He was about to break every rule of honorable behavior.

*Hell.* He didn't care.

Not with her mouth only inches from his. Framing her face, Jack savored for a heartbeat the porcelain smoothness of her skin beneath his callused palms. And then he kissed her.

Heat flared in his belly, spiraling upward and downward and everywhere in between. She made a sound but did not pull away as he touched the swell of her breasts. The rise and fall of her chest quickened and he was acutely aware of her body, soft and pliant against his.

"Sweet Jesus," he whispered, trailing kisses along the line of her jaw. "Our excavation must have freed some deep, dark ancient enchantment from the earth. How else to explain this magic?" His tongue dipped into the hollow of her throat. "This madness..."

———————

ALSO BY CARA ELLIOTT

*To Sin with a Scoundrel*

*For Douglas, Patricia, Meghan, and Devin*
*Thanks for all the laughter and love . . .*
*not to speak of all the pinot noir and Swiss chocolate.*

# Chapter One

Y ou tied my daughter to a *tree*?"

Rendered momentarily speechless, Alessandra della Giamatti flashed a very unladylike gesture at the gentleman who stood on the edge of the terrace, stomping great clumps of wet earth from his mud-spattered boots.

"*Si grande nero diavolo*—you big, black devil!"

He stilled, and his dark face tightened in a fearsome scowl. "Damnation, it was for her own good."

"For her own good," she repeated. "*Dio Madre*, if I had a penny for every time a man said *that* to a woman, I would be richer than Croesus."

Lord James Jacquehart Pierson muttered something under his breath.

Alessandra narrowed her eyes. "I'll have you know that I am fluent in German, sir. As well as French and Russian."

"Well, it seems that your command of the English language leaves something to be desired, marchesa," he shot back. "For you don't appear to have comprehended the situation quite clearly."

Squaring his broad shoulders—which were made even broader by the fluttering capes of his oilskin cloak—he set a hand on his hip and glowered. His olive complexion and wind-whipped tangle of raven-dark hair accentuated the shadows wreathing his chiseled features. In the fading light, his eyes appeared to be carved out of coal.

*No wonder the man was known throughout London Society as 'Black Jack' Pierson.*

Alessandra did not doubt that his pose was an intentional attempt to appear intimidating. However, the man really ought to know her better by now. A delicate English rose might wilt at the first sign of masculine ire, but she was only *half* English.

As for the rest of her...

Meeting his gaze, she deliberately mimicked the gesture, adding one slight variation. As her shoulders weren't quite as impressive as his, she stuck out her bosom.

His dark lashes flicked up a fraction.

*Tit for tat, sir*, she thought.

After another long moment of silent standoff, he cleared his throat. "Would you rather I had let her follow me to the cliffs? It was pelting rain, the winds were blowing at gale force, and one misstep on the splintered rocks would have meant a sheer drop into the surging surf." His black brows angled to a taunting tilt. "But perhaps she is a Nereid," he continued, referring to the sea nymphs from ancient Roman mythology. "Or maybe her father was Neptune, god of the oceans."

Alessandra sucked in her breath at the thinly veiled barb. *Men.* Most of them seemed to prefer females who were smiling, simpering—and stupid. So it was hardly a surprise that Lord James Jacquehart Pierson should choose to mock her. A noted scholar of classical archaeology, she was used to such a reaction when the opposite sex learned of her intellectual accomplishments.

And yet it still stung.

"Heaven knows," exclaimed Jack. "It would have required divine intervention to save her from certain death had she slipped."

That he was right only added an edge to Alessandra's indignation. "She said you handled her in a *very* ungentlemanly manner."

Her daughter looked up, lips quivering and a glint of tears in her eyes. "*Si.*"

Alessandra recognized that look of assumed innocence all too well. She was aware that Isabella deserved a good scold for what had happened. But for the moment, she was too relieved at finding the little girl unharmed to do more than brush a soft kiss to her curls. A lecture would come later. Right now, all her fears were still fierce—and the fury of her pent-up emotions was directed at Black Jack Pierson.

"His hands were like ice against my bare skin, Mama," added her daughter in a small voice.

Jack sputtered in disbelief. "Is she...are you...accusing me of impropriety? You are mad—both of you!"

"*Va' all' inferno,*" piped up Isabella.

"I can't believe my ears," he muttered. "I'm being cursed by a six-year-old."

"I am *eight,*" said Isabella, lifting her little nose into the air.

Alessandra winced as her daughter added several

more phrases in Tuscan cant. "*Isabella!*" Forgetting her anger with Jack for the moment, she looked down in chagrin. "Those are *very* bad words. Wherever did you learn them?"

"Marco says them," replied her daughter.

She felt a flush steal to her cheeks, well aware that Black Jack Pierson's frown had curled into a smirk. "That does *not* mean a young lady should repeat them."

"Foul language seems to run in the family," observed Jack.

It took every ounce of self-control for Alessandra to keep a rein on her tongue. She knew she was behaving badly. After all, the man *had* kept her impetuous daughter from plunging headlong into danger, however unorthodox his methods. But something about his manner set her teeth on edge. He always appeared so steely, so stiff—as if a bayonet were stuck up his...

*I am a lady*, she reminded herself. *And a lady ought not be thinking about certain unmentionable parts of a man's anatomy.*

Even if those parts were extremely impressive. Jack's cloak had fluttered up in a gust of wind, revealing well-muscled thighs and a solid, sculpted—

Forcing her gaze away from his lordly arse, she replied, "Italians are known for their volatile temperament, especially when upset."

"Oh, please accept my abject apologies for causing you mental distress," replied Jack with scathing politeness. He bowed. "Along with my humble regrets for keeping your daughter from smashing her skull into a thousand little pieces."

"I *did* say thank you, sir."

"It must have been in a language incomprehensible to mortal man."

*Uno, duo, tre*... Alessandra made herself count to ten in Italian before gathering what was left of her dignity and lifting Isabella into her arms. "If you will excuse me, my daughter is shivering. I must take her inside and get her out of these wet clothes."

"Oh yes, by all means take the little cherub up to her room, give her a nice, warm bath..." The flash of teeth was clearly not meant to be a smile. "And then wash her mouth out with soap."

# Chapter Two

*T*he splash of brandy burned a trail of liquid fire down his throat. Perching a hip on the stone railing, Jack took another quick swallow from the bottle, hoping to wash the stale taste from his mouth.

*Va' all' inferno*, he repeated to himself. *Go to hell.*

Those were precisely his sentiments, he decided. The ungrateful lady and her imp of Satan could fall into the deepest hole in Hades for all he cared. This was not the first time he had offered his sword—metaphorically speaking, of course—to the marchesa. Only to have it thrust back in his arse.

So much for *noblesse oblige.*

To tell the truth, he wasn't feeling terribly noble at the moment. Against all reason, the thought of swords coupled with the rapier-tongued Alessandra della Giamatti was stirring an unwilling, unwanted physical reaction.

*That fine-boned face, exquisite in every ethereal detail... emerald eyes, fringed with smoky lashes that set off their inner fire...sculpted cheekbones that looked carved out of creamy white marble...a perfect nose, supremely regal in its delicate shape.*

Oh, there was no denying that the spitfire was a stunning beauty—if one could ignore the Mouth. But on second thought, that proved impossible. Jack closed his eyes for an instant, recalling the firm, full lips, the rich, rosy color, the silky, sensuous curl of its corners...

*No, he must not let his mind stray to forbidden territory.*

The marchesa's lovely body would tempt a saint. But her fiery temper would singe Satan himself.

Swearing under his breath, Jack took another gulp of brandy. Indeed, she was the most infuriating, exasperating woman he had ever encountered. There was no rational reason to explain why she seemed hell-bent on deliberately misinterpreting his every action. Save to say she simply disliked him.

"So don't get your hopes up," he growled, staring balefully at the growing bulge in his breeches.

What a pity that a penis did not possess a brain. Then it might comprehend how utterly absurd it was to imagine that the aloof marchesa would ever consent to a physical liaison, no matter that widows were allowed certain freedoms if they were discreet.

An intimate joining of flesh? Ha! They couldn't be farther apart in temperament. It was as if they came from two different planets.

*Venus and Mars.*

An apt allusion, given her expertise in classical archaeology.

Looking up at the heavens, he let his gaze linger on

the constellations. Like the ancient Greek and Roman goddesses immortalized in the stars, Alessandra della Giamatti was a force to be reckoned with. That she had a mind made for scholarship and a body made for sin was intriguing. Her aura of cool self-assurance was alluring...

However, every meeting between them seemed to spark nothing but thunder and lightning. It was ironic—had they dug into the subject of classical antiquities, they might have discovered that they shared some common ground.

Jack pursed his lips. Along with a taste for fine brandy and beautiful women, he also had a passion for the architecture and art of ancient Rome—though he kept it a private one, save from his closest friends. But given their most recent clash, it seemed impossible to imagine that they would *ever* reveal their most intimate secrets to each other.

Sliding across the cold stone, Jack leaned back against one of the decorative pediments and stared out into the night. A mizzle of moonlight cast a faint glow over the gardens and lawns, its glimmer reflected by silvery tendrils of mist rising up from the nearby sea. Above the chirping crickets, he could just make out the sound of the surf and its rhythmic rise and fall against the cliffs.

*Lud, what a day.*

As one of his gambling cronies was wont to say, no good deed goes unpunished. The only reason he had come to be at daggers drawn with Alessandra della Giamatti was on account of trying to help his best friend, Lucas Bingham, the Earl of Hadley—who was engaged to Lady Ciara Sheffield, the marchesa's closest confidante.

Well, not *precisely* engaged, amended Jack. But that was a whole other story...

He expelled a wry sigh. Hell, the next time he was tempted to play the knight in shining armor, perhaps he should think twice, rather than risk his neck trying to do something noble. Scrambling over the rocks to help rescue Lady Sheffield's young son and the marchesa's daughter from danger had been no easy feat.

Thank God the adventure had resulted in no real harm, although there had been a few harrowing moments when his friend Lucas had been compelled to take a dive into the surging sea.

The more startling plunge had been his friend's announcement that he was, once and for all, renouncing the life of a rakehell bachelor and marrying Lady Sheffield for real this time.

Out of the corner of his eye, he saw the blaze of lights in the main wing of the manor house. Laughter drifted out through the diamond-paned windows, punctuated by the faint pop of champagne corks. The impending state of matrimony had set off a great deal of merriment this evening—in no small part because Lucas's elderly uncle had also become betrothed during the day.

Striking a flint, Jack lit a cheroot and drew in a mouthful of smoke. First Haddan, then Woodbridge, now Hadley...Was he really the only single man left from the pack of rowdy scamps who had banded together at Eton? He blew out a perfect ring, and watched it dissolve in the breeze.

Shaking off his black mood, Jack took another swig of brandy, telling himself he ought to be celebrating his freedom. He was damned lucky not to be legshackled to a wife.

"Won't you come join us?"

Jack looked around as his friend Lucas took a seat beside him on the railing. "Thank you, but no," he replied after exhaling another mouthful of smoke. "I fear I would only put a damper on the festivities."

Lucas held up a bottle of champagne. "If you insist on drowning your sorrows alone, at least submerge yourself in a superb vintage of wine." He took a drink himself before passing it over.

With a wordless grunt, Jack downed a long swallow.

Tilting back his head, Lucas smiled up at the night sky. "Did you know that Dom Perignon, the monk who discovered the secret to champagne's sparkle, compared it to drinking the heavenly stars?"

"No," he replied, not bothering to glance up. "Only a man besotted by romance would know such drivel."

"My, my, aren't we in a prickly mood," remarked his friend. "Any specific reason?"

Jack remained silent for a moment as the effervescence of the wine danced like tiny daggers against his tongue. Then, instead of answering, he asked abruptly, "Is Lady Giamatti celebrating with you?"

"No, like you, she cried off," replied Lucas slowly. "She claimed to be exhausted from all the excitement."

"Hmmph."

"She plans to leave for London at first light," added his friend.

"As do I. So if you don't mind, I think I'll retire for the night." Jack rose and ground the butt of his cheroot beneath his boot. "And take the bottle with me for company— seeing as there are no willing wenches to warm my bed."

"Ciara sends her thanks for all your help this afternoon," said Lucas, ignoring the comment. He allowed a brief pause. "She also said to ask you not to judge Lady Giamatti too harshly. They are the best of friends, and yet she has a feeling that there is something troubling the marchesa of late. Something the lady dares not discuss with even her closest confidantes."

"Assure your future bride that she need not worry over my opinion—I have none to speak of," snapped Jack. "The marchesa and her mysteries are no concern of mine."

"Ah," murmured Lucas. "And here I thought that I had detected a glimmer of interest in your eye."

"You must have been looking through the prism of your own lovestruck gaze," muttered Jack. "Not all of us have been struck blind to reason by Cupid's damn arrow." As he turned for the terrace doors, he hesitated. "But the needling aside, I wish you happy, Lucas."

A swirl of wind ruffled through the ivy leaves, nearly drowning out his friend's reply.

"The same to you, Jack."

He marched across the slate tiles, but as his hand touched the latch, he abruptly veered away, choosing instead to descend the side steps and take the long way around to the guest quarters. Perhaps a vigorous walk would shake off his dark mood.

*Damn.* He wasn't usually so snarly with a friend.

Lifting the bottle to his lips, Jack quaffed the rest of its content in one long gulp. There—that ought to loosen his mood, he thought grimly, tugging at the knot of his cravat. The crunch of gravel underfoot echoed the *clink* of glass against the stones. Hopefully, Sir Henry would forgive him for the lapse of manners in littering his lovely grounds. He rounded a privet hedge and stumbled past the garden statues...

One of the sculpted shapes appeared to move.

Jack stopped short. Surely the wine could not have gone to his head quite so quickly.

"You need not give me that basilisk stare, sir," said the stone.

*Of all the cursed luck.* It was not a figment of his foxed imagination but Alessandra della Giamatti in the flesh.

"Lucas said you had retired for the night," he blurted out, then immediately regretted making any response.

"I decided to come outside for a breath of fresh air before seeking my bed." Her hair was unpinned and fell in soft, shimmering ebony waves over her shoulders as she stepped out from the shadows of a laughing faun. "Or is there some arcane Anglo-Saxon rule that prohibits a lady from enjoying a solitary stroll after dark?"

Her words recalled an earlier clash. "Will you never cease snapping at me for having tried to do the honorable thing, marchesa?" demanded Jack. "I have already admitted that my interference in the arcade was a mistake. How many times must I offer an apology?"

A week ago in London he had stepped in to defend her from the advances of an aggressive male. Unfortunately, the fellow in question turned out to be her cousin.

"Not that I feel I was entirely in the wrong," he couldn't help adding. "An English gentleman does not allow another male to continue haranguing a lady, especially after she has asked him to leave her alone. Code of honor, you see."

Her jaw tightened. "It was a private discussion, sir."

"Then you should not have conducted it in public," replied Jack.

Alessandra drew in a sharp breath. "That is the trouble

with you Englishmen—you have such a rigid notion of honor."

"You would prefer that we act as cads?" His temper, which was dangerously frayed to begin with, suddenly snapped. "Very well."

Two quick strides covered the distance between them.

Her lips parted in shock, but before she could make a sound, his mouth crushed down upon hers.

For an instant Alessandra was too shocked to react. And then...

And then, though every brain cell was shouting at her to thrust him away, she found herself loath to listen. The taste of his mouth was intoxicating—the sweetness of the wine, the salt of the nearby sea, the smoky spice of masculine desire. Drinking it all in, she lay utterly limp in his arms, her senses overwhelmed with the different sensations.

In contrast to the searing heat of his kiss, his skin was cool and damp from the night mists. The stubbling of whiskers on his jaw prickled against her flesh, while his hair was surprisingly silky beneath her fingertips—

*Oh, Lud, were her hands really twining through the tangle of his sin-black hair?*

Alessandra choked back a moan. She had nearly forgotten how good it was to feel chiseled muscle and whipcord sinew hard against her body. The sloping stretch of Jack's shoulders—so strong, so solid—seemed to go on forever, enveloping her in a musky warmth.

A tower of strength.

*No, no, no.* What weak-willed delusion had taken hold of her? She could not be so stupid as to trust in the illusion of steadfast support. *A man to lean on?* She had been needy enough after her husband's death to reach for comfort. Only a fool made the same mistake twice.

She inhaled to protest, only to find that the earthy scent of him made her a little dizzy. Sandalwood and tobacco mixed with a dark spice that she could not quite define. Her knees buckled.

*Diavolo*—every bone in her body was suddenly soft as spaghetti.

Tightening his hold, Jack braced her against one of the decorative columns that flanked the pathway.

The initial explosion of male anger had burned down to a gentler heat. His touch left a trail of warmth along her night-chilled flesh.

Alessandra was woozily aware of his hands cupping the curves of her derriere. He pressed closer and she felt her nipples turn to points of fire as his chest slid slowly over the peaked flesh. She found the opening of his coat, her fingertips sliding over the soft linen.

He was so big, and so...utterly masculine, from the darkly dangerous name—*Black Jack*—to the broad chest, tapered waist, and muscular legs.

*Desire.* Like a serpent, it slowly uncoiled and slithered up from its place of hiding. With a liquid sigh, she opened herself to Jack's embrace, twining her tongue with his. With a rumbled groan, he thrust in deeper, filling her with his hot, hungry need.

Her pulse was now pounding out of control, but somehow, above the din in her ears, she heard the voice of Reason.

*Dangerous.*

As his mouth broke away to trail a line of lapping kisses along her throat, she finally got hold of her senses and shoved him back a fraction. Now was the moment for a scathing setdown, but strangely enough, as she searched her brain for something to say, her mind was a complete blank.

He, too, appeared paralyzed with shock. His dark lashes lay still against his olive skin, and aside from the harsh rasp of his breathing, he might have been carved out of stone. Sharpened by the slanting moonlight, the strong, sculpted lines of his face gave him the appearance of a Roman god.

Mars—the mighty, mythical warrior.

The only flaw was a tiny scar cutting just beneath his left eyebrow, a faint line nearly hidden by ravenwing arch. *A chink in his lordly armor?* She felt an impulsive urge to trace it with her fingertip, and then touch it with her tongue...

A swirl of breeze tugged at the tails of his cravat, and the flutter of white finally dispelled her momentary surrender of sanity.

Twisting free of his hold, Alessandra clutched at her cloak, drawing the folds in tight to cover her nightrail.

"That was unforgivable," he said softly. "I...I don't know what came over me—"

Mortified by her own actions—and reactions—she cut off his halting apology. "Or me. Save to say that the full moon is said to stir a certain madness."

How else to explain the elemental force that had drawn them together? Without waiting for a reply, Alessandra plunged into the pooling shadows, her slippered feet nearly tripping over the uneven ground in her haste to get away.

*As if she could outrun her embarrassment.*

To her relief, Black Jack Pierson made no move to follow her.

Plagued by fitful dreams, Alessandra rose early and hurried through the final packing for the journey back to Town.

*Slap.* A corset landed atop a pair of half boots. *Thump.* A book hit against her set of silver brushes. Snapping her portmanteau shut, she quickly turned away from the dressing table, eyes averted from the looking glass. She had already glimpsed the two hot spots of color on her cheeks, and needed no further reminder of her moment of midnight madness.

*For someone who prided herself on being intelligent, she certainly hadn't been very smart.* In the light of day, her behavior seemed even more incomprehensible. She didn't usually make such egregious mistakes in judgment. Except when it came to men.

"I think we are ready, Lucrezia." As far as she was concerned, they couldn't leave Sir Henry's estate quickly enough.

As her maid went off to fetch the footmen to carry down the trunks, Alessandra gathered her shawl and called her daughter to the staircase.

"Isabella, do not slide down—"

*Too late.*

The little girl was already whizzing down the curved length of polished oak. A peal of delighted laughter was followed by a loud thump.

"You are a menace to Society, child." An all-too-familiar voice rose up from the floor below.

Alessandra hurried down the stairs to find Black

Jack Pierson gingerly setting Isabella on her feet.

He looked up and for an instant she felt a frisson of heat curl in her belly. His dark eyes were the color of liquid chocolate, reminding her of how she had melted in his arms just hours ago. As their gazes met, he, too, appeared to be thinking of their midnight encounter. A wink of gold seemed to spark on the tips of his lashes, his expression hovering between embarrassment and...

Isabella's aggrieved voice broke the tentative connection. "You need not have caught me, sir," she complained, primly smoothing her skirts.

"No?" growled Jack. "If I had not, you would have flown straight into that suit of armor."

"You think so?" she asked hopefully. "Perry and I have a bet as to who can land farthest from the newel post. I would have won by a mile." Her face pinched into a scowl. "That is, if *you* hadn't stopped me."

Jack looked back up at Alessandra and grimaced. "I see you have no more control over your daughter's limbs than you do her language. I was under the impression that Italy was a civilized place, not a haven of hot-tempered hellions and hoydens."

*How unfair of the man to imply that she was wholly to blame for what had happened last night.* "That's rather the pot calling the kettle black," she retorted.

"I..." Looking a little uncomfortable, he slanted a glance at Isabella. "If anything about my recent behavior has struck you as less than gentlemanly, I am sorry for it."

"Oh, yes, I am sure you are, because Lord James Jacquehart Pierson is always the *perfect* gentleman."

"I try to be," he replied, his unfriendly tone implying the exact opposite.

Nettled by his scorn—and her own lingering sense of guilt—Alessandra reacted with deliberate rudeness. "Well, be advised that your manners leave much to be desired, sir."

He had the grace to flush. "That is only because I have been provoked by two of the most hellfire females in all of Christendom." Retrieving his hat from the carpet, he jammed it on his head. "Good day to you, ladies. Allow me to take my leave before I am subjected to any further assaults—be they verbal or physical."

"Arrogant oaf," whispered Alessandra, torn between feeling outraged and embarrassed as Jack turned away and stalked across the entrance hall. The thud of his steps was quickly echoed by the slam of the front door.

"What's an oaf, Mama?" asked Isabella.

She swallowed a sigh. "Never mind, *tesoro*." She wanted to resent Jack's criticism, but honesty compelled her to admit that his criticisms had been deserved. Looking back on their encounter of the previous evening, she was not proud of herself. Or her daughter.

"Come, our carriage is waiting," she said after putting several items from the side table into her travel valise.

"What are those?" asked Isabella.

"Primers on proper manners for young ladies." Alessandra added another book. "As well as a lexicon of English words that are allowed to be said in Polite Society."

"I liked it better in Italy," said Isabella. "There weren't so many rules there, especially when Papa was alive." Her lips quivered as she stared at the leatherbound spines. "Can't we go home?"

"England is our home now," said Alessandra, taking great

care to hide her anguish over her daughter's unhappiness. Oh, Lud, she missed Stefano, too—his wisdom, his wit, his warmth. He had been a solid, steadying force in her life. Since his death, she had felt a little like a child herself, naïve to the ways of the world.

Tightening her fingers around Isabella's hand, she added, "So we must make the best of it."

"Why?"

*A simple question, but how to answer?*

"Because..." She crouched down and smoothed the silky curls from Isabella's brow. "Because, *tesoro*, there is no going back. We must look to the future, not to the past."

A strange sentiment, given her expertise in ancient archaeology. But some things were best left buried.

"Let us have no long faces," she went on with forced cheerfulness. "Think of all the new and interesting things you are learning in England. You have started drawing lessons, you have toured the Tower of London, you have mastered the sport of cricket..."

Isabella's face brightened considerably at the mention of cricket. "Lord Hadley says he will give me and Perry boxing lessons when he returns from his wedding trip."

"There, you see." Alessandra smiled. "In Italy, little girls are not taught to fight with their fists."

"I like Lord Hadley," said Isabella decisively. "He is *much* nicer than his friend."

"Most gentlemen of the *ton* are not as comfortable with children as Lord Hadley," she replied.

Isabella scrunched her face into another scowl. "Hadley never called me an imp of Satan, not even when I hit him smack in the chest with a cricket ball and knocked him on his bum."

"Perhaps that is because you never called Hadley a pox-faced son of a shriveled sow," pointed out Alessandra. She frowned in consternation. Her own language was certainly not above reproach, but she did take care of what she said when her daughter was within hearing. "Lud, wherever do you pick up such horrible language?"

"I told you—from Marco," replied Isabella with a shameless smile. "He knows an awful lot of colorful curses. Even Perry is impressed. There is one about a squint-eyed slut—"

"That's quite enough," said Alessandra sharply, making a mental note to tell her cousin to watch his tongue around the children. "Thank goodness we have a great many hours of traveling ahead of us. Because, young lady, we have a great many lessons to learn about how to behave in English Society."

"*Merde.*" Isabella's chin took on a mulish jut. "Perry says that is French for sh—"

Alessandra quickly clamped her hand over her daughter's mouth. Much as she hated to admit it, perhaps Black Jack Pierson was right and her daughter's mouth needed a good rinsing with soap.

"I know *exactly* what it means," she snapped. "One more vulgar word out of you, and you will be blowing soap bubbles all the way to London."

A tear trickled down Isabella's cheek. "I *hate* London."

"Then you will be pleased to hear we are only staying there for a short while before heading on to Bath."

On that note, they took their leave.

# Chapter Three

*H*ave you been by Harley Street to see Mr. Turner's latest exhibit of paintings, Lord James?" Herr Gerhard Lutz added another bit of pigment to his paint palette and added several drops of water.

Jack shook his head. "I have not yet had the chance. I returned to Town only yesterday evening."

"Consider it one of your assignments to prepare for our next lesson," said the drawing master. In addition to his classes at the Royal Academy, Lutz gave private lessons to a few select students at his studio. Jack was one of them, though at times like the present, he wasn't sure whether it was on account of his talent or his family's title. His current work in progress looked stiff and clumsy to his eye, as if he had drawn it with his left foot.

"His latest work illustrates a new school of thought, a new way of looking at nature," continued Lutz.

Jack pursed his lips. "Are you hinting that I am merely a draftsman, clinging to the style of the past century?"

The remark drew a faint smile from the normally taciturn Swiss. "Not at all. You show great promise and are willing to try new things, else I should not have consented to take you on as a pupil. However, along with developing your drawing skills, I should like to see your work become more..." Lutz seemed to be searching for the right word. "Expressive," he finally said.

"Expressive." Jack maintained a stoic face. "Perhaps it is because of my military training, but I find that does not come naturally to me. We have it drummed into our heads that soldiers must be regimented in their thinking and their actions."

"*Ja.* The point is, you must stop thinking like a soldier and start acting like an artist."

"Hmmm." Jack squinted thoughtfully at the paper.

"The best art elicits some feeling, some emotion from the viewer. Loosen your lines. Don't be afraid to experiment with color." Lutz rinsed out the sable bristles of his brush and shrugged. "I can teach you things like proportion and perspective, but as to your own individual style—well, you will have to learn that on your own."

At first blush, art and soldiering didn't appear to have much in common, thought Jack. But both certainly tested one's mettle. It took courage to conquer fear—whether physical or mental—and march forward when one didn't quite know what lay ahead.

"A good example is Alexander Cozens, whose work you must know. Sir George Beaumont has an excellent collection of the artist's later sketches, and you ought to ask him if you might view them," continued Lutz. "You will learn a valuable lesson on giving your imagination a freer hand."

*A freer hand.*

After studying the rough pencil sketch from his travel notebook for another few moments, Jack tacked a fresh piece of paper to his drawing board and started a new watercolor interpretation. *A wash of pink for the sky, highlighted by a more daring shade of vermilion at the horizon...*

Absorbed in his work, Jack didn't hear the clock chime, indicating the end of the lesson.

"Lord James." Lutz looked up from sorting through his supply chest. "Much as I hate to interrupt, I have a class to teach at Somerset House." He regarded the unfinished painting. "Better, better," he murmured. "Practice your crosshatching exercises for our next session. And be sure to visit Mr. Turner's gallery."

"I will," replied Jack. After packing up his paint box, he propped the unfinished painting on one of the studio's easels. "Lud, it still looks all wrong," he said under his breath.

"Patience, milord. The Muse is like a beautiful but temperamental woman. You must court her carefully and prove yourself through hard work and constancy. She can't be won with false flatteries or overpowering advances."

*Bloody hell.* Given his recent encounters with the opposite sex, he might have to give up art for a position of sweeping horse dung from the streets of London.

Due to their depleted ranks, the Circle of Scientific Sibyls decided to end their regular weekly meeting a touch early.

"I think we should wait for our two friends to return to Town before drafting a rebuttal to Huntford's chemistry article," suggested Kate Woodbridge. "When we are at full force, the dons of Oxford can't stand up to our reasoning."

*Kate had a point*, thought Alessandra. The Circle—a group of five intellectually gifted females who had banded together for regular discussions on science—had compiled a rather impressive record of scholarly achievements in the time they had been together. But even more importantly, they had formed a close bond of friendship, despite their very different backgrounds.

Alessandra quirked a faint smile. As Society did not approve of ladies who pursued intellectual endeavors, the five of them had coined a more humorous informal name for their group—the Circle of Sin. And without the moral support of her fellow 'Sinners,' her life in London over the last two years would have been even more difficult.

"I agree." Lady Charlotte Fenimore scribbled a notation in the margin of her notebook. "We should definitely wait until Ciara returns from her wedding trip. And Ariel, too, of course, even though chemistry is her weakest subject."

Charlotte's sister, a spry sixty-five-year-old former spinster, had also recently been married and was currently enjoying an interlude in the country at her new husband's estate.

"That is the last item on the agenda," she finished. "Unless anyone wishes to raise a new topic."

"No, let's ring for tea," said Kate Woodbridge, quickly packing away her papers. "I'm famished."

"You are *always* famished." Alessandra regarded her friend's wraith-like figure and rolled her eyes. "Really, how is it that you can eat platters of pastries and never gain an ounce? It is very unfair."

"Perhaps we should make it our next research topic," replied Kate with a grin.

As the tea tray arrived, Alessandra took a moment to muse on her two companions. At age sixty-seven, Charlotte was hobbled by bad knees, but her mind had not lost a step. A widow with a tartly cynical outlook on life, she and her sister Ariel could always be counted on to share their hard-won worldly wisdom with the three younger 'Sinners.'

"Oh, good. Lemon custard tarts are my favorite!" While Charlotte was the oldest of the group, Kate was, at age twenty-two, the youngest. And most rebellious—at least outwardly. The daughter of a highborn English lady and a rakish American sea captain, she had spent much of her life sailing around the world. In the course of her travels, she had acquired an expertise in botany—along with a few more questionable talents...

"I had better forgo sweets today," said Charlotte as she sipped her tea. "I fear my gowns are growing uncomfortably tight." She paused. "Do you think it possible that Indian silk is subject to spontaneous shrinkage?"

"Doubtful," said Alessandra. "But we could add the question to our list of future experiments to try when Ciara and Ariel return to Town."

Kate curled an impish grin before popping a morsel of shortbread into her mouth. "Speaking of which, how long will you be away in Bath?" she asked.

"A month, maybe two, for this first phase of the excavation," replied Alessandra absently, her mind more on the note she had received that morning from her cousin Marco than on archaeology. His news had been very disturbing...

"Is something troubling you, my dear?" asked Charlotte. "You've seemed distracted all morning."

"N-no." Alessandra shook her head. "That is, Isabella has been in a difficult mood for the last little while—she misses Peregrine." Ciara's son was her daughter's best friend. "And Italy."

"Why not consider a visit to your old home? You, too, must miss your friends and your lands," suggested Kate.

"I have too many archaeological commitments at present," she said evasively. None of the 'Sinners' knew the real reason she had left Italy. Some secrets were too dark to share, even with her closest friends. "Perhaps sometime in the future."

"Life is too short to keep putting off the things that matter," persisted Kate with her usual bluntness. "Besides, you've been working too hard—I can't help but notice that you have lost several pounds over the last few weeks." She broke off another bit of shortbread. "And there are dark circles under your eyes."

"Helping Ciara to defend herself against the Sheffield family while we were away in Scotland must have been a very daunting task," murmured Charlotte. "Imagine how frightening it would be to face the accusation of murder."

As Kate choked on her crumbs, Alessandra felt the blood drain from her face.

"Actually, I'd rather not," quipped Kate, once she had recovered her voice. "In any case, we may all rest easy now that Ciara no longer faces any such threat." However, her expression remained strangely pinched and she pushed her plate away without finishing the pastry. "Getting back to the question of your work commitments, I think you should definitely consider begging off from the project in Bath. Take Isabella to Lake Como for the summer instead."

"It would be unprofessional to withdraw from the dig at the last moment," replied Alessandra. "We can't let it be said that female scholars are too fickle to entrust with real responsibilities."

Kate made a face, but Charlotte nodded in agreement.

Relieved that the argument had been nipped in the bud, Alessandra quickly changed the subject. "By the by, whose turn is it to take the Little Red Book?"

Along with their individual efforts of scholarly research, the 'Sinners' were working on a special joint project. Its official title was "The Immutable Laws of Male Logic—A Scientific Study Based on Empirical Observations." It was Charlotte who had given it the more informal name of "Men—An Essential Compendium to Managing the Brutes." They each took turns adding a chapter to the humorous *magnum opus*.

But of late, the book had been sadly neglected.

"I'll take it," said Kate. "I could use an amusing diversion to keep me busy while the Circle is stretched thin." She tapped a finger to the crimson leather cover. "Speaking of men, Alessandra, I could not help but notice that Hadley's dark-haired friend was watching you for much of the wedding breakfast. I think he is interested in you."

"Oh, yes—interested in how many ways he could devise to slice out my tongue," replied Alessandra tartly. "You are usually quite observant, but this time you have overlooked the obvious. Lord James Jacquehart Pierson does not like me. And the feeling is mutual."

"Why?" pressed Kate.

"I know why." Charlotte slanted a look at Alessandra. "You and Lord James exchanged words when you thought he was harassing Ciara." She coughed. "Very bad words, if I remember correctly."

Alessandra bit her lip. True, she had called him a number of very offensive names in Tuscan slang. Unfortunately, Black Jack Pierson spoke fluent Italian.

"However, first impressions can be misleading," continued Charlotte. "He turned out to be quite the hero in helping rescue the children."

*Tap. Tap. Tap.* Kate continued to drum on the Little Red Book. "In my experience, if a man truly dislikes a woman, he will ignore her. And vice versa. Anger sometimes indicates some other emotion."

"What an interesting observation. I suggest you add it to the book." Suddenly aghast at her waspish tone, Alessandra expelled a harried sigh. "I'm so sorry, Kate—my nerves are a little on edge today."

"I did not mean to tease you," replied her friend. "I simply meant that Black Jack Pierson might be more interesting than you think." She paused. "With those broad shoulders and brooding dark eyes, he looks like he's stepped straight from the pages of Lord Byron's romantic poems."

Alessandra reached for her reticule. "Romance is the *last* thing I need in my life."

Jack narrowed his gaze, focusing on the color of scudding squall clouds just visible above the treetops. They were not a plain lead gray, he decided, but a far more subtle shade that mixed a range of smoky blues with a touch of violet. Maybe even a hint of plum—

"Need spectacles, Lord James?" Lord Garrett Howe, an occasional companion in midnight rambles through the gaming hells of St. Giles, fell in step beside him. "Your shots seemed accurate enough at Manton's last week. I lost ten bloody guineas to you."

"Thought I saw a hawk," muttered Jack, unwilling to explain himself.

"You ought to be ogling the plumage on *terra firma*." His friend nudged him in the ribs. "That's a very lovely bird up ahead, eh? Apparently she doesn't fly around much in Society."

Jack spotted a flutter of indigo silk.

"But Gervin and I saw her in Bond Street yesterday and he tells me that she's a widow," continued Howe. "*Ergo*, she's fair game." A wink punctuated his lascivious leer. "She may not spread her wings in public, but perhaps I can convince her to spread her legs in private."

They walked on for a few more strides as Howe let out a slow hiss of breath. "Ye gods, just look at the way the skirt slides across that shapely arse. The sight is hypnotic." Another sigh. Or more precisely, a wolfish pant. "In fact, I think I'm fast forgetting that I am a gentleman."

*So am I*, thought Jack, as the lady in question slowed her steps on the path and turned in profile to untangle the fringe of her shawl.

For an instant he was tempted to grab his friend's throat and punch out his teeth. But reason prevailed and Jack shoved his hands in his coat pockets. "Then let me remind you of something that Gervin must have forgotten to mention. That is not some ladybird-for-hire up ahead. Rather it is the Marchesa della Giamatti, who is not only a paragon of propriety, but is also the closest friend of Hadley's new bride."

Howe's grin faded to a frown. "Since when have you become such a pompous prig? I wasn't about to toss up the lady's skirts in the middle of Green Park. I was merely expressing my admiration for her physical charms." He shot another glance at Alessandra. "You can't deny that the lady is an absolute stunner."

"No, I cannot," replied Jack through gritted teeth.

"Hell, I can't help it—she's got my whirligigs aflutter," said Howe. Giving a lewd hitch to his trousers, his friend added, "Perhaps that's why you are acting as ill-tempered as a bull with a gelding iron clamped to his pego. You tried your luck with the lady and she wouldn't have any part of you."

His fists flashed out of his pocket. "Damnation, Howe, unless you want your beak bloodied, you had better refrain from further crude comments about the lady."

"Satan's prick, you're in a devil of a mood." Looking offended, Howe abruptly reversed direction and stomped off.

Jack unclenched his fingers, unconsciously smoothing the soft leather of his gloves over his knuckles as he watched his friend's retreating rump. Not that there was anything remotely alluring about Howe's stiff-legged gait. It radiated aggrieved male anger. He winced, suddenly feeling foolish for reacting so churlishly over a bit of rakish chatter. Howe would, he hoped, accept an apology at their next meeting.

In the meantime...

His gaze slid back to Alessandra, who had finished unknotting her shawl and was now heading across the lawn.

*Time to beat a strategic retreat.*

Jack hesitated for a fraction before ignoring the voice in his head and quickening his pace to follow.

Falling in step a discreet distance behind her, he had an excellent view of Alessandra's figure. Howe was right—she moved with a sinuous grace, her hips swaying gently from side to side, as if tickled by some tropical breeze. It was subtle. Sensual. *Sexy.*

He felt the inside of his mouth go a little dry.

*Discipline*, he reminded himself. He ought not be imagining the contours of her curves, or the exact hue of her creamy skin. It was wicked to wonder how her thighs would look stretched out on a rumpled sheet of satin. And it was most definitely dishonorable to fantasize about the feel of her flesh against his palms. He was willing to wager a fortune that she would be firm, yet sweetly yielding. Like a perfectly ripe peach.

*Diavolo.* Now his mouth was watering.

Hell, it was depraved to be creeping after a lady, in order to undress her with his mind's eye. He was, after all, enjoying a very pleasant arrangement with a buxom blonde at Cupid's Cave. So it wasn't as if he was starved for the sight of a naked female.

A shiver of self-disgust slithered down his spine. Why couldn't he banish such bad, bewitching images from his brain?

Lud, he was trying. But she was a torment. *A temptation.*

Thank God the marchesa would never, ever guess the wayward direction of his thoughts.

Bedeviled by his inner demons, Jack didn't see the turn in the path until he stumbled on a patch of loose gravel. At the crunch of stones, Alessandra stopped abruptly and turned to see who was behind her.

As their eyes met, Jack realized his expression must be pinched in a black-as-hell scowl.

She froze him with an arctic stare. *Emerald ice.* Glittering like shards of frozen gemstones.

They stood face-to-face for a split second longer. Then Alessandra turned and walked on without a second look.

# Chapter Four

*E*xcellent essay, Lord James." Lord Fanning, head of the Architecture Committee of the Julius Caesar Society, took a moment to polish his spectacles on his sleeve. "And the accompanying sketches are first rate, sir. First rate!"

"Thank you," replied Jack.

"Might I keep them to show to Mr. Sprague?"

"If you wish."

"I am sure he will be delighted to discover we have a new member with such impressive artistic skills. Have you a portfolio of drawings from your trip to Italy, sir?"

Though he was usually reluctant to reveal his interest in art, the praise from a knowledgeable scholar loosened Jack's reserve. "Several, in fact. Including a number of larger studies done in watercolors."

Lord Fanning cleared his voice with a discreet cough. "Might we persuade you to put them on exhibit here in our gallery during Professor McNulty's visit from Edinburgh? Judging by your pencil sketches—they would make a marvelous addition to the symposium on the decorative detailing of classical columns."

"Sorry." He shook his head. "But my work is not for public display."

"Of course, sir, of course." Looking faintly embarrassed, Lord Fanning was quick to dismiss the idea. "I quite understand."

Jack doubted the other man guessed at the real reason behind his refusal. Pierson men—a long line of military heroes stretching back to the time of William the Conqueror—were made of steel and gunpowder, not books and watercolors. If word got back to his father that one of his sons was honing his skills with a paintbrush rather than blades or bullets, the elderly duke would likely explode. That Jack had served with distinction in the Peninsular War had made his family proud. Any show of a softer side would be a great disappointment.

Drinking, gambling, wenching—now those were all perfectly acceptable pursuits for a gentleman. Jack made a face as he accepted a glass of sparkling *prosecco* from one of the passing footmen. Why was it such a sin to be passionate about other things, too? He slanted a look around at the books and art. Not that he didn't partake in his share of rakehell pleasures. But he also enjoyed cerebral challenges.

As Fanning excused himself to go speak with another member, Jack lifted the glass to his lips. His father would likely answer that carousing was a natural release for a warrior's martial aggressions. And that war was a noble profession, one that forged a man's mettle, tested his resolve, challenged his courage. It was a force that created nations, protected traditions, preserved civilization from chaos.

Jack didn't disagree. He just didn't think that a man should be measured solely by the steel in his spine. A wry twitch pulled at his mouth. In his view, paint was as potent a force as gunpowder in shaping a better society...

"Why the black face, Lord Giacomo? Don't you approve of ancient Roman art?"

Jack recognized the drawling voice. Giovanni Marco Musto della Ghiradelli—the Conte of Como—was scion of one of the oldest titled families in all of Italy. He was also an insufferable prick.

"Perhaps you've joined our Society simply to admire the military achievements of my ancestors," continued the conte. "We do have a small room devoted entirely to the history of the empire's wars."

The teasing barb hit uncomfortably close to the truth. The only reason Jack had felt free to join the Julius Caesar Society was because he knew his father would assume it was a group devoted to the discussion of the Emperor's military exploits. But he was not about to admit it to the Milanese macaroni.

"I'm surprised to see you here, Ghiradelli," he countered. "Did you think that the ancient Roman name implied you would find an orgy of bacchanalian pleasures taking place within these walls?" The conte—who preferred the moniker Marco—had not been in London long, but he had already earned quite a reputation as a rake. "For wine and women you will have to look elsewhere."

"If I want those two things, *amico*, I know exactly where to find them," replied Marco with a smug smile. "Occasionally I do like to stimulate my mind, rather than some other part of my anatomy."

"I doubt your brain expands to any sizable dimension," growled Jack.

Marco laughed. "My mind may not be as well endowed as the rest of my body, but I daresay I won't come up short when measured against the other scholars in this room."

"You, a scholar?" Jack let out a low snort. "Don't make me laugh."

Ignoring the barb, Marco tapped a finger to the glass display case, where a selection of exquisite bronze portrait medallions were laid out on a length of black velvet. "Virgil, Livy, Horace," he murmured, identifying the ancient writers.

As Marco added a few knowledgeable comments on their work Jack's sneer became a touch less pronounced.

"Ah, but I have heard that you favor architecture over literature," continued Marco. "So tell me, what is your opinion of the Basilica Porcia?"

The conte might be an arrogant ass, but he did appear to know something about antiquities.

"Do you feel that such early works compare favorably with the Baths of Agrippa?" added Marco.

Jack so rarely had a chance to discuss classical architecture with someone who knew a Trajan column from a column of Trojans that the opportunity was too good to pass up. In spite of his dislike for the fellow, he found himself giving a grudging answer.

And to his surprise, Marco responded with a serious commentary on symmetry and proportion instead of his usual sarcasm.

"The stylistic development of mosaics and frescoes is, of course, a whole other field of study," finished Jack as he added his thoughts on the design of the Baths. "The decorative arts are not my specialty."

"Nor mine," said Marco. "It is the Marchesa della Giamatti who is considered one of the foremost experts on Roman art antiquities, especially bronzework." He paused for a fraction. "Perhaps I should invite her to join the Society. I wonder, is there any rule against female members?"

The thought of Alessandra della Giamatti intruding on the one sanctuary where he was able to enjoy a civilized exchange of scholarly ideas was not a happy one. "Not that I know of," replied Jack slowly. "However, I don't think it's a very good idea."

"No?" Marco cocked a questioning brow. "Have you something against intelligent women? I have noticed that the English tend to be a little intimidated by a beauty with brains."

Jack was dumbfounded for a moment. "What utter nonsense," he muttered. "It's not what's inside her head that bothers me, it's what comes out of her mouth when she's in a temper. Which, by the by, seems to be more often than not."

"Ah. Her temper." The conte gave an eloquent shrug. "Like most Italians, Alessandra has a passionate nature."

"Some might call it a violent nature," said Jack, recalling how her eyes had felt sharp as daggers. *If looks could kill.*

For a fleeting instant, Marco seemed to turn a little pale before regaining his usual bravado. "Now it is you, *amico,* who is indulging in the Latin penchant for exaggeration." He smiled, though to Jack it looked a little forced. "When she was younger, she sometimes let emotion get the better of her. But that has changed. Ask anyone here in

London—the marchesa is known for her cool composure. It is only you who seems to set off sparks with her."

"I can't imagine why," growled Jack. "I've done nothing but try to act the gentleman and offer her help when she appeared in need of it."

"Hmmm." Marco regarded him thoughtfully. "Maybe that is the trouble."

Behaving like a cad had not improved her opinion, but he kept that fact to himself. "I don't think she would care for my company no matter how I behave."

The conte—who was also the lady's cousin, as Jack had just recently learned—touched Jack's arm. But whether it was meant as a friendly pat or an oblique warning was impossible to tell. "Don't judge the lady too severely. She is wary of men who wear their nobility on their sleeve."

"What is *that* supposed to mean?" Jack frowned, recalling Lucas's oblique words on the same subject.

Before Marco could respond, a call from across the room requested the conte to come give his opinion on a marble bust of Bacchus. "*Ciao*, Lord Giacomo," he murmured.

Jack watched the man saunter away with a theatrical flourish. *Ciao*. The silky sound stirred a strange pricking at the back of his neck. Damnation, if he had any sense, he would say good-bye to further thoughts on Lady Alessandra.

*To hell with the marchesa and her moods, her mysteries...*

Taking up a fresh glass of sparkling wine, Jack turned away from the crowd and wandered into one of the side display rooms, looking to distract his mind with a closer study of the new exhibit. The recently acquired slab of an ancient fresco depicted a naked Minerva, the Roman goddess of wisdom and war, about to bathe in a pool of azure water. The artist had rendered the scene with exquisite skill, using subtle colors and delicate brushstrokes to make the figure seem alive.

"You are indeed a goddess—a lithe, lovely vision of female beauty," he murmured, leaning low over the glass case for a better look. He didn't usually talk to himself, but his recent encounters with Alessandra had left him feeling like howling at the moon.

Drawing in a mouthful of prosecco, he let its effervescence tickle over his tongue. "I wouldn't mind stripping off all my clothing and feeling your wet, willing, sun-warmed body next to mine."

From behind him fluttered the soft swoosh of skirts, followed by a sharp intake of breath. "Well, don't let me stop you, sir."

Jack turned around slowly. *Not that he needed a face-to-face confrontation to know who was standing behind him.*

The ancient deities were known for taking devilish delight in tormenting mere mortals. So perhaps that explained why mischievous Minerva goaded him into taking the offensive to cover his embarrassment.

"Is that an invitation, Lady Giamatti?" he said, deliberately assuming a provocative drawl. "Have you been secretly yearning to see me in the nude?"

The deep voice was lush and liquid, like cool water running over smooth stones. Her flesh began to tingle, and as Alessandra met his gaze, she had to repress a tiny shiver.

"It appears that you have wandered into the wrong building," she said evenly, hoping he hadn't noticed her response. "This is a place for the serious study of ancient art and culture, not for frolicking in the nude with lithe, lovely females—goddesses or otherwise."

Jack took a slow, sauntering step toward her. Like a panther, he moved with an animal grace, the flex of smooth muscle rippling beneath his finely tailored coat.

"Ah, but some people consider bacchanalian pleasures to be a highly refined art form," he replied in that same suggestive tone.

Recalling the brandied heat of his lips and the roving touch of his caresses, Alessandra couldn't help but agree.

"Yes—and they are called rakes, not scholars."

His mouth curled up ever so slightly at the corners.

*Dio Madre, he was a handsome devil.* Especially when he allowed a hint of a smile to soften the sculpted planes of his face.

"Which begs the question," she added quickly. "Why are *you* here?"

"Why am I here?" repeated Jack. His expression turned even more sardonic. "To ogle naked females, of course," he drawled. "That is what we big, black devils do when we aren't lurking in dark corners or breakfasting on small children."

Alessandra felt a flush of color creep to her cheeks. "Well, to my knowledge, the Julius Caesar Society has no lady members, so I fear you are in for a very dull night."

"Perhaps." Jack took a long drink of his wine. "Unless, of course, you wish to remove your gown and your corset." Lowering his voice to a husky whisper, he added, "Not to mention the other, even more intimate bits of lace and frills you may be wearing next to your creamy flesh."

Ignoring the provocative words, Alessandra looked away from his lidded gaze and snapped open her document case.

*Scholarship*, she reminded herself. She was here to deliver some research materials, not to think about Lord James Jacquehart Pierson's lean, chiseled body and what it would look like stripped bare of its civilizing layers of linen and wool.

*Printed journals filled with obscure Latin terms.* Her fingers fumbled with the papers. She would *not* be distracted by his hot chocolate eyes or his sweetly sensual mouth.

"I thought you prided yourself on always behaving like a proper, *perfect* gentleman," she said, once she had her skittering pulse back under control.

"Yes, I do. But strangely enough, when I am around you, some mysterious force seems to goad me into acting very *improperly*." Jack looked at her through his long, dark lashes. "You are a scientist, Lady Giamatti. Perhaps you can explain it?"

Alessandra could answer any number of complex scientific conundrums, but she couldn't give any coherent rationale for why sparks seemed to fly whenever they rubbed together. Like steel striking flint, he simply set off an explosive reaction.

"Science is based on reason, sir," she answered slowly. "Whereas your behavior defies...logic." *As did her own.*

"Ah, so you don't think my feeble brain can grasp abstract concepts?"

She looked up from her papers, startled to find he was

now close—close enough for her to smell the spice of wine on his breath. Close enough for her to see the dangerous glitter in his eyes.

Close enough for her to feel the touch of his fingertip against her cheek. "Maybe you were right to say men have misguided notions of honor," he added.

She recoiled, drawing a wicked whisper of laughter.

"Afraid I might kiss you again?"

Before she could answer, Sir Reginald Coxe, head of the Artifacts Committee, hurried into the gallery. "Lady Giamatti! Forgive me for keeping you waiting."

Grateful for the interruption, Alessandra quickly finished arranging the documents in her case and held them out. "I found the copy of *Hadrian's Quarterly Review* that you needed, along with some other older essays that may be useful for your research."

"I can't thank you enough," exclaimed Sir Reginald. "But you need not have troubled yourself to bring them by in person. I would have been happy to have my servant return for it."

"It was no trouble," replied Alessandra. "I was passing by here on my way to Lady Bevan's musical soiree."

Sir Reginald peeked at the papers and heaved a sigh of relief. "Your appearance is a gift from the ancient gods."

Out of the corner of her eye, Alessandra saw Jack pinch his lips in silent disagreement.

"Without your help, I should never be able to finish my article by the publisher's deadline," went on Sir Reginald.

"I am always happy to help a fellow scholar." Smoothing at the folds of her cloak, she turned, unable to keep from directing an oblique barb back at Jack. "Please don't let me keep you from your meeting. I am sure that such a group of learned gentlemen must be discussing a number of erudite subjects."

"Indeed we are!" answered Sir Reginald, blithely unaware of her subtle sarcasm. "Why, Lord James and I—"

"And I ought to be on my way," interrupted Alessandra, studiously avoiding looking at Jack. "It would be unconscionably rude of me to arrive late at Lady Bevan's soiree."

*Unconscionably rude.* The words, though spoken with silky softness, hit like a slap in the face. Jack gave an inward wince as he watched her walk away. In truth, he probably deserved a boot to the ballocks. 'Unspeakably crude' was a more apt description of his behavior.

*Bloody hell.* He wasn't usually so oafishly obnoxious with the opposite sex. Some perverse pagan spell seemed to take hold of him whenever Alessandra della Giamatti was near. Glancing back at the painting of Minerva, he thought wryly, *It's all your fault.*

As Alessandra had pointed out, there was no rational explanation for the friction between them. Or for his ill-mannered attempt to ignite her ire.

"A remarkable lady," murmured Sir Reginald admiringly. He puffed out his cheeks and ran a hand through his wispy silver hair. "If I were a fine young fellow like you, I might be tempted to pursue more than a scholarly friendship."

"Lady Giamatti does not encourage any intimacies," said Jack gruffly.

"Yes, she does seem to pride herself on being professional," mused Sir Reginald. "Yet given your mutual interest in ancient art…" He gave a small cough. "It appeared that the two of you were sharing your impressions of our newly acquired paintings."

"In a manner of speaking." Jack quaffed the rest of his wine in one swallow. "That's the beauty of art—it's such a subjective topic that it's open to all manner of interpretation."

Though Sir Reginald looked slightly puzzled, he nodded sagely. "Er, very true, Lord James. Very true." Shifting his hold on the portfolio, he sighed. "Well. I, too, had better be taking my leave. Despite Lady Giamatti's divine intervention, I shall need an act of Almighty Jupiter if I am to finish my article for the *Royal Archaeological Review* on time."

"May the gods smile on your efforts," murmured Jack.

"And on yours, Lord James," replied Sir Reginald as he started for the cloakroom.

Jack cast another baleful glance at Minerva. *Was it his imagination, or did the minx have the nerve to wink at him?*

"Women," he growled under his breath. Highborn ladies were proving to be nothing but trouble. Perhaps it was time to pay a visit to the nymphs of Cupid's Cave.

Things were simple within the silken grottos. *Need. Want. Desire.* All was easily arranged to everyone's satisfaction.

If only life outside the red velvet walls would go so smoothly.

# Chapter Five

Alessandra let out a sigh as she looked up from her shopping list. *Pigments, pastels, papers...* It had appeared simple enough at home when the newly hired Swiss drawing master had written down the basic supplies that Isabella needed to proceed with her art lessons. But here in S & J Fuller's emporium in Rathbone Place, the shelves held a daunting array of choices.

*Choices, choices.*

She hesitated for a moment, her thoughts straying from her list to her encounter with Marco the previous week. *Was she wrong to run off to Bath?* Her cousin had intimated that she was simply trying to avoid making certain difficult decisions. She swallowed hard. Maybe he was right. It was easy to hide from her troubles by immersing herself in work.

*But enough of such distractions.* This was neither the time nor the place to address such complex conundrums.

Looking around, she saw that the clerk was still

engaged with a customer in the alcove crammed with turpentines and linseed oils. By the sound of the discussion, he was likely to be occupied for some time.

"How hard can it be?" she murmured, edging around the thick rolls of raw canvas. Though her practical knowledge of art was rudimentary at best, she decided to go ahead and make the choices on her own. The clerk could correct any egregious errors when she went to pay for the items.

*Burnt sienna, alizarin crimson, cerulean blue . . .* Alessandra hesitated over the large selection of watercolor paints. Each hue—neatly formed cakes of dried pigment— offered a puzzling variety of what looked to be identical cubes. After a quick look at the prices, she arched a brow. Clearly there was quite a difference. Some were very cheap, while others were hideously expensive.

Bending down for a better look, she shifted a step to catch the light—

As her backside collided against a well-muscled pair of thighs, she heard a muffled grunt and clatter of mixing tins falling to the floor.

"Oh, I am *so* sorry—" Her apology ended abruptly as she spun around.

Lord James Jacquehart Pierson arched a brow. Shaded by the cluttered shelves, his expression appeared nearly as dark as the paint pigment labeled 'Mars Black.'

*How apt*, thought Alessandra, repressing a wry grimace—seeing as they seemed to be in a constant state of war with each other.

"What's going to hit me next?" He glanced around warily, as if expecting a salvo of cannonfire to explode from behind the containers of oxgall. "Is your daughter lying in ambush by the buckets of gesso?"

"Isabella is at home," she replied softly. "So you are safe from further attack, sir." Ducking her head, she began to pick up the fallen items. "And despite what you think, I did not deliberately knock into you. The aisle is narrow, and the shadows make it difficult to see."

"I suppose you are once again going to accuse me of lurking in a dark corner in order to spy on you," he said gruffly.

Alessandra felt her mouth quiver. Given their recent encounter at Sir Henry's country estate, Jack had every reason to think of her as a Harpy. Still, his sarcasm hurt. As for his shockingly rude comments of last night...

Biting her lip, she didn't answer but continued to gather up the last of the spilled items.

"That would be unfair," he continued in a low voice. "But I do deserve a ringing setdown for my behavior last night. Please accept my apologies."

"Yes, of course," she said quickly. *Where, oh where, was her dratted list?* Setting aside her basket, she began a search of the nooks and crannies beneath the shelves. All she wanted was to retrieve the paper and beat a hasty retreat. She would come back later, when her cheeks were not colored a bright cadmium red.

"What's this?"

Alessandra suddenly realized that Jack was on his knees beside her, helping to gather up the tins.

"My list," she said curtly, trying to snatch it from his hand.

He drew back and studied it for a moment. "I didn't know you were a painter, Lady Giamatti."

"I'm not," she admitted. "The supplies are for my daughter, who is beginning lessons with a drawing master this week."

A faint smile played on his lips as he handed over the paper. "I hope the fellow is deaf."

She knew the comment was meant half in jest, but given her unsettled mood, it struck a vulnerable nerve.

"For pity's sake, sir, she is only a child," she said tightly. "*A child!* All children make mistakes and misbehave. That does *not* mean Isabella is—how did you put it—a spawn of Satan." Sweeping up the last tin, she set it back in place with a force that rattled the metal. "Just ask your friend Lord Hadley. He gets along perfectly well with her."

Jack sat back on his haunches, his spine straight as a ramrod, his jaw steeling to a razored edge. The swirl of dust and shadow made his eyes unreadable. "Unfortunately, I do not have Hadley's gift of making himself agreeable to everyone, including children. He is lighthearted, while…" He paused to tuck a curling strand of raven hair behind his ear. "While, as you have taken pains to point out, I am dark as the Devil."

It was true—in the low light his olive skin and long black locks made him look like a specter from the Underworld.

"Hadley's charm has nothing to do with physical appearance," she replied. "His hair is as black as yours, sir. The difference is, he has a sense of humor. He smiles. He can laugh at himself." She paused. "You, on the other hand, march around with a fire-breathing scowl that would fry Satan's *testicolos* to a crisp."

She heard him draw in a sharp breath. And then let it out in an odd little rush of air. Surely she was mistaken—it couldn't have been a chuckle.

"Actually, as a cognoscente of Italian cuisine, I would choose to sauté them in olive oil," he said softly. "With a bit of minced garlic and oregano."

Alessandra bit the insides of her cheeks to keep from smiling. So, she was wrong about his wit. Black Jack Pierson was not such a martinet after all.

As he reached for a tin that had escaped her notice, his touch grazed her glove, leaving a trail of tingling heat.

*Dio Madre*, he had beautiful hands, with long, lithe fingers that were elegantly expressive. Yet there was nothing effeminate about their grace. *Hard and soft.* She remembered all too well the feel of their powerful grip imprinted on her flesh.

Drawing back with an involuntary shiver, Alessandra rubbed at her knuckles. *Why did this man spark such a visceral reaction in her?* She wasn't sure whether she wanted to slap him...or beg him to slide his perfectly shaped palms over the swell of her breasts.

Perhaps it was the subtle aura of strength that seemed to radiate from every pore. Jack was, she knew, a war hero who had won a chestful of medals for bravery in battle. Yet he appeared to care naught for flash and glitter. Quite the opposite. He seemed supremely self-confident in his own abilities, supremely comfortable in his own skin.

She forced her gaze away from his jawline, where the stark white of his starched collar and cravat accentuated the shadows wreathing his face.

"Forgive me for keeping you waiting so long, madam." The clerk came hurrying around the corner but stopped short on seeing her and Jack squatting inelegantly on the floor. "Er...may I be of some assistance?"

"Yes, thank you." Alessandra rose hastily and shook out her skirts, hoping she had not left her last shred of dignity in the dust. "I have a list of items I need to purchase."

Jack stood and brushed off his trousers. "An encounter with you is always a memorable experience," he said with exaggerated politeness. Spying her shopping basket in the shadows, he picked it up. "Good day, Lady—," he began, then fell silent as his gaze flicked to the cube of watercolor pigment that she had selected. "Is there a reason you chose this particular paint?" he asked.

"I...that is..." To her chagrin, Alessandra felt her face turning crimson again. "I assumed that the more expensive one was the best."

"That depends," he replied. "For a beginner, the pigment made by Newton is a better choice."

"Why is that?"

"Because the color is bolder and more opaque, which tends to suit the style of someone learning the basics of painting. The more expensive pigments use rarer ingredients, and usually provide a far more subtle range of hues. There is no need to waste your money."

Jack took a closer look at the basket's contents. "And these sticks of charcoal are much too soft for a child." He replaced them with a different box. "The harder ones will be much easier to handle. As for sketchbooks, I recommend the ones made by Whatman. Their paper is the smoothest and most durable."

"T-thank you," she murmured.

"Don't mention it." Dropping his voice a notch, Jack added, "The shock of a *grazie* from you might knock me flat on my *culo* again."

*Diavolo.* He did seem to bring out the worst in her.

Jack handed the basket to the clerk. "Lady Giamatti is purchasing supplies for her daughter, Jenkins. Make sure you help her select items that are appropriate for a child of eight." With that, he snapped a mock salute and left the shop.

"Er, yes, sir," said the clerk as the door fell shut.

It was only now that Alessandra thought to wonder what Jack was doing here in the first place. He was obviously acquainted with the clerk and the merchandise. "Is that gentleman a regular customer?" she asked.

"Yes, madam." Without looking up, the clerk started down the aisle, adding several brushes to her basket, followed by a box of colored pencils.

"Why?"

"Why?" The young man appeared a trifle confused. "Why, to purchase paints and brushes, madam. And paper, of course."

"Is he an artist?" Somehow Alessandra couldn't quite picture Lord James Jacquehart Pierson living in a garret studio painting pictures of dead pheasants or bowls of fruit.

"I dunno. I never asked him."

It seemed that there was a mystery surrounding the gentleman. But seeing she was not likely to get any more information, Alessandra let the subject drop.

*Everyone had secrets*, she told herself with an inward sigh.

With the young man's help, the list was quickly filled and the supplies assembled on the counter. The last selection that she made was a large inlaid mahogany case, specially designed to hold the assortment of paints and brushes. After paying for her purchases, Alessandra tucked the parcel under her arm and returned to her carriage. Still, as she settled back against the squabs, she couldn't put the strange encounter out of her mind. Perhaps her fellow

'Sinners' were right and there was more to Lord James Jacquehart Pierson than first met the eye...

*No, no, no.* She must *not* let herself think that the Prince of Darkness might have any redeeming qualities.

*Si grand nero diavolo.* He was too devilishly dangerous to allow into her life. Whatever the inexplicable force was that seemed to draw them together, she must fight it with all her might.

Black Jack couldn't be a friend. So he must remain an enemy.

Deciding he was not in the mood for female company after all, Jack rapped on the trap of his carriage and called out a change in destination. The high-priced nymphs at Cupid's Cave—Jeannette in particular—would, of course, have any number of delightful ways to elevate his spirits. However, the afternoon encounter with Lady Alessandra della Giamatti had left him feeling...unsettled.

He had, in truth, been in a brooding frame of mind for some time. Even his friend Lucas—who until recently had not been known for refraining from excess—had remarked that he was drinking and whoring too much. *Was it any wonder?* With little to stimulate his imagination, he found himself bored to flinders.

Jack fell back against the squabs, the pelter of a passing shower echoing his muttered oath. Shifting his seat, he pressed a palm to one of the rain-spattered windowpanes and slowly wiped the mist from the glass. The chill seeped through his skin, sending a tiny shiver snaking down his spine.

In the smoky light of the oil lamp he could just make out his own reflection. Leaning in closer, Jack curled his lips upward.

"Ha!"

*See, the marchesa was wrong—he was perfectly capable of smiling.*

The laugh might have been more of a snort, but that was beside the point. She had no right to criticize, not when her own expression took on such a razored edge whenever she looked at him.

*Cutting. Contemptuous.*

Yet he couldn't keep from picturing her emerald green eyes, alight with inner sparks of gold. And her sculptured cheekbones and elegantly arched brows, proportioned with perfect symmetry.

And her shapely hips, swaying like poetry in motion.

*Poetry?* Hell, he needed a drink.

Stepping down from the carriage, he stalked into his club's reading room and signaled the porter to bring him a bottle of brandy. A look around showed he would likely be drinking alone, which only exacerbated his feeling of malaise.

Draining his glass in one gulp, he poured another. And another.

"Why the dark phiz?"

Jack looked up to find his eldest brother standing over him. "I can't help it—I'm the black sheep of the family."

George eyed the near empty bottle and then pulled up a chair. Favored with flaxen hair and the pale, Nordic complexion of their Viking ancestors, the heir to the Ledyard dukedom was his opposite in looks.

"True, you're the only one of us who shows a hint of our Latin ancestors," he replied. "But you have to admit it's a very romantic story—a shipwrecked admiral from the Spanish Armada washed ashore on English soil, a lovestruck young noblewoman nursing him back to health—"

Jack made a rude noise. "I'm in no mood for fairy-tale stories of romance, if you don't mind."

"Mother assured me that the tale is true." George helped himself to the brandy. "What's the matter? Having trouble with Jenny—or is her name Jeannette?"

In answer, Jack ordered another bottle, a very expensive port. "And put it on the marquess's bill," he added. "His Lordship can well afford it."

"By all means. If you wish to drown your sorrows, might as well do it in tasteful style." George slanted him a sidelong look. "Maybe you've had enough for the night. You look like shite."

"Bloody hell, not you, too," he swore.

"Any specific reason for your ill-humor?"

Jack shrugged and slowly swallowed the last splash of his brandy. "Tell me something," he said abruptly. "Did I never laugh as a child?"

His brother arched a brow. "You had four older brothers who took great glee in kicking your arse. As I recall, you yelped a lot."

Jack grinned in spite of his foul humor. "I gave as good as I got."

"Aye, you were a tough little bugger." George tapped his fingertips together. "As for your question, you were the most serious of all of us. Which is not to say you were a stick in the mud. You weren't." He thought for a moment. "The truth is, you were always far more interesting than William or Charles or Edward."

The statement took him by surprise. "I always thought you liked Wills best."

"I like all my brothers. They are capital fellows. It's

just that you have more God-given talents than the rest of us." George propped a boot on the brass fender. "Now, why the question on laughter?"

Jack stared through his glass at the flickering fire. Strangely enough, his brother's praise left him feeling even more morose. "Never mind. It's not important."

They sat for some moments in companionable silence before George cleared his throat. "You know, I was speaking to Killingworth the other day, and he mentioned that Wright had asked you to accompany him to Egypt. Said something about a position as the expedition's artist, but that you turned it down."

"Can you imagine Father's face had I announced I was going to travel to a faraway desert in order to draw pictures of crumbling bits of stone?" Jack grimaced. "He would not have found the idea remotely amusing."

"So what?"

Jack straightened from his slouch.

"Father is a duke, not a deity, Jack. His wishes need not be taken as the word of God," said George. "You upheld family tradition by serving honorably, and with great distinction, in the military. You are allowed to make your own choices on how you will live the rest of your life."

"I—I always assumed you and the others would frown on the idea of having a scholar in the family."

"Because it isn't manly?" George shook his head. "Lud, I'd give a monkey to be as clever as you are, rather than just a clodpoll who knows how to shoot and ride and swing a saber."

Jack blinked, suddenly seeing his eldest brother in a whole new light.

"And as for Father, why don't you let me have a word or two with him on the subject of art."

"Don't do it when he's in the Gun Room, lest you want your arse peppered with buckshot," warned Jack.

"I'm the heir, so I'm not likely to be the target of flying bullets. Besides, I think he'll listen, especially when I tell him how many famous generals were also noted men of arts and letters. There are a number of excellent examples— Peter the Great, Frederick Barbarossa, the Holy Roman emperor Charles IV." George coughed. "And Hannibal."

"*Hannibal?*"

"Well, I made that one up. But Father isn't likely to check through the history books." George took a sip of his wine. "In any case, my point is, from now on, you need not hide your interest in classical antiquities under a rock, so to speak. Go ahead and explore what makes you happy. And if Wills or Chas or Neddy dare utter a disparaging word, I'll thrash them to a pulp."

Jack felt a strange flutter in his chest. But as Pierson men were known for their steely reserve, he refrained from throwing his arms around George and tossing him up to the plaster ceiling rosette. Instead, he waggled a hand at the passing porter. "On second thought, Hobbs, you may put the port on my account. It appears I owe my brother for a favor."

George acknowledged the oblique thanks with a grin. "A rather large one."

Jack raised his glass in salute.

"One last thing. Have you heard about the excavations set to start next week on a new site of Roman ruins near Bath?"

Jack nodded. "It was all people could talk about at the last meeting of the Julius Caesar Society. Preliminary indications are that it is a very important discovery. Several of our high-ranking members have been invited to serve on the Excavation Committee."

"Yes, well, I saw Lord Fanning at a diplomatic reception last night, and he mentioned that a sudden illness in the family was going to prevent him from participating." A pause. "So I took the liberty of suggesting to him that he ask you to go in his place."

"*Me!*" For an instant Jack held his breath, then slowly shook his head. "Hell, the position is one of great honor. There are far more experienced Society members who will get the nod over me."

"None of them have your unique skills at drawing, to go along with your knowledge of ancient architecture," replied his brother. "Fanning agreed that someone adept at keeping a visual record of the discoveries would be a valuable asset for the project."

*A chance to watch the foremost experts in the field at work?* It was the opportunity of a lifetime. "By Jove, I owe you a case of the port, George," he murmured.

"I'll settle for one of your watercolors of the Temple of Saturn."

"I can't help feeling that I am getting the best of the bargain," answered Jack. "You get a puling painting and I get an answer to my prayers."

His brother chuckled. "Maybe you should wait before thinking of me as your savior. There's always a chance that you won't find the excavation at all to your liking."

"I assure you, George, it will be heaven on earth."

A blond brow quirked in question. "Even though you will be parted from the fleshpots and gambling hells of London for several weeks?"

"I think I can survive without sex or carousing for that amount of time," said Jack dryly. "I shall channel all my baser urges into the serious study of art."

"You'll also be parted from Lady Mary Stiles," observed George after a small pause.

It took a moment for the remark to register. "Oh, that." Jack shrugged. "There is no formal agreement between us. It is Father who has been touting her as a possible match."

"And what is your feeling in the matter?"

"I have none to speak of. I am reaching the age when Duty—and the duke—demands that I think about marriage," muttered Jack.

After refilling his port, George gave the glass a meditative swirl.

"As a younger son, I don't have the same complex considerations as you did in choosing a bride," Jack continued, a little nettled by his brother's quizzical expression. "Father informs me that the only expectations for me are that I choose a young lady with a suitable pedigree and a handsome dowry, so as not to be dependent on your purse when he sticks his spoon in the wall."

A snort sounded above the crackling logs. "As if I would be such a nipcheese as to beggar my brothers when I come into the title."

"You're more than generous," said Jack. "However, I don't fancy living in your pocket for the rest of my life." He stared into his wine. "I suppose that Lady Mary would make a perfectly pleasant wife. She is pretty and her manners are polished."

He paused as a random picture of his future passed through his head. The breakfast room, conversing with Lady Mary about...about nothing more than platitudes.

*Perish the thought that a well-bred young lady might dare express an individual opinion or original observation.* Her duty was simply to manage his household and provide him with an heir.

"You don't sound very enthusiastic over the prospect." George pursed his lips. "But I suppose the fact that your comrade-in-devilry has just surrendered his freedom is coloring your feelings."

"Hadley won't find marriage boring," said Jack. "His new bride is...interesting."

"Yes, I've heard that she is rather unique."

"But be that as it may, I have no intention of taking a wife anytime soon," he muttered. "I've better things to do with my time."

"Like muck around in the mud," murmured George.

"Yes, like muck around in the mud." Jack thumped his glass down on the side table. "So Father may bloody well stick...a cork in his mouth when it comes to potential brides. When I decide to don a legshackle, I'll damn well choose my own ball and chain."

George raised his drink in smiling salute. "I applaud your mettle."

"Ass," growled Jack through his teeth.

Finishing off the port with an exaggerated swallow, his brother rose. "In that case, I'll toddle off to the card room, where my witticisms will be welcomed by a more appreciative audience. Enjoy your sojourn to Bath." He paused. "And try not to dig yourself into any trouble."

"Ass." This time it was said with a grudging grin. "Archaeology is not exactly a subject that is apt to stir up much trouble."

# Chapter Six

"Did you know there are more than seventeen different species of shorebirds on the Cornwall coast, not counting seagulls?" Charlotte looked up from the letter she was reading. "Ciara and Hadley are certainly enjoying their wedding trip. It says that they will stay in Penzance for another few days, then..."

Alessandra dutifully smiled, and tried to pay attention to the cheerful commentary on how their fellow 'Sinner' and her new husband were passing the first few weeks of wedded bliss. But her thoughts kept straying to her own unsettled life. She, too, had received a letter in the morning post, an oblique warning from her cousin that trouble might be brewing.

*Damn Marco.* Why was it that men were much more eloquent with blades and bullets than they were with ink and paper?

Instead of offering any helpful information, her cousin had merely dashed off a few lines of warning. And even those had been maddeningly vague. No details, no explanations, other than the fact that he had heard yet another disturbing bit of news from Italy hinting that the past had not been forgotten.

'Be alert for any danger,' he had cautioned, underlining the hurried scrawl.

*As if there were a moment when she had ever let down her guard during the last year.*

She heaved an inward sigh. He had promised to keep a close eye on things and send more news soon. However, he had also added that an urgent errand for Lord Lynsley required his presence in Scotland. He was, in fact, already on his way north.

The shortbread in her fingers broke, spilling a trail of crumbs across her plate. Alessandra was not precisely sure how her cousin was involved with Lord Lynsley, whose official government title was Assistant Minister to the Secretary of State for War. Marco's past was somewhat of a mystery. She suspected some of the wild tales she had heard about his exploits were not entirely exaggerated...

But right now, her only concern was her present predicament. That Marco was clever—as well as quick and deadly as a cobra in a fight—were skills she would welcome at this moment. But even a man known as *Il Serpente* to his friends could not move fast enough to be in two places at the same time.

No, she could not count on her cousin to protect her from trouble. Which brought her full circle back to the cold truth. She was on her own...

"Isn't that marvelous, Alessandra?"

Her head jerked up. "Sorry?"

"You haven't heard a word I've said, have you?" observed Charlotte with a quirk of her lips.

"Sorry," she repeated.

"Charlotte was just reading us the news that Ariel and Sir Henry have propagated a new bloom," piped up Kate.

"Good heavens—at their age!" exclaimed Alessandra.

"Kate was referring to *botany*, not biology, my dear," replied Charlotte, as Kate dissolved into a fit of giggles. "You know of their interest in exotic flowers. Well, they have succeeded in crossing two rare species of poppies."

"How lovely," murmured Alessandra.

"What's wrong?" demanded Kate after the rustling of the paper faded. "You've been acting queerly all meeting. It's as if your mind is miles away."

"F-forgive me," stammered Alessandra. "I—I suppose I am preoccupied with the upcoming excavation. And with keeping Isabella happy while we are in Bath." Groping for any excuse to change the subject, she quickly added, "By the by, her art lessons are going very well."

"Don't try to muddle the picture," said Kate with her usual bluntness. "I can tell that you're keeping something from us."

Alessandra dropped her gaze, carefully avoiding her friend's eyes. "Nothing to speak of. Just a private family matter." It wasn't exactly a lie, she told herself. "My cousin is upset about a past incident in Italy that he feels is cause for worry."

"All families have a skeleton in the closet," pointed out Charlotte.

Despite her friend's reassuring tone, Alessandra flinched. She quickly turned the tiny movement into a shrug. "Marco has a tendency to be melodramatic, so I'm sure it will turn out to be nothing. Hopefully it will have blown over by the time I am back from Bath." Reaching for her reticule, she put her notebooks away. "Speaking of which, I had better be getting home. We leave tomorrow and I have yet to pack up my tools and reference books."

A tiny frown tugged at Charlotte's lips, but she tactfully dropped the subject. "Well, do write often and keep us informed on your progress."

"I promise."

"Remember that Bath is a spa town, a place for relaxation and rejuvenation. So try to have some fun," remarked Kate. "Perhaps you will meet a tall, dark, handsome stranger."

The remark stirred a sudden vision of Black Jack Pierson.

*God forbid.*

"Perhaps you ought to stop reading those silly novels on love and romance," replied Alessandra dryly. "Besides, even if I did meet a prince in Bath, he would likely be an octogenarian afflicted with gout."

"Mama, are you sure my new paint box is safe?" Isabella craned her neck and tried to observe the packing of the baggage coach.

"Yes, *tesoro*," said Alessandra. "It was wrapped in lamb's wool before being placed in your trunk." Her own fragile technical materials, including an assortment of acids and special chemicals used to help determine the composition and age of an artifact, had also been carefully prepared for travel.

"I wish I could have kept it with me. I should like to practice my brushstrokes during the journey," said her daughter with a flourish of her fingers. The brightly varnished wooden case had hardly been out of Isabella's sight since its arrival from the art shop. Indeed, this morning, Alessandra had found it nestled in the pillows of her daughter's bed.

She gave silent thanks for the little girl's enthusiasm. It was a welcome change from her recent moody sulks. "I'm afraid that bumpy roads, jars of water, and paint do not mix well." She placed several sketchbooks and a box of pencils on the seat. "You will have lots of time in Bath to practice your painting. In the meantime, you can work on your pencil technique."

Isabella was already opening the book to a fresh page.

"It seems that you are enjoying your lessons with Herr Lutz," remarked Alessandra.

"He is very strict and serious." Isabella tapped the tip of her pencil to her chin. "But he says that to be a good artist, one must have a great deal of discipline."

With children, there was such a fine line between being too tough and too lenient. To Alessandra's surprise, the Swiss drawing master had somehow drawn up just the right course of study for her daughter. The first few lessons had been fun, and yet challenging. And when Isabella had understood that he would tolerate no nonsense from her, she had applied herself diligently to win his approval.

Biting her lip, Alessandra stared out through the misted panes of glass. *Oh, if only she could see things more clearly.*

For days she had been struggling to coax the pinched expression from Isabella's face. But all her efforts—a visit to the British Museum, sweets at Guenter's—had done little to lighten her daughter's unhappiness. She knew that the little girl was lonely, especially as her best friend, Peregrine, would not be returning from Kent for some weeks. London was still foreign to Isabella, and as Alessandra was somewhat of a recluse herself, they had few social invitations where a young girl might meet other playmates.

*Was she being terribly selfish to subject a child to such a life?* It wasn't as if she had much choice.

"Look, Mama, I've drawn your portrait."

Alessandra stared for a moment at the grim slash of a line that depicted her mouth, and quickly forced a smile. "How lovely. What a clever way you have of drawing hair."

Isabella beamed with pleasure. "Next I will try to draw a picture of Perry. Herr Lutz says it's a good exercise to try to draw something from memory. It teaches you to be more ob...ob..."

"Observant," finished Alessandra. She closed her eyes, imagining for a moment her villa and gardens overlooking the Lake of Como. "Yes, indeed it does."

"Is Herr Lutz really going to be in Bath for some of our visit?"

She shook off her momentary melancholy. "Yes, we are fortunate that he has a commitment to spend several weeks in the city while we are there. He was kind enough to schedule several lessons for you."

Isabella's dark curls bobbed as she bent her head over the paper. "Then I had better practice, so I can show him how much I am improving."

Art helped Isabella pass the long hours on the road, while Alessandra occupied herself with several scholarly books on the history of Roman rule in Britannia. But even with such distractions, both of them were happy when the carriage finally rolled into the city of Bath on the following afternoon.

"Oh, look at how the buildings curve!" Nose pressed to the glass, Isabella was eager to observe all the sights.

"That is the famous Royal Crescent, *tesoro*. It is a set of thirty houses designed by John Wood the Younger, and as you can see, he was greatly influenced by Roman architecture. That is because Bath is built on an ancient Roman town. It was one of the strongholds of the Imperial army, and they have left behind many fascinating reminders of their presence."

"Is that why you have come here?" asked Isabella. "To dig for buried treasure?"

Alessandra laughed. "Perry has been telling you too many tales of pirates. We are not after plunder, *tesoro*. We seek to uncover the artifacts that tell us about daily life, so that we may learn valuable lessons about the past."

Isabella rolled her eyes, having heard the lecture countless times before. "Can't we dig for information in a more interesting place—like the Caribbean islands?"

She brushed an errant curl from her daughter's cheek. "I'm afraid you will have to make do with Bath."

The carriage rounded the Circus and proceeded down Gay Street. "There are many interesting things to see and do here," explained Alessandra. "We shall visit the Pump Room, where all the fashionable people go to drink the mineral waters. It is built atop an ancient underground Roman bath, which has lots of beautiful art and mosaics for you to sketch."

Her daughter's expression brightened.

"And there is the Society of Roman Antiquities." Alessandra pointed out a handsome classical building in the middle of the block. "I shall be working there some of the time."

"Will you be digging for Roman ruins in its cellars?" asked Isabella.

"No, *tesoro*. Our excavation site is in the wilds of the countryside, several miles outside of town. For the most part, that is where I shall be. However, when the weather is bad, I shall clean and catalogue our artifacts in the Society's work rooms."

A few minutes later the horses turned off onto Trim Street and stopped in front of the small townhouse Alessandra had rented for the duration of the dig. Her longtime butler, who had come down a few days earlier to prepare the place, hurried down the marble stairs to greet them.

"A message came for you this morning from Mr. Dwight-Davis, *signora*," he said, reaching for Alessandra's valise. "He apologized for the change in plans, but wished to inform you that his welcoming reception for the Italian scholars will be held tonight at the townhouse of the Bath Society of Roman Antiquities, rather than tomorrow."

"Tonight?" She sighed, wishing she could think of some reason for avoiding the social gathering. But considering that Dwight-Davis had exerted considerable effort to have her appointed to the Excavation Committee, it would be rude to cry off. This phase of the dig—a joint effort involving a special delegation from Rome—was a particularly prestigious assignment.

"*Grazie*, Ferraro," she went on. "I had better tell Lucrezia."

"Luza and I shall take care of everything," he assured her. "Cook has refreshments waiting in the drawing room. You and the *angiolleto* must be hungry and thirsty."

"A cup of tea would be welcome," admitted Alessandra. She glanced back at the baggage coach, which had just pulled up behind her carriage. "As for the Little Angel—"

"*Buongiorno*, Ferraro!" Isabella jumped down from her seat. "Look, I have drawn a picture of you, and one of Miss Wolcott."

The butler eyed the pencil profile, which greatly exaggerated his prominent Roman nose. "You have, er, excellent technique, *bambina*."

Isabella beamed. "Miss Wolcott, come look—"

"Miss Wolcott will have ample time to review your portfolio after teatime," interrupted Alessandra. Seeing the little girl's governess approach, she handed over Isabella's sketchbook with an apologetic shrug. "I'm afraid you are going to learn more about art than you might wish."

The governess smiled. "Art is an excellent accomplishment for a young lady to have. And it appears there are a great many interesting sites for Isabella to sketch around Bath."

Reminded of her own reasons for coming here, Alessandra lifted her skirts and started up the stairs of her temporary home. Most people came for the famous curative waters and for the lively social scene, but her interest in Bath had nothing to do with such superficial pursuits.

Recalling Kate's teasing words about meeting a handsome prince, Alessandra made a wry face. *Men were the very last things on her mind.* She was here to submerge herself in serious work, not to engage in Pump Room flirtations or drink the sulfurous elixirs.

Her throat tightened.

Besides, it would take more than a bubbling thermal spring to wash away the ills that plagued her.

# Chapter Seven

*H*ow fortunate that you were free to join our committee on such short notice, Lord James."

Mr. Dwight-Davis straightened from his welcoming bow. A noted authority on the life of the emperor Augustus, the elderly scholar was a short, stout man whose rather odd outward appearance mirrored his inner zeal for the subject. His thinning white hair was styled *à la Brutus*, and despite the warmth of the room, he wore a long cloak artfully draped over one shoulder, the Imperial purple superfine wool falling in toga-like folds across his evening coat.

"Jupiter must be keeping a watchful eye on our endeavor," continued Dwight-Davis with a broad smile. "And has decided to give it his blessing."

"We all know that the gods can be fickle," murmured Jack. "So let us not tempt fate by speaking too quickly of good fortune. You have yet to quiz me on my expertise. You may find yourself sadly disappointed."

"Nonsense, sir! Lord Fanning sent me a selection of your essays and sketches. I consider us lucky indeed to have such a knowledgeable scholar on classical architecture appear, as it were, from out of the woodwork." Dwight-Davis chuckled at his own witticism. "Fanning's absence left a large hole in the excavation team. As I mentioned, we took great pains to include an expert in every aspect of ancient Roman history—mosaics, sculpture, numismatics…"

He gave an apologetic cough. "Er, sorry. As Horace said, *Quid quid praecipies, esto brevis*—whatever you want to teach, be brief. As you see, my enthusiasm for the subject sometimes leads me to rattle on like a loose screw."

"*Facile remedium est ubertati, sterilia nullo labore vincuntur*," replied Jack, handing over his hat and walking stick to a footman. "According to ancient philosopher Quintilian, exuberance is easily corrected, dullness is incurable."

"Ah, so a thorough knowledge of Latin is also one of your skills!" His host's smile stretched even wider. "Excellent! I see you have no need for my prosy lectures."

"On the contrary," said Jack. "I have much to learn about the proper methods of conducting an archaeological excavation, so I welcome all advice."

"My first words of wisdom are that you must be careful to whom you admit that, sir," warned Dwight-Davis. "We have a few gentlemen who will talk well into the next century if given the slightest encouragement."

"Ah." Jack smoothed a wrinkle from his lapel. "Then I shall try not to wear my ignorance on my sleeve."

The other man let out a genial laugh. "I can already

tell by the cut of your cloth that you will fit in quite splendidly, sir. Now, come this way to the drawing room, Lord James, and let me introduce you to some of your new colleagues before the Italian contingent makes its entrance."

Jack crossed the entrance hall, admiring the proportions of the arched ceiling and graceful marble columns flanking the curved staircase. Several wall niches held fragments of Roman sculpture and bronzework. He would have liked to linger over the artifacts but Dwight-Davis quickened his steps, clearly anxious to rejoin the party.

The rumble of voices, punctuated by a higher octave of clinking crystal, could be heard already. Jack repressed a smile. He had noticed early on that rigorous intellectual discussion seemed to require copious lubrication. In fact, the scholars he had met so far could drink his old army regiment under the table.

The room was quite crowded, and as Jack looked around, he saw no one he knew. That was not surprising, of course. He was a mere neophyte and these august gentlemen were...

*Was that a flutter of emerald skirts amid all the masculine coats and trousers?*

Jack looked back at the punch table, but the only sight that greeted his gaze was a quartet of freshly shaven faces, laughing together over some joke.

*A figment of his imagination.* Brought on, no doubt, by too many hours spent brooding over his recent encounters with Alessandra della Giamatti. It had been a long drive from London in his curricle, with no books or sketchpads to divert his thoughts from the tedium of the road. He ought to have left his piqued pride in Town—along with the lady herself. And yet, Jack couldn't seem to banish her from his mind.

"Haverstick, stop fussing with the roses and come meet Lord James, who is standing in for Lord Fanning." Dwight-Davis beckoned to a man who was busy re-arranging the flowers in a large marble urn.

"Servants have no eye for symmetry," grumbled the man as he tweaked the last stem into place. "James, you say?" His bushy brows drew together. "Hmmph. Never heard of him. What's he written?"

"Nothing to speak of," replied Jack, accepting a glass from one of the passing footmen. He was glad to see it was real champagne, and not the foul-tasting mineral water that many called 'Bath champagne.'

"Lord James is the youngest son of the Duke of Ledyard," explained Dwight-Davis. "And a promising scholar—"

"Ah, now I place you," interrupted Haverstick. "The war hero."

Jack shrugged off the sobriquet. "Hardly. Like many of my fellow soldiers, I was simply doing my duty."

Raising his quizzing glass, Haverstick subjected him to a lengthy scrutiny. "I suppose if we dig up any ghosts of ancient centurions, you might come in handy. Do you know how to handle a *pilum* or *pugio*?"

"In theory," replied Jack without hesitation. "My actual battlefield experience is confined to sabers and firearms, but I daresay I could learn rather quickly to use a legionnaire's spear or dagger."

"That's the spirit," said Dwight-Davis. To Haver-stick, he added, "I think you will be quite satisfied with Lord James's mettle as a scholar. And his drawing skills are superb."

"Hmmph." Haverstick smoothed the folds of his cravat. "Well, don't expect to pull rank here, young man," he warned. "You will be starting out as a foot soldier and will be required to work in the trenches."

"Nothing will please me more," said Jack. "I am here to learn."

Haverstick gave a curt nod, then turned away to follow two footmen who were carrying in the bottles of Chianti for a welcoming display in honor of the Italian delegation. "Now don't forget—arrange the wine in two precise rows, with the garland of thyme running straight down the center of the table..."

"He may appear a little abrasive," murmured Dwight-Davis as the directives trailed off. "But don't be intimidated, Lord James. He's like that with everyone."

"I am not easily intimidated," replied Jack. "My military experience has taught me how to stand my ground in the face of enemy fire."

"Right. I keep forgetting that you bring a rather, er, unique set of skills to our little band of scholars." Dwight-Davis cleared his throat and then lowered his voice. "But I hope you will not think of Haverstick as the enemy. As president of the Bath Society of Roman Antiquities, he is the overall head of the excavation, and so controls the assignment of tasks."

*In other words, don't cross swords with the pompous prig.*

Jack heaved an inward sigh. Dueling for power and prestige was apparently just as prevalent among intellectuals as it was among soldiers. "A wise soldier always makes an effort to get along with his commanding officer," he said in answer to the oblique warning.

"Enough said then." Dwight-Davis looked relieved to change the subject. After a quick gulp of his wine, he glanced over the display of flowers. "Ah, there is Knightley, head of the Mosaics Committee. His book on the Roman Baths of Britannia will be published next month and is a fascinating work. Come, you will enjoy meeting him."

Alessandra ducked into the alcove, grateful that her arrival had gone unnoticed by Dwight-Davis. He was a very nice gentleman, and extremely open-minded concerning the intellectual abilities of women. But in his enthusiasm for the subject of archaeology, he sometimes turned...overexuberant.

She sighed. He would insist on making her the center of attention, and though his gallantries were well-meaning, she much preferred to be singled out for her scholarship rather than her sex.

Looking around, she spotted several fellow members from the London chapter of the Society of Roman Antiquities standing nearby. As Mr. Knightley, the mosaics expert, glanced up and met her gaze, he excused himself from the group and came over to greet her.

"Lady Giamatti, I must say, I found your recent essay in the *Journal of Ancient Antiquities* very interesting."

Alessandra breathed a silent sigh of relief. Of all her colleagues, Knightley was the one who always treated her like an equal.

"I hear you have devised a new system for methodical digging," he went on. "You must tell me all about it..."

The head of the Mosaics Committee had his back turned and appeared to be in deep conversation with someone standing in one of the recessed alcoves.

"Perhaps we ought to wait until later, rather than interrupt," suggested Jack, loath to appear too presumptuous. As the son of a duke—no matter that he was merely the youngest of five—he was often treated with great deference. Society seemed to think that his family name entitled him to assume the trappings of power, prestige, and privilege.

He felt his jaw tighten. In truth, he had always preferred to earn respect on his own merits.

"No, no." Waving off Jack's words, Dwight-Davis started around the marble urn. "I assure you that Knightley and whoever he is with will be delighted at the opportunity to welcome our newest member."

As his host now had firm hold of his elbow, Jack had no choice but to follow.

"Knightley, allow me to introduce you to the gentleman who has so kindly agreed to step in for Lord Fanning."

The man turned, revealing his companion in conversation.

Somehow, Jack managed to mask his shock.

"Ah! Lady Giamatti! I did not see you come in," exclaimed Dwight-Davis. "I wasn't sure whether to expect you. How marvelous that you arrived in time to attend the reception."

*Bloody hell. The ancient gods had turned even more malicious in their mischief.*

"Your countrymen would have been greatly disappointed at your absence," went on Dwight-Davis. He chuckled. "As would all the other gentlemen in the room."

Alessandra acknowledged the compliment with a polite smile. After a fraction of a pause, she said, "How flattering to hear that my professional expertise would be so sorely missed."

"Er, yes, indeed it would be." Taking the hint, Dwight-Davis quickly assumed an expression of great seriousness. "We have the highest opinion of your intellect."

"Indeed," echoed Knightley. "Lady Giamatti was just explaining to me a new system she has devised for excavating in an orderly and precise fashion. It involves a mathematical grid, and..." He looked at Alessandra. "But I daresay I shall let you explain it. I have no head for complex numbers or geometry."

"Before we dig into the subject of archaeology, let us finish the introductions," said Dwight-Davis. "Lady Alessandra, allow me to present Lord James—"

"We are acquainted," she said, taking care to avoid any eye contact.

"Only slightly," amended Jack, matching her cool tone. "We have several mutual friends."

"Excellent, excellent." Dwight-Davis seemed unaware of the tension crackling through the air. "By Jove, what a fortuitous act of the gods that you find yourselves working together here in Bath."

Jack would have chosen several other adjectives, none of which a gentleman was allowed to say in front of a lady.

Dwight-Davis turned to Knightley and went through the same ritual of introduction. At least Jack assumed that was what his host was saying. His attention was on Alessandra. A sidelong glance showed that she still had not looked his way.

"So, Lord James, since you are stepping in for Fanning, I take it your expertise is in classical architecture?" asked Knightley.

Jack forced his gaze back to the other man. "I have some knowledge in the subject," he replied. "I trust I shall not disgrace myself."

Alessandra moved out of the shadows, the glittering light of the candelabra flickering over her smooth, sculpted face.

The other two men stared for an instant, their gazes drawn to her classical beauty like moths to a flame. Jack felt his own eyes linger in admiration. She reminded him of a bust of Venus that he had seen at the Villa Adriana in Tivoli. *A pale, polished, perfect piece of marble.*

And yet, despite her façade of stony reserve, he found the sight stirred a sudden recollection of her mouth, lush and liquid against his.

"Remind me again, Lord James," she asked slowly. "What other excavations have you taken part in?"

"This is the first, Lady Giamatti," replied Jack.

"Ah." The sound hung for a moment in the air. "I suppose that the duke is a generous benefactor of Fanning's Julius Caesar Society."

Jack felt himself stiffen, but refrained from showing his irritation. "My father supports a number of worthy institutions that appeal to him. But antiquities is not his field of interest—it is mine."

"And very glad we all are of it," exclaimed Dwight-Davis. "Lord James has visited a number of ancient sites throughout Italy, and I am sure he will prove a very quick study in the field."

Knightley asked a question about Jack's travels, drawing him into a polite exchange on the ruins around Rome. However, after several minutes the conversation was cut short as someone from across the room summoned the mosaics expert to answer a question on the Baths of Caracalla.

"I look forward to continuing our talk, Lord James," he said in taking his leave. "I am sure that you will find the coming weeks a very interesting experience. There is nothing quite like unearthing the secrets of the past with your own hands."

"I am looking forward to it," said Jack.

As Knightley moved away, Dwight-Davis darted a look at the mantel clock. "Oh, dear! The Italians will be arriving at any moment, so please excuse me while I check on a few last details. I am sure that the two of you wish to have a few moments alone to discuss your friends, as well as the upcoming excavation." He patted Jack's shoulder. "But be a sporting fellow and don't keep her to yourself all evening, sir. Given your previous friendship, you already have an unfair advantage over every other gentleman in the room."

*Ha!*

"What are *you* doing here?" she demanded in a low voice, as soon as their host had disappeared through the doorway.

"I'm hoping to see more erotic art," he replied, a little nettled that once again she had assumed that he had no right to be part of a scholarly group. "The ancient Roman gods and goddesses seem to enjoy frolicking in the nude."

A faint flush ridged her cheekbones. "Your schoolboy humor is wearing thin, sir. I don't find it amusing. If you have followed me to Bath—"

"Followed you?" He arched his brows. "I assure you, I had no idea you would be here. Lord Fanning invited me to take his place on the excavation, and I accepted."

"But...but what sort of expertise do you have to offer?" she asked haltingly.

Jack set his glass down on a decorative plinth and moved a step closer to her. "You question my qualifications?"

Alessandra went still as a statue, save for a faint flutter of her lashes. There was a long moment of silence before she responded. "An archaeological excavation is serious, scientific business, sir. I have been on several excavations in the past where a wealthy nobleman purchased a spot on the committee, only to grow impatient or bored." She drew in a deep breath. "Dilettantes only muck things up. They expect archaeology to be all about unearthing one glittering treasure after another, when in reality it is a painstaking process of uncovering mostly mundane items."

"Thank you for the lecture, Lady Giamatti," said Jack softly. "Much as it may surprise you, I'm not entirely ignorant of the discipline and dedication required to do a good job in the field. I may lack your experience in actual digging, but Lord Fanning and Mr. Dwight-Davis are satisfied that my knowledge is sufficient to the task. If you doubt that, our host has several of my essays on architecture. You are welcome to read them and judge for yourself."

A spark of emotion flared in her eyes. But like the rest of her reactions it was impossible to decipher. *If only there was a Rosetta Stone for the female mind*, he thought wryly.

"You are quite right, sir. A scientist should only draw conclusions from empirical observation," she said stiffly.

It was not the most gracious of apologies. However,

Jack took some measure of satisfaction in the concession.

"So I shall refrain from further judgment until I have a chance to observe you in action."

Determined not to let her have the last word, Jack assumed a deliberately smug smile. "I've never yet had a lady complain that my performance was unsatisfactory."

# Chapter Eight

*D*amn the man.

Alessandra felt her face flame as she turned away and made a show of signaling the footman for a glass of champagne. *Was there a paint pigment called Hellfire Red?* Mix two parts embarrassment and one part anger with a generous sprinkling of confusion, and that should result in the exact shade...

Lud, she had made a complete fool of herself. Yet again.

*Where, oh where was her wine?* The knowledge that she had behaved unprofessionally was a bitter pill to swallow. With everyone else she comported herself with cool composure. Yet against all reason, Lord Black Jack Pierson continued to spark a passionate reaction.

*Diavolo.* She *must* keep control of her emotions. After all, she knew how dangerous passions could be—

"Lady Giamatti."

Looking up, she found three men—four, including the footman—vying to press a glass into her hand.

Alessandra reached for the closest one and took a quick sip. "Is it just me?" she murmured, fanning her cheeks with a languid wave. "Or is it oppressively warm in here?"

"Stifling," agreed Mr. Eustace.

Sir Sydney was already at the bank of windows, tugging at the latches. "Allow me to open the casement for you, madam. If you come stand by me, you will feel a delightful breeze."

Elbowing the footman aside, Lord Hillhouse quickly offered his arm.

"Thank you, gentlemen." Alessandra allowed herself to be escorted to a spot by the mullioned glass. She usually discouraged such gallantries, wanting to be admired for her intellect rather than her cleavage. But at the moment, her self-esteem was a little fragile, so to have a trio of men tripping over their feet to please her was not unwelcome.

Black Jack Pierson might think her a conceited shrew; however, the other gentlemen of their scholarly group did not seem to judge her so harshly.

*Scholars.* Slanting a look at the alcove, Alessandra saw that Jack was still there, perusing a book he had taken up from the display table. His formidable physical appearance and wartime military experience seemed at odds with the notion that he possessed any expertise in the arts. But then, he had certainly appeared surprisingly knowledgeable in the paint shop.

Could it be that beneath the brawn and bravado, the man had a brain?

The idea was...intriguing.

As if sensing her scrutiny, Jack looked up.

Their eyes met.

Unwilling to appear intimidated, Alessandra angled her chin a notch higher and held her gaze steady. She would present a picture of regal refinement and...

His only reaction was to resume his reading.

"More wine, Lady Giamatti?" asked one of her swains.

She shook her head. A dull ache was already forming at her temples, and despite the swirl of evening air, she felt uncomfortably warm. The surrounding merriment—the peals of masculine laughter, the blazing lights, the clinking crystal—stirred a sudden longing to escape to the solitude of her own townhouse.

*Run. Hide.* Alessandra closed her eyes for an instant. Would such urges ever cease to control her life?

To her relief, Dwight-Davis reappeared at the doorway, leading a procession of eight gentlemen wearing matching azure velvet swallowtail coats and fawn-colored knee breeches.

"*I nostri amici sono arrivati*—our Italian colleagues have arrived!" he announced with a sweeping flourish of his purple cloak.

A round of applause greeted their entrance.

Haverstick stepped to the center of the room, obviously intent on establishing his importance in the hierarchy of the project. Clearing his throat, he commenced his introduction.

Alessandra gauged the time as she waited for the president to finish his speech. A quarter hour of small talk, she figured, and then she could gracefully withdraw and return home.

At the host's signal, the Chianti was uncorked and a welcoming toast was raised.

"Lady Giamatti!" As the wine began to flow, Dwight-Davis

gave an exuberant wave. "Do come and let me have the honor of introducing you to your fellow countrymen."

Drawing a deep breath, she crossed the carpet.

"The head of the delegation is Conte Orrichetti," began Dwight-Davis. But before he could continue, a courtly, silver-haired gentleman brushed aside all formalities and stepped forward to press a quick kiss to both her cheeks.

"My dear Alessandra! What a lovely surprise to see you," said Orrichetti. "Alas, I hate to say it, but the English climate seems to agree with you, for you are looking more beautiful than ever."

"*Saluti*, Pietro." She, too, had not expected to see an old acquaintance. Dwight-Davis had shown her a list of the delegation coming from the Antiquities Society of Rome, and she had not recognized any of the names.

"Ah, you know each other?" asked Dwight-Davis.

"Yes, the conte and my late husband were very good friends," replied Alessandra.

"*Si*, we all spent many a pleasant hour at your palazzo overlooking the lake." Orrichetti heaved a sigh. "Can we not coax you to come back to Como, Alessandra?"

"Perhaps at some time in the future," she said softly. "The memories are still . . . too painful."

"Of course. Forgive me for bringing up the past." Orrichetti patted her hand. "Let us enjoy the present."

"Indeed, indeed," said Dwight-Davis quickly. "I take it as a good omen that Luck has brought yet another familiar face for you to work with on this excavation."

*Luck was notoriously fickle*, thought Alessandra, while maintaining a dutiful smile.

"Like Lord Fanning, the original head of the Roman

delegation was compelled by family obligations to forgo an extended trip abroad," explained Dwight-Davis. "We are all fortunate that Conte Orrichetti was able to step in at the last moment and take over."

The conte inclined a bow to his host before offering Alessandra his arm. "Come, my dear, and let me introduce you to the others. I don't believe you are acquainted with Signor Luigi Mariello, who teaches Classical Poetry at the University of Rome..."

They proceeded down the line, repeating the ritual exchange of kisses and compliments. Though she tried to keep her attention focused, the faces of the strangers began to blur together. She was tired, and the encounter with Lord James Jacquehart Pierson had left her out of sorts.

The Bath contingent had begun to mix in with the foreigners, and as the babel of English and Italian— punctuated with classical Latin—grew louder, so did the pounding inside her head. Her gaze darted to the clock as Orrichetti looked around for the eighth and last scholar from Rome.

"I should warn you, I have one more surprise," murmured the conte.

"Indeed?" She was listening with only half an ear.

"*Si.* The last name on Mr. Dwight-Davis's list may have been unfamiliar, but I daresay you will recognize the face. I am not the only one of Stefano's old friends to make the journey to England."

A prickling sensation started up her spine, like daggerpoints dancing over her flesh.

"*Ciao*, Alessa."

*That honeyed voice.* Alessandra suddenly felt a wave

of nausea rise up from the pit of her stomach as she turned around. *That angelic face.*

Frederico Bellazoni smiled. "I always knew that Fate would bring us together again."

Lady Giamatti looked as if she had just seen a ghost. Even from halfway across the room, Jack could see that all the color had suddenly drained from her face.

*Give her brandy, you fools*, he thought, watching the Italians gesture to the footmen for a bottle of red wine.

Without thinking, he took a step toward her, then caught himself. Lady Giamatti would certainly not welcome his interfering yet again in her private affairs.

Not that she looked pleased at having *anyone* try to offer her assistance. Already she was shaking off Orrichetti's steadying hold on her arm.

Jack knew that common sense called for him to make a strategic retreat. But against all reason he found himself edging closer, close enough to overhear the conversation.

"I insist that you sit down, Alessandra." Orrichetti gestured for a chair. "Have you a vinaigrette in your reticule?"

"Oh, please, Pietro, I assure you that I have no need for smelling salts. I was feeling a little light-headed for a moment, but I am perfectly fine now."

Alessandra did indeed look a little better, though to Jack's eye there was still an odd tautness to the corners of her mouth.

"I am afraid that the fault is partly mine." Another blue-coated Italian was hovering by her side, his golden curls a gleaming contrast to Orrichetti's silver hair.

"I should not have shocked you by appearing here with no advance warning." He gave a rueful smile. "But I wanted to surprise you."

"Don't blame yourself, sir," replied Alessandra softly. "The room is overly warm, and I was traveling for most of the day, so it's simply a case of fatigue."

The blond Italian pressed a hand to his heart. "Dare I hope that means you are not unhappy to see me?"

The fringe of her dark lashes shadowed her expression for just an instant. "Old friends are always a welcome sight."

"You are a lucky fellow, Signor Bellazoni, to count the marchesa as an intimate acquaintance." Dwight-Davis beamed as he raised his glass in a toast. "To friends old and new!"

In echo of the sentiment, corks popped and jovial laughter rose from the rest of the room.

Jack knew he ought to go mingle with the scholars who were gathering around the punch table. And yet, he hesitated for a moment, his gaze lingering on Alessandra. If he didn't know better, he would say that she looked...flustered. *The cool, composed marchesa nervous as a schoolgirl?* Most likely it was just a quirk of the flickering candlelight.

"Here, Alessa, perhaps a glass of Bath's famous restorative water will help revive your strength." Bellazoni offered the glass with a graceful flourish.

Watching him, Jack was reminded of another Italian "B"—Botticelli. With his slender height, gilded ringlets, and full-lipped smile, Bellazoni looked as if he had stepped right out of a painting done by the Renaissance master.

"*Grazie*, Frederico," murmured Alessandra.

So, the two were intimate enough to be on a first-name basis?

*So, what of it?*

Jack quickly swallowed the last of his wine and turned away, feeling a little angry with himself for having stooped to being a *voyeur*. Lady Giamatti's personal life was really none of his concern. She was simply another colleague, and from now on he would take care that their exchanges would be purely professional.

No more sparks would flare between them, he vowed.

If she chose to reignite an old love affair, that was nobody's business but her own.

Alessandra took a sip of the water and then set it aside. "Thank you," she repeated. "But what I really need is a good night's rest."

An added sigh—admittedly exaggerated—drew an immediate apology from Dwight-Davis. "Do forgive me, Lady Giamatti! Knowing that you only arrived this afternoon, I should never have pressed you to attend this reception."

"On the contrary. In order for the excavation to go smoothly, it is important for all members of our team to become familiar with each other," she replied. "It is just that traveling with a young child can be more fatiguing than moving a mountain of stone. So I hope you will excuse me if I take an early leave. I assure you that I will be fully recovered by morning."

"I will accompany you to your carriage," announced Orrichetti.

She was in no mood for company, but a look at his face told her protest would only prolong the scene. Accepting his arm, she allowed him to escort her from the room.

"*Prego*, Alessandra," murmured the conte, once they were alone on the stairs. "Allow me to explain Frederico's presence here."

"Please do," she said, trying not to sound too shrill. "Since when has he become an expert in ancient history? I seem to recall that his chosen field was rhetoric—fiery rhetoric."

"*Si, si,* I know that his political speeches were sometimes a little radical. But remember, Stefano considered him one of his most gifted protégés."

*Oh yes, her late husband had admired Frederico's eloquence.* So had she. Idealism inspired a passionate response.

Orrichetti lowered his voice even more. "Were you aware that right after you left Italy, the Austrian authorities in Milan issued a warrant for his arrest?"

"Yes," she whispered.

The conte slanted her a sidelong look. "Frederico claims it was not he who sabotaged the Governor-General's carriage, and I believe him."

Alessandra felt her throat go very dry. She, too, had found Frederico's silver-tongued speeches seductive...

"In any case, he was forced to flee to Rome," continued Orrichetti. "Where I helped him get a position teaching at the university under an assumed name."

"That still does not explain why he is here in England as part of your delegation," she said slowly.

"He has renounced radicalism, and greatly regrets that his speeches might have sparked violence among those who favor an independent Italy," said Orrichetti. "For the past year, he has led a quiet life, devoting himself to

teaching and writing about the politics of ancient Rome."
The conte paused as a footman approached to hand him
Alessandra's cloak.

She drew up the velvet hood, hoping to mask her misgivings. Maybe Frederico *had* changed.

But she wouldn't bet her life on it.

Orrichetti stayed close, making a show of helping her
descend the townhouse steps. "However, several months
ago, Frederico was warned that the Austrians were on his
trail. He decided that it would be safer to leave the
country until the hunt died down." The conte blew out his
breath. "So when I was asked to take over as head of the
delegation at the last moment, I decided to grant his request to be added to the group. For old times' sake."

*For old times' sake.*

"I see." Alessandra kept her voice neutral.

The conte cocked his head. "I was under the impression that you and he were good friends, yet you do not
seem overly pleased by his presence."

*Thank God that Orrichetti did not know the full extent
of her relationship with Frederico.*

"You must excuse me, Pietro—I am tired and have a
beastly headache, so it is hard to appear enthusiastic
about anything."

He inclined a sympathetic nod. "Then don't let me keep
you a moment longer. Feel better, my dear. We shall have
plenty of time for reminiscences in the coming weeks."

Alessandra lost no time in climbing into her carriage.

*Oh, if only her horses could sprout wings and fly her
to the moon.* There seemed to be no place on earth
where she could hide from her past.

Leaning back against the squabs, she pressed her palms to her brow. The clatter of the iron wheels on the cobblestones seemed to echo her own harsh question over and over again.

*How had she made such a dreadful mistake as to turn to Frederico after the death of her husband?*

She drew in a deep breath. Perhaps part of the problem lay in her family history. Both her parents possessed a certain rebellious streak. Their love match had pleased neither family, but the pair had defied all objections and followed their hearts. Everyone said that Alessandra had inherited her mother's stunning good looks and her father's intellectual brilliance. The trouble was, an impetuous nature had also been passed on.

Happily, her marriage to one of her father's acquaintances, a Tuscan nobleman admired throughout the Continent for his erudite political essays, provided a welcome measure of stability. Twenty years her senior, Stefano had been both a wise and kind companion. With his encouragement, she had enjoyed an intellectual freedom unknown to most females. And after the birth of Isabella, life had seemed...idyllic. However, all that changed on the sudden death of the marchese from a heart ailment.

Alone and emotionally vulnerable, she had put her trust in the fiery words of her radical intellectual friends.

*Only to be badly burned.*

Alessandra uncovered her eyes, and watched the play of moonlight on the pale, polished stone of the Royal Crescent. She could not pretend to be blind to her own stupidity. Her own egregious error in judgment.

A chill snaked down her spine. Frederico was a protégé of her husband and a gifted orator who was oh-so clever with his words—and his kisses. *The gilded angel with the heavenly voice and celestial smile.* She had been seduced by his eloquent speeches promising liberty and equality, if only people would have the courage to fight for their principles.

But his promises had soon turned to lies.

Alessandra bit her lip. Even now, she was ashamed to think of how easily she had been duped. At first, the things he asked of her seemed harmless—a few small smoke devices to make a symbolic statement. Even after hearing rumors of the group's escalating violence, she had allowed Frederico to explain away her misgivings. It was only when he had asked for an incendiary device to place in a building used by the occupying Austrian army that she had come to her senses and refused to make any more things for him in her laboratory.

He had asked her for just one more favor...

*No.* She would not relive the pain of the past.

Alessandra shifted in her seat. She had come to England to make a new life for herself and for Isabella. No longer a naïve girl, she had learned her lesson about trusting a handsome face. Never again would she make *that* mistake.

Turning away to the shadows, Alessandra wished yet again that her cousin Marco were not on his way to Scotland. She had ignored all his earlier advice on how to deal with her past. Now, however, his counsel would be most welcome...

"*Dio Madre*," she whispered. Marco might be family, but he was still a man. And look at where putting blind trust in a member of the opposite sex had gotten her.

No, this time around, she would not count on any man

to make decisions for her. She had only herself to blame for the past. Now it was up to her—and her alone—to deal with the present.

Frederico's presence in Bath might be an innocent co-incidence. After all, what harm could he do her in England, save to remind her of what a fool she had been?

Alessandra didn't have the answer, but one thing was certain. She must be more on guard than ever.

# Chapter Nine

*H*ow do you like Bath so far, Herr Lutz?" asked Jack as he carefully cleaned his paintbrushes.

"The color of the buildings is quite interesting when the sun is shining," answered the drawing master. "As for the famous water, I am curious to see if the mineral content affects the lighter washes."

"Perhaps just a shade." Jack handed over his sketchbook. "You may see for yourself, though I haven't had time to do more than a few quick sketches of the Bath Abbey and Sidney Gardens."

"*Sehr gut*, Lord James," said the drawing master as he thumbed through the pages. "Your brushwork is improving nicely, but I still think you need some work on the art of creating perspective." He set the book aside and reached for a large leather portfolio. "I have brought a few examples to show you. Please have a look while I prepare a palette of colors."

Jack untied the strings and spread a series of Alpine

sketches over the table. "Yes, I think I see what you mean," he murmured after studying them for a bit. Looking up, he spotted a small paper folder tucked inside the main flaps.

No doubt it contained more examples.

He flipped it open, only to discover a set of charcoal sketches. His mouth quirked. They appeared to be of the lion at the Tower menagerie, and though clearly done by a child, the style had an eye-catching boldness and verve.

"These are actually quite good," he murmured.

"Thank you." Lutz did not look up. "The lake is the Silsersee, near Davos."

"No, I mean the lion." Jack chuckled. "Since when have you taken on children as pupils? I thought you told me that you didn't have the patience for dealing with tears and tantrums."

"I confess, I was loath to take on the assignment, but the mother was so earnest." He carefully added a pinch of Raw Sienna to the color he was mixing. "Not to speak of lovely. I found I could not say no."

"A pretty woman?" Jack grinned. "I am glad to hear you have blood flowing through your veins, and not paint."

Lutz flashed a rare smile. "Even dried pigment might develop a pulse around this particular lady." Dipping a sable-hair brush into a jar of water, he twirled it to a fine point. "We are ready, sir. Kindly step over here and I shall show you a few tricks for drawing perspective."

Sensing the other man's reluctance to speak of personal matters, Jack did not pursue the subject. His relationship with the stoic Swiss was cordial but a bit constrained. This was the first time they had ever exchanged a bit of banter.

"If you look closely at the landscape drawings of Rembrandt, you will see how he creates a feeling of depth through the use of line and tone." Lutz chose a wider brush for the newly mixed color. "He uses a light ochre wash—like so..." For the next quarter hour, the drawing master demonstrated a range of effects.

"Lud, if I could draw half so well as that, I should be a very happy man," murmured Jack. "How did you learn such skills—or do you just have a natural talent for art?"

"Some people may be fortunate enough to be gifted with talent, Lord James. But like most endeavors, art takes a great deal of study and hard work to master."

Jack straightened and sighed. "The next chance I get, I will look at art with a more discerning eye, rather than merely viewing it for pleasure."

"I have an acquaintance, an eccentric connoisseur of art, who lives nearby here. He has a great collection of Dutch landscape watercolors, as well as Italian architectural renderings, that you would find most interesting."

"Indeed?"

"In fact, he is the reason I have come to Bath. On occasion, I am called upon to serve as a consultant for prospective acquisitions. In addition to paintings, he has a treasure trove of rare books and prints from all over the world. If you can take an afternoon away from your archaeological duties, I may be able to arrange for you to accompany me on a visit."

"I should like that very much." Jack carefully collected the practice sketches to keep as reference. "It won't be a problem to request some time off."

"Then I will arrange it," replied Lutz. He began packing up his supplies. "I will be spending the next few days at the earl's estate. In the meantime, practice makes perfect, sir. Work on your washes for our next meeting. And use no other color but sepia."

"I will do that."

"*Sehr gut.*" Lutz rolled up his brushes. "*Guten tag,* Lord James."

"Good day," echoed Jack, disappointed that the lesson had passed so quickly. As the committee heads were still making a preliminary study of the site, the excavation would not begin for several days, and the lull after all the rushing around in London had left him a little restless.

It was, he mused, a bit like the feeling on the eve of battle—anticipation, anxiety. The resolve to prove oneself worthy of any challenge.

*Not that he was about to face a dangerous enemy.* Just a fiery female scholar who did not think him deserving of the promotion in rank.

A glance out the window showed that the earlier mists had blown through, leaving the surrounding buildings bathed in a mellow golden light. Taking up his paint box and sketchbook, Jack decided to walk to the Abbey and spend an hour or two sketching the façade. The carved stone, with its pale color and intricate patterns, was a perfect subject to paint with a monochromatic palette.

He took a seat on a low wall, and quickly became engrossed in his work. After finishing several different views, he leaned back and studied the results. *Not bad.* He was getting better at simplifying his brushstrokes.

Satisfied with his day's efforts, Jack flexed his stiff shoulders and repacked his case. He was just about to turn for the far gate when he spotted a child with a watercolor box, her half-hidden face scrunched in concentration.

On impulse, he altered his course for a quick glance at what she was working on.

The girl looked up.

*The imp of Satan.*

She didn't look any more pleased at the chance encounter than he was. Her small mouth pinched to a scowl. "It's not finished yet," she said defensively. "You aren't supposed to peek."

Jack had already caught a glimpse of the paper. "Why not?" he asked. "It's actually very good."

Her eyes widened. "Really?"

"Yes. Really." He craned his neck for a better view. "It is not easy to draw gargoyles, but you have caught their expression quite nicely." The fantastical creatures no doubt appealed to a youthful imagination. He smiled in spite of himself. "Indeed, your efforts are much better than mine."

She fixed him with a fishy stare. "*You* aren't an artist."

"No. Just a student, like yourself, Miss Isabella."

A giggle greeted his reply.

He knew he was asking for trouble. Still, he couldn't help but be curious. "What's so funny?"

Her gaze ran slowly from the tips of his boots to the top of his high crown beaver hat. "You look too big to be in the schoolroom. And too old."

"Education is for a lifetime," replied Jack. "If you recall, Lord Hadley was studying science with Lady Sheffield, and he is far more ancient than I am." The earl was, in truth, two months older.

The little girl's mouth pursed in thought.

"So you see, even old dogs can learn new tricks."

Isabella laughed again. "You aren't so horrid after all," she conceded. "Though not quite so much fun as Lord Hadley." She paused. "He is going to teach me and Perry how to box when he gets back from his wedding trip."

"Why do you want to learn fisticuffs?" asked Jack.

"So I can protect myself." Her chin rose a notch. "The next time a nasty villain tries to kidnap me, I will punch him in the nose."

It suddenly struck him how very frightening the recent experience must have been for the child. With a twinge of conscience, he realized that perhaps he had been a little harsh in his judgment of her. Looking down, he was aware of how very small and slender she was. And how very large and black he must appear.

*And weren't all children afraid of the dark?*

Jack cleared his throat. "You need not worry—you aren't in any danger here in Bath, Miss Isabella." He looked around. "Though I am not sure that you ought to be out here alone."

"I'm not alone," she answered. "Mama just went to the fountain to fetch some fresh water for my paints."

"Ah." All the more reason to move on. Instead, he sat down next to her. "May I see the rest of your sketchbook?"

She hesitated a moment and then shyly passed it over.

The sketches showed a great deal of talent. "Do you study with a drawing master?" he asked after perusing the pages.

"Yes. He is very good," she answered. "But very strict."

"No bad words allowed, eh?" he murmured.

Isabella made a face. "There are an awful lot of rules here in England, especially for girls. It's not very fair. Perry can say far worse things than I do and not get a spanking."

Jack chuckled. "Trust me, boys get their fair share of swats."

She blinked. "I bet no one ever tried to birch *your* bum."

"Oh, more times than I care to remember. I had four older brothers who found it very amusing to see that I took the blame for their mischief."

Her expression turned a little wistful. "I wouldn't mind having a brother or a sister. Even if they teased me."

Jack wasn't sure how to respond. As he had told the girl's mother, he had no idea how to act around children. Maybe he ought to be going...

A tug on his sleeve stopped him. "It's your turn to show me your sketchbook, sir."

"Very well." He passed it over.

After wiping her paint-smudged hands on her skirts, Isabella carefully opened the cover and began turning the pages.

As the silence stretched out, Jack began to feel absurdly nervous.

"You are very, very, good," she finally announced in a solemn voice.

"Thank you," he replied with equal gravity. "But my teacher says I have much to improve on—"

"Isabella!" Alessandra's agitated voice interrupted the exchange. "Please remember that you are not to converse with strangers—"

Jack looked around.

"Oh." The marchesa stopped in her tracks. "I didn't realize it was you, sir."

He unfolded his legs and rose. "Your daughter is a very talented artist, Lady Giamatti."

"Praise from your lips?" She quirked a tentative smile. "I may swoon from shock."

"You don't strike me as the sort of female who faints very often," he replied. "Though you did appear on the verge of it last night."

Alessandra paled for an instant before recovering her composure. "I was tired from traveling," she said curtly.

Jack had a feeling there was more to the story than that. However, he accepted the explanation with a polite nod. "I trust you are feeling more rested today."

"Yes. Thank you," she murmured, dropping her gaze and taking a seat on the ground cloth beside her daughter.

Jack sat down again, too, earning a slight frown.

"Mama, look at these drawings." Isabella held out his sketchbook before her mother could go on. "Lord James is a corking good artist, is he not?"

"You must not say 'corking,' *tesoro*," said Alessandra. "It is not considered ladylike language."

"I don't like being a lady." Isabella snorted a sigh. "Ladies aren't allowed to have any fun."

Jack couldn't help but smile. "What would you rather be?" he asked.

The little girl thought for a moment. "A pirate! Sailing the seas in search of buried treasure."

"So you like ships?"

"I—I am not sure," admitted Isabella. "I have only been on board one once, when we crossed from Calais to Dover."

He wasn't quite sure what prompted him to speak, save that the little girl seemed lonely. "My eldest brother keeps his yacht anchored at Bristol. If you would like to test the waters, so to speak, I would be happy to arrange for a day cruise. There are quite a number of interesting views of the coast to sketch."

"Oh, what a cork—that is, what a very nice offer, sir." She fixed her mother with a pleading look. "May we, Mama?"

"It is a generous offer, indeed," said Alessandra slowly.

Jack saw her take a cursory look at his book—but only because her daughter had angled the pages right under her nose.

"However, I cannot make any promises, Isa," she continued. "The excavation will require a great deal of work over the next few weeks. I will be very busy. And so will Lord James. I am not sure how much free time we will have for excursions."

The little girl's shoulders sagged but she said nothing as she carefully closed his sketchbook and placed it back in his lap.

Alessandra bit her lip. "It is nearly time for tea, *tesoro*. Shall we stop for strawberry ices on the way home?"

"I'm not very hungry," replied Isabella in a small voice.

Jack hadn't meant to make waves. But no doubt the lady thought that he had deliberately stirred up a squall.

However, when she looked up, there was no accusation in her lovely eyes. Just raw vulnerability. At that moment, Alessandra della Giamatti wasn't the worldly, self-assured scholar. Her mask had slipped, showing a glimpse of her inner feelings. Regrets, shaded by recrimination.

Jack felt a sudden stab of sympathy. Hell, her life must not be easy—a widow, far away from friends, trying to raise a child on her own. He wondered why she had chosen to leave all that was familiar for a foreign land...

"Then we shall go straight home, and Cook will make you a cup of hot chocolate," said Alessandra, smoothing the curls from her daughter's brow. "The ground is damp and you look a little chilled." She hurriedly packed up Isabella's painting supplies. "Good day, Lord James."

The message was clear as a ship's bell—she meant to weather the storm alone.

Any sailor worth his salt would have the sense to steer clear of this lady and child. Why try to navigate such dangerous waters?

Jack heaved a silent sigh and rose from his seat on the oilskin cloth.

"Allow me to carry that for you, Lady Giamatti."

Before Alessandra could object, Jack took up Isabella's paint box.

"Really, sir, you are already burdened with enough—"

His free hand was already on her arm, helping her to her feet.

Despite the layers of wool and muslin, she was acutely aware of the warm, steady strength radiating from his touch. *Lud, the man lifted her as if she was light as a feather.* But then, she had ample enough reason to know what sculpted muscles lay beneath his clothing. As her shoulder grazed his, she drew in a breath to protest again.

Only to be overwhelmed by his distinctive scent of sandalwood, tobacco, and starched linen.

The words died in her throat. The essence was intensely male, especially mixed with the earthy musk of his skin.

She jerked back, nearly tripping on her skirts.

"It's no bother," replied Jack softly. "We are headed in the same direction."

"I—I..." Realizing she was stuttering like a silly schoolgirl, Alessandra busied herself with fixing the collar of Isabella's coat.

"We are staying in Trim Street," announced her daughter. "Where are you residing, sir?"

"In Queen Street." Jack rolled up the ground cloth and added it to the rest of his load. "So it appears that we are neighbors."

Isabella mulled over the statement for a moment or two. "Well then, perhaps you would like to stop by our townhouse sometime and see my sketches of Perry and Lord Hadley. I—"

"Isabella," interrupted Alessandra, trying not to sound too shrill. "You must not pester Lord James. I am sure he is very busy in town. A gentleman has many demands on his time."

"I am never too busy to view art," said Jack. "I would be very happy to accept your invitation, assuming your mother has no objection." In a lower voice he added, "I give you my word that I will not tie your daughter to a tree, or any other immovable object."

"You may want to think twice before making any such rash promises, sir," she warned. "Clearly you have little experience with children, otherwise you would know that it's never wise to surrender any option."

Jack chuckled—a low, lush rumble that sent a strange shiver down her spine. "Are you saying that you've resorted to rope, Lady Giamatti?"

"There have been times when I've been tempted to do the unthinkable."

*Like right now.*

Against all reason, she found herself tempted to lean in a little closer to study the sculpted curves of his mouth. There was something sinfully sensual about the fullness of his lower lip, and the memory of its imprint upon her mouth—

*Sinful.* Alessandra quickly lowered her gaze. Yes, the man was a handsome devil. But hadn't she sinned enough?

He chuckled again. "It sounds like military tactics and child-rearing have more in common than one might think."

"Will you show me how to shoot a pistol?" demanded Isabella. "And wield a saber?" She skipped across the grass, waving an imaginary sword.

*Thank God for her daughter's interruption.* The lilting laughter was a pointed reminder that Isabella's future depended on her. She couldn't afford to make another mistake.

"If I am to be a pirate, I need to know how to capture a treasure ship," continued the little girl.

"Not a chance. Your mother would make me walk the plank," replied Jack. "However, I would be happy to show you how to mix up a better shade of blue for painting the sky."

Isabella considered the offer. "Oh, very well. Pirates

probably have lots of free time to paint while they are sailing the seas."

"I'm afraid Lady Sheffield's son was sharing his book on buccaneers with my daughter." Alessandra gave a wry grimace. "I hadn't realized until now what bloodthirsty little creatures boys are."

"As one of five boys, I assure you that you've used the mildest of adjectives, Lady Giamatti," said Jack. "My mother would probably agree with your earlier choice of *diavolo*, though not *nero*. The others are all fair-haired."

"You have four brothers?"

"Four *older* brothers." His black brows quirked, softening the chiseled lines of his face. "Whose heroes were dragon-slaying knights rather than swashbuckling pirates. And seeing as I was the runt of the litter, you can imagine who was poked and slashed with makeshift swords. It's a wonder that I survived my childhood."

She repressed a smile, trying to picture a pack of howling blond savages chasing after their smaller sibling. Somehow it was hard to imagine the tall, broad-shouldered Lord James as a small boy.

It was even harder to imagine him terrified of anything.

"Dragons!" Isabella twirled in circles. "I think I shall draw a dragon next. With great, big teeth, just like the lion I saw in London."

Alessandra saw a flicker of surprise in Jack's eyes. "A lion," he repeated. "Miss Isabella mentioned that she studied with a drawing master in London. Would his name perchance be Gerhard Lutz?"

"Why, yes. H-how did you guess?"

"I happened to see your daughter's sketches in his portfolio during my last lesson."

Alessandra frowned in confusion. In her experience with London Society, rakish blades of the *beau monde* did not spend their time taking art lessons. "You, a student of Herr Lutz? I think you are teasing me again, sir. I am well aware that your peers do not consider the study of art a very…manly pursuit."

"Manly." He curled a half smile. "Perhaps I don't feel the need to prove myself to anyone, Lady Giamatti. Including you."

"Why should you?" she replied, covering her uncertainty with a quick retort.

His lips twitched. "Not that anyone has ever questioned my manhood."

The teasing whisper stirred sudden thoughts of Jack's body unclothed. *Wicked thoughts.* Contrary to all rational laws of physics, her insides began to slide and twist into a terrible tangle.

Tearing her gaze away from his mesmerizing mouth, Alessandra quickly regained control of her wayward emotions. "I, too, couldn't care less about what others think of me."

"Then we actually agree on something," he said lightly.

She drew in a breath, and then let it out, unsure how to respond.

"Then again, it seems we are also in accord on the talents of Gerhard Lutz. Who knows what else we might have in common?"

The suggestion was like a lick of ice against her spine. Or was it fire?

If Jack noticed her agitation, he had the grace not to remark on it. "Lutz is a superb artist and excellent teacher," he went on. "And very much in demand. Both Miss Isabella and I are fortunate that he consented to take us on as pupils."

Alessandra finally managed to master her emotions. "How did you come to be studying with him?"

"Lutz and I met in Italy and spent a few days together, hiking and sketching the Alpine scenery. When I discovered that he was living in London, I asked to be taken on as a student."

"You attend his Academy classes?"

"No. I've engaged him for private tutorials."

No doubt Lord James Jacquehart Pierson, scion of pomp and privilege, did not wish to rub shoulders with those of less than noble birth. Which begged the question of why he was here at the excavation.

She didn't pretend to understand his motivations—and she didn't dare to delve too deeply into his inner thoughts. Her friend Ciara had hinted that Jack had hidden facets to his character, but as far as she was concerned, they were best left undiscovered.

*Why go digging for new trouble?*

"Ah," she replied. "I suppose you prefer not to mix with the other classes."

Though the brim of his hat shaded his face, Alessandra thought she detected a darkening of his gaze. *Anger?* She wasn't quite sure. He hid his emotions well.

"I prefer to concentrate on improving my weaknesses, which is best done under individual guidance," answered Jack slowly. "I have much to learn about rendering the nuances of perspective..."

As Jack went on to explain the technical aspects, Alessandra couldn't help recalling the brief glimpse of his sketchbook. From what little she had seen, he appeared to be a very skilled artist. She didn't want him to be, but he was.

*Why couldn't he fit into the simple outlines she had drawn for him?*

Stopping abruptly, Alessandra held out her hand for Isabella's paint box and ground cloth. "I just recalled a stop that I must make on Milsom Street. Thank you for carrying our things this far, sir, but we really must part company."

He eyed her for a moment with that dark look that always seemed so disapproving. "The items are rather weighty for a lady to be lugging through the streets."

Of course they were. What she was suggesting was absurd—which only made her respond more sharply. "I am an archaeologist, sir. I am used to hauling heavy objects, like stones and baskets of dirt."

"As a scientist, wouldn't you agree that a far more practical solution would be for me to drop these at your townhouse while you go about your business?" he replied.

She could hardly argue without appearing a total ninny.

"If you are sure it is no trouble..."

"None whatsoever."

"Thank you. How very kind."

The flicker in his gaze told her that he wasn't fooled at all by her feeble attempt at civility.

"Good day, Lady Giamatti." Jack gave a solemn nod. "And you, Miss Isabella. Enjoy your shopping."

\* \* \*

As he watched them walk away, Jack found himself smiling. It was hard to explain why he had gone out of his way to be friendly with the two most fiery females of his acquaintance. But strangely enough, this latest encounter had not left him feeling singed. In fact, he had rather enjoyed conversing with Isabella. He had forgotten how delightfully whimsical a child's imagination could be, flitting from here to there, unfettered by the constraints of adult logic or convention.

*Free-spirited.*

Perhaps there was nothing wrong with defying the rules from time to time. In some ways, Isabella's exuberant skipping and spinning brought to mind some of the watercolor sketches he had seen in Mr. Turner's studio—bold, blurred dabs of color, rendered with childlike spontaneity.

It was the *feeling* that mattered, not the object itself.

Jack stared thoughtfully at the rippling leaves across the lawns, suddenly recalling Lutz's words on developing an individual artistic style.

*Experiment. Don't be afraid to be different.*

His gaze shifted in time to catch the flutter of dark skirts swishing through the gates. No question that the marchesa dared to defy convention. Gifted with a remarkable intellect, she had decided to develop her talents, no matter that Society did not approve of a female who was smart.

That took courage, and conviction.

Shifting the load in his arms, Jack started walking. He wasn't sure whether he wanted to pursue such thoughts.

It was far simpler to think of Alessandra della Giamatti as a Harpy or a harridan than as ... a friend. After all, she had made it clear as crystal that she did not welcome his advances.

He did not consider himself a conceited coxcomb, but what man liked to have his gallantry shoved back in his face?

Take, for example, Lady Mary Stiles, who his father was hinting would make a perfectly proper match for a ducal son. She followed the rules of polite behavior to the letter, smiling prettily and agreeing with every utterance that came out of his mouth. There was something to be said for such biddable behavior.

*Yes, and the word was boring*, whispered a voice in the back of his brain.

Jack shook his head, seeking to silence the imp.

On the contrary, he told himself. Propriety was pleasant. A female—especially a wife—should be like a background wash in a painting. The color was simply there, a necessary element to anchor the more interesting elements of the composition. It didn't draw notice to itself.

*And wasn't that a pretty picture?*

He forced a smile. Yes, of course it was. One that wouldn't look a hair out of place in the family portrait gallery. Closing his eyes, he found that he could visualize the long line of ancestors with startling clarity. The problem was, each face was indistinguishable from another. They all seemed to blend together in a dull blur.

Maybe conformity did leave something to be desired.

# Chapter Ten

*H*ere in England, ladies have too many things to fret about, Mama," complained Isabella the next morning as they finished their breakfast.

At the moment Alessandra was inclined to agree with her daughter. She had spent the night worrying about how the presence of Frederico would affect her life. One of the reasons she had accepted the position at the Bath excavation was to hide from the present by immersing herself in the past.

But apparently her old life refused to stay buried.

"A lady must not speak unless spoken to. A lady must not contradict a gentleman. A lady must not slide down banisters. And that's just the beginning! The rules go on forever and ever." Isabella kicked at the carpet as Alessandra packed her trowels and hammers into a canvas bag. "I would much rather dig in the dirt with you than stay home with Miss Wolcott learning how to be dainty." Her chin took on a distinct jut. "And demure."

"I don't think we have to fear that you will be turned into a pattern card of propriety," she replied dryly.

"Marco says propriety is boring," responded her daughter.

"Marco says a great many things that aren't meant for the ears of an eight-year-old girl."

"I am almost *nine*."

"Perhaps when you are nine *and twenty* you may be allowed to listen to him without a scolding."

Isabella rolled her eyes.

"I am sorry, but an excavation is a dangerous place for a child, *tesoro*. There is much digging going on, and with all the trenches and open pits, it is easy for an accident to happen. I cannot supervise the workers and keep an eye on you."

"I could help Lord James with his drawings," said Isabella hopefully.

Alessandra repressed a sigh. "Lord James is new to the world of archaeological expeditions. He will be having enough difficulty trying to find his footing without having to oversee an apprentice." She could just picture Jack's face if she were to ask him to play nursemaid to her daughter. "Besides, I thought you didn't like *si grand nero diavolo*."

"He's not so terrible," she conceded. "And I didn't call him any more bad names, so there is no reason for him to tie me to a tree."

Alessandra could think of quite a few things a child might do to provoke a gentleman into reaching for rope. However, she kept them to herself. "I promise that I shall take you on a tour of the grounds on one of our rest days. We are starting to uncover a temple and underground baths, and there will likely be lovely mosaics and sculptures."

"And columns?" asked Isabella. "Lord James seems to like to draw columns."

"I daresay Lord James will find plenty of stonework to keep him busy." Alessandra took up her bag and pressed a kiss to her daughter's cheek. "Behave yourself. I shall see you at supper."

"Watch your step, sir. The ground is rather wet here," warned Dwight-Davis. "And you must take care not to stray off the path, for there's a bog just ahead and the footing is very treacherous. That is one of the reasons the place stayed undiscovered for so long."

Jack crossed the stream in one stride. "Thank you, but I need not be treated like a lad in leading strings. I've survived the Peninsular War, so I trust I can make it through an English swamp."

The other man turned beet red. "Forgive me, Lord James. *Magna res et vocis et silenti temperamentum*—the great thing is to know when to speak and when to keep quiet. I meant no insult to your intelligence—"

"No offense taken, Mr. Dwight-Davis. However, I wish to be treated the same as any other new member to the expedition. Pampering or special privileges will not endear me to my fellow workers."

"Hmmph. I understand your point." Dwight-Davis pulled a face. "It's just that I have never had the son of a duke mucking through the mud with me."

"Seeing I want to learn about archaeology from the ground up, it's a fitting place to start," quipped Jack. "Besides, I'm not the least bit afraid of getting my hands dirty."

"Well, if you are sure..."

A half hour later, as he missed his footing and slid into a steep trench puddled with foul-smelling, ankle-deep water, Jack was regretting such hubris.

"May I offer you a hand up, my lord?" A silky Italian accent floated down from above.

Jack looked up to see Alessandra's Italian friend— Bezzeroli? Berelloni? Bellazoni?—extend an arm. "Have a care, sir. The grounds are quite slippery."

"Thank you, but I can manage," he replied a little curtly.

"Might I suggest a pair of hobnailed boots next time?"

Jack realized he looked a little foolish dressed in his town clothes. He wasn't slated to start work until the morrow, but he had encountered Dwight-Davis near the Pump Room, and the invitation to take a quick tour of the area had been irresistible. He hadn't wanted to delay the other man by returning home to change into proper work attire.

"This was a spur-of-the-moment visit," he muttered, stomping the mud from his Hessians. "I already have all the necessary excavation gear. Signor..."

"Bellazoni, my lord. But as we are all to be working together out here under informal conditions, I would just as soon you call me Frederico."

"Speaking of formality, you need not address me as 'my lord.' I am a younger son, and am not given such a title." Even to his own ears, he sounded like a self-important prig. "Lord James is the correct form."

"Pray, accept my apologies. I am woefully ignorant when it comes to the nuances of nobility."

Frederico's tone was perfectly pleasant. Which made Jack feel even more like a churl. Good God, it was completely unlike him to care about the niggling little distinctions of rank and title. He had always preferred to be recognized by his own actions rather than an accident of birth. Was this odd response aroused by some primitive male instinct?

*Jealousy?*

His toes curled within the wet leather. The idea was ridiculous. He was a rational gentleman, not a snabbering beast...

"Forgive me for interrupting, but might you conduct your lecture on primogeniture somewhere else, Lord James?"

Jack didn't need to turn around. By some perverse pagan spell, his body seemed to sense Alessandra's presence whenever she was near.

"I am sure it is a fascinating subject," she continued. "However, I have an excavation grid to lay out and you gentlemen are standing in the way." After consulting her map, she waved to one of the workers. "Hopkins, I want the first hole dug here." She stuck a small stake in the ground, just inches from Jack's boot. "To the depth of a foot is fine for now."

Jack wished that he could sink into the ground—preferably all the way to Hades.

"I will then measure off one hundred paces to the west, marking each interval of ten."

"Aye, madam." The shovel cut into the damp earth.

"I would suggest wearing proper boots tomorrow, Lord James," said Alessandra as she turned to walk off. "Hoby's handiwork is quite impressive," she added, arching her brows as she eyed the rich—and now ruined—leather of his expensive Hessians. "But you are here to work, not cut a caper on the dance floor."

"For your information, a gentleman does not wear boots to a ball," he said through gritted teeth.

She did not hear him, but Frederico did. "You will only dig yourself into a deeper hole by trying to get in the last word with an Italian lady."

"She is half English," said Jack.

"*Si*. But that was a wholly Tuscan tongue speaking. And Tuscan ladies are notorious for their stubbornness and independent spirit." Frederico smiled. "Speaking from experience, I would say that they respond better to charm than to confrontation."

*Splendido*, thought Jack. He had just sunk to a new low. Not only was he being lectured on the basics of archaeology by a feisty female, but he was also receiving amorous advice from the lady's erstwhile lover.

As to their current relationship...

"Then it's a good thing I've absolutely no desire to seek her favor, isn't it?" Turning on his heel, Jack stalked away before he could make an even bigger arse of himself. He hadn't felt like such an idiot since his days as a spotty-faced schoolboy.

"Bloody hell." Cursing under his breath, Jack veered off the footpath and cut through the stacks of storage crates and tools. Beyond the loading area was a steep hillock, which separated the two main sections of the ancient enclave. Mindless of the prickly gorse, he started to climb. An overnight rain had softened the earth and the ground was slick in spots. Mud spattered his breeches, thorns snagged at his coat. He slapped at the branches, anger goading him to a faster pace.

*Damn.*

Still brooding over his ignominious entrance into the world of archaeology, he nearly lost his footing on the wet rocks leading down to the eastern edge of the excavation site.

*Steady, steady.* A swan dive into the ruins of the Roman temple below would only corroborate what many of his fellow expedition members were probably thinking—Lord James Jacquehart Pierson was simply a rich dilettante, indulging in a whim. And in taking a coveted spot, he was keeping a more deserving scholar from contributing his expertise.

Jack made a wry face. So far, he hadn't done much to convince them otherwise.

He stood for a moment, watching the bustle of activity around the pale stone columns that were slowly appearing as the peaty soil was dug away. His own petty problems were quickly forgotten as he took in the scene. Under the supervision of Mr. Hightower, an expert from Cambridge, several skilled workers were carefully dislodging the dirt from the entrance to the sacred shrine. Nearby, a line of young boys were lugging baskets filled with earth and rock fragments to be sifted through by a trio of local scholars. Pottery shards, bits of tile, bronze spearheads, silver coins—all artifacts would be carefully cleaned and catalogued.

The digging on this section had started last season, so its shape was beginning to take form. Even to Jack's inexperienced eye, it was clear that the discovery of this site was of monumental importance. He had read the preliminary research papers speculating that the place was likely the southern headquarters for the Second Legion

Augustus. Jack mulled over what he knew of the Roman army's occupation of Britannia.

The main expeditionary force had been quartered in Wales, near Caerleon. That site was perhaps the most famous Roman ruin in Britain—in no small part because it was also said to be the legendary home of King Arthur's Camelot. For nearly four hundred years, beginning around AD 47, the Romans had ruled much of British soil, keeping two to four legions stationed around the country. With each legion consisting of six thousand men, it was a force to be reckoned with.

Viewing the site in person, Jack could see why the scholars were convinced that it was an important base. The location was right—a flat meadow, nestled among limestone hills and woodlands. He shifted his gaze. Close by was the River Avon, its waters rushing through a narrow gorge in the rocks...

"Help!"

The cry floated up from the water's edge. A boy was waving his arms, frantically pointing at the roiling eddies near an outcropping of rocks in the middle of the water.

"Damn." Jack saw a small head bobbing in the foaming current. Charging down the slope, he hurdled a work barrow and slid down the muddy bank.

"Davey! 'E can't swim!" The boy's face was white with fear. "M' brother can't swim!"

Without a heartbeat of hesitation, Jack stripped off his coat and plunged into the frigid water.

Alessandra looked up from her map. "What's going on?" she asked, suddenly aware of cries coming from the other side of the knoll.

"I dunno, madam." The workman cocked an ear. "But it sounds like trouble."

*Indeed it did.* A dig was a dangerous place. Holes could cave in, ropes could snap, ancient rocks could shift, easily crushing a man...

Lifting her skirts, she broke into a run. Unlike Lord James, she had worn sensible footwear—a sturdy pair of half boots with hobnailed soles. The metal clattered against the stones as she left the path and scrambled through the gorse to the crest of the hill. From there she could see a crowd gathered at the river's edge.

*Dear God.*

Fed by spring rains, it was a rushing torrent of ink-black water. Alessandra could see the swirling patterns of the powerful currents, spraying the jagged rocks with flecks of foam. Her breath turned even more ragged as she hurried down the steep slope. She always took great care to establish stringent safety measures around her excavations.

But accidents happened.

Pushing her way through the milling workers, she found the head of the Transportation Committee shouting orders for men and rope to be rushed downstream.

"What's happened?" she demanded.

"One of the basket lads fell in while larking around on the rocks," replied Eustace. "His friends say he can't swim."

Alessandra felt her heart lurch. A child was in danger? She scanned the roiling waters, desperately searching for a sign of life. Between the shifting shadows and refracted sunlight, it was hard to make out any distinct shapes. Finally, in midstream, she spotted one head...then two.

"What—," she began, only to be cut off by a shout from Eustace's assistant.

"Look! I think Lord James has nearly got the lad!"

"Lord James?" repeated Alessandra.

"Aye, the gentleman came charging down the hill and dove straight in from these rocks," said the assistant. "He must have nerves of steel."

"For God's sake, someone help him!" she cried.

The men around her shuffled uncomfortably. "The current is too swift, even for a strong swimmer," said Eustace. "I've sent a party down to the shallows. With luck, they will be able to pull Lord James and the lad to safety."

"But that may be too late!" Alessandra looked around wildly.

"It's too dangerous to try anything else, Lady Giamatti," said Eustace softly. "Let us pray..."

A sudden cheer went up.

She wrenched her gaze back to the water and saw that Jack had managed to snag the boy by his collar and was now angling for the riverbank. His stroke was powerful, despite being hampered by the awkward burden, but the swirling eddies and frigid waters looked to be sapping his strength.

"Kick, sir, kick!" called one of the workers.

Alessandra bit her lip, so hard that she tasted blood.

"By Jove, I think he is going to make it," exclaimed Eustace. "Be prepared to pull them ashore."

Ready hands reached down.

"Blankets," she called out. "Someone fetch blankets."

"And brandy," added Eustace's assistant.

A last splash brought Jack within arm's reach of land.

One of the workmen grabbed the boy, while two others caught hold of Jack's shirt and fished him out of the water.

Gasping for breath, he lay for a moment on the rocks before pushing up to his knees and shaking the sopping hair from his eyes.

A shower of drops flew through the air and splattered over Alessandra's skirts.

A second cheer went up as Jack levered to his feet.

Standing in a puddle of mud, with water dripping from his face and his long locks spilling in a sodden tangle around his shoulders, he should have cut a rather pathetic figure. Instead he somehow looked... magnificent. The very picture of raw virility.

Alessandra couldn't help but stare. His shirt was ripped in several places and clung to every contour of his chest, showing an indecent amount of muscle and a peppering of coarse black curls. Through the nearly transparent linen, she could see that they tapered in an intriguing trail down to his navel.

Her gaze dropped lower. *A big mistake.* The wet buckskin breeches fitted like a second skin, leaving little to the imagination. He had very well-formed thighs, bulging with thick, corded sinew and firm, hard...

*Lower. Look lower.*

"Y-your boots," she stammered.

"Yes, yes, I know," growled Jack. "My boots are not proper swimming attire, but they were already ruined."

She bit her lip in confusion, realizing that her halting words had been interpreted as criticism.

"Lord James! Thank Jupiter you are safe!" The arrival of Dwight-Davis put an end to the awkward moment.

Skidding to a stop, the scholar wheezed for breath as he mopped at his brow. "That was a deucedly remarkable display of bravery, sir! We are fortunate indeed to have such a hero in our ranks."

A murmur of assent went up from the cluster of workers.

"The river is not so deep, and the currents look worse than they really are," replied Jack.

Alessandra could not help but notice that he looked uncomfortable with the lavish praise.

"It was nothing out of the ordinary," he went on. "How is the lad?"

"Cold and frightened, but completely unhurt," piped up Eustace. "Thanks to you, sir."

"Someone should accompany him home to his mother," said Alessandra. "I'll go."

"An excellent suggestion, Lady Giamatti," said Dwight-Davis. "And I shall take Lord James back to town before he catches his death of cold."

"A dip in the river is hardly cause for such a fuss," he muttered, allowing a blanket to be draped over his shoulders.

"Nonetheless, I should hate to see a promising career in the classics cut short before it is properly begun." Dwight-Davis dabbed at his brow. "Not to speak of having to inform the Duke of Ledyard that having survived the battlefields of Portugal and Spain, you had sacrificed your life in the peaceful farmlands of Somerset."

"Don't worry, His Grace has sons to spare," replied Jack.

"Here, sir." One of Haverstick's assistants shoved a flask of brandy into Jack's hands.

"Make way, make way," called Dwight-Davis, raising his shovel with a flourish, as if it were an Imperial standard.

The crowd parted amid another round of cheers.

*Hail Caesar.* Alessandra watched the procession for a moment longer before turning to find the rescued child.

# Chapter Eleven

Jack ran a hand through his still-damp hair, undoing what little order his brush had just achieved. He grimaced at the looking glass, wishing he could shuck off his coat, unknot his cravat, and spend the evening painting instead of attending the supper soiree at the local Historical Society.

*Duty*, he reminded himself. He was fast learning that scholarship and soldiering had much in common—there were times when it was required to parade around in fancy dress.

All of Bath was eager to entertain the Italian delegation. Jack cast a baleful look at the stack of invitations on his mantel. Assemblies, concerts, picnics...Hell, if he had a choice, he would pitch a tent by the river and dispense with the formalities and flatteries.

After a final tug to the folds of starched linen, he squared his shoulders and quitted his rented quarters for the short walk across Queen Square.

"Welcome, welcome, Lord James!" Mr. Lattimer, the head of the local Historical Society, greeted him effusively as he came through the portico. "I trust that you are suffering no ill-effects from your heroic rescue mission."

"None whatsoever," replied Jack, wondering how he could put a damper on any further mention of the afternoon. "I think that the incident has been greatly exaggerated."

"Again, you are being far too modest, sir!" Dwight-Davis hurried over and insisted on giving him a hearty handshake.

"Indeed, the gentleman deserves a medal for bravery." Frederico Bellazoni turned around from one of the glass display cases and lifted his glass in salute.

"A splendid suggestion." Dwight-Davis's eyes lit up. "I'm sure we could fashion a lovely one with a Roman coin and some—"

"Signor Bellazoni was just making a little joke," said Jack, countering the Italian's silky smile with a curt shrug. He shifted his gaze to a shelf lined with marble fragments. "Now tell me, are those statues of Sulis Minerva from the temple here in town?"

As he had hoped, the two scholars were quickly distracted by his question and plunged into a detailed explanation of their history. Frederico listened politely for several minutes before drifting off to join a group by the refreshment table.

An informal supper was served, along with a great many toasts. Quelling the urge to consult his pocketwatch, Jack sipped his wine and tried to pay attention to the elderly wife of a local Society member, who was prosing on in excruciating detail on the armaments of an ancient centurion. There were a handful of other ladies present, their occasional laughter breaking the monotony of male voices.

As for Alessandra della Giamatti...

Jack slanted a look around. She had arrived late and was immediately surrounded by her fellow countrymen. They were still paying court to her, and judging by the smiles and the ebullient snippets of Italian drifting up from their table, the group was having a gay time.

He speared a lobster patty and signaled for a footman to refill his glass.


Her cheeks ached from the effort of keeping a smile in place. And slowly but surely, Alessandra felt the niggling pain creeping up to her temples. Lud, she *never* had headaches.

"Will you try a taste of the creamed pheasant, Alessa?" asked Orrichetti. "We hear horror stories about English cooking, but it is really quite tasty."

"Thank you, Pietro, but I have a full plate."

"From which you have scarcely taken a bite." The conte wagged an elegant finger. "I shall have to invite you to my residence and have the cook prepare a proper *fettuccine Alfredo*."

She managed a small laugh. "On such a diet, I would soon be as fat as the Prince Regent. However, you must be sure to sample the cream from Devonshire while you are here. Even the French are forced to admit it is superb."

"*Si*, but the *Inglieze* have nothing to compare to *mozzarella di Bufala* from Caserta," exclaimed Professor Mariello.

"The cheddar cheese is not half bad..."

Her lips quirked. Italians were almost as opinionated about cuisine as they were about politics. It was no surprise that a lively discussion on food continued for the rest of the meal.

Card tables had been set up in the adjoining room and the guests were invited to have their tea while enjoying a game of whist. Alessandra demurred, choosing instead to take a seat at the pianoforte set in the shade of the potted palms.

She began to play, using the interlude to compose her emotions. Perhaps Beethoven would be a better choice than Vivaldi, she thought wryly. *Dark versus light.* The conflict mirrored her own strange mood.

Lord James Jacquehart Pierson was having an unnerving effect on her. She wished she could dismiss him as just another aristocratic ass—a rich, dull-witted dilettante who would soon grow bored with the demanding discipline required by archaeology. But it was becoming harder and harder to think of him that way. Just before supper, Dwight-Davis had shown Jack's portfolio of architectural watercolors to her and the Roman delegation.

They were, in a word, superb.

Like the man himself, the paintings possessed a muscular grace. *Strong. Sure.* There was great delicacy to detailing, but it was not at all effeminate. That he possessed an impressive artistic talent upset her assumptions. She wished she could see his air of confidence as mere arrogance...perhaps because she secretly envied such inner self-assurance. Yes, he was unyielding in some ways. Yet it confounded her expectations that a battle-hardened blade of the *ton* could have a sensitive soul. That his recent attentions to her daughter had shown an unexpected kindness had also compounded her confusion.

She didn't want him to be nice, she wanted—

A shadow fell across the sheets of music, a solid silhouette of a man's profile that easily overpowered the fluttering pattern of the leafy fronds.

*For a big man, Black Jack Pierson moved with the stealth of a cat.*

Alessandra was incredibly aware of his presence—how could she not be? He was so large, and so *looming*. She didn't have to look up to know his long hair was falling down over his starched shirtpoints, the curling ends kissing the fine merino wool of his evening coat.

*Diavolo*. She could almost swear that the heat of his gaze was prickling like red-hot pitchforks against her flesh.

Her fingers jerked on the ivory keys, striking a wrong note.

She glanced up in confusion. "Is there a reason you choose to stand there and glower at me, Lord James?"

"Forgive me if my expression displeases you," replied Jack quietly. "I was not aware I was glowering."

Alessandra resumed her playing, hoping to hide the erratic thump of her pulse. *Why, oh why, was her body refusing to stay in rhythm with her mind?*

"According to you, I cannot smile, so I fear I have few options left," he added. There was a hint of humor in his tone.

She didn't trust herself to speak. Surely if she didn't answer he would go away.

His palm pressed against the polished wood as he leaned in a little closer. "Have I done something new to offend you, Lady Giamatti?"

Alessandra switched to a Salieri sonata.

"I've not really had a chance to properly apologize for my risqué remarks at the Julius Caesar Society. Please allow me to do so now. It was ungentlemanly to indulge in such petty teasing."

"No further apologies are necessary," replied Alessandra. "I implied that you did not belong there. You had a right to feel insulted."

Jack cocked his head. "Then I assume you continue to dislike me because of our first few encounters."

She felt a tinge of red creep over her cheekbones. "Though we converse in English, we seem to be speaking to each other in foreign tongues, sir. I don't dislike you, Lord James."

"You simply resent my heavy-handed attempts to do the right thing?"

Her lashes lowered, curtaining her eyes. "English notions of chivalry are different from those of Italian men."

"You would prefer Machiavelli?" he asked slowly.

"I would prefer that men of every nationality would stop pestering me!" exclaimed Alessandra in a low voice. "*Santa Cielo!* You all act as if I am a helpless, brainless creature, incapable of looking out for myself. Once and for all, if I ever need help, I shall ask for it."

"Be assured that even if you were speaking in Urdu, I would understand the message quite clearly, Lady Giamatti," replied Jack.

"I doubt you understand at all." A sigh stole out from her lips. She was tired. She was tense. That still did not quite explain how the next words spilled out. "Sometimes I am not quite sure what it is I mean. Or want."

Appalled at the slip of her tongue, Alessandra steeled herself for a sarcastic retort.

Instead, Jack made a wry face. "Actually, I know the feeling."

Her hands stilled in shock. "I—I don't see how you could. A man of wealth and privilege, who has every advantage in life. Why, the world is your oyster."

"Perhaps I don't care for seafood." A half smile played on his mouth. "You know, I don't like it any more than you do when someone makes presumptions about my life, Lady Giamatti."

The candlelight flickered softly across his face. Like his beautiful paintings, Black Jack Pierson appeared deceptively simple at first. But the closer she looked, the more she saw the complex layers and subtle textures that gave shape to the whole.

"Isn't a scientist supposed to refrain from jumping to conclusions?" he asked lightly.

Alessandra was finding it hard to think of scientific rules or textbook theorems as she watched a smile play at the corners of his mouth. "Yes, a serious scholar should always base any judgment on careful research."

"And empirical observation." Jack lowered his lashes. "I expect that you shall be watching me closely over the coming weeks."

*Dio Madre.* It was hard enough to keep her eyes off him now. The thought of intimately observing the flex of his long, lithe muscles as he worked made her mouth go a little dry.

"I shall try to ensure that you have no grounds for complaint," he finished.

Feeling even more confused, she wasn't quite sure how to answer. "I...that is, you..."

"May I join you?" Flicking at the palm fronds, Frederico brushed by the decorative greenery and perched a hip on the piano. "Or am I intruding on a private conversation?"

Jack stepped back. "Not at all. We were just discussing philosophy."

"Philosophy?" Frederico arched a gilded brow. "But the evening is supposed to be a social interlude, not a time for serious subjects." He shifted his stance and gave a light laugh. "So I'm sure you won't mind if I steal Alessa away for a stroll on the terrace."

*Ha! She would just as soon walk through the gates of hell.*

"Come, *cara*. English gardens look so lovely in moonlight." The pressure of Frederico's hand on the small of her back belied the softness of his voice. Alessandra could sense that he did not intend to take no for an answer.

Much as she wanted to swat away his fingers, she rose.

"Enjoy the view." Jack turned without further comment and walked away.

For an instant she wished she were the little boy from the afternoon, held safe in the circle of Jack's muscled arms.

*A childish notion.* She could not look to anyone but herself for rescue from the sordid cesspool of the past.

*And from the moonlit English gardens, would the Italian be strolling his way into the marchesa's bed?*

Jack drowned the snide question in a long quaff of brandy. *Why should he care?* he chided himself. It wasn't as if he would be asked into her boudoir anytime soon.

Quelling a growl—and the urge to punch out several of Frederico Bellazoni's perfect teeth—he took another swallow. And yet...

He slanted a sidelong glance at the couple. Strange, but she looked more like a lady being dragged to an execution than an eager lover on her way to a romantic tryst.

Then again, perception was all in the eye of the beholder. He had been woefully wrong before, and it wasn't a mistake he cared to repeat. Even without her warning, he now knew better than to plunge yet again into her private affairs.

Jack stared into the dregs of his glass. The truth was, he couldn't begin to fathom her feelings—and he wasn't sure whether that angered or intrigued him. There seemed to be strong currents swirling just below the surface of her outward self-assurance.

*But maybe he was simply imagining things.*

His mouth thinned. Unfortunately, he was cursed with a very vivid imagination, for even as he turned away to study a display of Roman coins, he couldn't help but recall their midnight kiss. Her rigid reserve had suddenly dissolved into a wave of passion. Hell, the taste of sweetness and sparks still lingered on his lips...

"Lord James! How good to see that you are dry! But your glass should be wet!" Dwight-Davis waved to a passing footman. "More brandy. And let us all raise a toast to our hero."

Jack gritted his teeth. *Hip, hip, hooray.*

\* \* \*

Gravel crunched underfoot as Alessandra shook off Frederico's touch and quickened her pace along the garden path. The scent of roses perfumed the night, with a hint of lilac wafting in and out of the bordering trellises. Up ahead she saw a marble fountain pooled in moonlight, its pale stone framed by a boxwood hedge.

Drawing a steadying breath, she took up a position with her back against its railing. "I take it you have a reason for wishing to speak with me alone?"

"What makes you think I desire anything more than the pleasure of your lovely company?"

"Please don't waste your golden words on me anymore. What is it you want?"

"Come now, Alessa, we used to be friends." Frederico paused. "Very good friends."

"That is all in the past," she muttered.

He pursed his lips. "Much as we may not like it, the past is always a part of our present lives."

"Pietro said you had taken up the study of history." Alessandra made no attempt to keep the sarcasm out of her voice. "I would have advised the study of ethics."

Flicking aside the tails of his coat, he took a seat on the stone and crossed one elegant ankle over the other. "Oh, I am familiar with the subject. Enough to know there is no such thing as absolute right and wrong."

She bit her lip.

He cocked his head and looked up at the stars, as if savoring the subtle night music—the splash of the water, the chirp of the crickets, the rustle of the breeze through the leaves.

A shiver stole up her spine. She was ashamed to

remember that once their thoughts had been in perfect harmony.

Frederico seemed to sense her thoughts. "Very well, seeing as you are in no mood to reminisce, I shall not keep you much longer. It is true, I have a favor to ask of you."

"You must be joking."

"It's a small one. A harmless one—"

"No," declared Alessandra, somehow keeping her outrage in check.

"Still so impetuous, I see. A lady alight with spark and fire." He fanned his cheeks, a gesture she found insufferably patronizing. "You haven't heard what I have to say."

"I don't have to," she said. "Nothing—*nothing*—could persuade me to help you."

The falling water muffled the scrape of his shoes as he rose and came close. "Are you sure of that?"

"The last time I did as you asked, a man ended up dead. How does that feel on your conscience?"

"*My* conscience? How can you say that, when in truth it was you who mixed the lethal concoction..." His words trailed off with an eloquent shrug.

"The mixture was altered without my knowledge," stammered Alessandra. "I—I only did what you asked."

"Ah, *cara*." A soulful sigh caressed her cheek. "I think perhaps that you misunderstood my words that night," he said in that same silky tone she recalled so well. That boudoir voice—soft, sensuous, soothing. Sliding over her misgivings like the finest gossamer silk.

Now it made her skin crawl.

"No, I did not misunderstand," she whispered. "You lied to me."

"So you say," he replied with a choirboy smile. "But in a court of law, it will be your word against mine. And my oratorical skills are far more polished than yours. Need I remind you that I have a great deal of practice in making pretty speeches?"

Alessandra felt the bile rise in her throat.

"Who do you think they will believe?" he crooned.

"You are a fugitive, wanted for murder," she croaked.

His smile stretched a little wider. "So are you, my dear."

"Damn you to hell."

"Tsk, tsk." Frederico contrived to look injured. "There is no need to be nasty, *cara*. It's a simple thing I ask. And if you do your part, no one will get hurt. I promise." He reached out and ran his thumb lightly along her jaw. "Don't you remember how well we worked together? You may find that you like it—"

Alessandra pushed his hand away. "That time and that naïve young girl are long gone, sir. I was a fool once. I won't make the same mistake twice."

Anger flared in Frederico's eyes, turning their topaz color into a swirl of liquid fire.

How had she been so blind to his arrogance? In the past, she had seen his passion as idealistic. A force for freedom and equality. When all he really wanted to do was change one tyrant for another.

His gaze quickly hardened, turning flat and cold as stone. "It's not quite so easy to dismiss those days—and nights—in Italy. You speak as if what went on between us was ancient history, Alessa. But it is still very much alive." He paused for effect. "Just ask the Austrian authorities."

Alessandra sucked in a breath, taking a moment to still

the pounding of her heart against her ribs. "Your clever little speeches fall on deaf ears. Your threats no longer have the power to frighten me, sir. The English are not about to hand me over to a foreign power. Go ahead and denounce me in public. My mother's family is not without influence in this country. I will survive any scandal."

"A pretty speech, *cara*. It appears you have learned to stand up and speak for yourself." He stepped back and set a hand on his hip. "Or have you? As I recall, you used to depend on Stefano to protect you from life's harsh realities, leaving you free to indulge in your passion for antiquities and abstract ideas. And then, when he was gone, you turned to me."

The truth of his words hit her as hard as a physical blow. Summoning all her strength, Alessandra willed herself to stand firm. She would not give him the satisfaction of seeing her flinch.

"So I can't help but wonder," continued Frederico. "Does a person ever really change? Or have you just found some new protector to cling to? Someone who you think will shield you from your own impetuous nature?" His lips twisted into a cunning curl. "You think that fancy aristocrat—Lord James—might be willing to play the knight in shining armor?"

"Clearly *you* have not changed," replied Alessandra, refusing to dignify the ugly innuendo concerning Jack. "You are still the same selfish, manipulative demagogue as before."

His smirk became more pronounced. "You didn't seem so averse to my manipulations at your villa at Como."

Once—*just once*—she had allowed him into her bed. The night of her birthday, when the flames of the lakeside terrace torchères had lit a feeling of overwhelming longing inside her. *Loneliness. Loss.* Alessandra closed her eyes for an instant, recalling the silvery shimmer of moonlight on the water, the dampness of the mists against her skin. She had been a young widow, suffering through the doubts and fears of her recent loss.

And Frederico, her husband's brilliant protégé, had taken shameless advantage of her weakness...

*No, the blame did not lie entirely with him.* She bore the responsibility for her own decisions.

Which was all the more reason to put an end to this meeting.

"You disgust me," she said in a fierce undertone.

His smirk disappeared.

"You have an exaggerated opinion of your prowess," she went on. "Just as you have an exaggerated notion of your hold over me. My answer is no. And that is final." Turning in a ruffled swoosh of silk, she started to walk away.

"Not so fast, Alessa."

She kept going, but he caught up to her in several swift strides and grabbed hold of her arm. "Do you think I have traveled all the way to this cursed cold island just to let you turn your back on me?"

"I've told you, I don't care what you say about me," countered Alessandra. "You cannot force me to help you."

"Oh, yes. I can." His smile was back in place. "You might not care about yourself, or your reputation. But what about your daughter? Dear Isabella is such a pretty little girl. It would be a pity if anything were to happen to your only child."

"You *wouldn't*!"

Yet she knew he would. He had killed without compunction before.

"As you saw the other day at the river, accidents happen easily, especially to children. And there won't always be a noble *cavaliere* to ride to the rescue." He brushed a leaf from his trousers. "The *Inglieze* are so conventional. Do you really think that a war hero would offer his sword to a cold-blooded murderess?"

Her throat froze.

Sensing her fear, Frederico pressed on. "Trust me, I am not acting alone on this, Alessa." A low laugh stirred the air by her cheek. "Indeed, you would be greatly surprised to know just how powerful an ally I have. So if I were you, I would not risk opposing us."

"You—you leave me little choice," she whispered.

"There, you see. It is not so difficult to agree with each other, is it?"

Alessandra stared down at the dark stones beneath her feet.

"Don't look so stricken, *cara*," replied Frederico. "I shall see that you don't regret the decision."

It took all of her courage to ask, "W-what is it you want me to do?"

"No rush, *cara*, now that we have come to an understanding." Frederico drew out his snuffbox and inhaled a pinch. "Let the excavation settle into a comfortable routine. I shall let you know the specifics when the time is right."

A sudden swirl of wind spattered some spray from the fountain against her cheek. Squeezing her eyes shut, Alessandra blotted a teardrop from her lashes.

"Of course, it goes without saying that any word of

this to another person would have serious consequences, eh? And don't think that you can run and hide. We would find you, and poor little Isabella would suffer for your sins."

*Murder.* If she had the physical strength, she would throttle him on the spot.

"So...how do the *Inglieze* say it—mum is the word." His lips curved in a scimitar smile. "It will be our little secret."

# Chapter Twelve

*T*hank you, my dear. How very thoughtful of you. I wasn't aware that the latest shipment from America had arrived." Charlotte unwrapped the package of books that Kate had brought with her from Hatchards.

"There looks to be a new volume of experiments by Benjamin Silliman, the chemistry professor at Yale." Kate poured herself a cup of tea. After choosing a slice of almond cake, she added, "Lud, things are sadly flat around here with all of our friends away. I miss the excitement—the intellectual excitement, that is."

"Yes, I daresay the scandal that swirled around Ciara was frightening enough. We can do without any more of us being accused of murder," replied Charlotte dryly.

Kate choked back a cough.

"Have a sip of tea. And remember—take ladylike bites."

"Right," murmured Kate, brushing a crumb from her lip. "I keep forgetting all the rules on polite behavior."

"Most of London is away in the country, now that the

Season is ended," observed Charlotte. "Are you terribly bored without the evening entertainments?"

"Hell, no!"

"Language, my dear," chided Charlotte.

Kate made a face. "I'm actually relieved to have a respite from the silly soirees and fancy balls. Grandfather seems determined to have me married off to the first suitor who meets *his* lofty standards. Never mind *my* feelings on the matter." A biscuit snapped in her fingers. "I would have thought he had learned a lesson with my mother. But apparently not."

Charlotte sighed in sympathy. She knew that the story of Kate's family history was a turbulent one. The iron-willed Duke of Cluyne had clashed with his daughter—Kate's mother—over her choice for a husband, and the young lady had eloped with an American sea captain. A lifelong estrangement had followed. However, a deathbed promise to her parents had led Kate to seek reconciliation with her grandfather.

But things were not sailing along very smoothly.

"Has someone caught your fancy?" inquired Charlotte. "Someone His Grace might consider ineligible?"

"No." Kate shuddered. "The truth is, I've no desire to get married. I much prefer my independence. Such as it is." Another grimace pinched at her mouth. "English ladies are subject to far more rules than I am used to. Given my background, I—I am not sure that I will ever fit in here."

"It may take a little time, but you will meet kindred spirits in England, my dear," counseled Charlotte. "After all, you found us, the Circle of Sin."

"Thank god for the 'Sinners,'" said Kate. "Without your friendship, I would have long ago mutinied against

Grandfather's rules and commandeered his pleasure yacht to sail to...somewhere far from Polite Society." Her expression brightened. "Come to think of it, the Barbary Coast is a haven for pirates and rebels."

"Only for men. They lock women in harems and veil them from head to foot, save when their lord and master wishes to take his pleasure," pointed out Charlotte. "I can't quite picture you as a submissive sexual slave."

A peal of laughter slipped from Kate's lips. "You are right—I wouldn't fit in very well there either."

The two of them shared a smile.

"That's what's so wonderful about you, Charlotte. You are never shocked by what I say." Kate stirred her luke-warm tea. "There are times when I feel that my comments make our other friends...uncomfortable. But you always seem to understand."

"I suppose that's because I tend to be a tad more cynical than the others. I sometimes fear that I am setting a bad example for you." Her eyes twinkled. "At my age, I can get away with murder, so to speak. You can't."

Kate jerked her gaze up from her cup. "S-surely you would never think that I would kill in cold blood—"

"I was joking, of course," said Charlotte quickly. "Though you have slain a number of Society's strictures without compunction."

"Ha, ha, ha." Kate's laugh was a little brittle. "I will try to temper my tongue. But it seems stupid to swathe my real self in silks and superficial sweetness. I—I would rather be accepted for who I am."

"Trust me, each of the 'Sinners' knows that feeling, my dear. We are all your true friends." Charlotte patted her hand. "And I am sure you will find others who share your outlook on life."

"Mmmm." Kate swallowed a small morsel of jam tart.

"Perhaps a change of scenery would do you good. Tomorrow, I am traveling to Kent to stay with Helena Gosford for a week. Why not join us?"

"Thank you, but I think I shall forgo the pleasure. Much as I like science, geology bores me to tears. And Helena..."

"Never stops talking about the subject." Charlotte's lips twitched. "Helena is an old friend and I owe her a visit. But you need not sacrifice yourself."

"Perhaps I'll visit Bath and see how Alessandra's excavation is coming," mused Kate. "Grandfather would likely welcome the suggestion, thinking that I might meet an eligible gentleman taking the waters."

A discreet knock on the parlor door interrupted their conversation. "The afternoon post, milady," said the footman as he set a small tray on the table.

Charlotte glanced through the pile. "Ah, speaking of Alessandra, here is a letter from her..."

A last bit of stippling added an undertone of gray to the oak tree's foliage. Finally satisfied with the color, Jack set his paintbrush and sketchbook aside and reached for one of the bottles of Moselle wine he had cooling in the stream.

A heavy rainstorm during the previous night had closed down the excavation site for the day, so he had decided to give himself a holiday—a chance to forget about all the niggling expectations of his father and his new professional colleagues. He had packed a picnic—including ample liquid libations to celebrate the sense of freedom—and set out to explore the countryside. The rolling pastures, rocky hills, and ancient woodlands provided a number of interesting vistas.

Uncorking the wine, Jack took a drink. The clouds had cleared, allowing the sun to burn the dampness from the air. He leaned back against the slab of stone, feeling its heat slowly seep through the muscles of his back. He must have been hunched over his work for some time, judging by the stiffness of his shoulders. Funny how he lost all track of time when he was painting.

The truth was, he hadn't missed the sybaritic pleasures of London at all. His recent boredom had given way to the heady joy of creating colors and composition. Of capturing what he saw on paper. Each sketch was a new challenge, a unique opportunity for individual expression.

He gave an inner wince, imagining how his father would scoff at such artistic drivel. He could just hear the ducal bellow—*My son an artist? I'll not have such a blot on the family history.*

Blast and damnation, Pierson men did not wax poetic over the sight of wind ruffling through the meadow grass. They wouldn't know azure blue from turquoise. The only hue that mattered was blood red. The color that flowed through a true gentleman's veins.

Jack rubbed at his neck. Of course he was proud of his family's heritage and the reputation for steadfast courage and loyalty that had been carved out over the centuries. He simply wished that his father might be a bit less rigid in his ideas on what constituted a good soldier.

*And pigs might fly.*

Sighing, Jack lifted the bottle to his lips again. *Hope springs eternal*, he thought wryly. In the meantime, he would savor this interlude of freedom.

His thirst quenched for the moment, he wedged the wine back between the rocks and turned his eye to a copse of silvery beech trees atop a nearby knoll. The play of light was creating an interesting mix of textures and color...

A flutter of burgundy suddenly appeared among the shades of green. He squinted, and then swore under his breath.

He had been looking forward to another few hours of uninterrupted solitude, but suddenly the pastoral scene no longer seemed quite so peaceful. Not with Minerva, the goddess of wisdom—and war—walking his way.

However, as Alessandra della Giamatti drew closer, he saw that instead of wearing her usual purposeful expression, she appeared distracted. In another world.

And beneath the flush of exercise, her face looked pale. Strange, but he could almost swear that pearls of moisture were clinging to her lashes.

*Talk about a vivid imagination.*

Chiding himself for romantic nodcock, Jack ducked his head and shifted his position against the stones. The marchesa was definitely not a damsel in distress. With any luck, she would pass by without noticing his presence.

Alessandra bit her lip, determined to keep her churning emotions under control. She had shed enough tears in the past over Frederico's betrayal of her trust. This time around, instead of indulging in self-pity, she would—*she must*—take action.

Perhaps the most important lesson she had learned from her fellow 'Sinners' was that a female must not allow herself to be a passive victim of circumstances. Her friend Ciara had been brave enough to stand up to the vicious rumors concerning her first husband's sudden death. And as for Kate...

She smiled in spite of her troubles. Some of the stories that Kate told about her adventures while sailing around the world were enough to make a lady's hair stand on end. But then, Kate made no pretensions about being a real lady.

*Throw caution to the wind.* It was one of Kate's favorite sayings, and not for the first time, Alessandra found herself wondering whether she should take it to heart. Perhaps she should rush away to the coast and book passage on a ship to...to ports unknown. A place far, far from Frederico where she and Isabella could start a new life, free from the clouds of the past.

*Don't be a fool*, she chided. There was no spot on earth where the sun shone all the time.

Glancing up as the way grew steeper, she suddenly spotted Jack among the weathered boulders and rippling fescue. He was sitting in the shade, his coat off, his collar open, his shirtsleeves rolled up to the elbows.

Alessandra knew she should avert her eyes and quicken her pace, pretending she didn't see him.

And yet her steps veered off the path, as if her body had a mind of its own.

Jack didn't look up from his sketchbook. He might as well have lettered "*Go Away*" on the paper.

She paused, her gaze stealing to the wash of colors and intricate brushstrokes.

"Oh, Lud, that is lovely." The words slipped out before she quite knew what she was saying.

Jack slowly raised his head.

"How do you create such a subtle gradation of tone?"

He hesitated, his eyes narrowing in suspicion. "If you have stopped to express your low opinion of my skills, Lady Giamatti, I would prefer that you simply turn around and keep going. The day is far too pleasant to be spoiled by mockery, however subtle."

"I—I was not mocking you, sir," she said softly.

His expression relaxed ever so slightly. "No? If the heavens were not clear, I would think that you had been struck by a stray thunderbolt from Jupiter."

"Now who is mocking whom?"

Jack allowed a twitch of his lips. "We do seem to set off sparks whenever we come together. Forgive me."

"I shall, sir," replied Alessandra. "On the condition that you will consent to answer my question."

Rather than speak, Jack turned to a fresh page. "How much do you know about the art of painting in watercolors?"

"Not very much," she admitted.

Shifting his position, he motioned for her to sit down beside him. "Well, considering your scientific mind, let's begin with a brief technical explanation. The pigments used are finely ground minerals or other organic matter, which are mixed with gum arabic and oxgall, and then dried to form the cubes of color, like the ones you purchased at S and J Fuller's shop."

Dipping his brush in his palette, and then in water, he laid a faint wash of color over the textured paper. "The paint dissolves in water, allowing a brush to spread the particles across the paper. As it dries, the gum arabic makes the color adhere to the surface. As you see, the pigments are translucent, so one achieves depth and texture by layering them. It's key to start out with a light tone." Mixing a darker tone, he sketched in the contours of the distant hills. "Depending on how damp the paper is, one can create subtle gradations like this."

Fascinated, Alessandra leaned in a little closer, watching the edges blur to a hazy edge. "Why, it has the feeling of looking at the scene through the morning mists."

He nodded. "Or, if one lets the paper dry completely, one can sketch in sharp detail." He demonstrated by sketching in a delicate tracing of tree branches at the corner of the page. "Of course, there is an infinite range of possibilities in between."

With a deft flick of his wrist, Jack added a stippling of meadow grasses. "To me that's the beauty of this medium. There is a spontaneity and luminosity that can't be duplicated in oil paints." A subtle dab of violet indicated the patch of wildflowers growing in the foreground. "You have only to look at the brilliant work of Mr. Turner."

Alessandra stared in amazement. A few quick strokes, a few splashes of color, and somehow he had captured the essence of the moment. She could almost feel the sunlight dancing over the fields, and the breeze ruffling through the trees.

"To my eye, you are quite as talented as Mr. Turner."

An odd glint seemed to spark in his gaze, and then he gave a self-deprecating laugh. "That's very kind of you, Lady Giamatti. However, I assure you that I have a great deal to learn before I can ever dream of matching his skills."

She stared at his long, tapered fingers, marveling at his natural grace and how delicately he held the slender paintbrush. *How many men would be so modest?* Clearly he possessed a great talent, and yet he felt no need to boast of his skills.

"I also like the work of David Cox, who is a master at depicting sun, wind, and rain," he went on.

As Alessandra looked up, he smiled. There was a faint smudge of blue on his bronzed cheek, giving his face a boyishly lopsided look. For an instant she was tempted to trace its shape and savor the feel of his skin beneath her fingertips.

Instead she touched the edge of his sketchbook. "The paper is quite different from writing paper."

"Yes, indeed," he answered. "And the various choices affect the look of a finished painting. Laid paper has a rough texture with deep furrows, while wove paper, which uses a fine wire-mesh screen in the mold, has a more uniform surface."

"How did you become so interested in art?" she asked.

Jack pursed his lips. "It's hard to say. As a boy, I used to spend hours in the family library, poring over the portfolios of color prints." He brushed the hair back from his brow. "And then there was the ancestral portrait gallery. I liked looking at the faces, and the textures of the oil paints and canvas."

His broad shoulders lifted in a shrug "Family tradition did not exactly encourage artistic sensibility. My brothers teased me unmercifully, but didn't manage to beat a passion for painting out of me."

Alessandra studied the sketch a moment longer. "I hope they appreciate your talents now, sir."

A look of surprise tinged his features. "My eldest brother, George, has offered encouragement—much to my shock, I might add. Indeed, I owe my chance to participate in this excavation to his influence." He made a wry face. "So you were right in a sense. I am a rich dilettante whose spot was gained through intercession rather than any proven merit of my own."

She was suddenly ashamed of her accusations. He deserved better. "I apologize for my earlier rudeness. It was unprofessional to judge your qualifications before examining your work." She smoothed at her skirts, feeling awkward, unsure. "I looked over your essays last night, along with your sketches from Italy. And, well, we... we are fortunate to have an artist of your caliber as part of the expedition."

"Thank you." Jack dipped his brush in his mixing palette and added a light wash of blue to the sky. "I appreciate that, Lady Giamatti. But I am aware that I must prove myself here in the field."

"Fieldwork is demanding," she agreed. "However, Mr. Dwight-Davis also gave me several of your essays on the principles of archaeology, and it's clear from your writings that you understand the importance of recording the details of the past."

"It's essential to pass such fragile knowledge on to future generations," he replied.

"And yet, too many so-called experts are interested only in plundering its treasures." Alessandra sighed. "It is shameful that people feel free to loot ancient art and artifacts for their own personal pleasure, no matter that doing so destroys valuable information for scholars. To me, it ought to be a crime, for the knowledge is lost forever."

Jack nodded. "I couldn't agree more. There is nothing worse than someone who pretends to take the high moral ground and then turns out to be a snake in the grass. It's contemptible."

As a silence settled over them, she told herself it was time to move on. But somehow her feet seemed rooted to the damp earth.

"Tell me," he added, after a lengthy pause. "How did you come to be interested in archaeology? It is an unusual pursuit for a lady."

She felt her mouth quirk. "Mine was a rather unconventional upbringing. My mother believed that females ought to have many of the same freedoms as men in making decisions about their lives. And my father heartily agreed. He was an intellectual, who encouraged my early interest in art and Italian history." Seeing as Jack had shared his family history with her, Alessandra felt it was only fair to do the same. "And so did my husband."

"Was your husband an artist?" asked Jack.

"No, like my father, he was an intellectual, a noted political essayist." A sigh slipped from her lips. "Stefano was quite brilliant and much admired throughout the Continent for his incisive mind."

"He sounds... very special."

"Yes, he was," said Alessandra softly.

Looking down, Jack busied himself with mixing up a dusky shade of green. His long hair fell over his face, curtaining his expression. "I take it you had a happy marriage?"

"Yes." She stared out at the distant hills. "Very."

"That is good." He kept on working, his brush moving expertly over the paper, sketching in delicate shading that gave the foliage depth. "So few people do. Society doesn't encourage love matches."

"No," she replied. "I was very lucky to meet a man who shared my interests, and treated me as an equal, rather than a possession. You have only to look at Ciara and her first husband to see how miserable a marriage can be." She wasn't quite sure what made her add, "Do you think she has a chance to be happy with Lord Hadley?"

Jack took his time in replying. "Yes, in fact I do. Lucas was just waiting for the right person to bring the better part of his nature to the fore."

"He does seem a very decent man at heart," mused Alessandra.

"He's more than decent," said Jack. "He's kind and funny and staunchly loyal. She will have no cause to question his constancy."

*Talk about loyalty.* By all accounts, Black Jack Pierson had stood by his friend, despite having doubts about Lucas's involvement with a lady accused of murder.

Out of the blue, she found herself wondering whether Jack had any marriage plans on the horizon. He didn't have a title, but the younger son of a duke would still be considered quite a catch on the Marriage Mart. She could, of course, ask, but afraid that the conversation was becoming far too personal, Alessandra quickly changed the subject back to archaeology.

A query on his impressions of the Grotto of Neptune at Tivoli elicited a lengthy reply, and from there they exchanged opinions on a number of classical buildings.

"You are very knowledgeable on nuances of ancient architecture," she remarked after he finished a lengthy stylistic description of Doric column design.

"What you mean is, I tend to prose on *ad infinitum*." Jack smiled. "I suppose that comes from having a passion for the subject. I have probably bored you to perdition."

"Not at all. It's been extremely . . . enlightening. Bronze-work and mosaics are my specialties, but I always enjoy learning something new."

"As do I." The wet wash of color glistened on the paper as a shaft of sunlight broke through the clouds. "You have chosen a good time to take a break from your work. With the wind blowing in from the east, the skies should stay clear for the rest of the afternoon."

"I am not simply out for a breath of fresh air," replied Alessandra. "It's always important to survey the area around a discovery, to see if there are any other potential sites."

He looked thoughtfully at the distant hills. "Isn't that rather like searching for a needle in a haystack? The odds against spotting any artifacts must be astronomical."

"Not really," she said. "What I mean is, what I'm looking for are certain signs that might indicate that the land has been disturbed by some force other than nature. A mound that is out of place, a rock formation that's been chiseled by tools."

"Fascinating," he mused. Through the fringe of his dark lashes, she saw his gaze sharpen with interest.

"You have an artist's eye, sir. With a little training on what to look for, I am sure you would be very good at it."

"Walking works up a thirst." He suddenly set aside his palette. "Would you care to share some refreshments? It's just simple fare—bread, cheese, and wine."

Alessandra hesitated.

"But if you would rather not fraternize with the enemy…"

She hugged her knees to her chest. "Perhaps we could negotiate a truce."

"Don't tell me that you are suggesting we become friends?" he murmured.

*Friends.* The word struck a chord of longing inside her. "Let's just say that as colleagues we ought not see each other as being on opposite sides."

"Ah." Jack kept his tone light. "So we can meet somewhere in the middle?"

"Yes, I suppose so."

*Just as long as she didn't find herself caught between a rock and a stone.*

# Chapter Thirteen

So, the marchesa was not quite willing to let down her guard, thought Jack as he retrieved the wine from the stream and began unpacking his rucksack. *A prudent strategy.* His military experience had taught him that one should never be too quick to trust the offer of an olive branch.

Especially when there was a history of hostility between two forces.

He set to slicing the bread and the wedge of cheddar. It had been pleasant talking of art and archaeology rather than crossing verbal swords. And her interest in watercolors seemed unfeigned, as did her professional praise.

And yet...

Jack found himself feeling a little wary. Perhaps war had sharpened his cynicism, for he couldn't help wondering whether there was an ulterior motive to the change in her attitude. However, he couldn't think of what it could be. There was nothing she needed from him. If anything, it was *he* who should be seeking to curry *her* favor. After all, she outranked him.

Venturing a sidelong look, he saw she had picked up his sketchbook and was looking through the pages.

"I am sorry." On catching his eye, Alessandra quickly put it down. "I should have asked first."

"You are welcome to examine its contents, Lady Giamatti. I have nothing to hide."

She flinched, and two hot spots of color appeared on her cheeks, as if she had suddenly been singed by the sun. It seemed an odd reaction to a mild jest, but there was much about the marchesa that baffled him.

"I—I was merely making a closer study of your technique, in order to have a better understanding of what you just told me," she explained. "My daughter is becoming more and more enthusiastic about painting. And though I have no idea if she has any true aptitude for the subject, I would like to encourage her interest."

"Be assured that Miss Isabella possesses a real talent," said Jack.

"You think so?"

He nodded.

"Unfortunately, I know very little about the subject," mused Alessandra. "So it is difficult to offer any guidance."

"You should ask Herr Lutz to show his portfolio and explain some of the basic principles to you. He is not only a superb draftsman but also an excellent teacher."

"I fear I would be imposing on his goodwill," she said. "You are not the only one who has told me that his time is in great demand."

"Lutz likes talking about art with people who appreciate

his knowledge." Jack did not add that the Swiss drawing master would find a face-to-face meeting attractive for other reasons. "He is here in Bath for several weeks."

"Yes, I know," she replied. "He has kindly consented to continue with Isabella's lessons during his stay."

"Consider that another sign that your daughter has a real aptitude for art. Lutz would not make the extra effort unless he felt she was a special student."

"He must consider you a very gifted pupil, too."

Jack gave an inner wince, suddenly aware that his words might have been interpreted as braggadocio. Using the food as a distraction, he arranged the slices of bread and cheese on an oilskin square and set it between them.

"Help yourself." He chose a piece of cheddar, and took a long drink of wine. Carefully uncorking the second bottle, he offered it to her. "Sorry, no cups."

Alessandra hesitated, then tentatively accepted it.

"Come, we are both on holiday for the afternoon," he said lightly after taking another drink of his own wine. The cool, fruity taste was wonderfully tart on his tongue. "We are allowed to indulge a little."

Alessandra lifted the bottle to her lips and took a small swallow. "Why, that's quite lovely."

*Not nearly as lovely as she was.* Watching the breeze tug at her hair and the soft light play across her upturned face, Jack felt his breath catch in his throat. Forcing his eyes away, he took another long swallow. "The Royal Academy's exhibitions may be too formal for a child," he said quickly, returning to the topic of art. "However, the shows by the Society of Painters in Water-Colours might be of interest to Miss Isabella..."

As they sat sipping the chilled wine, he went on to describe some of the other galleries. Alessandra seemed to be enjoying herself. The tension had eased from her features and she had shed her shawl and undone the top two buttons of her high-collared walking dress. The gesture revealed nothing but a scant half inch of throat, but the mere suggestion of what lay beneath the sprigged muslin was stirring improper thoughts. *Highly* improper thoughts.

Perhaps another drink of the ice-cold Moselle would help drown his rising desire.

"Thank you for the suggestions, sir," she said when he finished his commentary. She broke off a small piece of bread, but he noticed that she didn't take a bite.

"Sorry it's a bit primitive, but I was not expecting company." Jack made a wry face. "I apologize if it offends your sensibilities."

Alessandra seemed to interpret his words as a challenge. She quickly took a tiny bite and another drink. "Unlike the perfectly polished young ladies who populate London, I am quite capable of tolerating rough conditions."

"I don't doubt it. Nothing seems to intimidate you, Lady Giamatti."

"I—I suppose you find that offensive."

*Damn.* That daggered look.

"I didn't say that—," he began.

She cut him off. "You didn't have to. Our temporary truce aside, it's clear that you disapprove of me." A pause. "And my daughter."

"You are different," said Jack slowly.

"And heaven knows, English Society frowns on

anyone who does not conform to convention," replied Alessandra a little bitterly.

Her mood had changed in the blink of an eye and he wasn't sure why.

"Rules are rules," he replied. "Granted they may chafe at times, but without them we would have chaos."

"What a very regimented notion of the world, Lord James." She gestured at his sketchbook. "Don't you find such thinking at odds with the spirit of creativity?"

"Art has rules. One must learn them and master them before breaking them."

There was a moment of silence, save for the crackle of crust turning to crumbs between her fingers. "Perhaps that is true for those who have the inquisitiveness to question conventional wisdom," she conceded. "For most people, however, a strict adherence to conformity tends to strangle the life out of them."

Jack couldn't help countering with another quip, no matter that he knew it would spark a heated response. "You and your daughter might consider putting a tighter rein on your tongues."

As expected, her eyes flared. "True. We both have an occasional lapse in judgment. But I would rather that Isabella misbehave at times than to have her lose her individuality." She drew in a sharp breath. "The young ladies of the *ton* all seem to lack personality," she continued. "No wonder you men grow bored and seek mistresses. I imagine they, at least, are interesting in bed."

Jack choked on a swallow of wine.

"How you prefer vapid conversation to intelligent discourse is beyond me."

"I don't," he protested.

"Really? Just look at all the belles of your fancy London balls—they have been leached of all color! They are naught but pale, pastel shapes, impossible to tell apart."

He frowned.

"As an artist, you must see that."

The comment took him aback, as it echoed his own earlier musings. He couldn't help but picture Lady Mary Stiles in her demure white gowns.

*Colorless*. An apt description.

"You make an interesting observation," admitted Jack. "I had not looked at it in quite that light." He lifted the wine bottle and cocked a small salute before draining the last drops. "I wish you good luck in adhering to your ideals. As your daughter grows older, it will become more and more difficult to be different."

Alessandra looked away, but not before he caught a glint of moisture on her lashes.

The sight was more shocking than any of her words. He had come to think of the marchesa as a pillar of strength. Impervious to emotion. Yet at this moment, she looked vulnerable as a child.

"I—I...," he began.

"You have made your point, sir." Fisting her skirts, Alessandra started to rise. "It won't be easy, but I'll find a way to shield her from scorn. Somehow, I'll manage to give her the freedom to explore ideas and..." Her voice broke as she choked back a sob.

Jack felt a sudden surge of conflicting emotions. *Guilt. Anger. Sympathy. Desire.* And something he couldn't quite name. Coupled with the wine, it was a volatile combination.

He caught her sleeve and drew her down into his arms.

"Come, I didn't mean to upset you. Let us have no tears." The rasp of her breathing was like a tongue of fire on his cheek, and the beat of her heart drummed against his chest. "You are right—where there is a will there is a way."

"You are a war hero, so courage comes naturally to you," she stammered. "But for me..."

Lifting her chin, Jack traced a thumb along her quivering lip. "Trust me, fear is a formidable opponent, even when one is a seasoned soldier. On the eve of battle, the only ones who don't question their heart are fools or madmen."

"You are kind to offer such encouragement," whispered Alessandra. "Even if it is not true."

"I'm not being kind, Lady Giamatti." He leaned in closer. Close enough so that the subtle scent of spice and neroli perfumed his nostrils. "Far from it."

*Hell.* He was about to break every rule of honorable behavior.

*Hell.* He didn't care.

Not with the Mouth only inches from his. Those sinuous, sensual lips, exotic in shape, enticing in color. Lud, he would like to paint a picture of them, and then tear the paper into tiny pieces and let them dissolve on his tongue.

Instead, Jack framed her face, savoring for a heartbeat the porcelain smoothness of her skin beneath his calloused palms.

And then he kissed her.

Heat flared in his belly, spiraling upward and downward and everywhere in between. He had experienced pleasure with quite a few women, but nothing like this sensation. It possessed him. Turned his mind to mush.

He found the ties of her bonnet and pulled the knot free, itching to curl his fingers in the silky texture of her hair.

*Entwined. Ensnared.* With a wordless groan, Jack scattered a handful of hairpins across the stones. The dark curls cascaded over her slim shoulders, tangling with the fastenings of her dress. He loosened them as well, and slid his hands beneath the soft muslin.

She made a sound against his mouth but did not pull away as he touched the swell of her breasts. He felt them yield to his pressure, the tips hardening against his teasing thumbs as he dipped below the top of her corset. Her eyes widened, and flooded with a gently shimmering light. The rise and fall of her chest quickened and he was acutely aware of her body, soft and pliant against his.

"Sweet Jesus," he whispered, trailing kisses along the line of her jaw. Her skin tasted fresh and indescribably sweet, like the petals of a wildflower after an early morning rain. "Our excavation must have freed some deep, dark ancient enchantment from the earth. How else to explain this magic?" His tongue dipped into the hollow of her throat. "This madness."

*Madness.*

Alessandra felt as if her mind was possessed by some overpowering force. Some impossible need that never should have seen the light of day.

*Run! Hide!* whispered the ragged voice of Reason. But somehow, she made no move to disentangle herself from Jack's arms. Instead, against her better judgment, she looped her arms around his neck and drew closer, savoring the smooth, slabbed planes of his chest, the chiseled contours of his ribs.

Oh, Lord, he felt so good, so solid. Twined together, perhaps she could cling to the illusion that she might draw on a touch of his strength.

*If ever she needed a hero.*

Looking up into his dark eyes, she found his expression inscrutable. Impenetrable. She didn't dare dwell on what he must be thinking of her. Dropping her gaze to his mouth, she was overcome with longing. Her lips parted in a silent plea.

And then he was kissing her again. He tasted of wine and the warmth of the sun. She surrendered to the sweetness, molding herself to his muscle, tracing the ridge of his shoulder blades, caressing the curling strands of his hair.

Jack deepened the embrace, thrusting his tongue deep inside her. She moaned against his mouth, and his response was immediate as he shifted her bottom across his lap. She could feel the heat of his arousal through her skirts, and the thud of his heart against her searching hands.

Her own pulse was skittering out of control.

*Madness.*

Her head was spinning wildly, weakened with wine and the wanton, wonderful feel of his rampant masculinity. Stubbled whiskers, calloused palms, jutting manhood—hard, rough, demanding. Desperation fanned the flames of desire. All at once, the future was too terrifying to contemplate. Perhaps if she clung hard enough to Jack—a man whose honor was woven into every sinew of his being—she could draw on his courage and strength to hold her fears at bay.

She had been wrong before about a man, yet somehow she knew in every fiber of her being that Jack would not hurt her.

And without his arms holding her tight, her sanity might shatter into a thousand tiny shards.

Closing her mind to all but the present moment, Alessandra twisted in his arms and lay back in the sun-warmed grass, drawing him down on top of her. She said nothing—how could she even begin to articulate her need? Her hands would have to be eloquent enough to express it.

A tentative touch to the flap of his trousers drew a rasped groan from Jack. As her fingers worked the first button free, they seemed to unravel the last thread of his self-control.

Hitching his hips, he fisted her skirts and dragged them up over her thighs. He pressed his broad palms to the bare flesh above her stockings and spread her legs. His mouth possessed hers again, his tongue dipping, delving, matching the probing of his touch through her feminine folds.

She moaned as shivering heat shot through her body. The sensations were exquisitely erotic. Earth, wind, fire—and pure primal passion.

The elements ignited in a sudden burst of flame as Jack thrust himself inside her. She arched up, sheathing him to the hilt. His body tightened, a low growl thrumming in his throat as he stroked into her again, his movements coming hard and fast. Alessandra responded with matching urgency. There was nothing gentle or languid about their coupling. *No whispered endearments, no soulful sighs.* This was raw emotion, stripped of all pretense.

Squeezing her eyes shut to the bright sunbeams dancing over their bodies, Alessandra was aware only of Jack and his beautiful, strong maleness filling the emptiness inside her. The heady musk of his arousal filled her nostrils, and she felt his skin turning slick with sweat.

A wet heat was cresting in her flesh as well. *Higher, higher.* And then with a last, desperate surge, she clutched at his shoulders and let a wave of swirling, shimmering oblivion wash over her.

An instant later, he pulled back, his hoarse shout echoing her own cry as his seed spilled on the grass. Then his big, warm body was once again sprawled against hers. Legs and clothing still tangled together, they both lay very still.

*Dio Madre.*

As her heartbeat slowly returned to normal, so did her sanity. Slipping free of Jack's arms, Alessandra sucked in a lungful of air, trying not to choke on her dismay. *What had she done?* For a moment, she felt overwhelmed with embarrassment.

*No, she would not sink even deeper into the morass of guilt.* She had needed to touch and be touched by an honorable man, else she would have gone out of her mind. If Jack thought her a wanton jade...

"Oh, Lud, the wine," she mumbled, her fingers brushing one of the empty bottles as she rolled free of his arm.

"The wine." Jack, too, sounded a little dazed. "I didn't...that is, you must not think that I intended—"

"No, of course not." Alessandra awkwardly smoothed her tangled skirts down over her legs and pulled her bodice back into place.

She heard the hurried rustle of wool and linen as he fixed his own clothing. "Lady Giamatti—Alessandra. Allow me to say—"

"Please don't feel you have to say anything," she whispered. "I don't blame you. I blame..." A ragged sigh slipped from her lips. "Oh, what does it matter who or what is to blame!" Evading his outstretched hand, she began groping for her hairpins.

"As a gentleman, I ought to have acted more honorably," began Jack in a halting voice.

"Good heavens, I flung myself at you, teary-eyed and trembling," she interrupted, forcing herself to meet his gaze. "Your honor is not in question. As for my own..." She drew a deep breath. "I—I can't explain what came over us. As you said, it was a moment of madness. Let us leave it at that."

"Leave it at that?" Shadows hung on his dark lashes, hiding any hint of emotion.

"Yes. After all, we both have had sex before, so there's no need for guilt or abject apologies." Alessandra hesitated. "Neither of us did anything shameful. No virtue was stolen, no innocence was lost."

"Indeed, there is nothing shameful about passion," he said in a husky murmur.

Alessandra flinched.

"It is what makes us feel alive," he went on.

"Passion can also be frightening," she whispered.

"Are you afraid?" asked Jack. He fixed her with a searching stare. "Of what?"

*Darkness. Specters. Her own frightening weakness.* Aloud she said, "Sometimes loneliness is overpowering."

"Perhaps I can offer some company, to help keep your fears at bay," he said carefully. "A widow is allowed a certain degree of freedom in English Society."

"Are you suggesting a...liaison?" asked Alessandra.

Jack was very still, save for a tiny throb of pulse at the base of his throat. After a heartbeat of silence, he replied, "You cannot deny that there seems to be some elemental force that draws us together."

"No, I cannot." She bit at her lip. "But..."

"It goes without saying that any meeting would be at your discretion," said Jack. "You may trust that I would take great care that no hint of impropriety shadows your name."

Alessandra sucked in a long breath. Oh, how she was tempted to say yes. Tempted by his honor, his strength... his sinfully beautiful body.

Jack remained silent, solemn. If he had pressed her, she would have refused. But he didn't. He was leaving the decision to her.

"Yes, I will see you again," she whispered. "But I cannot promise when."

"Neither of us need make any promises," he replied. "It is understood that an assignation does not imply any deeper commitments."

"As long as we are in agreement on that..." Alessandra rose, a little unsteadily, and gathered up the last hairpins from the grass. Aware that she must look like a tart fresh from a tumble in the hay, she hastily arranged her hair in a simple twist and prayed that the fastenings would hold. After finding her bonnet and shawl, she hesitated for a moment, searching for something else to say. But further words seemed absurd, so she simply turned and walked away.

Jack made no move to stop her.

She waited until the path threaded through a copse of

trccs before allowing her steps to quicken and a heaving of angry little sobs to ricochet off the rocks.

*Had she simply repeated her mistake of the past?*

A clench of self-loathing tightened around her chest. She was so weak, and Black Jack Pierson was so strong. His aura of quiet confidence was...seductive. Oh, how she admired his sense of self. He was a man comfortable with who he was. There wasn't a false bone in his body.

*Or was she just indulging in girlish fantasy?* Seeing only what she wished to see?

Alessandra made a face as she stumbled up the crest of a hill. There was a time when she had been as self-confident as Jack. She still could recall the elation of publishing her first scientific essay. Her proud husband had arranged a gala dinner at their palazzo to celebrate the occasion, and as they had stood overlooking the lake, she had felt as if she could walk on water.

Now, she feared that she had lost her nerve...

*No. She couldn't afford to think that.*

Tears prickled against her lids. Maybe she was just an unprincipled jade, seeking to grab at whatever a man could give her.

The thought sent a desperate shiver skating down her spine. *No, no, no.* Forcing her chin up, Alessandra reminded herself that she had learned much since that fateful interlude with Frederico. She was not the same weak-willed woman as before. Adversity had taught her to be strong.

Strong enough to outwit Frederico.

Strong enough to protect Isabella.

Strong enough to keep Black Jack Pierson from getting too close to her deep, dark secret.

# Chapter Fourteen

His hands simply refused to obey his brain. Jack stared down at the paper and muttered an oath under his breath. He was supposed to be sketching the scenic Pulteney Bridge in Bath. However, the perverse little paintbrush kept drawing a cascade of dark hair framing a feminine face. *Haunting green eyes, a lush, lovely mouth—*

"Very interesting, Lord James." Peering at the image, Lutz coughed and raised a brow. "I did encourage you to use your imagination—I see you are taking my advice to heart."

Jack quickly turned the page. "Sorry. My thoughts seem to be elsewhere this afternoon."

"Well, I cannot blame them for straying from stone and water to such a lovely lady." The Swiss drawing master cocked his head. "Your mistress, perhaps?"

"No," he replied quickly, hoping that his teacher had not recognized Alessandra's features. "Just an acquaintance."

"If I were you, I would seek a closer friendship," quipped Lutz before turning his attention to the arched stone bridge spanning the River Avon. "Look how the light is creating an interesting play of texture and shadow. It won't last for long."

"Right." Jack rinsed out his brush. "I'll get to work."

The graceful curves and classical pediment slowly took shape on the paper, but his fingers were moving mechanically. His mind's eye was still seeing Alessandra lying on a bed of gold and green meadow grasses, her hair falling in glorious disarray around her slim shoulders.

His body tightened in response. It was now two days later and the interlude still sparked a flare of conflicting emotions. He wasn't sure what to think. What to feel.

*Was he a cad for taking shameless advantage of her?* The sun, the wine, and some elusive emotion he couldn't yet define had lowered her defenses. And like a ruthless savage, he had charged straight ahead, saber swinging, and demanded a full surrender. Jack gave an inward grimace. He wasn't proud of himself—for any number of reasons.

Still, he couldn't quite bring himself to regret his actions. Recalling the sun-warmed feel of her naked flesh beneath his body sent a lick of heat spiraling through his belly. He was not vain enough to think that Alessandra had suddenly fallen head over heels in love with him. And yet, she had been willing—even a little desperate—to surrender herself to him. He couldn't quite make sense of it, but for now, he wasn't about to argue with the elemental forces of nature.

Passion had no rhyme or reason.

That she had agreed to see him again offered a chance to delve deeper into her mystery. There was a dark side to the marchesa, hidden somewhere beneath the layers…

"Clouds," called Lutz.

Jack looked up to see that the bridge was now lost in shadows.

"We might as well call an end to the session," said his teacher after consulting his pocketwatch. "The light is gone for the day. We shall have to wait for another time to finish up."

"The emerald gown, milady?" asked her maid.

Alessandra wished she could don her nightrail instead. Curling up in bed with a good book would be vastly preferable to yet another party. The entertainments for the visiting Italian contingent were becoming exhausting. Tonight they were all scheduled to attend the dances at the Assembly Room. It was bad enough to see Frederico's smirking countenance during the day. To be forced to dance and make merry with the dastard was a true torment.

And then, of course, there was Jack to consider. He was sure to be there tonight, but as she had cried off from the last two evening entertainments, she knew that she must summon her courage and make an appearance.

"I think I shall wear the burgundy," she finally replied. Perhaps it would reflect a bit of color to her cheeks. Or perhaps she had better resort to a touch of rouge. No matter how she felt inside, it would not do to appear as a living corpse.

Alessandra glanced at the looking glass, and then quickly averted her eyes. Her face was unnaturally pale, and her skin seemed to have tightened over the bones, sharpening every angle and shadow.

*She looked like hell.*

Which was only fitting, seeing as she had been living in a dark, demonic underworld of fear ever since Frederico had made his threat.

For an instant she was tempted to slip the jeweled penknife from her escritoire into her reticule. As he pulled her close in a twirling dance, the blade would slide in oh-so-easily between his ribs.

*What did one more body matter?* She could only be hanged once.

"Lift your chin, milady," murmured her maid. "And raise your arms, please."

Closing her eyes to such bleak thoughts, Alessandra squared her shoulders. No matter what, she must not give in to despair.

The silk sighed as it slid over Alessandra's bare skin. "I shall have to see about ordering a new corset," added Lucrezia with a slight frown. "I'm afraid that this one can't be laced any tighter. You are turning into nothing but skin and bones."

"Come, you are clever—improvise," she murmured, speaking as much to herself as to her maid.

She felt the strings pull and then the stays tightened against her ribs.

"*Ecco,*" said Lucrezia through a mouthful of pins. "That should hold for now."

"Now, if only you can work some magic with my hair," said Alessandra. "It's been defying all attempts to tame it with a brush."

Her maid gave a small sniff. "Leave it to me, milady. I promise that you will be the belle of the ball."

The compliments from her group echoed the same

sentiment as Alessandra entered the Assembly Room an hour later. Offering his arm, Conte Orrichetti escorted her past the octagonal card room and fetched her a glass of ratafia punch.

"The *Inglieze* are always said to be stiff and staid, but they do appear to enjoy dancing," he remarked.

"Yes," she replied, sipping her drink. The dance floor was crowded with couples capering through a lively country jig. Candles flickered wildly and the sound of laughter mingled with the swirling scents of perfume, pomades, and earthy exertion. "And Bath is more informal than London, so there is less constraint on exuberance."

He eyed the skipping steps and flashed an apologetic smile. "I am not sure my old bones can keep pace with you young people. Otherwise I should ask for your hand in the next set."

"I would much rather watch for now," Alessandra assured him. She fluttered her fan, finding the atmosphere oppressive. The overheated room with its cloying air and wilting roses...the brittle cacophony of violins and clinking crystal...the swirling, silken crush of bodies...

Somewhere among them was Black Jack Pierson. Her insides clenched at the thought of facing him. For the last few days it had been easy enough to avoid him at the site. But she couldn't continue to be so cowardly. *Courage*, she chided herself. She knew that he would honor his word to behave with perfect politeness in public.

And yet, the knowledge of their intimate arrangement stirred a pebbling of gooseflesh along her bare arms. A part of her wished to avoid any contact, and a part of her yearned to feel—

A light touch grazed her wrist. "Are you well, my dear?"

She looked up into Orrichetti's kindly dove-gray eyes.

"Forgive me for saying so, but you have appeared tense these last few days," he went on softly.

"Have I?" Alessandra swallowed her misgivings with a throaty laugh. "I suppose I am always a bit on edge when a new project begins," she said evasively. "And to be honest, Isabella has been a bit difficult of late."

"*Bambini*," he murmured. "It is only natural for you to be concerned. Family is very important."

"Yes," she replied. "Very."

The lines on his face etched a little deeper. "I hope you know that as one of Stefano's closest friends, I am always here to listen, should you feel the need to talk."

"*Grazie*, Pietro. That is very good of you." Using the painted paper as a shield, she stirred a breath of air against her cheeks. "It's nothing, really. I am sure things will sort themselves out soon."

"If you are sure..." Lips pursing in thought, he tapped a long, elegant finger to his chin.

For an instant, Alessandra was tempted to confide in him. But the impulse quickly died as a glimmer of light from the chandeliers caught Orrichetti's patrician profile. *Hair silvery as moonlit snow, skin pale and lined as old parchment, hands soft and scholarly*...She looked away quickly, ashamed of her weakness. What could he do? Challenge Frederico to a duel?

*God perish the thought.*

No, it would only worry her old friend if she told him about the full depths of Frederico's depravity. It might even put him in danger.

"Quite sure, Pietro." Tightening her grip on the ivory sticks, Alessandra snapped her fan shut. "Please, no more talk of troubles. This evening is a time for gaiety and laughter. You are here to enjoy the experience of English entertainment, so let us find our colleagues and make merry." The words, bitter as bile, left a bad taste in her mouth, but in looking around at the flushed faces and broad smiles, she saw that the other members of their expedition seemed to be enjoying themselves immensely.

"Ah, I see that Mr. Haverstick is signaling us to join his circle," observed Orrichetti.

Heaving an inward sigh, Alessandra let herself be led to a spot near the punch table.

"Behold, we have a goddess in our midst," exclaimed Dwight-Davis, who sounded as though he had already drunk several glasses of champagne. "*Femina praeferri portuit tibi nulla*—no woman is lovelier than you, Lady Giamatti. Our own incomparable Minerva!" He tugged at the sleeve of the gentleman standing next to him. "Don't you agree, Lord James?"

Jack slowly turned from talking with Signor Mariello, the classical poetry professor. "Roman mythology sometimes gets a little confusing," he said slowly. "Minerva was the goddess of wisdom, but under certain circumstances, she was also considered the goddess of war."

*Blood, pain, death*...Willing away such frightful thoughts, Alessandra forced herself to smile. "I shall try to be smart enough to avoid causing any conflict among our learned band of scholars, sir."

Dwight-Davis laughed heartily as he bowed over her hand. "Indeed, indeed. The only thing we shall be battling over is the right to claim a dance with you this evening. May I ask for the honor of the next set?"

"*Si*," seconded Mariello. "And may I have the next one?"

She nodded her assent, noting that Jack remained silent. Slanting a sidelong look through her lowered lashes, she saw that he was surveying the crowd with a show of calm detachment.

*Was he having second thoughts about any involvement with her?* Alessandra hardly dared to imagine what he must think of her after their last encounter. A strumpet, willing to lie with any man who grabbed her for a quick tumble?

She dropped her gaze, wishing that she could sink into some deep, dark hole, far from his piercing scrutiny. How could she blame him if he thought ill of her? He had seen the worst of her character—

*No.* Not the very worst. That, she prayed, would remain buried in the lies of her current life.

"Ah, I see the musicians are taking a break," said Dwight-Davis as he dabbed at his brow with a handkerchief. "Come, Mariello, let us fortify ourselves for the coming dances by refilling our glasses. May we fetch you another serving, Lady Giamatti?"

The idea of being left alone with Jack caused her throat to constrict. "No, but—"

Her words, however, were lost in the shuffle. The two scholars moved off through the crowd.

*Diavolo.* Now what?

Jack answered her unspoken question by continuing his silent study of the Assembly Room.

Following his lead, Alessandra angled her eyes to the opposite wall, relieved that she did not have to face his dark, dangerous eyes right now. A trickle of sweat dampened the lacing of her corset as she held herself very still. It was silly, she knew, but there were times when she was very much afraid that his gaze had the power to undress her. To strip away the layers of silk and sarcenet, to unravel the intricate weaving of lace and lies.

Despite the warmth, she slid her shawl up over her bare arms.

"La, Lord James!" Aglow with laughter, two ladies suddenly broke away from a cluster of giggling females standing nearby and waved a greeting. "How delightful to find you here in Bath!"

"Miss Anne. Lady Margaret." Jack inclined a polite bow.

Alessandra sensed that he didn't wish to introduce them to her, but good manners dictated that he do so.

She wrenched her attention away from the curl of his mouth, its expression as inscrutable as ever, as he finished the formalities and began to exchange pleasantries with his friends.

"Lady Mary will be *so* sorry she did not accept my invitation to visit me here for the week before joining her aunt in the Lake District." Miss Anne, a plump brunette with a pretty, heart-shaped face, tapped her fan to Jack's sleeve with a knowing wink.

"Devastated," agreed Lady Margaret, a petite blonde with the porcelain complexion of a china doll. "How was her journey? She's an awful correspondent with *us*, but I am sure *you* have had a letter."

It could have been only a flickering of the light, but to Alessandra's eye, Jack looked a little uncomfortable. "I am not sure why she would favor me over her best friends," he replied.

The two ladies looked at each other and rolled their eyes.

"In any case," went on Jack. "My decision to depart London was a last-minute one."

"We'll be sure to tell her of your change of plans," said Lady Margaret. "I know Mary will want to write to you quite often. The Lake District is *such* a romantic place and she has *such* a sensitive nature. Naturally, she will be anxious to share her thoughts with her good friends."

*Black Jack Pierson was courting?* It should not come as any great surprise, realized Alessandra. He was from an august family, and would be considered a prime catch on the Marriage Mart. Younger sons were, after all, expected to marry—and marry well—so as not to be a drain on the family coffers.

Still, the knowledge only exacerbated her troubled mood.

However, her outrage lasted only an instant. *Dances within dances.* Polite Society permitted all manner of dalliances, as long as they were choreographed correctly. Jack was breaking no rule by coming to her bed. And neither was she, Alessandra reminded herself. She was free to slide her hands over his hard, naked muscles. To open herself to his aroused flesh...

"If you ladies will excuse us." Jack suddenly took her hand as the musicians struck up the first notes of a gavotte. "The marchesa and I should join our colleagues on the dance floor."

*A fancy bit of footwork*, thought Alessandra as he threaded through the twirling couples and joined a line of dancers at the far end of the room. She wondered if he would say anything about the encounter. However, when he spoke, it was not about his female friends.

"I've just received an order of art supplies from London, and took the liberty of having the shop include several brushes that would be suitable for your daughter. If you like, I could drop them by your townhouse." He stepped smoothly through a turn. "At your convenience, of course."

Her insides gave a little lurch. *Jack wanted another intimate encounter?* The music had quickened and it took her a moment to catch her breath. So did she, no matter the risk. He appeared the only steady, solid element in her life right now. Everything else seemed to be spinning out of control.

"I will be leaving here soon," she whispered. "And plan to be working late in my study. If you come through the back gardens around midnight, you will find the terrace door unlocked."

Jack's face betrayed nothing. "I, too, shall be taking an early leave of these festivities," he murmured. They danced on in silence until the final flourish floated through the air. "Until later, then," he murmured as he escorted her to the perimeter of the dance floor.

The trill of the violins forestalled any further conversation. Inclining a small bow, Jack turned and disappeared into the swirl of silks.

"The next set is starting!" Dwight-Davis hurried over and offered his arm. "Shall we?"

Alessandra reached out a hand, only to be halted by a voice from behind her.

"*Prego, signor.*" Frederico glided through the crowd and favored the group with a gleaming smile. "Excuse me for stealing a march on you, but I would be very grateful if you would allow Lady Alessandra to show me the steps of this English dance."

"Of course, of course, sir." Dwight-Davis ceded his place with a courtly flourish. "I'm sure the lady would far prefer a more agile partner."

She felt her skin crawl at Frederico's touch. *If only she could announce to the world what a slithering snake he was.*

His grin stretched a touch wider. "Come, *cara.* I am sure that with your help, I will have no trouble picking up the right moves, *si?*"

Biting the inside of her lip, Alessandra followed his lead.

"Smile, Alessa," murmured Frederico. "You must try not to look as though you are on your way to a funeral."

"Is there a reason you have dragged me out on the dance floor?" she demanded.

"Other than to enjoy the pleasure of your body moving in tune with mine?" His gilded brows rose in a mocking arch. Drawing her closer, he tightened his hold on her hand. "But yes, as a matter of fact, there is."

A shiver skated up her spine as the musicians struck up the first chords of a country reel.

The first few figures of the dance drew them apart. But all too soon, Alessandra found herself back in Frederico's grasp, and for an instant they were separated from the couples. Leaning close, he whispered, "The time has come for us to begin the real work, Alessa."

Only his vise-like grip kept her knees from buckling.

"Steady, sweetheart." His breath tickled against her cheek. "Let us have no missteps, eh? Remember, I'm not working alone—and against us, you don't stand a chance."

"What is it you want?" she rasped.

"I shall explain it all tomorrow," replied Frederico.

He was taking cruel delight in making her dance to his tune. Oh, yes, he had mastered the art of manipulation. But even a master could be made to stumble.

Clinging to that hope was what kept her feet moving.

"In the meantime, *cara*, let us enjoy the festivities." Laughing, Frederico moved back with a graceful spin and hooked arms with another lady. "La," he said loudly. "There is no place on earth that I would rather be at this moment than here in Bath."

# Chapter Fifteen

*T*he night mist swirled like liquid silver, washing over his boots as he moved lightly across the damp grass. The back of Alessandra's townhouse was dark, save for a glimmer of light from a glass-paned door at the far corner of the terrace.

Jack paused for a moment, shifting the small package from hand to hand as he watched the scudding moonbeams play off the pale stonework. *Light and shadows.* Like the lady herself, the subtle interplay of elements was intriguing, teasing the eye with its constantly shifting shapes.

Approaching the door, he found it slightly ajar. Slipping inside, Jack found himself in a spacious study dominated by a massive oak desk piled high with books and papers. A single branch of candles was lit on the side table by the sofa. In its glow, the wood paneling appeared dark as aged sherry.

Alessandra turned slowly from the banked fire in the hearth. Her hair was down, held back by a single ribbon, and she was dressed in a silk wrapper, sashed loosely at her waist. On seeing the hint of lace peeking out from its front, Jack felt his throat constrict. She must be naked beneath the light fabric, save for her nightshift.

Jack was no stranger to midnight trysts, but oddly enough, he found himself feeling a bit nervous.

She, too, seemed on edge. Gesturing to the sideboard, she asked, "Would you care for some brandy?"

"Thank you." Crossing the carpet, Jack poured himself a glass, and then filled one for her. As he passed it over, their hands touched and he felt her flinch.

"Perhaps a sip of spirits will help you relax," he murmured.

Her lashes lowered, the dark fringe accentuating the paleness of her face. "Like you, I am entering a new field of study." Raising the glass to her lips, Alessandra added, "I have little experience in illicit affairs, so forgive me if I appear a little awkward."

To Jack's eyes, she looked sweetly shy. And achingly vulnerable.

"If you are regretting the invitation," he began.

"No," she said quickly. "Please—don't go."

Strange, but she sounded a little desperate.

Following her gesture, he took a seat on the sofa. Alessandra joined him, though her body remained rigid.

Jack took a swallow of brandy and looked around the study, wondering how to put her at ease. Spotting a small stone statue on her desk, he raised his glass in salute. "Ah, I see our friend Minerva has followed us from London, though this time she is wearing a different guise."

The candlelight caught a glimmer of a smile. "Seeing as she is the patron goddess of the Bath, it's no surprise that we find her here." Alessandra's shoulders softened. "This one was discovered in the small temple we are unearthing by the river. I brought it home to do a few tests with my acids, to determine whether the stone came from here or Italy."

"Interesting," he replied. "Have you come to any conclusion?"

Giving an answer seemed to break the ice. Her face grew more animated, and her color returned as she explained the technical tests. Clearly antiquities was a strong passion.

As she continued, he couldn't help but be distracted by the play of the flickering flames over her features.

"Lady Giamatti—that is, Alessandra," he murmured, interrupting her words. "Your face is so lovely—I would love to paint you sometime."

She blushed and seemed surprised.

"Surely I'm not the only man who has told you how beautiful you are?"

"No," she replied softly. "But... well, coming from you, with your artist's eye, it is quite a compliment."

"It's not false flattery, Alessandra." Reaching out, Jack curled a strand of her hair around his finger and held it close to the candles. "Look, at first glance, your hair may seem black as a raven's wing, but in the firelight, see how the sparks light a range of subtle tones. If you look closely..." He shifted on the sofa, so that his legs were now touching hers. "You can see hints of indigo and cinnabar."

"You see things most other people miss," she whispered.

"War teaches one to be very observant," he said lightly, then immediately regretted the remark. It seemed to make her tense again. *Damn.* Recalling the package in his pocket, he set down his glass and quickly took it out. "Speaking of art, I brought some supplies to add to Miss Isabella's collection." Unwrapping the paper, he displayed several sable-hair paintbrushes of varying widths. "A painter can never have too many tools of the trade at hand."

"How very kind of you," said Alessandra.

On impulse, Jack took up one and feathered the soft bristles against her cheek. "If I were painting your face, I'd begin with a wash of pale peach."

Her eyes widened, but she didn't draw away.

"Then I'd start sketching in the details, starting with your lovely, luminous emerald eyes." Choosing the smaller brush, he feathered it against her lids.

"It seems you are a poet as well as a painter, Lord James."

"Jack," he corrected, touching the bristles to her lip.

Her lashes fluttered. "Do you always use art to seduce your women?"

"No," he replied, tracing the line of her jaw. "I've never tried this technique before." Untying the fastenings of her wrapper, he let the silk fall open, revealing the thin scrim of her nightshift. He flicked the soft sable over her collarbone. "Is it working?"

"The preliminary sketch is promising." Her voice was a little ragged, a little breathless. "It all depends on how you fill in the details."

The sound—a smoky, sexy whisper—stirred a lick of heat in his belly. "Why, Alessandra—are you flirting with me?"

"Am I?" Alessandra took up one of the other paintbrushes and twirled it to a fine point. "I—I suppose I am."

She dappled it across his jawline to the top of his shirt-points. "Against the white of your linen, your skin has the burnished bronze glow of an ancient statue," she murmured. "Mars, I think. Or perhaps Apollo." A tentative tug untied the knot of his cravat.

Jack shrugged out of his coat and waistcoat. Slowly unwinding the length of starched linen, he let it fall to the carpet. He undid the top button of his collar and then hesitated. "May I remove my shirt?" he asked softly.

She nodded. "But we must be quiet, and... and I cannot linger here overlong." Her gaze dropped and her eyes were lost in shadow. "I must also warn you, Isabella sometimes has nightmares, so if I have to leave abruptly—"

"I understand," he interrupted. "It is for you to make the rules. I shall respect them."

When she voiced no further objection, Jack eased the garment over his head. The air felt cool against his bare chest—or maybe his skin was overheated. The sight of her shapely body and breasts through the gauzy cotton had him burning with desire. But he made himself go slowly. *Discipline, discipline.* No matter that holding his lust in check was proving exquisitely difficult.

Alessandra looked up, and for a moment the firegold reflection of the candle flames seemed to hang on her lashes. Ever so slowly, she lifted her brush and ran it along the ridge of his collarbone. "I don't imagine most London bucks of the *ton* have muscles like these." The gossamer touch glided over his nipples and down over the contours of his ribs.

He felt himself growing aroused.

"I don't live an indolent life, Alessandra. I fence, I box, I ride."

A hint of a smile played on her lips. "All admirable pursuits, it would appear."

"I will exert myself to win your approval, both professional and personal, throughout this excavation," he said.

"So far, you have passed every test with flying colors." Alessandra traced the line of dark hair down to where it dipped into his trousers. "As I said before, we are lucky to have an artist of your ability working with us."

The silk wrapper had come loose, and as she moved, it slid down off her shoulders and pooled around her waist. A line of tiny pearl buttons ran down the front of her nightshift, framed by a delicate frothing of lace. "Speaking of art," he rasped, "I've an idea for a picture I would like to paint."

"You've no paper," she whispered. "Or pigments."

"Ah, well then," replied Jack. "I'll just have to use my imagination."

As his fingers grazed her shift and slowly set to unfastening the buttons, Alessandra closed her eyes, trying not to think of all the wicked, wanton things she wished for him to do to her body. Frederico's touch had frozen her insides with terror. However wrong it might be, she desperately needed Jack's intimate warmth to melt her fears, if only for a fleeting interlude.

"Raise your arms, sweeting," murmured Jack.

She arched, allowing him to ease the garment up over her head. Now scandalously naked, she nestled back down into the damask pillows, the silken folds of her wrapper smooth beneath her bare bum.

A soft thud sounded, followed by a second as Jack peeled

off his boots and let them fall to the carpet. The rustle of wool stirred a naughty image of Jack unclothed...

Her lashes fluttered open.

*Oh, Lud, he was a magnificent man.*

Candlelight gilded the chiseled contours of his chest, and the hard, flat plane of his belly. But it was his jutting erection that held her gaze in thrall. A ruddy, red-gold shaft of aroused maleness, rising from a dark tangle of coarse curls.

A sound must have slipped from her lips, for Jack stilled. "Do I frighten you?" Shielding his cock, he added, "I know that you find me a big black devil."

"No, I'm not afraid of you." Alessandra reached out and nudged his hand away. "I see the Prince of Darkness, not the devil."

"I'm not a prince, merely a humble painter," murmured Jack. "Who wishes to see if he can do justice to your ethereal beauty."

She watched in fascination as he dipped his brush into brandy. What was he...

*Oh, diavolo.*

A drop of the amber spirits splashed onto her nipple. Jack flicked his brush in a slow, sensuous circle, spreading its warmth over her rosy areola.

"Hmm, I'm not sure that's quite right—perhaps I had better blot it off and start again." His mouth, wet and warm, covered the tip of her breast, suckling the tingling liquid from her skin.

"*Dio Madre*, you *are* a devil after all," she whispered as he turned his tantalizing attentions to her other breast.

A husky chuckle rumbled deep in Jack's throat. "Oh, I've not yet begun to be devilish."

His tongue licked over her hardening nipple, coaxing, caressing it until Alessandra thought that she might burst into flame. Surely, he could not do anything more wicked than this.

But suddenly he was easing her legs apart, and drawing the brush through the folds of her most intimate flesh.

"Jack!" She gasped and tried to sit up.

His palm pressed down on her belly, holding her in place. "Please—let me pleasure you."

The temptation was too great. And she was too weak to resist it.

Surrendering herself to the moment, she lay back and let the delicious sensations wash over her.

Gently probing, Jack found her hidden pearl and his brushstrokes started to quicken.

Alessandra gave a low cry as the fire seared right to her core. Squeezing her eyes shut, she let it burn away her fears. Frederico's repulsive touch had made her skin crawl, leaving her feeling soiled. While Jack…Jack made her spirits sing. Her passions had betrayed her before, but somehow she felt safe in his hands.

"Alessandra," he said, his brandy-sweet lips capturing hers in a long, lush kiss. The soft bristles kept up their teasing tempo and she felt herself growing slick with need.

"Jack," she moaned against his mouth. Her hand found his cock and closed around its velvety steel.

He groaned, a dark, masculine sound that reverberated right through her. She released him, just long enough to dip her fingers into the brandy glass, and then ran a caress along the length of his shaft. His whole body stiffened in response. Emboldened, Alessandra traced the flared head of his arousal, reveling in his shape. *Hard and soft. Coarse and smooth.* The textures of his body were so very beautiful.

"*Bellissimo*," growled Jack in Italian, echoing her own thought.

"*Si.*" She reached up and threaded her hands through the silky tangle of his hair. Suddenly aware of how fleeting, how fragile the moment was, she drew him closer, reveling in the musky spice of his scent, the faint stubbling of whiskers shading his jaw, the heady heat of his desire.

"Make love to me, Jack," she said in a ragged whisper. *Keep the darkness at bay for just a little longer.*

The paintbrush fell atop their discarded clothing as he shifted and lowered himself between her legs.

He, too, seemed gripped by a sense of urgency. No more teasing play, no more gossamer kisses. As Alessandra wrapped her arms around his broad back, she felt the tension rippling through his muscles. They sank deeper into the sofa pillows, entwined as one. She drew up her knees, clenching tight to his lean, lithe hips. *If only she could hold on to his strength forever.*

And then, he was inside her, filling her honeyed passage with his gliding thrusts. There was nothing languorous about their coupling. It was fast, furious. The rise and fall of their bodies set the candle flames to dancing wildly in the midnight shadows.

Her climax came quickly, exploding in a blinding shower of white-hot sparks.

With one last surge, Jack rocked his hips in and then out, biting back a groan as he spilled his seed over her belly.

A little dazed, Alessandra lay still and gasped for

breath, the pounding of her heart sounding loud as cannonfire in her ears. Above her, scudding flickers of light and dark played over Jack's sweat-sheened face. His expression was obscured by the curling fall of his hair.

As he brushed back a strand, their eyes met.

"I..." Alessandra was uncertain of what to say. "I am sorry, but I cannot invite you to stay much longer."

"I understand." Jack sat up on his knees and found his cravat in the rumple of clothing on the carpet. "You may depend on my discretion, Alessandra," he said, carefully wiping her skin with the length of linen. "I won't do anything to hurt you."

His quiet assurance sent a stab of longing through her. "Thank you." She hesitated, but before she could speak again, a faint noise sounded from upstairs.

"Dear God." Twisting free, Alessandra grabbed up her nightshift and tugged it on. "Please, I must—"

"Go," he whispered. "I will let myself out."

# Chapter Sixteen

*T*ap, tap, tap.

Angling his chisel, Jack carefully chipped away a tangled tree root and eased the stone fragment out from the mud. He removed his work gloves and rinsed it in a bucket of water, then set it in the felt-lined tray beside the other artifacts he had unearthed. Three long hours of work—his colleagues had not been exaggerating when they had warned him that archaeology was mostly a painstaking process of tedious labor. Still, he had no complaints. He was playing a part, however insignificant, in bringing history to light. The feeling was immensely satisfying.

Opening his sketchbook to a fresh page, he noted the date and location of his find. But as he drew in the rough outlines of the first object, it was not the mysteries of the past that occupied his thoughts, but rather the living, breathing present.

*Alessandra.*

Lady Giamatti was still a great conundrum to him. *Hot*

*and cold. Fire and ice.* Whatever strange chemistry drew them together, he could not begin to define it. But already he was fantasizing about their next tryst, and the feel of her naked body against his heated flesh. His pencil bit a touch deeper into the paper. She bedeviled him, beguiled him. *Bewitched him.*

The memory of her flame-warmed skin, her arching hips, her heated whispers sent a rush of lust coursing through his blood. She was utterly unlike any woman he had ever met before—alluring beauty and provocative intelligence edged with a dark, dangerous hint of mystery.

Pursing his lips, he added a slash of shadowing to the sketch. The contrast between the marchesa and his London friends was like...night and day. To her, the two ladies must have appeared silly, superficial. He had been embarrassed by their banal remarks—their comments had sounded as shallow as spilled milk.

At least they had to him. Now that he had been around serious scholars, giddy girls fresh from the schoolroom seemed boring beyond words. Which didn't exactly bode well for his future, considering that his father appeared to be stepping up his campaign to find him a bride. The duke must have mentioned the possibility of a match to Lord Saye, who in turn dropped hints to his daughter, Lady Mary...

*Bloody hell.* Jack tightened his jaw. After this expedition ended, he would have to pay a visit to the ancestral estate and forestall the attack on his freedom. His father would, of course, counterattack. Jack could almost smell a whiff of gunpowder...

Hurriedly finishing his drawings, Jack moved his

things to another section of the outer walls where he was working.

*No use fighting imaginary battles.* He had his hands full at the moment. And much could happen in the coming weeks.

"Begging yer pardon, milady, but I can't finish laying out the grid of squares fer digging as ye asked."

"No?" Alessandra looked up from her sheaf of site maps, welcoming the distraction. She had been staring at the same page for the last half hour, her mind numb with worry over the upcoming meeting with Frederico. "What's the trouble, Mr. Grove? If we have run out of rope and stakes, you can borrow some from Mr. Dwight-Davis."

"It's not that, milady." He held out the paper she had given him earlier and pointed at the neatly drawn diagram. "If I follow these directions, I will land smack in the middle of the river."

Alessandra quickly thumbed through the packet of work orders she had drawn up that morning. "So sorry, Mr. Grove." She touched her fingertips to her temples. "I must have handed you the wrong plan by mistake."

"I figgered as much." He grinned as she passed him a different set of orders. "Wouldn't want Lord James te have te fish *me* out of the drink."

"No, indeed." At the mention of Jack, the dull thud in her head took on added force. It now felt as if a hammer were pounding against her skull.

"Ah, there you are, Lady Giamatti."

As the workman withdrew from the shelter of her canvas tent, his place was taken by Haverstick, Eustace, and Dwight-Davis.

"Do you have a moment to give us your opinion on these reports?" asked Haverstick. "To me, the Italians seem a little slipshod in their observations."

She reached mechanically for the papers. "Yes, of course." Only belatedly did she notice that her hands were shaking.

"I fear we are running you ragged," said Dwight-Davis. "You look a little peaked."

"I did not sleep overly well last night," she admitted, knowing full well what a fright she must look. "I think I shall beg off from further festivities for the next few days."

"Perhaps you should take a day off," suggested Dwight-Davis. He pondered the thought for a moment. "By Jove, perhaps we have been pushing everyone too hard to make up for the time lost to the rains. *Salus populi suprema lex esto*. As the Romans said, let the good of the people be the supreme law..." His countenance brightened somewhat. "A holiday may be in order."

Haverstick frowned but Eustace fingered his chin. "The idea merits some consideration. I suggest that we go discuss it with the other committee heads."

"Indeed, indeed," chimed in Dwight-Davis.

"I shall return at the end of the day," called Haverstick over his shoulder as the two other men led him off.

Alessandra stared dully at the writing on the top page of Haverstick's documents, hardly noticing their departure. *Concentrate*, she scolded. But her nerves were drawn too taut. Like a cat with a mouse, Frederico seemed to be playing a cruel game, working her into a state of terror before he pounced.

Deciding she could no longer sit still, she set aside the

papers and went to check on how the excavation was progressing down by the river. The brisk walk did help dispel the tension, and for the next hour she was able to bury herself in the work.

It was almost time for the midday meal when Frederico strolled over to where she was inspecting a pair of spear-heads dug up by one of the local scholars.

"Lady Giamatti, I have a question about the section of outer wall where I am working," he announced loudly. "Might I ask you to come have a look?"

Taking hold of her toolbag to avoid his outstretched hand, she rose. He was fortunate there wasn't a pistol among the mallets and chisels. At this point she would have cheerfully put a bullet in his brain.

If she burned in hell, she would at least have company.

*Think of Isabella. Think of Isabella.* Repeating the words was the only way to force her feet forward.

"The English countryside is far more scenic than I expected." At the crest of the hill, Frederico shaded his eyes as he surveyed the surroundings. "Though not nearly as lovely as the vista from your villa at Lake Como."

"Feel free to return there and drown in the view," she muttered.

"Tut, tut, *cara*. No need to be so sarcastic."

"In public I shall watch my tongue, but in private..." She shot a look down at the iron-clawed hammer in her bag. "Don't go out of your way to provoke me, Frederico."

"Still the hot-tempered hellion, I see." A peek of pearly teeth showed through his lazy smile. "But then, I have always preferred a little fire in my women."

She bit back a retort. "Get to the point. What is it you want from me?"

"In a minute. Let us find a more sheltered spot." He picked his way past a tangle of thorns and led her to an outcropping of rocks. The weathered slabs hid them from the workers sifting soil down by the river, while to their rear was nothing but a glade of trees and a crumbling stone wall, nearly hidden by a tangled overgrowth of vines and mosses.

Alessandra turned, pressing her back against a jutting of limestone for support. "Now, enough of your games."

"*Si, cara,* I am ready to be deadly serious. And you would do well to remember what I told you—it's not just me you are dealing with."

If her heartbeat grew any more furious, it might shatter a rib.

But rather than rush on, Frederico brushed a bit of leaf from his sleeve. "You know, I have learned a great deal about ancient Rome during the time I have spent working in the university library."

"Spare me the history lesson," she said through gritted teeth.

"You don't care to relive the past?" he said softly. "I thought that was your passion—among other things, of course."

*Temper, temper.* Tormenting her seemed to amuse him, so Alessandra stayed silent.

When she didn't react to the barb, he shrugged and went on. "Orrichetti had his friend assign me to cataloguing the archives, which kept me well hidden from prying eyes. As you can imagine, there were countless old parchments and papers. Out of sheer boredom, I started reading some of them."

She couldn't help but mutter under her breath, "What a pity you did not learn anything of value."

"Oh, but I did, Alessa." The cocky curl of his lips was beginning to make her stomach curdle. "By chance, I happened to find an old brass box, buried under a pile of musty old medieval books. Inside was a manuscript."

The smile stretched wider. "Julius Caesar was not the only soldier who kept an account of his experiences fighting in a foreign land. The document I discovered was the memoirs of a centurion, who was part of the force stationed here in Britannia during the last days of Roman rule. Among the things he recounted was commanding an expeditionary force that was sent from the legion's head-quarters at Caerleon to occupy an outpost near Aquae Sulis—the present-day town of Bath."

"I am familiar with the ancient name for the city," she said.

"Yes, but I doubt you know about the final battle that forced the Roman soldiers to withdraw from the area. By the fourth century, the times had grown troubled, and when a force of local tribes rose up in rebellion, the garrison stationed here"—he gestured at the overgrown wall—"at this very spot, was forced to flee in the dead of night."

Alessandra felt a prickling at the back of her neck.

Frederico moved a step closer. "They left more than rusting swords and spearheads, Alessa. More than your stupid shards of sculpture and broken bits of mosaics. They left a solid gold *imago*—the mask depicting the Emperor that a legion carries into battle. Not one has survived from ancient times—except this one. Have you any idea what a priceless treasure that would be today?"

"If it's money you are after, name a price. I am, as you know, quite rich."

"Oh, it's not just money I want, Alessa. It's power as well. There is a collector in Rome, a very wealthy and influential aristocrat, who is willing to fund my campaign against the Austrians, as well as use his political connections to have me appointed as spokesman of the Italian nationalists."

Frederico had always craved power over people, but to envision himself as a modern-day Caesar was...delusional. However, Alessandra kept such thoughts to herself.

"All provided I can get him the *imago*," he finished.

"Have you any idea how impossible it would be to find it?" she countered. The man was mad. And yet, she breathed a little easier. They could dig until Doomsday and still not locate what he was looking for. "Along with your moldering manuscripts, you've been reading too many lurid novels. Finding buried treasure happens in pirate tales, not in real life."

Paper crackled as Frederico withdrew a folded sheet from his pocket. "Ah, but what if 'X' marks the spot, *cara*? What if I have a map that shows exactly where we should look?"

Alessandra opened her mouth, but found herself speechless.

He smoothed out the creases, caressing the worn folds with a lover's touch. "Have a look."

She closed her eyes. "Good heavens, it's not that simple. It's been centuries...the landscape changes...the man's memory might have been jumbled...or he might have been lying."

"I've researched the matter. Other accounts corroborate the fact that the *imago* was lost when the Romans fled from this fort."

"Even if it is true, it is absurd to think that a crude map, drawn on recollections from the heat of battle, is accurate. The mask is likely a lie, or long gone. And if it is not, the odds of finding it are about the same as a snowball's chances of surviving in hell."

Frederico's mouth thinned to a grim line. "You had better hope, for Isabella's sake, that they are a lot better than that."

Lying flat on his belly, Jack wriggled a little closer to the stone wall. Something sticking out from a crevice in the stones had caught his eye, and using a soft brush, he began carefully loosening the surrounding clumps of moss and dirt. As he shifted sideways, the snap of twigs underfoot sounded on the other side of the wall.

"Frederico, you must understand."

*Of all the cursed luck.* Jack swore an inward oath as Alessandra's voice continued. "It won't be easy."

"Ah, but *cara*, your beauty is equaled by your brains."

Ye gods, was that the Italian's idea of charming flattery? A spotty-faced schoolboy would know better than to spout such banal drivel. He gritted his teeth, restraining the urge to leap up and flatten Frederico's perfect nose with his fist. He had no hold on Alessandra, he reminded himself roughly. Their arrangement had entailed no promises, no commitments. If she chose to take another lover, that was entirely her own business.

Still, she ought to have better taste in men...

Then again, he was one to talk. It was disgusting to be eavesdropping, especially as she had accused him of such slimy behavior before. If he went slowly, he should be able to slide back into the tall meadow grasses without being noticed, and from there drop back into the trees.

Jack was about to put his plan in motion when Frederico's next words froze him in his tracks.

"I've made copies of all the papers. Once you have had a chance to think it over, I'm sure you will have an idea of where we should start looking."

"It's a large site, and the terrain is going to make things difficult." Alessandra was speaking so softly he could hardly hear her.

"Time is limited," said Frederico. "We have to move quickly."

"Yes," she replied, her voice dropping another notch. "But we also must take care not to draw attention to ourselves." A pause. "We can do some poking around during the break for nuncheon."

"I've studied the description quite carefully—"

"The description is vague to begin with, and I told you, the landscape has undoubtedly changed over the centuries," snapped Alessandra. "I'll need to make another survey of the site and see if I can spot a likely place."

"You are the expert, *cara.*"

To Jack's ears, the Italian's voice had an edge of mockery.

"Whatever you do," continued Frederico, "do it quickly."

Jack couldn't make out her answer.

"I trust, Alessa, that I need not remind you..." The rest of his words were lost in a gust of wind.

*Damn.* Jack inched a little closer.

"...I had better get back, before my absence is noticed," replied Alessandra.

Jack waited until the steps died away before raising his eyes level with the top of the wall. Through the creeping vines, he watched the two figures move halfway down the hill and then part ways.

*What the devil was that all about?*

He returned to the task of freeing the small fragment of metal from the stones, but his mind was on what he had just overheard.

*Was Alessandra in league with her friend to steal antiquities from the excavation?*

It defied belief. Yet how else to interpret the furtive exchange? It would certainly explain the air of tension about her. Frowning, Jack recalled that her closest friend had recently remarked that something appeared to be troubling Alessandra.

*Her conscience, perhaps?*

Taking up his trowel, Jack shoved it deep into the damp earth. Had she played him for a fool? His stomach turned a little queasy.

He hated to think that the marchesa might be a fraud. She had spoken so passionately about preserving the past. Was she merely a clever liar? A consummate actress whose kisses and lovemaking were meant to distract him?

Jack stared down at his clenched hands. During the Peninsular War, he had led a number of covert missions to gather intelligence on the enemy and one didn't survive long in that line of work by misjudging a man's character.

But perhaps therein lay the problem. *Instinct.* Was he being guided by lust rather than logic? As he had observed before, a penis did not possess a brain.

Hopefully the other parts of his anatomy could rise to the occasion. Whatever it took, he meant to get to the bottom of this mystery. And one thing was for certain, doing so would mean keeping a very close eye on Lady Alessandra della Giamatti.

Somehow, Alessandra managed to get through the rest of the day. Force of habit allowed her to go through the motions of updating the excavation charts and supervising the storage of the newly uncovered artifacts. Her mind, however, might as well have been on Mars.

Oh, if only the God of War would swoop down in a chariot of fire and vanquish her enemy.

But the gods only helped mortals in myths. Much as she needed divine intervention...

"Lady Giamatti?"

The voice was distinctly human. And distinctly male. She looked up from her charts.

"Where would you like me to put this?" Jack unwrapped a blanket of cotton wool to reveal a fragment of bronze.

Peering closer, she saw it was a piece of an ornamental wolf. Despite her worries, she felt a flutter of excitement. "Why, it looks to be the bronze hilt of a *pugio*, a legionnaire's knife. Where did you find this?"

He gave a vague wave. "On the hill."

"I trust you have recorded the details with more precision than that," she said, still entranced by the rare find.

"I listen well," he replied rather darkly. "I have noted

all the particulars, as you instructed. And I've made a sketch."

It was obvious that she had offended him. Ah, well, better to be at daggers drawn than yearning for...

Alessandra wrenched her gaze away from his dark eyes. "You may leave it with me, Lord James. I should like to examine it more carefully before turning it over to Mr. Dwight-Davis for safekeeping."

A muscle in his jaw twitched. "As you wish."

As if summoned by the sound of his name, the stout little scholar appeared from around a stack of packing crates, followed by Haverstick and Orrichetti.

"Here she is, gentlemen—still hard at work!" Turning to her, Dwight-Davis shook his head in mild reproof. "The committee heads have agreed that a day off from the dig is in order, Lady Giamatti. Indeed, we are running short on some supplies, so tomorrow, we shall let the carters do their work, while we enjoy some leisure activities."

"*Si*," said Orrichetti. "I have noticed that you are looking too pale, Alessa. And my delegation would enjoy seeing some of the local sights. The sea is close by, *non*?"

"Yes," replied Dwight-Davis. "What a pity we do not have access to a sailing vessel. An afternoon cruise would be delightful."

"I can arrange for that." It was Jack who spoke up. He was still standing near the edge of her worktable, arms crossed, his expression unreadable in the shade of the canvas. "My brother keeps his pleasure yacht in Bristol. I know he would have no objection to my making use of it."

"Excellent, excellent!" exclaimed Dwight-Davis. "I say, why don't we make an overnight stay of it? There is a charming inn near the harbor, and that way, Lady Giamatti will not have to make the long carriage ride twice in one day."

"That is a fine suggestion," seconded Orrichetti, before Alessandra could voice any objection. "I am sure that Isabella would enjoy such a treat."

Recalling her daughter's eagerness to accept Jack's earlier invitation, she swallowed her reluctance and nodded. "Yes, I daresay she would."

"Then it's all settled." Dwight-Davis clapped his hands together. "Let's see, present company makes five...six with your daughter, Lady Giamatti."

"I shall forgo the trip," said Haverstick. "I am not overly fond of boats."

"Ravenna also suffers from seasickness, so I imagine he will cry off," added Orrichetti. "As for the others—"

"You may count me as part of the party. It sounds like a delightful outing." From out of nowhere, Frederico joined the group.

Alessandra felt her heart sink. Was there no escape from his shadow?

"There are, I see, great benefits to having a wealthy benefactor among the group," continued Frederico.

Jack's expression didn't alter, but a subtle change came over him. Beneath his muddied workcoat, every lean line of muscle and sinew sharpened, as if centuries of Pierson steel had suddenly reforged itself from flesh and blood.

She took some satisfaction in seeing the Italian's smirk shrivel slightly.

Oblivious to the undercurrent of tension, Dwight-Davis beamed. "Yes, yes, we are *very* fortunate that

Lord James was able to join the excavation." He resumed his planning. "Lord Orrichetti, if you will check with your delegation and give me a final count by suppertime, I will send one of my men to make arrangements with the inn."

"I had better send word to the ship's captain." A small salute—or perhaps he was simply adjusting the brim of his hat—and Jack was gone.

"Are all English peers so... how do you say it... starchy?" inquired Frederico, exaggerating a grimace. "The fellow always looks as if he has just swallowed a bite of bad fish."

*Or smelled something rotten*, thought Alessandra. "Lord James is taking his tasks seriously," she said evenly. "He wishes to learn how to do things right, an attitude that I find highly commendable."

"Well said, well said," agreed Dwight-Davis. "And he has certainly shown himself to be a quick study."

Alessandra couldn't say why, but she kept the bronze *pugio* covered, unwilling to share Jack's discovery with the others just yet.

"I was skeptical about the last-minute arrangement," conceded Haverstick. "However, his drawings appear quite competent."

"Well, far be it from me to contradict you learned scholars," said Frederico with a silky smile. "Apparently Lord James is a paragon of virtue."

Orrichetti appeared a little embarrassed at his countryman's rudeness and shot him a warning look. But the subtle sarcasm appeared to sail right over the heads of the English gentlemen.

"I would gladly have a century of legionary soldiers

like Lord James working here at the site," said Dwight-Davis.

"But tomorrow is a day for leisure, *non*?" Orrichetti diplomatically changed the subject. "At what hour should we plan to leave?"

Now in his element, Dwight-Davis began planning the details of the scheduling. "What fun. This promises to be a memorable experience."

# Chapter Seventeen

*B*ack the sheets." Captain Mellon squinted up at the sails. "And ease the bow five degrees to starboard."

Jack leaned on the taffrail and watched the yacht work its way through the tidal lock leading out to the Bristol Channel. The currents could be tricky, but the man in charge of his brother's vessel was a former naval officer who had cruised for years in the notoriously fickle waters of the West Indies.

"Watch the eddy up ahead, Jennings," murmured the captain to the crewman at the wheel. He touched the varnished spoke, turning it a hair more to the right.

"Aye, sir."

The yacht passed through the last stretch of swirling water and headed out to sea.

"A fine piece of seamanship, sir," called Dwight-Davis. "I am told that it requires a skillful hand to navigate through the floating harbor."

Mellon puffed on his pipe. "One must keep a weather

eye on the tides, the currents, and the wind."

The Bath party, which numbered nine, was gathered in the stern of the yacht, watching the crew move smartly through the task of adjusting the sails to the freshening breeze.

"What, precisely, is the floating harbor?" inquired Alessandra, looking back at the dam that regulated the tidal rise and fall of the River Avon. "I have heard that it's quite a feat of engineering."

Mellon nodded. "Aye, milady, it is. What with the tobacco trade from America, and the coal, stone, and timber from Wales, the original port was too small and too treacherous to handle the traffic. So Parliament approved funds to build the Cumberland Basin, which is essentially a canal with locks on either end. By controlling the water level during the ebb and flow of the tides, it creates a 'floating harbor' if you will."

"How interesting." Holding her daughter firmly by the hand, Alessandra moved closer to the railing to get a clearer look at the gears and gates.

Isabella appeared much more intrigued by the sailor scrambling up through the ratlines.

*Batten down the hatches.* Jack had a sneaking suspicion he knew what was coming.

"May I climb to the top of the mast?" asked the little girl.

The captain chuckled indulgently. "It's not really an endeavor for little girls to try, Miss Isabella. Not only does it require strength, but you might get a smudge of pine tar on that pretty dress."

"I am strong enough to bowl over a wicket in cricket, sir," countered Isabella. "And a smudge can be laundered."

Mellon blinked, clearly outgunned. "Er, well, Miss…"

"Isa," warned Alessandra. "Please remember what I told you. You mustn't make a nuisance of yourself, or misbehave in any way."

Her daughter looked up in confusion. "But I asked politely, Mama. I don't see why I can't try something new, just because I am a girl."

Recalling the countless times that he, as the youngest of five boys, was denied the chance to join in some dashing adventure, Jack felt a twinge in his chest. That look of longing was all too familiar.

"What about the bosun's chair?" he suggested.

All heads swiveled around.

"It's a canvas seat," he explained to Alessandra, "that is used to make repairs in the rigging. It attaches to a block and tackle, and allows a sailor to be hoisted aloft." He looked to Mellon. "If one of your men were to take Isabella up, she could experience the heights in perfect safety."

"Yes," agreed the captain. "That would work."

His gaze returned to Alessandra. "Isabella would not be in any danger."

She hesitated. "But I should not like to trouble the captain."

"It only takes a few minutes," he said.

Mellon was already calling out the order. "Williams! Make ready with the topsail halyard! McArthur, fetch the harness." Canvas cracked and a coil of heavy hemp thumped against the deck. "Gentlemen," he added to the rest of the excavation party. "Our steward is serving rum punch on the foredeck, so might I ask you all to move forward, so that we may clear a space here by the mainmast."

As the others drifted off, Jack turned back to the rail,

intent on resuming his study of the passing shoreline. A moment later he felt a tug on his sleeve.

"Thank you." Isabella's smile was bright as the sunbeams dancing across the azure waves. "You are...well, you are quite as nice as Lord Hadley."

Jack was suddenly aware of feeling absurdly pleased with himself. *How odd that a compliment from an eight-year-old could make his stomach do a series of funny little flip-flops.*

Seasickness, no doubt.

Pursing his lips, Jack replied, "I trust you won't make me regret it, Miss Isabella. You must obey Mr. McArthur at all times—no hijinks, no squirming." He lowered his voice. "And most definitely no swearing."

She nodded very solemnly. "Yes, sir."

The first mate of the yacht's crew was now buckled into the bosun's chair. He held out his arms. "Come, missy. I've two young bairns at home, so I willna let ye slip through me fingers."

Isabella flung herself into his lap with a squeal of delight, then stilled and primly smoothed her skirts.

Jack bit back a laugh.

"Ready?" At the captain's signal, the little girl and her guardian rose into the air. Up, up, up they went, swinging gently against the snowy sails.

"Oh!" Alessandra expelled a gasp as the ship heeled over in response to a gust of wind.

"There is no reason for alarm." Jack steadied her sway. "The roll of a ship is a natural motion."

She jerked her arm free. "Thank you, but I'm aware of that. I have lived on a lake—" Just as abruptly, she clamped her mouth shut.

Jack studied the patterns of sun and shadow playing across her profile, deliberately drawing out the pause. "Is there a reason you are so on edge, Lady Giamatti?"

Her mouth quivered for an instant before setting in a grim line. Instead of answering him she looked up at the crisscrossed lines of spars and rigging. "Do be careful, Isa!" she called. "You must sit very still!"

"Yes, Mama!" The reply floated down, along with a peal of laughter. "The sea and the sky seem to stretch on forever!" Ignoring her mother's caution, Isabella flapped her arms. "I wish I could soar over the ocean like the gulls. Do you think they can fly all the way to Italy, Mr. McArthur?"

The first mate chuckled. "Aye, missy. But it be a long, long journey, with scary squalls and storm-tossed seas. Fer now, we ought not stray too far from English shores."

"Oh, very well." The little girl spotted the ruins of an ancient castle. "I think I will draw a picture of the cliffs for my friend Perry."

McArthur called for the crewmen to lower the canvas chair. "Shall we go to the gallery for a cup of hot chocolate afore ye fetch yer sketchbook?"

Isabella slanted a pleading look at her mother, who nodded ever so slightly. "Mind that you obey Mr. McArthur's orders," she called as her daughter skipped away, with the hulking first mate following close in her wake.

"She's in good hands," murmured Jack. "You can relax."

The splash of salt spray did not account for the sudden sting of color on Alessandra's cheeks. "I have no idea why you think that I am on edge."

"To begin with, if you were gripping the railing any tighter, it would crack into kindling."

She loosened her hold on the varnished wood. "My equilibrium is a little off. I do not want to fall flat on my face."

*Nor do I*, thought Jack. So he decided to tread very carefully. "Indeed, it's easy to be thrown off balance by an unexpected jolt."

Her gaze turned shuttered. Shadowed. As if she had withdrawn to a dark place deep within.

For a heartbeat he felt the urge to dive in after her and pull her back up to the surface. That beautiful Botticelli face ought to be bathed in naught but a shower of sungold light.

"If you will excuse me, sir, I think I shall go join the others."

"Just a moment." Jack shifted his stance just enough to block her path. "I am curious—what do Dwight-Davis and Haverstick think of the bronze *pugio* that I uncovered?"

"I…" She wet her lips. "I…that is, they are not yet aware of the discovery."

"Keeping secrets, Lady Giamatti?" said Jack softly.

She looked as though she might keel over. "No! Of course not. I've simply not yet had a chance to discuss the dig with them."

He didn't press the point. "Are you satisfied with how the excavation is shaping up?"

Her answer was evasive. "It's still too early to make any judgments, sir."

"I was not asking for a final report, just an opinion. I shall not hold your feet to the coals if you wish to change your mind at a later time."

If he hadn't been watching her closely, he might have missed the momentary spark of emotion in her eye.

*Fear.* To a veteran soldier, the demon was a familiar sight.

But fear of what? Of failing to find whatever valuables she and her cohort were seeking? Of having their perfidy exposed? Of ending up in prison?

"Very well," she said slowly. "I think it goes without saying that this site holds a wealth of priceless information for scholars. Never before has a military outpost of this size been found in such well-preserved condition. Most have been looted of art, or had their stones carted off for use in local buildings."

*Treasure. Wealth. Loot.* The words reverberated inside his head, an insidious drumbeat of suspicion.

Jack chose his words carefully. "Yes, it's quite a unique opportunity."

Waves slapped against the hull and wind thrummed through the rigging, amplifying the silence. When finally she did respond, it was not at all what he anticipated.

"By the by, allow me to offer my felicitations," she said with a sardonic little quirk of her mouth. "I was not aware you were on the verge of announcing your engagement."

He pressed his lips to a thin smile. "I have no such agreement, formal or otherwise. The lady in question is naught but a casual acquaintance. Apparently my father has other ideas."

"And you, as a dutiful son, will no doubt honor his orders," she replied. "God forbid there be a mutiny in the ranks."

"Duty is one thing, blind obedience is quite another," he said with deliberate care. "Be assured that when

I choose to marry, it will not be my father who picks out the bride."

Her expression betrayed surprise. "You would go against his wishes?"

Jack leaned his elbows on the railing and drew in a long breath of the bracing sea air. "Charging straight into cannonfire is not the only way to achieve victory in battle. Some generals choose to depend more on strategy and well-planned skirmishes to vanquish their foe. The advantage of such tactics is that they usually result in far less bloodshed."

"You sound as if you were a very good soldier, Lord James."

"Yes, as a matter of fact, I was."

She looked about to speak and then hesitated, seemingly distracted by the shrill cries of the circling seabirds. A large herring gull wheeled off from the others and plunged into the waves, emerging an instant later in the shower of spray with a wriggling fish in its beak.

"Most creatures care only about looking out for themselves, yet you..." She drew in a deep breath. "Let me thank you again for being so kind to Isabella. Believe me, I am grateful."

"She is an engaging imp," he said gruffly.

A faint smile tugged at her lips. "Of Satan, you forgot to add."

*Damn.* He had forgotten about making that unfortunate comment.

"Stefano was not Satan," she went on. "Quite the contrary. He was a wonderful man—kind, patient, wise beyond words. Isabella adored him and..." Her voice cracked. "And how dare he leave us!" Her hand flew up to her mouth and remorse flooded her face. "Oh, Lord, what a horrible thing to say," she whispered. "What a horrible thing to feel."

Jack caught the fluttering tail of her shawl and tucked it around her shoulders. "Not at all," he replied. "I was nine when my mother died, and it took me years to forgive her for leaving such a void in all of our lives. Anger is easier to deal with than grief."

Alessandra gave a watery sniff. "How true." She looked up. Salt clung to her lashes, luminous pearls of light winking out from the fringe of darkness. "Once again, I must thank you for your understanding. I...I fear that of late, I've been..." The arch of her pale throat looked achingly vulnerable against the wind-whipped waves. "...Not quite myself."

Jack tried not to look at her quivering mouth. A part of his brain sneered that he would be a fool to swallow this show of feminine weakness.

*Truth or lies.*

Either she was a consummate actress, or she was in trouble.

"But that is hardly of any concern to you," she added, so softly that her voice was nearly lost in the thrumming of the rigging.

"Alessandra." Jack hesitated, unsure whether to go on. "If there is something you wish..."

She was no longer looking at him. Her gaze suddenly shifted to a distant spot over his left shoulder and her eyes widened in shock. "*Isabella!*"

He whirled around to see Frederico and the little girl up in the bow of the yacht. The Italian had her in his arms and was dangling her legs out over the side. Both of them were laughing as the wind snatched at her skirts, turning the muslin and lace into a wild, flapping tangle of cloth.

"*Bella! Bella!*" Leaning lower, Frederico swung her up and down, dodging the waves of foaming spray by mere inches.

A look of panic spasming over her face, Alessandra pushed past him and started to run.

Jack darted quickly over the hatchway and around the mainmast, reaching the bow a step before she did.

"It's dangerous to be so cavalier on a boat, Signor Bellazoni," he said calmly. "Please pass Miss Isabella to me."

The Italian ignored him, and took an even more precarious perch by the ratlines. "We are just having a little fun."

Out of the corner of his eye, Jack saw Alessandra, her face white as death, clutch at the jib halyard to keep herself upright.

He shot out his hand, seizing Frederico's wrist. During the war, he had learned a number of useful holds for controlling unruly prisoners. A squeeze of pressure, a subtle twist...

His smirk pinching in pain, the Italian went momentarily limp.

In the same smooth motion, Jack released Frederico's arm and freed Isabella from his hold. "Apparently you are unfamiliar with boats, Signor Bellazoni." Pressing the girl to his chest, Jack was struck by how small and fragile she was. "What with the slapping sails and unstable footing, it is far too easy for accidents to happen."

"Ah, *scuzie.*" Frederico quickly assumed a contrite face. "How careless of me. You are right, of course— accidents do happen, especially to children." He reached out and patted Isabella's tangled curls. "*Ciao, bambina.* I shall cede my place to your noble protector for now." A glint of gold flashed as he winked at the little girl. "We'll play again sometime soon."

"*Ciao*, Freddi," she trilled.

Seeing the Italian smile, Jack wanted to knock the pearly teeth right down his gullet. Instead he merely murmured, "Just make sure the game is not a dangerous one."

Alessandra shrank back against the capstan to let Frederico pass, and then held out her arms for her daughter. "Oh, Isa," she whispered, sounding perilously close to tears.

"There is no reason to be upset, Lady Giamatti," he said, handing her over. "Miss Isabella was in no real danger of falling overboard. And even if she had fallen into the water, I would have had her back on board in a trice. Like Hadley, I'm an excellent swimmer."

Rather than look reassured, Alessandra turned a greenish shade of white.

Jack gave himself a mental kick for reminding her that Isabella's best friend had nearly drowned in the ocean not long ago. "Shall we go see what treats have been packed in the picnic hampers?" he added quickly. "I'm famished."

"I hope there are strawberry tarts," piped up Isabella.

Her mother still looked queasy.

Jack knew that Alessandra della Giamatti was one of the least likely ladies on earth to fall into a fit of unprovoked hysterics. Yet her nerves were clearly stretched to the point of snapping.

Again, he asked himself why.

# Chapter Eighteen

*A*lessandra accepted a mug of mulled wine, hoping it might relax her nerves.

All around, the others were enjoying the rich selection of refreshments provided by the yacht's crew. Orrichetti, Da Riffini, and Frederico were by the railing, sipping rum punch as they amiably argued over the merits of Michelangelo's love sonnets. Dwight-Davis and Eustace were downing a platter of freshly shucked oysters while the captain explained the workings of a sextant.

Only Mariello appeared to be enjoying the outing as little as she was. He excused himself and went below to lie down.

She sighed, watching him crab away to the main hatchway. If only she, too, might bury herself under a ship's blanket. Or in a deep hole. Preferably one that dropped all the way down to China.

Perhaps she could become an expert in Ming dynasty pottery or carved jade. As far as she was concerned, the

Roman Empire was crumbling down around her ears.

"May I have another tart, Mama?"

"Very well, but just one," said Alessandra, forcing a smile. "I don't want you to make yourself sick."

"Perry got sick just riding in a rowboat on the Thames." Isabella sniggered. "He pu—"

"Language, Isa," she warned.

Her daughter frowned. "You mean 'puke' is a bad word? Perry says it all the time."

"It's not precisely a bad word, but it's not considered…" Jack crouched down beside her and lowered his voice to a murmur "…ladylike."

Isabella's mouth scrunched. "Nothing fun is ladylike," she groused.

"Drawing is fun, isn't it?" asked Jack. "And painting. Both of which are considered exceedingly ladylike."

"Oh. Right." Her daughter's expression brightened in an instant.

Jack produced a pencil and small sketchbook from the folds of his coat. "Shall we take turns drawing a scene from the shore?" Indicating two teak chairs by the stern rail, he added to Alessandra, "I shall see that she doesn't stray from her seat."

"Oh yes, please!" Isabella wiped her sticky hands on her skirts. "May I draw a picture of the mast first, so I may show Perry just how high I went?"

"That sounds like a splendid idea." His long, wind-tangled hair fell over his collar, and with the belcher kerchief knotted at his throat, Jack looked a little like a storybook pirate.

*Dark and dangerous.* In contrast to the man who spoke so calmly about conforming to the rules. So much about him seemed a contradiction. Hard and soft. Soldier and scholar. Aristocrat and painter. Yet he always seemed remarkably comfortable within his own skin.

*Lover and...*

Alessandra felt a lump form in her throat as Isabella placed her little hand in his. Those long, lithe fingers looked so very strong and capable as he led her to the chairs. Lud, she knew only too well the feel of their touch.

*Don't think about his artist hands. Don't think about his hero smile.*

Looking a little bored, Frederico left the conte and strolled over to Jack and Isabella. "Tell me, Lord James, is there a reason your *Inglieze* friends call you Black Jack?"

Jack continued sharpening the pencil with his penknife. "I should think that would be rather obvious, Signor Bellazoni."

"I thought perhaps that you were...how do you say it... a *malateste.* Someone prone to dark moods. Someone whom others fear to anger."

At that, Jack looked up. "Have you done something bad?"

Frederico's smile faded for an instant, then he laughed. "Good heavens, no. I have had little chance to get into any mischief in England, *si*?"

"Then you have nothing to fear from me."

It was Frederico who broke eye contact first.

"You do look a little like a Caribbean pirate," observed Isabella, with unabashed candor. "At least that is the way they are described in Perry's book—very dark and very scary."

Jack chuckled, softening the planes of his face. "Family legend does say that I have a bit of Spanish marauder's blood in my veins."

"*Really?*" Isabella looked impressed.

"Yes, it is said that one of my ancestors was an admiral in the Spanish Armada. When his ship was sunk in the battle with Queen Elizabeth's fleet, he washed ashore in Cornwall, where he was nursed back to health by the daughter of a local nobleman. They fell in love and married." Jack brushed the tangle of raven-dark hair back from his brow. "And so every once in a while, a black sheep appears among the bevy of blond Norse warriors who bear the Pierson name."

"Fascinating," remarked Dwight-Davis. "By Jove, you are a living piece of English history, Lord James."

"How *very* romantic," said Frederico.

"Yes, actually it is," blurted out Alessandra, unable to keep silent in the face of his sarcasm.

"Well, well, I see that your story has won the admiration of the ladies present, Lord James," drawled Frederico, after shooting her a malevolent glance. "But then, females have a great weakness for tales of love conquering all. Somehow they all seem to yearn for a hero with whom to live happily ever after."

Jack shrugged. "You must have far more experience with the feminine mind than I do. I wouldn't dare make sweeping presumptions about what women want."

The other men laughed.

"A wise philosophy, sir," said Orrichetti. "Bellazoni, perhaps you ought to temper your judgment."

"Perhaps." Frederico gave a sulky smile. "But in my experience, I have yet to be proved wrong." Brushing a lock of hair from his brow, he called for Da Riffini, the expert in ancient stonework, to take a stroll around the deck and identify the ruins atop the coastal cliffs.

"You must forgive my colleague," apologized Orrichetti, once the two had moved away. "Like many Italians, Signor Bellazoni has a passionate nature and sometimes gets carried away in voicing his opinions. I hope you will take no offense."

"Actions speak louder than words. As long as Signor Bellazoni performs his excavation duties to the best of his ability, I have no quarrel with him." Jack shut his knife. "I take it you are satisfied with his work so far, Lady Giamatti?"

"Yes," replied Alessandra, trying to muster some force to her voice.

"Indeed, indeed," chimed in Dwight-Davis. "It is marvelous to see everyone working together for a lofty common goal. *Unus pro omnibus, omnes pro uno*—one for all, all for one." He lifted his glass in a toast. "There is no greater treasure than knowledge."

"Speaking of which," said Eustace. "I have a technical question concerning the winches we are setting up by the grotto..."

The scholars all circled together at the railing to discuss the query, but Alessandra remained where she was, preferring to be alone with her thoughts.

After a moment, however, Orrichetti drifted off from the others and took a seat on the hatchway combing. Turning up the collar of his coat, he fussed a bit longer with the silk muffler wound around his neck before asking, "May I fetch you a blanket, my dear? You must be chilled."

Alessandra quirked a rueful smile. "I don't need to be

wrapped in cotton wool, Pietro. I am not quite so fragile as everyone seems to think."

"I did not mean to imply you were." He cleared his throat with a cough. "Indeed, I see a strength in you now that was not there when you were in Italy."

"I went from being my father's daughter to Stefano's wife," she said softly. "Neither of which required me to bear much responsibility. But once I was on my own, I had to make a choice." She glanced out to sea, where shimmering, silvery patterns of light rippled across the surface. "Sink or swim."

Orrichetti reached and took her hand, twining his fingers with hers. The buttery soft Florentine leather of his gloves—the exact same shade favored by her husband— brought back a flood of memories.

"Am I upsetting you, my dear?"

She shook her head. "I was just thinking of Como, and how the scent of Stefano's cigars would drift out from his study to the terraces overlooking the lake. It was very soothing, you know. I would sit there in late afternoon and watch the sun set behind the mountains, the pinks and golds gradually fading to the deep, smoky gray of twilight."

As the wind shifted, the captain called the order to tack, and with a thunderous crack, the mainsail swung around to the opposite side of the boat.

"It's strange," she continued. "I have trouble picturing the palazzo now." A mizzle of sea spray fell from the canvas. "Perhaps because *I* have changed beyond recognition."

"*Non, non*, my dear. I see the same lovely young girl." A smile played at the corners of his mouth. "But there is a…how shall I say it…" He cocked his head and subjected her to a searching look. "A new firmness to you."

"Lud, you make me sound like a loaf of bread that has gone slightly stale," she murmured.

Orrichetti chuckled. "You don't need an old man like me to tell you that your beauty has only grown more refined with each year." A flicker of regret shaded his soft gray eyes. "Stefano would be very proud of you."

Alessandra drew in a long, painful breath, and then let it out with a shuddering sigh. "Thank you, Pietro. What lovely words." A lock of hair fell across her cheek and she pushed it aside, slowly twirling the dark strand around her fingertip. Fearful of allowing the moment to become too maudlin, she quickly added, "Does Frederico know he has a rival in oratorical skills?"

As she hoped, he chuckled again, yet as the sound died away his expression turned very serious. "Frederico," he repeated. "I had thought you would not mind the company of an old friend. However, I fear I might have been mistaken."

Alessandra shied away from meeting his gaze. "We did not part on the best of terms, but pray, do not upset yourself over your decision. It's nothing to be concerned about. We have agreed that there is no reason we cannot have a cordial working relationship."

The conte inched a touch closer. "Has this bad blood anything to do with Frederico's political activities in Milan?"

For his own protection, the less her friend knew of the truth, the better. "Please, Pietro, I would rather not dredge up the past."

He gave her hand a squeeze, and the warmth of his

palm through the thin layer of leather was comforting. "Then I shall speak no more of it, my dear." All around them was the rhythmic creaking of wood as the hull rolled with the ocean swells. "Save to say that if you ever feel the need to confide in someone, you know I am here."

In the glint of the gleaming brasswork, the conte's silvery head took on a more muted, mellow glow. Strands of his pale hair fluttered in the gusty breeze, the curling ends coming close to caressing the marchesa's cheek.

Jack shifted his gaze back to the page of his sketchbook, fighting back a twinge of irritation. It was only natural that Alessandra would choose to confide in an old friend rather than a near stranger. Orrichetti's air of courtly calm would no doubt be reassuring to a damsel in distress.

Clenching his teeth, he quickly added another few pencil strokes to the fanciful drawing of a pirate that he was doing for Isabella, much to her delight.

"Oh, that's a *corking* good snarl," she exclaimed, then clapped a hand over her own pursed lips. "I forgot, I'm not supposed to say 'corking.'"

"Your secret is safe with me," he whispered back.

The little girl giggled. "I think he needs a scar on his cheek, and an earring. And a bloody big cutlass."

"Don't push your luck, imp," he warned. "I could have the captain clap you in irons." He sketched in a parrot on his paper pirate's shoulder and then passed the sketchbook to Isabella. "Here, why don't you finish him."

As Isabella set to work, Jack stretched his legs and propped an elbow on the back of her chair. "Conte Orrichetti and your mama appear to be well acquainted," he murmured.

"Oh yes, he came very often to our villa on the lake. Mama says he was my papa's closest friend."

"Ah." Jack felt a twinge of guilt at seeking to pry information out of a child. But war was a dirty business, and until he discovered just what he was fighting, he would use whatever tactics he could. "And Signor Bellazoni? I take it he was a frequent visitor as well?"

"Freddi?" Isabella chewed thoughtfully on the end of the pencil. "He was very nice to me and Mama after Papa passed away. He brought me toys, and...he made Mama laugh." A tiny furrow formed between her brows. "But I once heard our butler telling Mama's maid that he was a fork-tongued demi...demo..." She trailed off with a small shrug. "Whatever *that* means."

*Demagogue*, thought Jack. He, too, wondered what the marchesa's butler had been implying, and made a mental note to make a few discreet inquiries about the fair-haired Italian's background.

"I haven't a clue," he said aloud. "But people often say silly things, so if I were you, I wouldn't fret about it."

Isabella drew in a pair of high-top boots and began to color in the outlines. "I miss Italy," she said softly. "But Mama says we can never go back."

Jack's ears pricked up. "Oh? And why is that?"

The little girl's shoulders lifted in another shrug that nearly touched her ears. "She won't say. Whenever I ask, I get the same answer." Pursing her lips, Isabella lowered her voice to a frighteningly accurate imitation of her mother's most solemn tone. "We must look to the future, *tesoro*, not to the past."

If the subject hadn't been so serious, Jack would have laughed. Instead, he stared thoughtfully at the seagulls circling overhead. *Yet another mystery surrounding the marchesa.*

"Well, I daresay she has a good reason."

The little girl began to draw a wicked-looking pistol. "Maybe she killed someone in a duel."

At that, Jack couldn't hold back a smile. "You have a very vivid imagination, Miss Isabella, which is a great asset in art. However, in real life, you must take care not to say such wild things."

"I'm not just imagining things." Darting a furtive look at her mother, Isabella leaned in a little closer and whispered, "I'm not supposed to talk about it, but we left Casa Neroli in a great rush. It was the middle of the night, and I didn't even have a chance to pack my favorite doll."

Jack ruffled her curls. "There are any number of reasons for leaving at an odd hour. Travelers must always consider things like ferry schedules, border crossings, and traversing the mountain passes in the light of day."

Isabella looked unconvinced. "I suppose. But Perry thinks it sounds awfully havey-cavey."

"You know what I think?" murmured Jack.

The pencil ceased its scratching.

"I think that you and Perry ought to stop reading all those bloodthirsty horror tales." And yet, even as he said it, his own imagination was racing through a gamut of macabre motifs for the marchesa's strange behavior.

*Pistols at twenty paces?*

No, not in his wildest fantasies did he think Alessandra della Giamatti capable of killing someone. However, Isabella's playmate was right—something havey-cavey was going on.

\*     \*     \*

*The bronze fragments would need an acid bath to dissolve the sediments, the glass mosaic tile needed to be tested to determine its origin...* Alessandra tried to concentrate on her upcoming work, but her mind's eye kept forming the picture of a sword-wielding knight fighting a fire-breathing dragon.

*If only.*

If only storybook fantasies could come alive. She slanted a look at Jack, who was wielding a pencil with consummate skill, judging by her daughter's admiring expression. His handsome face no longer looked as forbidding as it once had. If one looked closely, the chiseled lines had a subtle softness, the dark eyes had a rich warmth. *Like melted chocolate.*

Alessandra sipped her wine, savoring the sweet memory of his mouth. His kisses had released all sorts of sensations that were...best left locked away in her heart, along with her past.

She couldn't help wonder, though, what Jack had been about to say just before Frederico had spoiled the moment with his reckless play. There had been an odd spark in his eye. As if, despite all her previous rebuffs, he was willing to offer her help.

A fresh gust of wind blew over the water, the sharp, salty air swirling through the hemp and canvas. Lifting her face, she let its sting slap against her skin. Her gaze followed the rise and fall of the ocean, the deep, dark seagreen waves moved by some inexorable force, some mysterious rhythm.

Oh, if only she dared appeal to his sense of honor now...
*Spill her secrets?*

Her insides gave a lurch. Oh, no, she dared not. He would be disgusted at the truth. Better to have him dislike her than to despise her. She couldn't imagine what he would think if he knew she had been a party to murder.

*A violent criminal.* And now, about to become a conniving thief. Someone willing to betray every principle he held dear.

Black Jack Pierson might be a hero for some lucky lady. But not, alas, for her.

# Chapter Nineteen

$B$loody hell," murmured Kate as she stared down at Alessandra's latest letter. The smudges marring the neatly penned lines looked awfully suspicious.

"I beg your pardon, Miss Katharine?" The elderly butler turned around with the tea tray, a symphony in silver, from his perfectly combed mane of hair to the ornate pots and glittering heirloom platter cradled in his dove-gray gloves.

She squinted into the brilliant reflections, a habit from her seafaring days that annoyed her imperious grandfather to no end. "Nothing, Simpson," she answered. "I was merely talking to myself."

Which was another little quirk that drove the duke to distraction. But thankfully he was ensconced in his study, reviewing account books with the steward from his Kentshire estate.

"Very good, ma'am." The butler bowed and slipped silently from the room, despite the heavy load of precious metal in his arms.

Sighing, Kate returned her attention to the letter. "I wish Charlotte had not left London," she muttered to herself a moment later. "I fear we have a far more pressing problem than Huntford's essay on our hands." She was quite sure that she was reading between the lines correctly. Alessandra sounded like a stranger—a cheerful, chatty stranger who was as different from the real marchesa as chalk was from cheese.

She lifted the letter up to the light. Besides, after years of sailing the seas, she knew damn well what a splash of salt water looked like.

If Alessandra was reduced to tears, something was seriously amiss. And yet, she had not dared to confide in the Circle.

Kate's brow creased.

*What could possibly be so dreadful?*

It took the sharp crackling of paper to make Kate aware that her hands had clenched into fists. On second thought, she conceded that some secrets were not easy to share, even with one's closest friends.

"Damn." The curse came out a great deal louder than before.

The tweeny who had tiptoed into the sitting room to dust the hearth gave a terrified squeak and nearly fell into the coal scuttle.

"Not you, Mary," added Kate hastily.

Ye gods, the servants moved like ghosts through the ornate townhouse. And no wonder, seeing that the place was like a crypt. Stuffy, silent. Everything about it seemed devoid of life—the formal portraits, the ancient furniture, the hideously expensive *objets d'art*.

"Will you kindly take word to my maid that I wish to

make a trip to Hatchards." All of a sudden, Kate was in dire need of a breath of fresh air to think properly. "And please have her inform Simpson that I am going out."

"Yes, ma'am." The girl curtsied. "Right away."

Kate made a face at the haughty ancestor hanging above the escritoire, unsure if she would ever get used to being treated like royalty.

The long-dead duchess stared back in rigid disapproval.

A grin slowly replaced Kate's grimace. Rank and privilege did, however, offer some practical advantages. She took up the ivory pen and dashed off a note before hurrying from the room.

Alessandra felt a brackish chill seep through her boots as she struggled to climb to the top of the hill. The weather had been blustery for several days, and during the night, a thunderstorm had swept through the countryside, its torrential rains leaving the excavation site mired in mud.

"The cart paths are naught but a swamp," said Eustace's assistant, staring balefully at the waterlogged ropes and half-submerged winch in one of the main pits. "I had to send the wagons back to town."

Dwight Davis mumbled something in Latin, while Haverstick looked up at the heavens. "We may very well get another squall blowing through. It seems pointless to start work under these conditions."

The other committee heads nodded in glum assent.

Eustace puffed out his cheeks. "We are falling behind schedule. But there's naught we can do when the elements conspire against us."

"So." Orrichetti shifted from foot to foot, his wet boots stirring a soft squelch of mud. "Back to Bath?"

"And a dram of brandy," muttered Haverstick. His ears were turning red in the raw, swirling wind.

"You all go on. I think I will stay for a while and catch up on my notes," said Alessandra. "If the rains hold off, I may even take a look at the upper grotto walls. I've not yet had a chance to collect some samples of the mosaic tiles and cement for chemical testing."

Jack had leaned a muscled shoulder against a tree and was thumbing through his sketchbook, for all appearances completely uninterested in the discussion.

"Do take care, Lady Giamatti. The rocks will be slippery." Dwight-Davis blew on his hands, sending up tendrils of ghostly white vapor in the morning chill. "Perhaps I should stay with you. I don't like the idea of you wandering around the site alone. It could be dangerous."

"Oh, please, there is no need for gallantry, sir, though I do appreciate the offer. In all likelihood I shall not stray from my tent."

"Well, if you are sure…"

"Quite," she replied firmly. "I prefer to write up my reports on-site. In case there are any questions, I can easily check on the details. As you know, the more accurate we can be, the more valuable the information."

"Very commendable." Haverstick looked impatient to be off. He had been limping earlier and Alessandra suspected that the expensive hobnailed shoes he had ordered from Bavaria were pinching his feet.

"There is plenty of work to be done at the Antiquities Society," pointed out Alessandra. Knowing that the task would appeal to Dwight-Davis's organizational zeal, she added, "There are boxes and boxes of artifacts that need to be sorted and labeled."

"Indeed, indeed!" The scholar visibly brightened. "We shall need to establish a set of categories, and make sure we have plenty of cotton wool and pasteboard..."

"Then it's settled," said Haverstick. "Come along, everyone, let us inform the others that we shall be working in town today."

Still mumbling to himself, Dwight-Davis fell in line and marched off.

As the group faded to shadowy shapes in the mist, Alessandra turned and saw that Jack was gone, too. A sigh of relief slipped from her lips. The last thing she needed was his penetrating gaze following her every move.

As she left the bookstore, Kate paused and looked up at the sky. "Seeing as the weather is so nice, Alice, why don't we take a stroll up Bond Street, before heading home."

Her maid nodded dutifully and fell in step beside her. The woman was new to the position, the old one having resigned in despair the previous week over the state of Kate's wardrobe. Work in the laboratory tended to result in a number of peculiar odors. But it was probably the bloodstains from dissecting the frog that had done the trick, thought Kate. So far, Alice was showing more backbone.

Setting a brisk pace—which raised several eyebrows along Piccadilly—Kate skirted the Royal Academy and turned right.

"Perhaps we should stop and shop for a pair of gloves to match your new ballgown," began her maid.

Kate kept walking. "I'm not interested in shopping, Alice." Her gaze skimmed over the fancy store windows, ignoring the expensive fashions and furbelows on display. Spotting an arched façade of pale Portland stone up ahead, she crossed the street and came to a halt in front of the doorway.

Her maid peered at the sign and Kate heard a sharp intake of breath.

"We must move on, milady. You can't be seen standing here."

Kate cut her off with a quelling look.

A few minutes of strained silence ticked by as Alice struggled to contain her mounting agitation.

"Miss Katharine!" The warning was no longer a whisper. "This is a gentlemen's club—a gentlemen's *sporting club.* A place where they prance around half naked—"

"Which half?" quipped Kate, which earned her a look of horror.

"A gently bred lady *cannot* be seen loitering around its entrance," insisted her maid, gamely trying to press her point.

"You ought to know me by now."

"Aye, miss." Alice chuffed a harried sigh. "And I also know your grandfather. Of the two, you are less likely to cut out my liver and feed it to the Tower ravens."

"I'm actually quite skilled with a sword and a stiletto."

Alice did not look amused.

"I promise you will suffer no consequences for my actions," added Kate. "Grandfather knows by now that none of his staff is to blame for my unladylike behavior."

Their exchange was cut short by the *thunk* of the paneled portal swinging open. Two young bucks emerged from the salon, still looking a little pink in the face from exertion.

Smiling sweetly, Kate moved to block their path. "Pardon me, sirs. Is Mr. Angelo holding fencing classes this afternoon? Or is it Mr. Jackson's day to give boxing lessons?"

"It's—it's fencing day," stuttered the ginger-haired gentleman.

"Aye," added his companion, whose round face and slightly bulging eyes gave him an unfortunate resemblance to a frog. "But if you are looking for lessons, you are out of luck. The Master doesn't accept female students—does he now, Derwitt?"

Ginger Hair tittered.

"Oh, that's quite all right—I doubt I'd need any pointers on how to carve your spleen into fish bait," she replied pleasantly. "You see, if I need to wield a blade, I'm certainly not going to fight by the rules."

Their grins turned a trifle uncertain.

"But speaking of rules, I wouldn't want to overset the delicate sensibilities of the club's members by setting foot inside. So would you kindly deliver this note to Mr. Angelo for me." She jabbed the paper in Frog Face's chest before he could object.

"Er, well…"

"Hop to it, sir," snapped Kate. "I haven't got all day."

Both gentlemen did a quick about-face and scurried back into the academy.

The wait was lengthy enough to set her foot tapping. "Damnation," she muttered under her breath. It would be a cursed nuisance if she had to wait until the day after the morrow to try again.

Her maid gave an audible sniff, but refrained from comment.

Finally, the portal swung open again, and out swaggered Conte Marco Musto della Ghiradelli, coatless and with his black hair damp and curling in Renaissance ringlets around his shirt collar.

Kate sucked in her breath as he lowered the towel from her brow.

*Oh, no.* Of all the bloody, *bloody* luck.

In her travels through the seamier seaports of the world, she had encountered a good many rogues. Why in the name of Lucifer did her good friend's cousin have to be one of them? In Naples she had known him only as *Il Serpente*. While he had thought her to be . . .

*Never mind that.*

There was no reason to think he might recognize her now. The room had been hazed with cigar smoke, the single candle had been naught but a weak flicker of cheap tallow, and the conte had been three sheets to the wind. Maybe four. If she recalled correctly, fine French brandy had been his preferred poison that evening.

"I confess, I am used to ladies pursuing me, but this is a rather novel approach." Marco's cocky voice brought her back to the present.

Kate looked up through her lashes. In the light of day, it was clear why the rascal was rumored to have females following him all over Town, ready to swoon at his feet.

His *bare* feet, she noticed, dropping her gaze. He had obviously been interrupted in the middle of a match, but most men would not saunter out into the streets in such a shameless state of undress.

But then, the conte was known for his flagrantly outrageous behavior.

"By the by," he went on, his deep voice tinged with an

intriguing accent. "How did you know where to find me? I only arrived back in Town yesterday afternoon."

"A lucky guess," she murmured. Actually, she had read a snippet of gossip in the morning newspaper mentioning the divine Lord G's return. And as Alessandra had mentioned her cousin's prowess with a sword, Angelo's Fencing Academy seemed a logical place to look for him. "But that's neither here nor there," she hastened to add. "I need to have a word with you in private. It's a matter of some importance."

"Have we met?" inquired Marco after subjecting her to a lengthy scrutiny.

"No," she replied quickly, dropping her head a touch more. "But I've heard a great deal about you."

He toyed with the folds of his rolled-up sleeve, revealing another inch or two of well-muscled forearm. "Somehow, that doesn't surprise me. I've been told I'm a popular topic of conversation when the ladies of London make their rounds of morning calls."

*Still the same arrogant ass,* thought Kate impatiently. However, for Alessandra's sake, she managed to keep her assessment to herself. "I wouldn't know, seeing as I don't waste my time in mindless tittle-tattle. Now please, would you mind getting dressed, sir? We really need to talk."

Setting a hand on his hip, Marco let out a sigh. "Can't it wait another quarter hour? I am leading Angelo on points going into the final round, and it is considered bad form among gentlemen to quit while you are ahead."

"No," replied Kate testily. "It cannot. And it has nothing to do with your manly thighs or muscles, so you can stop waggling your arse in those skintight buckskins." Ignoring Alice's horrified hiss, she lowered her voice. "I am a friend of Alessandra, one of her fellow 'Sinners.'"

His beautiful topaz eyes sharpened, and for an instant she saw a different facet to their glittering golden hue. "Gentlemanly scruples demand that I not leave a lady in the lurch." He sketched a bow. "Being of Italian descent, Angelo will understand. Allow me five minutes."

Jack moved quietly through the grove of oaks and elms, using the pockets of lingering fog and the soft, soggy ground to hide his approach to Alessandra's shelter. The air was heavy with the smell of damp decay, its humidity forming tiny beads of moisture on his cheeks and brow. Shadows snaked through the dark branches, and in the washed-out light of the overcast sky, the leaves appeared more pewter gray than green.

Picking a path through brambles, Jack covered the last few yards in a low crouch and crept close to the rear of the tent. A breeze stirred, spattering the canvas with a shower of raindrops from the overhanging trees. He had spotted Frederico coming up the footpath. In another moment or two...

The wet slap of the front flaps announced the Italian's arrival. Ignoring the trickle of cold, clammy water seeping under his collar, Jack cocked an ear close to the woven wall. Whatever the two conspirators were up to, whatever secrets lay between them, he meant to discover the truth, come what may.

The crackle of paper sounded unnaturally loud in the stillness.

"So, did you check that section yet?" It was Frederico's voice, sharp with impatience.

"Yes," replied Alessandra, sounding strangely muffled.

"After the meeting where it was decided to take several days off, I waited until the workmen had left for the day." Metal scraped against the wood planking as she shifted a tool. "It's not the right spot."

"You are sure?"

"Yes! My probing rod showed that beneath the thin layer of soil is nothing but solid rock."

"But the description—," began Frederico.

"The description is vague at best, and as I keep telling you, the landscape has no doubt changed over the centuries," snapped Alessandra. "I'll need to make another survey of the site and see if I can find another likely location."

"*Diavolo*. Do it quickly." The Italian sounded angry. "I trust, Alessa, that I need not remind you..."

The rest of his words were muddled as a gust of wind shivered the tent.

*Damn.* Drawing a shallow breath, Jack shifted his position.

"I am well aware of that." Her voice had dropped to a near whisper. "Trust me, I am just as anxious as you are to find it. I am doing my best, but archaeology is not an exact science. And we must also face the fact that we may be searching for something that doesn't exist. The map may be a fake, the object may have been discovered long ago—"

Frederico cut her off with a low laugh. "Let us hope that is not the case, *cara*. That would be disappointing, to say the least."

Jack couldn't tell whether Alessandra said anything in reply. He heard footsteps scuff over the bare earth. "Curse this foul English weather," muttered Frederico. "Time is short enough as it is, without any further delays."

"I know. I'm doing everything I can to speed things along, but I have to be extremely careful. You wouldn't want the others to become suspicious of what I am doing."

He grunted. "*Si*, I know that. What about today?"

"I am going to have a look along the river," she replied.

"Shall I come along to help?"

"No, it's best that we are not seen together. Go back to town and join the others. Use your charm to keep them amused." She paused. "And try not to antagonize Lord James. Of all the men on this dig, he is the most dangerous."

"Dangerous?" The soft slap of leather sounded as the Italian flicked his gloves against his palm. "Believe me, I am not afraid of a pampered prig."

"You ought to be," she countered. "Don't forget that he is a decorated veteran of the war in Spain."

"Yes, I'm sure his medals look very pretty on his fancy scarlet tunic. But surely by now you know that in England, such military commissions are purchased." His words hung for an instant in the air. "And you yourself have implied that his position here has more to do with family wealth and influence than any individual qualifications."

Alessandra did not reply.

"But perhaps it is you, *cara*, who are in danger from the man. I have seen the way you watch him—"

"Don't be absurd," cut in Alessandra. "Yes, I keep my eye on him. In order to make sure he is not coming too close to our secret."

"Hmmph." Jack heard Frederico's pacing quicken, the swirl of damp wool slapping against his boots. "Very well. But remember, I count on you to keep him distracted. Use whatever means necessary, but on no account can he be allowed to uncover our real reason for being here."

Deciding he had heard enough, Jack retreated to the cover of the trees.

Frederico stalked off a few minutes later, his stride a little shaky, his handsome face twisted in a ferocious frown.

*So, the conspirators were nervous.*

All the better, thought Jack. Impelled by fear, people tended to make mistakes. Turning up his coat collar, he sat back on his haunches. The Peninsular conflict had taught him patience. He was prepared to wait all day if need be for the marchesa to make her move.

But it wasn't long, no more than a quarter hour, before the tent flaps fluttered open. Covered in a long, hooded cloak, Alessandra was naught but a spectral shape as she glided into the mist. She moved swiftly, silently, only the faint chink of her toolbag disturbing the stillness of the deserted site.

Jack hurried to keep her in sight. The clouds had thickened, and the muted colors and textures of the surrounding landscape were growing hazy in the subdued light. At the same time he was careful to keep his distance. He wanted to catch her in the act.

Following the footpath down to the river, Alessandra picked her way along the rocky bank, pausing here and there to study the eddying currents. It appeared she was heading to the entrance of a newly discovered grotto. Just last week, a pile of tumbled stones had been shifted, revealing a well-preserved underground thermal bath, smaller than the main structure, so probably made for the use of the officers. The walls were decorated with striking mosaic murals and several lovely statues of the goddess Minerva. The ancient sculptures had been taken to Bath for safekeeping. But given what he had just overheard, Jack suspected there must be something of far greater value still hidden within the shadows.

The rocks were still wet with rain, slowing him to a snail's pace in order to avoid any slip that might give him away. Rounding an outcropping of limestone, he saw her disappear into a sliver of space between the shadowed rocks.

Jack counted to ten and then followed her lead.

The opening was so narrow that he had to turn sideways to slip inside. Pressing his shoulderblades up against the rough surface, he paused for a moment to allow his eyes to adjust to the murky light. Having made a brief tour of the grotto on the day of its discovery, he knew that there were a half dozen shallow stairs leading down to a stone floor, perhaps twelve feet square. Beyond that was a deep pool of a similar size, lined with skillfully mortised stone blocks. Holding his breath, he could hear the murmur of the bubbling thermal waters rising up from the underground spring that fed them.

The sound reverberated off the walls, and combined with the warm, moist air, it created the sensation of being inside the mouth of a sleeping dragon.

Jack shook off the strange thought. He had not come to slay a dragon, he had come to catch a thief.

The strike of a flint against steel echoed through the dark shadows and a small flame flared to life. Alessandra set the lantern down beside her bag and began rummaging among her tools.

He stepped forward, the scattering of pebbles on the floor crunching under his boots.

She whirled around, a look of surprise freezing her features.

"Do you want to explain what you are doing?" he asked.

Her hand flew to a spot high on her chest, and he saw the tiny muscles of her throat tighten in a convulsive swallow. "I—I don't have to answer to you, Lord James."

"Oh, but I think you do." He stepped closer, watching the swirl of fear in her eyes darken into something more desperate. Hell, he wanted very badly to believe in her innocence. But the facts belied his hope.

Disappointment goaded him to speak roughly. "I heard you with your old friend, plotting to rob the site. What a pretty team you make. Tell me, how long have the two of you been doing this? How many priceless treasures have you stolen?"

"I'm not...He's not..."

"He's not what? Your lover? Your partner in crime?"

"Y-you are mistaken," she whispered.

Jack slashed an angry gesture through the air. "Enough lies, Alessandra. By Jove, I mean to have the truth out of you."

"The truth?" A shrill laugh slipped from her lips as she suddenly slumped to her knees and buried her head in her hands. "Oh, God," came her muffled groan. "I'm not even sure what that is anymore."

# Chapter Twenty

*L*ud, that devil is too handsome for his own good," muttered Alice as they waited for Marco to reappear.

That was putting it mildly, thought Kate.

"And you, Miss Katharine. I would be remiss in my duties if I didn't remind you that a proper female never, *ever* makes reference to a gentleman's...anatomical features."

"His arse is rather nice," murmured Kate.

There was a hesitation, followed by a sigh. "Divine."

"Alice, I have a feeling we are going to rub along together quite well, once you become used to my little quirks." Kate checked her reflection in one of the shop windows, taking a moment to pull the poke of her bonnet a little lower on her brow. "First and foremost is the fact that I may be a duke's granddaughter, but there isn't a proper bone in my body."

The maid pursed her lips thoughtfully. "What's the second?"

"I don't give a damn whether that upsets anyone. Including the Duke of Cluyne."

"Ah." Alice maintained a straight face. "Is there a third?"

Kate grinned. "No, I think that about sums it up."

"So, let me see if I have this straight, ma'am." The maid smoothed the front of her cloak. "I will cheerfully remind you of the rules, and you will cheerfully break them to flinders."

"Correct."

Allowing a soupçon of a smile, Alice also let her speech slide into a hint of Irish brogue. "And here I thought that being lady's maid to a duke's granddaughter was going to be a crashing bore."

True to his word, the conte reappeared within minutes, no longer looking like a raffish corsair. The cut of his exquisitely tailored coat accentuated his sculpted shoulders and narrow waist to perfection, while his tapered trousers showed off the long, lean lines of his legs.

"Shall we take a stroll, *signora*?" After setting his curly brim beaver hat on his still-damp curls, Marco offered his arm. "I'm afraid you have the advantage of me—you know my name, and yet I don't know yours."

"Kate Woodbridge," she replied quickly.

"Miss Katharine Woodbridge, granddaughter of the Duke of Cluyne," corrected Alice, who was trailing close behind.

"It is a great pleasure to meet you, Miss Kate-Katharine," said Marco with a roguish wink.

Kate rather doubted he would be smiling so sweetly if he knew who she really was. But that was not something she intended to let him discover. Ducking her head, she kept her eyes on the pavement. *The less he saw of her face, the better.*

"If you don't mind, let's not waste time in frivolous flirtations, sir. I sought you out because I am worried about Alessandra."

Beneath the whisper-fine wool of his sleeve, Kate felt his muscles tense. "I thought she was in Bath, working with a group of other scholars on the excavation of an ancient Roman fort."

"She is," replied Kate. "But before she left, she was clearly worried over something. And now, after reading her last letter, I am convinced that she is in trouble."

"You are probably reading too much into it," murmured Marco. "Alessa can occasionally let her emotions get the better of her."

"On the contrary, Alessandra is the most calm, controlled person I know," she shot back. "For her to betray a frisson of fear means that something is seriously wrong."

A wink of gold cut across her gaze as he toyed with the fobs on his watch chain. Despite his show of studied nonchalance, she sensed him turning wary, watchful. "What makes you say that?"

"It's hard to explain," said Kate slowly. "It wasn't exactly the words she used. It was more the tone." When said aloud, her suspicions suddenly sounded a little silly. "Which was painfully cheerful."

"Maybe she is having a good time."

"No," insisted Kate. "I tell you, something is not right."

"She should be safe in Bath," he muttered under his breath.

"Safe?" echoed Kate. "Are you saying that Alessandra is in some sort of *danger*?"

Marco lifted his elegant shoulders in a shrug, a gesture that caused the tails of his snowy-white cravat to catch in the breeze. "A figure of speech. It's nothing to be concerned about." He smoothed the starched linen back into place. "A private family matter."

"What fustian," she retorted. "You are lying through your pretty teeth."

His well-shaped mouth stretched a touch wider, but the smile did not come close to reaching his eyes. They remained shadowed by the curl of his dark lashes. "And why would I do that, Miss Kate-Katharine?"

"I have no bloody idea." She clenched her jaw, careful to keep her face at an oblique angle to his. "But I mean to find out. With or without your help."

"*Cara...*," he began.

"Stubble the sweet talk," she snapped. "I don't suppose you are going to share with me what she said in her letter to you."

She saw the corners of his mouth tighten. "What letter?"

"Didn't you get it? Alessandra mentioned that she wrote to you in Scotland."

He shook his head. "I finished my business there sooner than expected."

"Well, it seemed that she was quite anxious to hear from you. In fact, she repeated it twice." Kate blew out her cheeks. "That's another reason I smell a rat."

"You have been reading too many novels," said Marco. "There are no deep, dark dungeons and dastardly villains in Bath. My cousin is surrounded by bookish scholars, enjoying the fresh air and pastoral English countryside. She likely is looking forward to hearing from me because she is . . . bored."

"And the moon is made of green cheese," muttered Kate.

"I heard it was *mozzarella di Bufala*."

She shot him a quelling look. "I've a good mind to leave for Bath at first light."

"Slow down." His hand tightened on her arm, bringing her to a sudden halt. "Leave this to me."

"Because a female might faint at the first sign of trouble?" she said sarcastically. "Trust me, I am not some helpless peagoose. I know how to take care of myself. And my friends."

"*Al diavolo*. Women!" he growled through his teeth. "You are as stubbornly strong-willed as my cousin."

"Men!" countered Kate. "What you mean to say is, both of us have a brain and are not afraid to use it."

He slowly released her and flexed his fingers. She watched, mesmerized for a moment by the sinuous shape of them snaking through the air. *Il Serpente*. It was not all on account of his amorous exploits that he had earned the moniker. In Naples, he was rumored to be quick and deadly as a cobra in a fight. Rubbing unconsciously at her arm, Kate reminded herself to be careful and keep well out of range of his fangs.

Marco moved closer, forcing her back a step. "*Non*, what I mean is, there are reasons—reasons I am not at liberty to discuss with anyone—for keeping this a private matter. Since you consider yourself so smart, I ask you to think about this, Miss Kate-Katharine, before you run off half-cocked. Why do you suppose Alessandra has not confided in you?"

Kate opened her mouth and then closed it. She had asked herself the same question.

"Could it be that some secrets are too painful, too personal to share, even with close friends?"

She wanted to come up with a clever quip, a cutting retort, but in her heart she knew that his words had the ring of truth. "What are you going to do?" she demanded. "Assuming I agree to leave things in your hands."

He curled a fist and set it on his hip. "I need to make a few inquiries among some friends before I can answer that. It's imperative not to do anything rash. You have no idea how dangerous that could be."

*As if she were any stranger to danger.*

Kate bit her lip, knowing how foolish it would be to say so aloud. And whatever else her faults, she was no fool. Much to her irritation, she had to admit that in this case Marco was right. Any impetuous intrusion on her part into Alessandra's affairs might do more harm than good.

"Very well." She couldn't help but add, "However, you had better act in the next few days, or I'll be forced to take charge."

He narrowed his eyes. "Who do you think you are, to order me around like a lapdog?"

The words were a sharp reminder of how little she wanted him to dwell on *that* question. Sometimes discretion was the better part of valor. Even though the platitude chafed against her natural inclination to race to the rescue of a friend. *Discretion*, she repeated. All things considered, it made no sense to risk the chance of stirring Marco's memory of the past.

"I'll move as fast as I can, but it may take me several days to contact all my sources," he continued. "Trust me, even if trouble is threatening, Alessandra is better off in Bath than here."

"I suppose I shall have to take your word for it," replied Kate grudgingly. "Is there nothing I can do to help?"

"If I think of anything, I shall let you know."

The offhand dismissal rankled, but Kate swallowed the urge to start another argument with him. "Do," she said curtly before turning on her heel. "Come, Alice. We need to pick out a pair of gloves." Blood-red ones, to match the color of her angry flush.

Marco cut a sardonic bow. "Until later, Miss Kate-Katharine."

On second thought, perhaps she would purchase a gauntlet—to slap across his arrogant face.


Jack dropped to his knees next to Alessandra. Tendrils of steam floated up from the bubbling spring, misting the glass globe of the lantern. Her cloak had come undone, the ties tangling with the fallen hood as it slipped to the ground. In the blurred light, her hair shimmered like waves of silk as it spilled over her sagging shoulders.

Anger licked up inside him, hot little tongues of fire crackling in a chorus of jeers. *Fool, fool, fool.* The realization burned like a blaze of furious hellfire twisting through his gut. Blinded—no, besotted—by her beguiling beauty and intellect, he had failed to see through her sophisticated lies.

And yet, against all reason, a part of him still refused to believe her guilty of such cold-blooded deception.

*Burning anger, desperate need.* It was a very volatile combination...

At the sight of that quivering Marchesa Mouth, looking impossibly innocent, something inside him exploded.

"Damnation." He grabbed her arms, aware that his fingers were digging into her flesh.

She made no protest, her body still save for a slight flicker of her lashes. Her eyes were luminous in the watery light. Like liquid emeralds.

*No, no, no.* Don't drown in their depths.

"Don't play me for a fool, Alessandra," he rasped. "The truth is not so hard to define. Or have you been living a lie for so long that the word has lost all meaning?"

"Lies." The sound was more of a sob, its echo reverberating against the rough-cut stones. "Yes, my life is a lie, but not in the way you think."

"Tell me." Jack slid his hands higher, to the ridge of her shoulders. "Trust me."

"I—I can't."

"*Why?*" he demanded, trying to control his pent-up frustration. His grip tightened, pressing hard against the fragile blades of her bones.

She flinched. "Oh, please. Don't ask. I don't have the strength to fight you, too."

Her anguish seemed oh-so real. *Or was he merely being manipulated again?*

"I wish...," whispered Alessandra. "I wish that I might borrow a little of your steel." She reached up and feathered a finger along the line of his jaw. "A little of your courage." Her bare flesh was cold as ice. "And your honor." A twist engulfed her face in shadow. "Mine, I fear, was lost long ago."

"Take what you need from me," he answered hoarsely.

Suddenly, at that instant, it didn't seem to matter whether she was playing him false.

Alessandra turned back to him, the flickering lantern painting a faint line of light over the tenuous curve of her mouth.

"Would that I could."

Her perfume swirled around his head, filling his nostrils with the tantalizing scent of exotic spices. Jack pulled her close, drawing a deep, shuddering breath. "What's to stop you?"

Her lips parted, as if on the verge of speech. But all of a sudden the spark seemed to die in her eyes and all that came out was a ghost of a sigh.

"Alessandra."

"I..."

"Go on," he urged.

A tiny swallow pinched her throat. She hesitated for a heartbeat, and then arched up to brush a kiss to his cheek.

*Distraction.* Jack dimly recalled Frederico's exhortation. *Use whatever means necessary.* He had seen the enemy use such a tactic countless times on the battlefields of Spain. But distraction was a two-edged sword to wield against an experienced foe. Danger could cut both ways.

Framing her face with his palms, Jack leaned in and flicked his tongue over her lower lip. With a tiny moan, Alessandra clutched at his shirt and opened herself to his probing embrace.

His self-control was already teetering on a razor-thin blade. Her lips touching his sent him over the edge.

Seized by an overpowering need, Jack tightened his

hold and twisted hard, his knees scraping the rough stone floor as he drew her down and straddled her body. A hiss of heat seemed to rise from the stones, enveloping him in a vaporous haze. He hitched his hips, pinning her to the rock tiles.

She gave a soft cry, the sound nearly swallowed by the bubbling of the hot spring.

Jack stilled for an instant, feeling like a brute.

But then, Alessandra's arms were around his neck, her slim fingers twining in his hair. "Jack. *Si grande nero Giacomo.*"

*Oh yes, he was big, bad Black Jack.* A dark, dark devil with a heart singed in sin.

He knew she was reacting out of desperation. But he was cad enough to take shameless advantage of her weakness. His mouth captured hers again, delving deep in a lush kiss. She tasted of smoke, of spice, of every sensuous fantasy he had ever imagined. Sweet beyond words.

A groan rumbled deep in his throat as he trailed a line of kisses to the hollow of her throat. Beneath his groping touch, her breasts swelled against his palms, the tips like tiny points of fire.

"Sweet Jesus." Bracing himself on his elbows, Jack found the fastenings of her gown. His movements fast and furious, he freed the tabs and loosened the lacing of her corset. Any lingering twinge of guilt gave way to pure, primal lust as Alessandra began tugging at his clothing.

No words, no thoughts. His mind was a haze of longing.

She worked his coat off and slid her hands under his shirt, her nails scoring a trail of heat across his shoulder blades. Jack groaned again—or was it a growl—and shifted his weight. Groping for her skirts, he hiked them up around her waist. A hem snagged and he heard a rip as the fabric bunched in a torrid tangle of muslin and shirttails.

*Honor be damned.*

Above the creamy stretch of her stockings was a pure white frothing of lace. It took only a moment to peel off her garters, exposing her flesh. The insides of her thighs were soft and sensuous as a sun-warmed rose petal. In contrast to his bronzed hands, their color was a delicate shade of blush pink.

"Lift your hips, sweeting," he rasped.

Her back arched, allowing Jack to slide his coat beneath her. She had only to say no, he rationalized. A single word and he would stop, no matter that he was half wild with need.

As if sensing his question, Alessandra looped her arms around his waist, entwining them closer. Her lips brushed the corner of his mouth.

"*Si*, Jack. *Si*."

*Yes. Yes.* Like the soft swirls of steam, the whisper licked against his flesh. He levered himself up, the lantern's dancing flame casting sinuous shadows across the grotto walls. *Dark. Dangerous.* Was it magic or madness drawing him on? Hell, he no longer cared. Only this moment mattered.

Stripping off his shirt, Jack pressed his palms against her legs, urging them wider. Through the wisp of lace he caught a peek of silken curls and nearly came undone. Holding her open with his knees, he fumbled with the buttons of his breeches. The flap fell free, releasing his rigid cock.

Muscles taut and glistening in the winking glow, he

was acutely aware of the tiny drops of water beading on his bare skin, the tickle of his tangled hair kissing his shoulders. He was wickedly, wantonly naked save for his boots and the breeches scrunched around his knees.

Alessandra lifted her lashes, her gaze a glitter of green as she stared at his fully aroused manhood. She touched his belly, trailing her hand down the line of dark hair to the nest of coarse black curls and the heavy sac of his sex.

*Diavolo.* He could hold back no longer.

Exhaling a pent-up breath, Jack surged forward and positioned himself at the opening of her passage. A tingle of honeyed heat teased against the tip of his cock. Fire pulsed through him, singeing his senses. He was dimly aware of his heartbeat, pounding loud as cannonfire in his ears.

Biting back a cry of triumph, he thrust in deeply, sheathing himself in her core.

Alessandra was suddenly filled with a thick, throbbing heat. It felt...so right, this joining of their bodies.

Was it so wrong to lose herself in a surge of sweet oblivion, before surrendering to her past sins?

For yet another brief interlude she could hold on to a world untarnished by sordid deception. Black Jack Pierson was a pillar of shining strength, a soul of unquestionable honor. She didn't deserve his goodness. But selfishly, she would seize it.

"Alessandra." The stubbling of his jaw scraped lightly against her cheek. His scent—a heady mix of masculine musk and earthy arousal—swirled up from his sweat-sheened body. Beneath her flattened palms, she felt the rippling of muscle, the pulsing rhythm of his heartbeat.

"Jack." His closeness filled her with longing.

*Jack.* He had made her achingly aware of the void in her life—one that was not merely physical. His sculpted strength transcended flesh and blood. Oh, if only she might take heart from touching his essence.

But a fleeting coupling was all she could hope for. And shamelessly, she would take it. No matter how empty she would feel in the aftermath.

He kissed her, a sweet, gossamer grazing of his lips that left her yearning for more. "Why won't you trust me?" he whispered. "I want to help."

Tears welled up in her eyes. "Later. We will speak of it later." Her voice trembled. Yet another lie. How could she explain, when the answers he sought were too horrible to speak aloud?

"Later," he echoed. "*Va bene.*"

Good? No, it was evil of her.

But her soul had long since been damned to perdition. This last sweet moment of wickedness would hardly add to her sins.

*Sin.* Oh, it was sinful what his tongue was now doing to her body. Teasing a languid trail down the arch of her neck, the warm wicked tip flicked at her nipple, slowly at first and then with a more demanding urgency. Alessandra wriggled against him, moaning softly as he hooked his finger in her bodice and bared her breasts.

"*Sei così bella*—you are so beautiful." The words were hardly more than a breath of air as his mouth closed over her and suckled the peaked flesh.

Drawing her fingertips in slow, swirling circles down the line of his spine, Alessandra cupped a caress to his taut buttocks. A prick of her nails and she felt him swell and surge inside her.

Muffling her cry in the dark, tumbled fall of his hair, she arched up to match his quickening tempo. Heat spiraled through her core, the sweet friction teasing her feminine pearl to a throbbing point of fire. She was no stranger to lovemaking. Her late husband had enjoyed the physical pleasures of the marriage bed. But while Stefano had been a gentle, languid partner, Jack possessed her with a hot, demanding passion.

*Passion.* For so long she had kept herself under tight check. The fierceness of her own emotions sometimes frightened her. She had seen how dangerous it could be to let the heart overrule the head. But as Jack's teeth nipped her neck, the last shred of willpower unraveled in a moan.

*Danger be damned.*

Jack lifted himself, allowing a whisper of moist air between their bodies. The wispy steam was cool against her burning flesh. Too cool. Mouthing a soft sigh, Alessandra shifted her hips, seeking to close the sliver of space between them.

He sucked in his breath and let it out in a ragged, rasping groan. "Another instant and I'll fall over the edge, sweeting. I must. Hold back." His hand slipped through her honeyed curls and found her throbbing spot. "But let me take you to the peak of pleasure."

She twisted beneath his stroking touch, the tension inside her coiling to an exquisite, unbearable tautness. Mindless of all else but the need to have him around her, inside her, Alessandra arched up, driving him deeper.

As his hoarse shout reverberated off the rock walls, the stones seemed to shudder beneath her, and in the next heartbeat, her body convulsed in the shower of firegold sparks.

# Chapter Twenty-one

$L$ying in languorous repose, Jack listened to the gentle gurgling of the thermal spring. There was something soothing about the water sounds, and the tendrils of heated mist floating through the air. Through half-opened eyes he watched them swirl above his head in lazy circles and then dissolve into the darkness. In the pale pool of lamplight, the grotto walls shimmered with droplets of water.

He stretched and traced the tips of his fingers along the curve of Alessandra's hip. She stirred with a low murmur and slid her hand lower on his chest, but did not wake. Her face was softened by sleep, untouched by worry. As he feathered his lips to her brow, she hitched a little closer, her lovely mouth curling up at the corners.

*Damnation, what was she hiding?*

If only he could decipher her smile, her secrets.

*Was she really a scheming thief, an unprincipled liar?* Her words said one thing, her body quite another. Perhaps it was hubris, but he could not believe in his heart she was really in league with Frederico Bellazoni. Not after their passionate lovemaking. There *had* to be some other explanation.

Jack gazed at the fringe of her lashes, black as midnight against the pallor of her skin. She had tried to put on a brave face, but fear was a hard emotion to hide. It was always there, just beneath the surface, subtly shading her every expression. As a soldier, he recognized it. As a friend, he meant to slay it.

*If only she would let him.*

She had come close—oh-so close—to confiding in him. However, he had let lust get in the way. Never a wise strategy. The heat of battle required a cool head.

Shifting his bare shoulders against the makeshift blanket of his coat, Jack shot a rueful glance down the length of his nakedness, to the rumpled scrunch of his breeches tangled with damp leather and laces. Seeing the twisted folds of her shift clinging to her thighs sent a small stab of guilt through him. Alessandra deserved a less primitive setting for lovemaking. Candlelight and champagne, feather pillows and silk sheets, not hard rock and rough wool.

He should...

The sound of the thermal spring stirred an idea.

Sitting up, Jack slowly stripped off the rest of his clothing. "Alessandra," he murmured, his breath ruffling the strands of hair around her ear.

"Mmmm." Her voice was still smoky with sex.

As she turned, he could see the sweet curves of breasts limned in the flickering lamplight. Feel their imprint against his skin. His palms prickled, itching to touch her again.

It took all of his willpower to keep himself under control.

Her eyes fluttered open, embarrassment slowly darkening the emerald glitter.

"Lift your arms, sweetheart." He had already untied the fastenings of her shift and was sliding it up over her head.

"*Jack!*" She tried to pull away.

Tossing aside the crumpled cotton, he took her hand. "Come. When in Rome…" He let out a husky laugh as his bare feet slipped on the wet stones. Three quick strides brought them to the edge of the pool.

The wet warmth of the steam was intensely erotic against his skin. A froth of silvery bubbles rose up from the depths of the dark water. The effect was enchanting. Like a cauldron of simmering magic. Which was apt, as he intended to cast a spell that would coax her into revealing her secrets.

After dipping a toe to test the temperature, Jack plunged into the water. He surfaced and shook the hair back from his face. "Come on, it's lovely!" he urged.

Alessandra hesitated, her arms folded shyly across her thighs. "We should be getting back, before anyone discovers—"

He grabbed her ankle and pulled her in.

The splash echoed off the walls, melding a moment later with her sputtering mirth.

"Oh, you wicked, *wicked* man," she cried, water streaming down her face as she blew out a mouthful of silvery spray. With her hair falling in sleek, sinuous curls around her shoulders, she looked like one of Neptune's nereids, a mythical sea sprite rising from the inky depths.

He pulled her close, their naked bodies kissing up against each other in a swirl of heat. Waves lapped around them, the sound like lush, liquid laughter. Fire pooled in his groin. "I've not begun to be truly wicked," he murmured.

Her arms looped around his neck, a soft slap of warm, wet flesh. Jack felt her chest heave, her muscles tighten. But when she spoke, her voice was suddenly drained of all emotion. "While I have been wicked enough for several lifetimes," she whispered. "I—I must go..."

Jack silenced her words with a hard, possessive kiss. Holding back her protest, he spun them around in the water and set her back against the edge of the pool. The ancient stones were smooth as glass beneath his palms. He gripped the rounded lip, trapping her within his arms.

"I'm not letting you escape, sweetheart." Jack released her mouth a little roughly. "Not until you tell me what's wrong."

She shook her head, evading his gaze.

"I was often put in charge of interrogating prisoners during the war," he rasped. "Trust me, there are myriad ways of eliciting information." He ran his tongue along the edge of her lower lip. "Some are more pleasant than others."

Her look of longing quickly disappeared in despair.

"Alessandra." He pressed a kiss to the pulsing point of flesh at the base of her throat.

A moan reverberated against his lips. "You must think me a whore. And I suppose I am." Her voice broke. "If only I had listened to my brain and not my body back then."

"I think it's time to tell me everything," he said softly. "You have no reason to keep anything hidden."

"Stripped of all pretenses?" She gave a mirthless laugh. "I—I fear it will break this fragile peace between us."

"Friendship is not fragile, Alessandra. It can suffer through all sorts of hardships and adversity and emerge unscathed."

"I—I cannot ask you to be my friend."

"Why not?" he demanded.

She looked away. "Because I couldn't bear to see the look of disgust on your face if I told you the truth."

"Have you so little faith in me?" he asked softly. Skimming his hands up the length of her arms, Jack began massaging the knotted muscles of her shoulder, slowly working his fingers to the nape of her neck. Her wet hair tangled in his touch and along with the earthy musk of the mineral water rose the scent of her spice. Her wonderful, womanly essence.

"Whatever you have done, it is not beyond redemption."

*Oh, how she wished to believe that.*

Squeezing her eyes shut, Alessandra choked back a sob. His touch was so strong, so soothing. Impossible as it seemed, the tension started to drain from her body. She felt weightless, her body floating in some underworld paradise. Not heaven, not hell.

She wasn't sure what to call it.

The word 'love' came to mind, but she thrust it aside. She couldn't—wouldn't—taint his honor with her sins. Better he should think her a whore than a murderess.

In the gently swirling water, she felt the rise and fall of his stiffening cock against her thigh. She must wield her body as a weapon. Tempt him, tease him—anything to fight off his questions.

"No, I am a bad girl," she murmured, jutting out her hips and rubbing against him.

His lids grew heavy, hooding his eyes in dark, unfathomable shadows.

"How bad?" he asked.

"Very bad," responded Alessandra, opening her legs and letting them float up around his hips. "Very, *very* bad."

"One has to be extra firm with bad prisoners." His voice was deceptively mild. "Otherwise, they might suddenly turn dangerous."

"*Si.*" She tilted herself a fraction higher and clenched her knees. "Dangerous. You must know ways to subdue such impulses."

"Lots. Sometimes the situation calls for a subtle approach. And sometimes it's best to use a straightforward show of power." The head of his erection nudged into her feminine folds.

A current of awareness thrummed through her body. His closeness stirred unspeakable needs. Impossible longings.

He was now inside her passage, filling her with his heat.

Alessandra bit his shoulder to keep from crying aloud. The salty sweetness of his skin mingled with the taste of her tears. Slowly, silently, they surged together, their rhythm as elemental as the ocean tides. *Ebb and flow.* The only sounds were the seductive splashing of water and the zephyrous bubbling of steamy vapors.

Her need crested and then climaxed in a burst of shimmering light. Wave after wave of pleasure rippled through her body. She heard his shout, and felt him fill her with his essence.

If only she could float forever in this watery idyll, hidden from the present and safe from her past.

But dreams could not keep the real world at bay. After an interlude of peaceful bliss, Jack raised his head. Perhaps if he had spoken in English, the words would not have had the same effect. But his sensual mouth quirked and he whispered a sonnet from Dante.

"It wounds me that you have so little faith in me, Alessandra," he added. "And my word of honor to stand as your friend, no matter what."

She could not bear to see the look of hurt in his eyes. "It is not your honor I question, but rather my own. But you are right, I owe you the truth—on one condition. If what I tell you is too terrible to accept, you must consider yourself released from your word and walk away."

He nodded gravely.

Alessandra shivered in spite of the water's warmth. "I..." Might as well spill it out, she decided. "I murdered someone. In Italy. That is why I fled the country."

Jack's face remained impassive. "I imagine you had a compelling reason. I can't quite picture you killing for the mere thrill of it."

"That's the horror of it," she whispered. "I didn't. Have a reason, that is. It was a horrible mistake."

A tiny furrow formed between his brows. "That is not murder—"

"It was!" she insisted, her voice turning a little shrill.

"I *knew* Frederico was engaged in violence, yet I let him seduce me into helping him."

"Bellazoni was involved?"

Alessandra couldn't bring herself to meet his gaze. "Yes. He was a protégé of my late husband. Stefano admired his oratory and his zeal, even though he didn't agree with Frederico's ideas." She sucked in a breath. "After Stefano died, I let myself fall under the spell of Frederico's radical views. He and his friends spoke so passionately about freedom, and the need to fight for liberty and justice."

"Such idealism is hardly a crime, Alessandra," said Jack. "Those are noble principles."

"Yes, in theory. But Frederico twisted them into an excuse for violence against the Austrian occupying force in Milan." She took a moment to steady her voice. "I was such a fool, Jack. I...I let him into my bed. Just once, as if that makes it any less reprehensible."

His arms came around her, drawing her close. "You must have been frightened. And lonely."

"That doesn't excuse my lapse in judgment," she said. "I should have seen him for the snake he was."

"Your husband considered him a friend, and from what I gather, Stefano was not a fool." Jack brushed a bead of water from her cheek. "Now, tell me about the murder."

"Frederico knew all about my work with metals, of course. He asked me to make up an acid in my laboratory. Something strong enough to cut through the locks of an Austrian warehouse. I did it, even though I had vowed to myself that I wouldn't be part of their plans anymore. This was the last time."

"And?" encouraged Jack.

"And instead of opening a lock with the acid, Frederico used it to cut through the axle of an Austrian official's carriage while he was stopped at an inn near Como. There was a steep hill, leading down to a bridge spanning a river gorge. The driver managed to throw himself off the perch when the wheels snapped off, but the official plunged to his death. His mangled body was pulled out of the water the next day, along with the remains of the vehicle. The woodwork was shattered beyond recognition, but the evidence of foul play with the iron axle was clear-cut."

"Christ Almighty, Alessandra—you must not blame yourself. You are innocent of murder," he growled.

"Innocent," she echoed. "Oh, Jack, you did not see the man's wife and young daughter weeping as the soldiers carried his broken corpse up from the rocks."

"I have seen more than my share of death and destruction," he replied. "So much of war causes senseless suffering. You, too, are a victim."

She hung her head. "No, I cannot shrug off responsibility for my actions. I knew it was wrong, yet rather than listen to my conscience, I did it anyway."

Jack set his strong, graceful hands on her shoulders and gave her a gentle shake. "Look at me, Alessandra."

Her chin lifted.

"Stop torturing yourself. Yes, you made a mistake. But that does not make you a murderer. It's Bellazoni who is the guilty party." His mouth compressed. "I take it he's using the past to coerce you into helping him steal some treasure from this site."

"How did you guess?"

Jack's expression turned a little sheepish. "I happened to overhear the two of you talking the other day—quite by accident, I might add—while I was working by the outer walls. I only caught snatches of the conversation, but it made me suspicious that something sinister was afoot. It also explained why you had been looking so tense. So I decided to keep an eye on you, and learn what you were up to." His jaw hardened. "After I thrash Bellazoni to a pulp, I'll see he is handed over to the authorities and expelled from the country—"

"No!" she exclaimed. "I've not yet told you the worst. It's not just me he's threatened. I would never, ever have agreed to help him on my own account." Alessandra couldn't keep her voice from cracking. "But you see, he's threatened to harm Isabella if I don't cooperate. He claims he is not alone here in England, and I dare not call his bluff. He's killed before."

"He threatened Isabella?" Jack's dark face looked carved out of stone.

"Yes," she whispered. "I've been so frightened, I can't think straight."

"It is *I* who may soon be accused of murder." His gaze was cold as steel. "I just might kill him with my bare hands."

Fear still kept its grip inside her, but as Jack unclenched his fists and framed her face, Alessandra couldn't help feeling as if a terrible weight had been lifted from her shoulders.

"You now have me to help you, sweetheart," he murmured. "I won't let him harm either of you."

That she no longer had to bear the burden of such shameful secrets alone gave her a glimmer of hope. Was it possible that there might come a time when the past would no longer hold her life in thrall?

"I am selfish enough to cling to you for help," she whispered. "But I—I don't want to soil you with my scandal. You have your family, your reputation to think of."

"Don't worry about me. I am quite capable of fighting whatever battles we must face." His warm, firm lips blotted the beads of salt from her lashes. "Pierson men are born soldiers, formed from steel and gunpowder. And Bellazoni is a cowardly cur who makes war on innocent women and children. He doesn't stand a chance."

"Oh, Jack." Alessandra wasn't sure if she was laughing or crying. "You are more than a soldier, you are a hero—a flesh-and-blood hero. I've always known that in my heart, I think, and that's why I treated you so badly. I wanted your help, but didn't dare admit it." She pressed her cheek flush to the warm, hard plane of his breast. Through the slabbed muscles and sculpted contours she could hear the steady thud of his heart. His olive skin, golden in the lamplight, glowed like sun-kissed bronze.

An ancient god come to life.

"Can you ever forgive me for being so beastly to you?"

A deep chuckle rumbled in his throat. "I shall think of some ways you can make it up to me."

She smiled, and looped her arms around his waist, reveling in the feel of his tapered leanness, his chiseled strength.

"But in the meantime," said Jack, "we had better get back on *terra firma*, before our flesh shrivels up."

"Shrivels?"

His hand guided hers to an underwater spot.

"Oh." She bit back a burble of laughter.

"It's no joking matter," he chided. "A soldier must guard his sword from adverse conditions. Though cold is more a cause for concern than heat." He waggled a brow. "After all, steel is forged in fire."

Seeing this teasing side of Jack warmed her heart. "Hot or cold, I am sure that it can rise to the occasion," she quipped. "But you are right. We must have a—"

"A council of war," he finished. The lighthearted laughter was gone from his face. He lifted himself out of the water and helped her up to a seat on the stones. After drying her back with his shirt, he handed over her shift. "Gentlemanly scruples demand I turn around," he murmured as she wriggled into the damp garment. "However, I may just sneak a peek."

"I must look like a drowned rat," she sighed.

He, on the other hand, cut a sinfully sensual figure, clad only in a wisp of white linen. The wet cloth hugged every corded contour of his torso like a second skin and the tails barely brushed his thighs, leaving his long, muscled legs on full view.

Alessandra averted her gaze.

"Maidenly modesty?" His mouth quirked as he spotted the slight movement.

"A far less laudable motive," she admitted. "When I look at you undressed, I find myself...distracted."

"I shall take shameless advantage of that information at some point in the future." He slipped on his breeches and carried his boots over to where she was sitting.

"Another pair ruined?" She sighed, eyeing the muddied leather. "Feel free to send your bootmaker's bill to me."

"We younger sons are a feckless lot, but my quarterly

allowance does allow me to pay for my own footwear."

For an instant, Alessandra feared she had wounded his pride. But the flicker of lamplight showed only a look of fierce concentration on his face. The hobnailed soles scraped against stone as he kicked the boots aside. "Strategy," he muttered. "We need to come up with a strategy to see the dastard is locked away in prison here in England, where he can't harm anyone again. He is too dangerous to let get away."

"But what can we do?" asked Alessandra. "The murder of an Austrian official in Italy is of no concern to the authorities here. And as for his blackmail threats, I have no proof. It would be my word against his."

"Tell me what he is after, here in Bath."

Alessandra quickly explained about the ancient *imago*, the centurion's map, and how a wealthy Italian nobleman was willing to fund Frederico's political aims in return for the priceless artifact.

"They dream of setting up a state that is ruled by a modern-day Caesar?" He shook his head. "I know that the Italian people are anxious to free themselves from foreign rule, but Bellazoni and his friends are delusional to think the glories of ancient Rome can be revived."

"Yes, Frederico's mind is unhinged," replied Alessandra. "But he is sane enough to be devilishly dangerous. I have seen him in action, Jack. He is clever and cunning."

He lifted a dark brow. "I am not half bad when it comes to thrusting and parrying."

She felt her cheeks grow rosy. "The King ought to award you another medal for your services."

"The Order of the Garter?" he suggested.

Alessandra threw a balled-up stocking at him. "Keep

your mind on the battlefield, not the boudoir."

Jack rubbed at his jaw. "In the military strategy, the key is to take away an enemy's strongest weapon. For Bellazoni, that would be you," he mused. "And now that you have told me, he has lost the advantage."

"But he also has Isabella," she pointed out, the thought of him anywhere near her daughter causing her stomach to knot.

"Yes, Isabella adds an extra worry, but I am convinced she will be safe, as long as he doesn't suspect that his plans have been exposed."

"You mean, we must pretend that nothing is amiss?"

"For the moment." Jack stared meditatively at the bubbles rising up from the watery depths. "To catch him in the act of stealing from the site would not be so hard to set up. However, the penalty for making off with some ancient artifacts would be laughably light. I want to see him arrested for a serious offense, and that will be a little more difficult to do."

"By difficult, you mean dangerous."

He shrugged.

The vapors suddenly turned cold and clammy inside her lungs, making it difficult to breathe. "No, I won't have you taking risks for me and my daughter. Maybe..." She chafed her hands together, trying to dispel the sensation of ice in her veins. "Maybe you could help us find somewhere safe to hide until he leaves." Even as she said it, Alessandra knew it was not the answer.

Jack was quick to point out the flaw. "And leave him free to come after you in the future? Or hurt someone else?"

She felt ashamed of herself. "You are right, of course. I was being selfish. And cowardly."

Jack closed the gap between them, twining his hand with hers. "You are the bravest person I know, to face such terror on your own for so long." He lifted her fingers to his lips, kissing each tip in turn. "Why did you never tell Lady Ciara and your other fellow 'Sinners'?"

"I could not bear to burden them with such an awful secret. They could do nothing, save worry. And Ciara was facing her own troubles." Alessandra thought for a moment. "And so, I fear, is Kate, though she appears to be the most free-spirited of our little group. I see it in her eyes sometimes, though she thinks she keeps it well hidden." The mist was thinning, the ghostly tendrils giving way to a fresh breeze blowing in from the mouth of the grotto. "I, of all people, recognize the tiny signs of subterfuge."

"You don't have to hide anything from me anymore," he replied.

Alessandra didn't trust herself to speak. She hoped her nonchalant smile would mask the futile lurchings of her heart. It seemed that she could hear it thumping against her ribs.

*Silence*, she chided. Love was a word that must never be spoken of. Never be thought of. Never be dreamed of. Jack's family expected him to marry a sweet, innocent English miss, not a widowed foreigner with a scandalous past.

"My cousin Marco is the only one who knows about the murder," she said, once she had composed her emotions. "Ironically enough, the argument you interrupted was about dealing with the matter. He was of the opinion that I ought to have taken some action to clear my name before the secret could be used against me."

"Perhaps we should contact him," said Jack after some thought. "Through his friends in Italy, he may have some idea on what pressures we can bring to bear on Bellazoni."

"I've tried," replied Alessandra. "But at the moment, he is somewhere in Scotland. He left London rather suddenly, though I am not sure why." She sighed. "I think he is involved with Lord Lynsley, whose position as a minor minister at Whitehall seems to cover some unusual activities. The Sinners have answered some *very* esoteric questions for him."

Jack nodded. "I am under the impression that he is involved in clandestine work for the government." He thought for a bit longer. "I will write to my brother George, who is well acquainted with Lynsley. He can pass on a message to the marquess that we need to speak with Marco right away."

Alessandra hesitated, feeling a pinch of worry. "Must you? The fewer people who know about the threat to my daughter, the better. I am truly afraid of Frederico. He will do anything—*anything*—to get what he wants."

"Yes, but now he must deal with *me*, sweetheart." Jack dismissed her objection with a flick of his hand. "I won't tell George any of the details. I will simply tell him to find Lynsley and pass on the message about Marco. No other explanation will be necessary."

She frowned. "And he will?"

"Of course." Jack seemed puzzled by the question. "If I say it's important, he won't ask questions."

"Very well." Alessandra suddenly realized in a rush of gratitude how wonderful it was to have him take charge. His self-assurance steadied her own uncertainties. And his selfless kindness was overwhelming. He was willing to risk his life for her and Isabella.

She had to quell the urge to throw her arms around him and never let go.

"Are you all right?" Jack looked up from reaching for his boots, a quizzical expression shading his features.

"Yes," she murmured. "Fine."

"You look a little pale. Don't catch a chill." He fetched her gown and cloak. "You had better dress. Let me help you."

She fumbled with the folds, trying not to think of how nimbly his fingers worked the female fastenings. He was a handsome, virile man—of course he had dressed and undressed a legion of women. She had no right to feel a stab of jealousy.

"As I said, there is no reason to tip our hand right now." Unlike her, Jack was focused on strategy. "The excavation is slated to continue for several more weeks. As long as you go through the motions of trying to find the artifact, Frederico won't suspect that anything is amiss."

"Yes, that won't be so difficult." Drawing a calming breath, Alessandra felt his confidence rubbing off on her.

"I will make sure that you spend as little time alone with him as possible, both at the site and during the evening entertainments. In the meantime, I would like to get a look at the original journal pages and map. Do you think you can manage that?"

"Frederico keeps them to himself, but I daresay I can find a reason to ask for some time with them."

"Good." Turning his back, Jack reached for his coat. Through the scrim of his still-damp shirt, Alessandra watched the supple movement of his body—the bladed bones, the corded muscles, the broad shoulders, looked like they could bear the weight of the world.

Lost in longing, she didn't look away quickly enough.

"What?"

"I—I was just trying to think of what excuse I can make for my bedraggled appearance." She regarded her disheveled garments in dismay. "Lud, how will I ever explain this?"

A look of unholy amusement played on his lips. "Why not tell the truth?" he replied. "You slipped while working in the grotto and fell into the thermal pool."

# Chapter Twenty-two

$T$he next day dawned with a peek of blue showing through the clouds as the lingering line of squalls finally blew over the excavation site. Jack slipped the knife back into the sheath in his boot and looked up to gauge the wind threading through the overhanging trees. The rope holding the tent canvas should snap shortly, the frayed ends leaving no trace of his blade's cut.

Retreating into the long, leafy shadows, he quickly made his way down the back side of the hill. Still slippery from the recent rains, the ground was redolent with the moldy smell of wet earth and wild lichen. His steps silenced by the soft earth and moss, he picked his way through the dense grove of oaks and slipped in among the stacks of supplies being unloaded from the baggage carts.

"Ah, you are here bright and early, Lord James." Dwight-Davis looked up from cross-checking the lists in his notebook. "We look to be getting a spot of sun at last, so we ought to make the most of it."

"Indeed," answered Jack. "Unless you have a specific job in mind for me today, I thought I might start making sketches of the sculpture fragments that Eustace and his team have recovered from the temple."

"Excellent, excellent! Your drawings of the pottery shards were first rate. If only our full force were as dedicated as you, sir." He blew out his cheeks, allowing a note of frustration to shade his normally cheerful voice. "I do not mean to criticize, but our Italian contingent has been less than diligent in their work." Punctuating his comment with a peek at his pocketwatch, he shook his head mournfully. "Perhaps we will see them in time for luncheon."

"You could put them on bread and water until they shape up," said Jack dryly.

"Ha! And risk another pitched battle between Romans and Britons?" Dwight-Davis chuckled. "I fear they take their food more seriously than their scholarship."

Their exchange was interrupted by Eustace and Lattimer, whose querulous argument could be heard above the scrape of their steps on the rocky footpath.

"You are making a mountain out of a molehill," groused Eustace. "The workmen will have the tent repaired by the time Lady Giamatti arrives."

"I still say we should move her field office to a more protected location," countered Lattimer. "She could have been injured by the falling poles."

"Injured?" Dwight-Davis stiffened in alarm. "Have we had another accident?"

"Nothing to speak of." Jack couldn't tell whether Eustace's face was red from exertion or irritation. "The ropes securing the marchesa's shelter broke during the night."

Jack reacted with deliberate surprise. "Was anything damaged?"

"No, no," growled Eustace. "All her tools and supplies were packed away in the storage boxes."

"Still, perhaps Lattimer is right." Dwight-Davis mopped at his brow. "Perhaps we ought to think of relocating the shelter."

"There's no other logical place," objected Eustace. "The ground is too muddy near the river."

"But we must think of Lady Giamatti's well-being," insisted Dwight-Davis. "If it had happened while she was working—"

Jack cleared his throat. "You all are the experts, of course. But if I may offer a suggestion?"

The three other men all nodded in unison.

"If we construct a timber frame, instead of relying on ropes to hold up the heavy tent, then the structure would be far more sturdy, and the canvas can be lashed securely to the wood to create walls. The clearing is large enough, and flat enough..." He paused, widening his eyes as if struck by a novel thought. "And if we make it a little bigger, there would be a protected space for Mr. Merrill to sort his pottery, which would ensure that Lady Giamatti is not alone if any sort of accident should happen again. Two birds with one stone, if you will."

"By Jove, what an excellent suggestion!" exclaimed Dwight-Davis.

Eustace relented with a gruff snort. "I suppose that makes sense, and shouldn't take too much time away from the excavation."

"We often did the same thing to make ourselves more comfortable during military maneuvers," said Jack.

"A team of three or four workers should have it done in a trice. If you like, I would be happy to supervise."

"Excellent, excellent!" Dwight-Davis clapped his hands together, the sound a sharp counterpoint to the shuffling of the workers and the squelch of carriage wheels rolling to a halt beside them.

"Have we something to celebrate?" asked Orrichetti as he helped Alessandra down the iron step.

"Lord James's ingenuity!" replied Dwight-Davis, a happy smile brightening his ruddy, guileless face. "As I have said before, we are extremely fortunate to have a gentleman of his many talents among us. Just now, his military experience has proven invaluable."

"How so?" Eyes narrowing as he emerged into the glare of the sun, Frederico paused on the top rung. The breeze ruffled his golden hair, creating something of a halo effect. "Has the site been attacked by the ghosts of ancient savages?" he asked sarcastically.

Jack watched him jump gracefully to the ground. *No, the threat was very much alive.*

Dwight-Davis, cheerfully oblivious to the nasty edge of the question, gave a hoot of laughter. "No, no, the assault came from Favonius—god of the west wind. Lady Giamatti's tent was knocked down." The scholar swung around and snapped a salute to Alessandra. "But never fear, milady, Lord James has suggested an excellent solution. We are going to build a more solid structure, with room for Merrill and his pottery. That way, you won't be alone should another unfortunate accident occur."

"Perhaps you ought to consult Lady Giamatti as to her wishes," said Frederico slowly, flicking a meaningful look at Alessandra. "I imagine she would find the extra commotion a great distraction to her work."

Jack kept his own face impassive as he watched the subtle interplay of emotions. Dwight-Davis looked uncertain and Alessandra wary, while Frederico smoothed a wrinkle from his sleeve, apparently confident of imposing his will on the others.

"It's not really our place to question the committee decisions, Frederico," said Orrichetti quietly. "I am sure they know best."

A wink of light caught the spasm of anger that creased Frederico's handsome countenance. However, he set his teeth, and remained silent.

The conte gave a conciliatory wave of his gloved hand. "We are grateful for your concern for the marchesa's safety. I think it a very prudent suggestion."

"I'll organize the men and all the necessary supplies." Touching his pencil to his lip, Dwight-Davis thumbed to a fresh page in his notebook. "Let's see…a load of lumber, including four stout posts, nails, cording, canvas…"

Leaving the scholar to his lists, Jack gave a casual nod to the others and strolled away, careful to avoid Alessandra's eye. She hadn't known his exact plan, only that he had promised to find a way to make it hard for Frederico to be alone with her. As for their own meetings, they had agreed that nothing must hint at any sort of intimacy.

*Distant. Detached.* Damn, it would not be easy. At the first sight of Frederico's smirking face, his initial impulse had been to grab the Italian by the throat and thrash him to a bloody pulp.

Drawing on his work gloves, Jack felt his hands prickle. He tapped his palms together several times, the soft slap of leather a whispered reminder of the need for discipline. The element of surprise was on their side— better to win the war than to lose the advantage in a meaningless skirmish.

Hoisting two boxes of drawing supplies to his shoulder, Jack wove a path through the work carts and cut behind the storage sheds.

"Ho, Davey," he called, crooking a finger at the gaggle of lads preparing their workbaskets for the day's excavation.

The boy he had pulled from the river dropped his gear and scampered over. "Sor!" he said, snapping a smart salute.

"At ease, lad," he said. "Here, will you give me a hand with this?" Passing over one of the boxes, he indicated the footpath leading down to the main pit.

"Yes, sor!" Davey fell in step by his side, looking up like an eager puppy. "D'ya need me te help ye teday?" he asked hopefully.

"As a matter of fact..." Checking that the thicket of thorny gorse screened them from view, Jack stopped and squatted down on his haunches. "I do have an assignment for you—an important one. But you must keep quiet about it to anyone else, and report back only to me. Can you do that?"

"Aye." The boy mimed locking his lips. "Mum's the word, sor!"

"Good. I knew I could count on you."

"What's ye need me te do?"

"Keep an eye on Lady Giamatti while she is working. Just to make sure she doesn't wander into any trouble." Jack cleared his throat. "Mind you, she is a very independent female, so she wouldn't like that I am concerned. That's why it's best that she doesn't know about it."

Davey nodded sagely. "Wimmen. Papa says they can drive a man to drink."

"Among other things." Repressing a smile, Jack took a shilling from his pocket and pressed it into the boy's hand. "I will arrange it with Mr. Eustace that you are assigned to her shelter. If you see anything amiss, you're to come find me right away."

The boy stared at the silver in speechless wonder.

"Remember, I'd rather no one guess what you are up to. But you strike me as a clever lad. I'm sure I can count on you."

"Don't ye worry, sor," stammered Davey, finally recovering his tongue. "I'll watch her like a hawk."

"That's the spirit." He stood up and took back his box. "Run along now. I'll contact you each day for a full report."

"It's as busy as a bloody coaching inn here," muttered Frederico, watching the workmen hitch a wooden post into place and begin hammering.

Alessandra lifted a shoulder as she turned away from the construction. Merrill and his two assistants were already lugging their crates of pottery fragments up the steep footpath, the thumps and yelps over bruised shins adding to the general cacophony of the clearing. "I can hardly object without raising questions."

"I suppose," he conceded. "But how the devil are we going to get on with the project?"

"Ssshhh, keep your voice down," she warned. Crossing the trampled grass, Alessandra took a seat on a light-dappled rock outcropping. The sun had finally begun to burn off the haze and oppressive humidity. As the air cleared, the surroundings seemed to lose the dull wash of gray that had muddied the colors.

Or perhaps it was merely that her own spirits felt brightened, despite the daunting challenges that still lay ahead. Frederico's threatening presence was like a cold, clammy finger teasing at the nape of her neck. And yet, knowing that she did not have to face him alone freed her from the worst of her fears.

Without looking up, she untied the strings of her document case. "I'm working on mapping out a new section to survey," she said in a low voice. "But as I told you before, we must be patient, and do nothing to arouse suspicion."

Frederico moved closer and tugged at his watch chain, setting off a jingling ripple of gold and carnelian. Twisting in the light, the intaglio fobs gleamed bloodred against the pale cream silk of his waistcoat. "We don't have forever."

"I am well aware of that." She watched the polished stones slowly cease their movement. "It would help appearances if you would make some semblance of showing up here ready to work."

"I *am* working," he replied with a smug little tweak of his coat lapels. "Haverstick asked me to accompany him to a luncheon with the Countess of Milford, a local patron of the arts who is interested in hearing about our project. Her estate is close by, so I shall return for an hour or two of digging at the end of the day." He shifted his stance, unable to control his restless energy. "In the meantime, I trust you will find a way to do some more exploring."

Alessandra shuffled through some of the papers,

angling the leather flap to hide her hands from the casual observer. "Speaking of which, I would like to take another look at the centurion's account, along with the map."

His gaze squeezed to a calculating squint. "Why?"

She let out her breath in an exasperated huff. "Because that is what scholars do—they look over things again and again to make sure they are not missing some vital clue. A fresh look often sparks a new idea. Yet I've been allowed only a cursory glance at the contents."

A jaw muscle twitched as Frederico considered the request.

*Would her bluff succeed?* Jack was anxious to have a look at the original documents, but so far, Frederico had not let them out of his hands.

"But if you would rather not improve the odds of us finding the artifact, suit yourself," she added sardonically.

He lifted his golden lashes and his eyes were chilling to behold. "Very well. However, if anything happens to them, there will be serious consequences. So if I were you, I'd guard them with my life."

She maintained an unflinching expression, though the words were like a blade, cutting a razor-thin 'X' above her heart. "That goes without saying."

He slipped the papers from his pocket and passed them over. "Try to have some new information to hand back with them, Alessa. I am getting tired of staring at the same old moldy scraps."

The ancient pages unfolded with a whispery crackle. Hunched behind the shelter of a limestone ledge, Jack smoothed them on his knee and studied the spidery writing. The ink had faded over the years, and the arcane grammar made it even more difficult to decipher.

"I never thought I would give thanks to my Eton Latin master and the years he spent drumming verbs and conjugations into my head," he muttered. Knowledge of the obscure military terms came from the duke, and family suppertime discussions that demanded an intimate acquaintance with Caesarian battle tactics.

Under the guise of making a quick review of his sketches, Alessandra had slipped him the documents, admitting that as her Latin was mostly scientific, the contents were a bit baffling to her. She had relied on Frederico and his translation of the original text in mapping out possible locations.

Quite likely he was simply covering the same ground, but...

Lifting the page to the light, Jack stared thoughtfully at the smudged words, and then down at the site map that Alessandra had drawn for him. Pencil shadings indicated the two places where she was doing some exploratory digging, and a circle marked the area where Frederico was concentrating his efforts. However subtle, nuances of language could easily change the meaning of a sentence. 'Stride' and 'distance' meant different things to a soldier and to a civilian.

Jack reread the page several more times, then carefully pocketed the papers. Taking up his canvas bag of tools, he circled back to the footpath and followed it down to the flat verge of swampy soil that bordered the river. The eddying waters pooled in the shallows along the bank, gurgling softly over the smooth stones. In the distance he heard the song of a linnet, and the *slush* of shovels digging out the sculpted Roman columns.

Following his instincts, Jack turned left, away from Alessandra's markings and the main excavation site and began to count his strides.

*One, two, three…*

"I was beginning to worry." Alessandra fumbled with her document case, hurriedly sliding the ancient papers in between two committee reports. "Frederico will be back at any moment," she whispered. "You had best not linger."

"Actually, I have good reason to be here," he replied with a hint of a smile. "I've been assigned to help Merrill sort through the pottery and help choose the best example for a drawing to go in the Society's exhibition gallery."

She was glad of his company but couldn't quell a flutter of worry over the Italian's reaction. "Frederico won't like it."

"Frederico can *va' all' inferno.*"

A burble of laughter rose in her throat, but Alessandra quickly choked it down. Folding back a square of oilskin cloth, she busied herself with arranging her site plans on the makeshift trestle table. The workmen had just finished lashing down the canvas roof and walls on the new shelter and were helping to move the crates of pottery inside while she readied her things. "Please don't make light of the danger. He is still a deadly threat."

"Not for much longer." Jack reached over to help her shift a wooden box of writing supplies. He had removed his gloves, and she saw mud was embedded beneath his nails and scrapes covered the flat of his palms. "I was hoping to uncover some hard evidence of Bellazoni's misdeeds, but I've decided that we ought not wait. Given that we've not heard from your cousin, I am going to slip off to London tomorrow, after making an appearance here in the morning."

A firegold glimmer in his dark eyes made her inhale sharply. "*Santa Cielo*, you've discovered something."

He nodded. "A classical education does prove useful once in a while. As do military marching drills. In putting the two together..."

Alessandra listened in stunned silence as Jack explained his hunch, and how he had followed it to a bend in the river below the main excavation site. Pacing out the distances according to his own calculations, he had come to a spot that seemed to match the ancient description.

"It was there?" she demanded, jumping one step ahead of his explanation. "The gold *imago* of the Second Legion Augusta in Britannia actually exists?"

"Yes."

She felt a surge of scholarly excitement. "Is it—"

"Undamaged, and absolutely magnificent," finished Jack. He smiled. "It is an incredibly important archaeological discovery."

Her breathing became a ragged, rapid-fire series of tiny gulps. For an instant, she felt a little giddy, as if she were floating on air. And then fear brought her back to earth.

"We *can't* let him get his hands on it," she whispered.

"Never fear." He touched the back of her fisted hand, the fleeting flare of warmth loosening its clench. "It's buried in a spot where no one will think to look. And the fact that it is real works greatly in our favor, not his." Sensing her confusion, he went on quickly. "His plan no longer seems such a fanciful dream. If he succeeds in raising money, he has a chance of fomenting an uprising in Italy. Something that our government would find troubling, to say the least. So I think Lord Lynsley will listen very seriously when I explain the situation."

His argument was logical, and yet Alessandra was not entirely convinced. "If only we had some shred of evidence that proved his malice. He is here in England under an assumed name—his real name is Frederico Bertoni—so even something so simple as a document showing his false identity would give credence to our story."

"It would help," allowed Jack. "But your word—our word—will suffice for now."

She pressed her lips together.

"You must trust me on this."

Keeping her voice steady, she braced her hands on the rough planking and looked up to meet his gaze. Those deep, dark eyes had once seemed so opaque, so intimidating, but she had learned from a master artist how to see the subtle nuances of color and texture. "Of course I do. Without question."

"I promise you, we will beat him at his own game, sweetheart."

His calm confidence fanned a spark of hope inside her. *A future free of the terrible past?* She hardly dared to let it flicker, for fear that it would somehow turn to ashes.

"I…" Alessandra forced her mind to focus on the present. "I am ready. Tell me what I must do."

"Simply go through the motions of your daily routine." Jack lowered his voice as the sound of footsteps on the path rose above the rustling of the oak leaves. "Just for another day or two." His fingertips met hers in a swift, sweet caress. "As I said, I'll show up here in the morning, just to be seen, and then sneak away to London. No one will know I have gone."

Outside, Frederico's silky laugh snaked up through the thicket of gorse.

"Go back to Merrill's worktable," she urged softly. "No point in stirring Frederico's suspicions by having him see us conversing."

Jack listened for a moment as the Italian's voice grew louder and louder, then turned away. As he crossed to the other side of the shelter, muscles rippling with the lithe, light-footed grace of a large cat, Alessandra caught a glimpse of his unsmiling face, his features honed to a hard edge.

"We shall soon see how the predator likes becoming the prey," he murmured.

# Chapter Twenty-three

*T*he next day seemed to go on forever. Restless and on edge, Alessandra went through the motions of her work at the site. Jack had slipped away unnoticed after the morning committee meeting. While he raced to a rendezvous in London with Lord Lynsley, she could only sit and wait.

Between meetings with Dwight-Davis and supervising a new section of the excavation grid, she managed to dodge any contact with Frederico. But he continued to crowd her thoughts, his shadow swirling around her consciousness like a thick, choking London fog.

A sharp sound startled her from such reveries. Looking down, she realized that the pencil had snapped in her grip. She drew a steadying breath, and stared at the splinters. *No more running, no more hiding.* She had cowered in fear for far too long, a passive victim, flinching at the sound of every knock or footstep.

Surely she could do something more useful than fretting.

Pushing the tiny slivers of wood into an orderly row, Alessandra forced herself to think dispassionately about the situation, and how she and Jack could prove their allegations that Frederico was a criminal. Words were all very well, but a piece of incriminating evidence would give much more credence to their charges. There must be some proof, some paper...

*Pietro.* The conte had arranged for Frederico to be part of the Italian delegation. Once he knew how his longtime friendship had been abused, he would gladly help her by turning over any document in his possession. A false name, a forged credential—a lie, set down in stark black and white, would be hard for the authorities to ignore.

Alessandra listened to the flapping of the canvas, the chink of the brass buckles against the wood posts, echoing her own misgivings. She might well be drawing Pietro into danger. A small slip on his part might tip off Frederico to the trap about to spring. And Frederico was clever and cold-blooded enough to do whatever was necessary to save his own skin.

Gooseflesh prickled up and down the length of her arms. Chafing her hands together, she slowly rubbed some warmth back into her palms. Pietro would want to do what was right, regardless of the danger, she decided. The workday was almost over and he would be returning to his quarters for several hours before going out for the evening...

The curricle's wheel bounced over the ruts and puddles, spraying a brackish mixture of muck over the lacquered wood. Bracing his now-filthy boots against the iron rungs, Jack turned up the collar of his driving coat to ward off the chill bite. As the sun played hide-and-seek among the gathering clouds, the rising wind was growing sharper with the threat of impending rain.

He eyed the heavens, hoping the ominous black line hovering at the horizon would hold fast long enough for him to reach London. *Wishful thinking, no doubt.* Given the rotten state of the roads, he couldn't expect to make very good time.

Dropping his chin into the thick folds of melton wool, Jack resigned himself to the fact that he had hours of bruising travel ahead of him.

The workday finally over, Alessandra had returned to town. But rather than return home, she had her carriage drop her at the Society's townhouse. Ducking into the back stairwell, she pulled the latch shut and started up the steep steps. Pietro's suite of rooms was on the top floor, and while a visit to his private quarters might raise a few eyebrows if she were spotted, it could be explained away.

Time was of the essence.

Tiptoeing up the last two treads, she peeked into the corridor. The small arched window on the opposite wall let in only a single blade of the afternoon sun. Dust motes danced in the muted glow, the only sign of movement. Still a bit breathless, Alessandra swallowed a small gulp of air, trying to slow her thumping heart. *No need to be nervous.* Pietro would no doubt be shocked to learn the depths of Frederico's depravity, but he would believe her.

Shifting her stance, she saw that the door to the conte's sitting room was slightly open, spilling a pool of lamplight across the dark polished parquet. Relieved that he was not out on some errand, she slipped from the shadows and started forward, tiptoeing silently over the thick Turkey runner.

But as she approached, she heard a muffled oath.

"*Me ne infischio*—I don't give a damn!"

Alessandra froze in her tracks. That all-too-familiar silver-tongued voice! Yet now it was twisted in a snarl.

"Don't patronize me, Pietro!" continued Frederico. "Come take a look for yourself."

"Calm down, *amico*," counseled Orrichetti with his usual patience. "There is no need for histrionics."

"Easy for you to say," grumbled the other man, though his voice did drop a notch. "You ought not let the *Inglieze* give all the orders here."

Alessandra heard her old friend heave a long-suffering sigh. "Very well, let us go down and talk to Dwight-Davis. Give me a moment to get my coat."

She dared not let Frederico see her here. Looking around wildly, she saw the door to a small linen closet set into the wood paneling. It yielded to her push, allowing just enough room for her to squeeze inside.

"It is only to be expected that some problems will arise on a joint venture like this one. You must trust that I know how to deal with them." Orrichetti spoke as if trying to soothe a sulky child. "Try to remember that I am in charge here."

"*Si*," grunted Frederico. "But that does not mean..."

The words faded into the sound of bootheels clicking over the marble steps of the main stairs.

Alessandra waited several moments before emerging from her hiding place. *Retreat and wait for him to return?* That would be risky. As the afternoon faded into evening, so would her chances of finding the conte alone.

She looked around uncertainly, the surrounding silence seeming to amplify the quickening thud of her pulse. Perhaps from the window she could see where the men were headed.

A few tentative steps brought her abreast of the door. Orrichetti had left it slightly ajar, allowing a glimpse of coals crackling in the hearth and a pair of highback chairs arranged close to the fire. Between them stood a dark mahogany tea table, a leather portfolio case bulging with papers resting upon its polished top.

*Papers.* That was what she had come for. Perhaps it would even be better if she could discover any useful information on Frederico without exposing her old friend to any danger.

He would forgive the intrusion, she told herself as she slipped into the room.

Taking the portfolio to the alcoved window, she seated herself on the cushions and began skimming through the folders. The first few held naught but itineraries and expense records. Feeling a little guilty at snooping through her old friend's confidential papers, she tried to hurry her search.

Her fumbling fingers nearly missed the slim packet wedged between the wine merchant's bills and a list of books ordered from London. Hope flared in her breast, but on untying the ribbon, Alessandra was disappointed to see the first few papers appeared to be private letters. Still, she could not afford to overlook the chance of finding any documents on Frederico's background and qualifications. All personal correspondence she would skip over without a second glance.

But as she thumbed through the sheaf of papers, her eyes caught a name and held it.

*Stefano.*

Torn between guilt and longing, she hesitated, and then couldn't resist reading what was written about her late husband. Orrichetti had been his closest friend and confidant. Any reminiscences he had exchanged with other acquaintances would be a welcome complement to her own memories of Stefano.

Smoothing the deckled edges of the letter, she began to read.

*"Dio Madre,"* she whispered, before quickly moving on to the next missive.

At some point the portfolio slipped from her lap, scattering the papers across the carpet. She was oblivious to any sound, save for the crackle of creamy stationery between her nerveless hands. A wave of light-headedness washed over her, blurring the lines of ink into one long, looping serpent. Squeezing her eyes shut, she feared she was going to be sick.

*Somehow, she must have mistaken or misinterpreted the words.*

For one mad moment, Alessandra wondered whether the last few weeks of worry had unhinged her mind. But on forcing herself to swallow the taste of bile and reread the letters, she saw her eyes had not deceived her. The truth was there, undeniably etched in black and white.

Orrichetti was a methodical man. He had kept copies of his own letters, filed along with the replies received from a man named Luigi Vignelli. She knew of him—he was a rich, reclusive nobleman who dreamed of one day restoring the glories of ancient Rome under a modern Caesar.

*A dreamer.* But a dangerous dreamer, according to the twisted thoughts he had put down on paper.

Like spiders, the men had spun a sinister web of intrigue and innuendo. *Bribery, slander, and yes, even murder.* According to these missives, Vignelli had helped fund Frederico's violence against the Austrians in return for a promise of political influence in the cabal that he and Orrichetti were planning.

She made herself study the sordid details, and it soon became clear that their conspiracy stretched back several years. Which meant that while Orrichetti and Frederico had been enjoying her late husband's hospitality, they had also been betraying his principles. And his friendship.

*Lies, all lies.*

Sinking back against the mullioned windowpanes, Alessandra pressed her palms to her throbbing brow. A swirl of wind rattled the casement, the chill air seeping through the glass and taking hold of her heart.

The truth was horrifying, not only for itself but also for the doubts it cast on her own judgment. She had trusted these men without question, looked to them for counsel and support. And she had let them manipulate her with laughable ease, following their advice like a docile little lamb being led to slaughter.

Pietro's perfidy was perhaps the more shattering. He had known her late husband for years. They smoked together, drank together, talked philosophy long into the night together. He had always expressed admiration for Stefano's political writings. How could he have disguised his true nature for so long?

But she knew well enough how one could hide an evil secret, if one were disciplined and determined.

Somehow, she had the presence of mind to pluck the

most damning of the letters from the sheaf in her lap and tuck it inside her cuff.

"Alessa?" Orrichetti was naught but a dark shape, his silhouette limned by the fire. "Is something amiss, my dear?"

She looked up, tears trickling down her cheeks. "How *could* you?"

His gaze flicked from her face to the papers on the floor. "Shut the door, Frederico."

Smoke wafted out from the half-open door, along with the pungent smells of spilled ale, wet earth, and the unwashed bodies of the local farmers. Jack tugged the brim of his hat lower and shouldered his way inside the taproom. The inn was one of the less reputable stops on the road to London, which was exactly the reason he had chosen it. He didn't want to chance encountering a familiar face. The fewer people who knew he had left Bath, the better.

Peeling off his driving gloves, he ordered a tankard of porter and took a seat by the window. The coins he had passed to the ostler should ensure that a fresh team of horses would be harnessed to his curricle within five minutes. Still, he shifted impatiently on the rough bench, watching the twisting shadows in the stableyard with a growing sense of unease.

*Stop seeing specters*, he chided himself. Looking away from the dingy panes of glass, Jack lifted the mug to his lips, silently recounting all the reasons it was necessary to leave Alessandra alone while he made a quick trip to Town. The possible rewards far outweighed the risks. That damn rogue Marco may still be missing, but with his brother vouching for him, he should be able to arrange a meeting with Lord Lynsley. The marquess had the resources and authority to deal with dangerous situations. And he owed the Circle of Sin a debt for past services.

*Quid pro quo.*

The thought should have settled his nerves. And yet as he leaned back, a chill prickled down his spine.

Steeling his jaw, he crossed one booted leg over the other and began drumming his fingers on the scarred tabletop. A minute passed.

And then another.

*Damn.* A growl reverberating in his throat, Jack pushed up from his seat and hurried for the door, the flap of his heavy caped coat stirring up swirls of sawdust. He was alive today because he had listened to his instincts, even when they countermanded common sense.

"Here now, sor." The ostler looked up from the horses. "I've just one more buckle an—"

Jack pushed away the man's hands from the harness and quickly threaded the stiff leather through the brass. Silencing the protest with a handful of silver, he vaulted onto the driver's perch and grabbed for his whip.

Alessandra heard the soft thunk of oak and the click of the key. "You murdered Stefano," she whispered.

"Tut, tut, my dear. Murder is such an *ugly* word, as you well know," replied Orrichetti. "Stefano had a weak heart. I simply helped to hasten the inevitable."

Alessandra choked down a wave of nausea. "But *why?*"

"His voice of moderation was growing too strong. His influence was spreading, which threatened to ruin all our plans."

"Stefano was wrong," added Frederico. "And too stubborn to see the truth. Italy needs to bc led by a strong ruler, not the voice of the rabble."

"And *you*, I suppose, will speak for the new Caesar?"

Frederico smirked. "I do have a gift for oratory."

"You are cursed with an overweening pride in your own worth," she replied. "But remember—pride goeth before a fall."

"And who is going to trip me up? *You?*" He laughed. "I think we both know that you are no match for my skills."

Ignoring the gibe, Alessandra turned back to the conte. "How did you do it?" she asked. "Poison?"

"Again, such a nasty word." Orrichetti clucked his tongue. "Let us just say a botanical cordial. How familiar are you with the medicinal properties of plants?"

She shook her head mutely, not daring to let herself speak.

"Ah, yes, it was your colleague—Lady Sheffield—who stood accused of doing away with her husband by adding a toxic substance to his drink." He straightened his cuff. "Ask her what a dose of hemlock dissolved in brandy does to someone with a weak heart. By the by, she will assure you that it is quite painless."

At the reference to the sordid stories that had swirled around Ciara, Alessandra found her hands were trembling with rage. He dared kill her husband and then make light of it?

She pressed her palms together, summoning a sense of calm to replace her initial shock. *Strategy*, she whispered to herself. Jack would not waste his time wailing or weeping. He would concentrate on planning a counterattack.

"That is right," said Frederico. "I doubt that Stefano had any idea what was happening to him." He snapped his fingers. "It was over in an instant. Leaving a grieving widow to be consoled by his friends."

Alessandra bowed her head so he would not see the murderous spark in her eye. Let him think her the same spineless creature as before.

A flutter of linen fell in her lap. "Allow me to offer a handkerchief, Alessa. I know how easily you are moved to tears."

Exaggerating a sniff, she picked it up and dabbed it to her dry cheeks.

Frederico's voice lost a touch of his smugness as he directed his next words at the conte. "Now what?"

Orrichetti didn't answer right away.

"I don't see why we can't go on with business as usual. Alessa won't dare say anything. Not with dear little Isabella to consider."

"Perhaps not." The conte moved to the sideboard and poured himself a brandy. Swirling the amber spirits, he lifted the glass to the waning light. "But the situation raises the possibility of complications. I've been watching Lord James lately, and he seems to be taking a little too much interest in the excavation."

"Bah!" Frederico dismissed the idea with a snort. "He's a dull prig who takes his work too seriously. He's trying to impress Haverstick and Dwight-Davis—no doubt so that he will be appointed head of some stupid committee."

"That may be true." Orrichetti took a sip of his wine, savoring the mouthful before swallowing. "But you see, we have been successful because I leave nothing to chance."

Crossing his arms, Frederico responded with a toss of

his gilded curls and a sulky stare. His eyes were no longer looking so angelic, leaving Alessandra to wonder how she had missed seeing the brimstone malevolence burning just beneath their golden hue.

Orrichetti set down his empty glass and tapped his fingertips together. "Chance," he repeated. "And opportunity."

Frederico's lashes flicked up and down in impatience. "This is no time to talk in riddles. We need to act."

Moving with unhurried ease, the conte stepped around the tufted settee and placed a hand on the polished pearwood side table by the bookshelves. "And we will, Freddi. Trust me, we will." A wink of brass played over the curl of his lips. Turning the tiny key, he unlocked the wooden case centered between two decorative marble plinths.

Nestled on a bed of black velvet was a matched set of pistols.

Alessandra watched as Orrichetti carefully checked the priming and then aimed one of them at her heart. "Go call for my carriage," he said slowly to Frederico. "All things considered, I think it's time to make a change in plans. We can be in Bristol by dark, and from there we can make a quick passage by boat to France." His smile stretched wider. "I am sure Lord James won't mind if we borrow his brother's yacht and crew for another cruise."

"What! Flee from England?" Frederico shot her a venomous look. "And allow all our plans to sink in the stinking English mud?"

"My dear Freddi, that is why you do the talking, and I do the thinking. As she has done in the past, Lady Giamatti is going to use her considerable scientific talents to help us achieve what we want."

"But the ancient *imago*," protested Frederico. "I am sure she is not feigning ignorance. We have no clue yet as to where it is buried."

"And we don't care." Orrichetti straightened his cuff. "You see, in mulling over the situation, I suddenly realized that I had been overlooking the obvious. Why go to all the trouble of digging for something that might or might not exist, when we have an expert in ancient metalwork right here at our fingertips."

Frederico looked confused, but Alessandra had an inkling of what he was suggesting.

"Come, come, Freddi." Orrichetti's smile gleamed like a crescent moon in the lamplight. "Think. You are a clever fellow."

As the realization dawned on his face, Frederico gave a nasty laugh. "Brilliant!" he exclaimed. "Why, of course! You mean to have dear Alessa fabricate a fake. After all, we know of her expertise and experience with metals and acids."

Alessandra felt a churning in the pit of her stomach. *No, not again.*

"Precisely. Vignelli is a discerning collector of Roman artifacts, but someone intimately acquainted with the materials and processes used in ancient times should be able to fool even a well-trained eye."

Getting an iron grip on her emotions, she met the conte's gaze and held it. "Child's play," she said coolly. "But this time around, I'm not a gullible girl. If I am to cooperate, I want something in return."

"You're in no position to bargain," growled Frederico.

"On the contrary." She cast a sardonic glance at the pistol. "It won't be quite so easy to cover up my death if you are forced to pull the trigger, Pietro. A shot will have a crowd of people here within minutes. Even with your considerable skills at deception, you would find it hard to arrange a scenario that won't create unpleasant questions."

The gun barrel wavered ever so slightly. "What are you proposing, my dear?" asked Orrichetti.

"There's no need to negotiate," snarled Frederico, clenching a fist. "One blow will render her unconscious."

Alessandra picked up the brass candlestick by her side. "Move one muscle and this smashes through the window, followed an instant later by my screams."

"You wouldn't dare," said Frederico. "What about dear little Isabella? You think I would have any trouble getting my hands on her?"

"Yes, actually I do. She is at her art lesson right now. With the same drawing master who teaches Lord James." She gave a deliberate look at the mantel clock. "Seeing as his lesson follows hers, I would imagine he is walking into the studio right now."

"Y-you are bluffing."

*Yes, she was.* Jack was in London, but she didn't think they knew that. *Tactics and strategy.* She whispered a silent prayer that something of his military training had rubbed off.

"Would you care to try me?"

"Well, well, well, our little kitten has grown a sharp set of claws." The conte cocked his head. "Violence is so primitive—unlike my colleague, I prefer to use it only as a last resort."

A curt wave of the pistol signaled Frederico to retreat.

"So I'm perfectly willing to listen to your demands, my dear. What is it that you want?"

# Chapter Twenty-four

$W$ind gusted through the tall hedgerows, its high, keening whistle punctuated by the faint rumblings of thunder up ahead. Storm clouds scudded and swirled, turning the sky an angry shade of slate gray.

"Damn," muttered Jack as a moment later the heavens opened up, lashing his face with a stinging rain. Fisting the reins, he hunched lower, trying to see the road through the thickening fog.

The horses snorted, their hooves kicking up great clots of mud as they rounded a rutted turn. The wheels skidded and the curricle sloughed dangerously close to the rocky verge. Breakneck speed was foolish, he told himself. And yet, a mounting sense of unease drove him to snap the whip again, urging the team to an even more reckless pace.

Better to raise eyebrows by rolling into Bath looking like a drowned river rat than ignore the sensation of daggerpoints dancing down his spine. Besides, he was getting rather used to the feeling of water against his skin.

A lick of heat warmed through the wet chill as he recalled the steamy thermal springs and the beauty of Alessandra's naked body in the rippling lamplight. The sight had left him breathless. Speechless. Senseless. Was there a word for such pure, primal emotion? Lust came to mind. And yet...

All of a sudden it hit him, like a spinning, surging, roaring wave of water. His feelings had nothing to do with lust. Oh yes, by God, he had taken fierce pleasure in their passionate coupling. But his need ran far deeper than physical desire. The truth was, he had fallen head over heels in love with Alessandra.

*Love.* He loved her scintillating intellect, her indomitable courage, her quiet strength. Hell, he even loved her tart tongue.

*And Isabella?* Jack blinked the drops from his wind-whipped lashes, unsure whether it was rain or tears coursing down his cheeks. He had *two* ladies in his life. If anything happened to them...

Above the noise of the squall rose the sound of galloping hooves bearing down on him from the rear. Nerves already on edge, he turned on the perch, feeling for the pistol tucked inside his coat. Come hell or high water, nothing was going to stand in the way of his keeping Alessandra and her daughter safe.

A black blur materialized from the fog—a lone rider bent low over a dark stallion, drawing closer and closer with every pounding stride. Silhouetted against the pearly mist, the flapping oilskin cape looked like the wings of a giant bat.

Jack kept his weapon shielded from the rain, but cocked the hammer. *Just in case.* He had no reason to suspect trouble, but he wasn't taking any chances. Easing his team to a slower pace, he made room for the rider to pass the curricle.

A gust caught the man's wide-brimmed hat as he galloped by, lifting it just enough to reveal a peek of his profile.

"*Diavolo*," muttered Jack. Releasing his weapon, he shouted out a loud hail. "Ghiradelli!"

Marco glanced over and then reined his mount to a slow trot. "Fancy meeting you here, Lord Giacomo," he called, swiping a sodden lock of wind-snarled hair from his cheek. "Only mad dogs and Englishmen would choose to be out in this weather."

"Given the choice, I would be sipping a brandy in front of a blazing fire," snapped Jack. "Damnation, where have you been? Didn't you get Alessandra's letter?"

"Not until this morning."

Jack made a rude sound. "Perhaps you ought to button up your breeches and emerge from the boudoirs every so often, especially when you know your cousin might have need of your counsel."

"Hell, don't you start cutting up at me, too. Alessa's fellow 'Sinner'—Miss Kate-Katharine—has a tongue sharper than a saber. She all but threatened to slice off my balls if I didn't ride neck and leather down to Bath."

"I've a lovely Andalusian dagger I can lend her."

The quip earned him a pained grimace. "*Et tu, Brutus?* Well, for your information, I haven't been spending my hours in frivolous pleasure. Much as it disappointed my legion of ardent admirers, I have been hard at work tracking down some vital information about...a few of Alessa's old friends." The rain was tapering off to a fine

mizzle. Looking up at the sky, Marco shook out the folds
of his cape. "How much do you know of my cousin's
past?"

"Everything," replied Jack.

"Indeed?" Marco shot him a speculative look. "Aside
from me, she hasn't trusted any man with her secret. Not
even her closest female friends know the truth."

The man was an unrepentant rake, but he was also
Italian—and Italians could be very volatile when it came
to the women of their family. Deciding that discretion
was the better part of valor, Jack moved quickly to keep
the conversation from delving too deeply into his relationship with Alessandra.

"Seeing as she hadn't heard from you, she had to turn
to someone. Alessandra has had good reason to mistrust
men, but she knows her secrets are safe with me." The
road wound through a grove of silvery beech trees and
then straightened through a stretch of wheat field. With a
flick of his whip, he urged his team to a faster clip. "We
were hoping you might speak with Lynsley on her behalf.
But seeing as you appeared to be missing in action, so to
speak, I decided to make the trip to London."

Spurring his stallion to keep pace with the curricle,
Marco took a moment to reply. "I am, of course, on for-
eign soil, but I was under the misguided impression that
London lies in the opposite direction."

"I—I changed my mind."

Despite the haze, he saw Marco's features sharpen.
"Why?" demanded the conte. "Is Alessa in any danger?"

"Do you think I would have left her if she was?" he
retorted.

Marco grunted a curt apology, but as he shifted in his

saddle, his hand brushed the brace of cavalry pistols hanging in the holster.

"I've no reason to think that has changed," added Jack. "And yet, I can't help feeling…" He hesitated, wondering whether to admit his vague fears. "Laugh if you will, but I suddenly thought it best to return to Bath."

"A gut feeling?"

He nodded.

"Like a stab of steel here?" The stallion blew out a foam-flecked snort as Marco fisted the reins and thumped his belly.

"*Si*, like a stab of steel," echoed Jack.

"Then why the devil are we wasting time in idle talk? Come, let us fly!"

Alessandra did her best to assume an expression of cold calculation, hoping the two men would not guess how fragile a mask it was. "I'll go with you quietly," she said. "But only on the condition that you leave my daughter here in Bath."

Orrichetti pursed his lips in thought. "That's a reasonable request," he said after some moments.

"But what is to guarantee that she will cooperate, once we've reached the Continent?" demanded Frederico.

"Freddi, you really must learn more about women," chided the conte. "It's all very well to dip your pego into the Grotto of Venus, but you ought to study how they *think*."

"Why? When swiving them gets me what I need?"

Orrichetti gave a pained look. "Because that method is so crude. Alessa has become much more sophisticated, so we must appeal to more than the little nubbin between her legs." He paused to adjust the angle of the pistol's flint. "As a mother, she wishes to see her daughter grow to womanhood."

In the waning light, his profile looked smooth as polished marble. A thin veneer of civility could hide a multitude of inner rot, thought Alessandra grimly.

"So she will do as we ask. Because she understands that we will have no reason to harm her once we possess the *imago*. It's simply a business arrangement." His dove-gray eyes turned to her. "You *do* know that I have no intention of harming you, Alessa, don't you? I have always been very fond of you, my dear."

She bit back an acid question. *Just as you were very fond of Stefano?*

Frederico looked unconvinced. "The authorities—"

"The English authorities cannot touch us, and as for the Austrian authorities…" He gave a very Italian shrug, eloquent in its casual dismissal. "She is far too intelligent to think of stirring up the past."

"Quite right," she replied with cold contempt. "The past is the past. I would be doing myself no favors to try to dredge up interest in old crimes."

"There, you see how reasonable we can be?" said the conte to his cohort. "This does not have to be an unpleasant interlude."

She maintained a mask of rigid self-control, though his smile made her itch to rear back and slap him with all of her strength.

Frederico glowered, a tiny tic pulsing at his temple, but for once he seemed bereft of clever words.

The lamp flickered as the afternoon breeze ruffled the ivy leaves hanging around the leaded windowpanes.

"The carriage, Freddi," prompted Orrichetti. Though his voice was silky soft, there was no mistaking the note of command.

A hiss of breath signaling his surrender, Frederico stalked off.

"You will forgive me if I keep this out until we are on our way," said the conte, as if he were talking about a snuffbox or pocketwatch rather than a lethal weapon. "It's not that I don't trust you, but I am in the habit of being just a touch cynical about human nature in general."

"Something I would have done well to emulate," she said tightly.

He expelled a soulful sigh. "Don't be too angry with me about Stefano. He really was ill, and the doctors told me that he did not have many months to live."

"That did not give you the right to play God," she whispered.

"I would do a better job than whatever Supreme Being allows such chaos to sweep across Europe." His eyes turned hard, darkening to the color of tempered steel. "A firm hand is needed to restore order and prosperity. Stefano could never understand that."

Argument was pointless. All demagogues thought themselves possessed of almighty powers. Let him bask in the reflected glory of his own delusions, decided Alessandra, rather than goad him into anger. Bending down, she began to gather up the fallen papers.

Taking her silence as a sign of uncertainty, he smoothly changed his tone back to the affable, erudite aristocrat who could converse so knowledgeably on fine art and rare wines. "We will have a good deal of time to talk during our voyage. I am sure you will come to understand what I mean."

*And hell might freeze over.*

She carefully looped the ribbons around the portfolio and tied it shut.

"Thank you, my dear." He approached, careful to keep the pistol out of reach, and held out his hand.

It wasn't hard to feign nervousness. She shifted, hoping the swoosh of her skirts would cover any crackling of the letter she had hidden in her sleeve.

"Come, let us go downstairs. I take it you have a cloak?"

"Yes," she replied. "In the storeroom."

"We'll fetch it. However, I regret that it will not be possible to stop for any additional items. I apologize for the discomfort, but once we reach the Continent, I shall see that you are provided with a proper traveling wardrobe."

"How very kind," she murmured, trying not to let sarcasm edge out sincerity.

A nudge of steel touched her back as they turned into the corridor. "I have great faith in your intelligence, Alessa. But as a reminder, do not try anything stupid." Taking her arm, he dropped the weapon to a more discreet position within the folds of his coat. "You would not want Isabella to grow up as an orphan."

Anger skated down her spine, but she kept her steps measured, her voice calm. "We are in perfect agreement about that."

"Don't worry, my dear," he soothed. "You will soon be reunited with your daughter."

She was under no illusion that the conte intended to

let her live. Once they reached Bristol, she would try to escape. Or maybe Jack...

She stumbled, her legs suddenly going a little numb. *Don't think of Jack.*

*Don't imagine the feel of his dark curling hair.*

*Don't long for the taste of his kiss.*

*Don't yearn for the strength of his honor.*

Steadying herself on the carved banister, Alessandra moved down the curved staircase, Orrichetti by her side. The clicking of his heels on the marble treads seemed overloud as they descended into the shaded stillness of the tiled foyer. Save for themselves, the townhouse stood deserted, the last of the scholars having left an hour ago.

To reach the street, they had to pass through the main gallery. The lights were unlit, save for a pair of flickering wall sconces flanking the archway leading to the storage rooms. Shadows wreathed the display pedestals, the marble busts of the ancient Roman emperors rising like ghosts out of the gloom. Piled high with wooden trays and tools, the dark worktables cut a slightly sinister silhouette against the bank of leaded windows.

Orrichetti paused for a moment, his gaze flicking over the room, and then moved for the side aisle. "Let us be quick in finding your cloak, my dear," he murmured. "As you saw, Freddi is a trifle on edge. It would be best not to leave him waiting for too long."

Alessandra shot a sidelong look at the tables, wondering whether she could brush up against one of them long enough to slip a knife or scalpel into her skirts. But much as a weapon might come in handy later on, the risk was not worth the reward. Despite the deceptively pleasant smile, the conte appeared alert to any sign of trouble.

Sure enough, Orrichetti froze as a floorboard creaked within the storage area. His grip tightened on her arm and she felt the barrel of the pistol shift out from the folds of his coat.

*Snick.* The hammer cocked back as a shape flitted out from the darkness.

"For God's sake, put that away," she said in a low hiss. "It's just one of the basket lads." In the hide-and-seek light, she recognized him as the one Jack had rescued from the river.

"You there," called the conte sharply. "Why are you still here at this hour?"

"Mr. Dwight-Davis ordered me te fold up the tarps and sweep up the closets, sir. But I—I fell asleep, sor." The boy scrubbed a fist to his face. "Please, ye won't tell him, will ye? I don't want te lose my place here."

"You've done no harm, Davey," she said gently. "Would you fetch my cloak for me? Then you may run along home."

"Yes, ma'am!" The boy darted back into the storage area and emerged a moment later with her garment in his arms.

Orrichetti released his hold, allowing her to step forward and gather the jumbled folds of merino wool.

As her hands brushed against Davey's upturned palms, Alessandra decided to take a desperate chance. She slipped the incriminating letter she had taken from Orrichetti's file up his sleeve. "For Lord James," she whispered, hardly daring to breathe the words.

To her relief, the boy blinked but stayed silent.

In the same sweeping motion, she hitched the cloak over her shoulders, hoping the pounding of her heart was not really as loud as cannonfire. "Thank you," she added quickly.

"Now off you go," said the conte, with a curt wave.

The boy darted across the gallery without a backward look.

As she smoothed out the twist of her hood, the conte waited for the *thunk* of the front door falling shut before taking her arm again. "Well done, Alessa," he murmured. "You see—if you play your role properly, there is no reason for anyone to get hurt."

# Chapter Twenty-five

$T$he iron gate to Alessandra's townhouse swung shut behind him, its heavy clang echoing the note of his own inner alarm bell. Quickening his steps, Jack hurried across the street to where Marco was walking the lathered horses.

"Her butler says that her carriage dropped her at the Society headquarters, but she has not returned."

"Alessa often loses track of time when she is working," pointed out Marco.

He shook his head. "No—not when Isabella is concerned. Alessandra was supposed to pick her up from her art lesson, but never appeared. Herr Lutz walked Isa home instead."

Marco swore under his breath. "Where is the Society's townhouse?"

"Not far." Jack checked the priming of his pistol. "Grab your weapons. I suggest we go on foot, just to be safe—though I can't imagine Bellazoni would dare try anything there. Not with Orrichetti quartered on the top floor."

"She must be there. Surely she wouldn't have gone back to the excavation site alone."

"I..." Jack felt his heart start to hammer against his ribs. "I can't imagine she would be that foolhardy." The trouble was, he *could* imagine it. There were any number of ways that Bellazoni could lure her into abandoning any thought for her own safety. If she feared that Isabella was in trouble...if she thought that one of the workers had been injured...

Gulping down his fears, he spun around. "Follow me. There's a shortcut through Beauford Square."

As they reached Gay Street, Jack saw that the only light in the building was a faint glow in one of the upper windows. "The workrooms are dark—where the devil has she gone?" he muttered, his sense of unease rising another notch. "Thank God Orrichetti looks to be at home. Maybe he can help us."

But a quick search of the place revealed that both the galleries on the ground floor and Orrichetti's suite of rooms were vacant.

"There's not a soul around," confirmed Marco, emerging from the back stairwell. "The storage rooms are empty and the attics are locked from the outside." He took a last look at Orrichetti's sitting room before shutting the door. "Nothing looks amiss. It appears that he has just stepped out for a short while."

Jack was already heading out the door. "Let's check back at Alessandra's townhouse, then I shall go ask Haverstick if he has any idea of where she might be. After that, I'll saddle a fresh horse and head for the site."

"Wait—I'm coming with you," called Marco.

Too preoccupied to answer, Jack began trying to map out a strategy. But there were so many unanswered questions...Had something sparked Frederico to panic? Had Alessandra been frightened into taking a dangerous risk?

Slapping his gloves against his palm, he swore a silent oath. And then added a prayer. The site seemed the logical place to check next, but in his gut, he knew that she could be anywhere. *Anywhere.*

Fighting down a sense of helplessness, he crossed the street and cut back into Beauford Square. Action would, at least, keep fear at bay.

"Lord Giacomo—Jack." Marco caught up to him and put a hand on his sleeve. "We may not find Alessa at the site—"

"I damn well know that," he growled, shaking off the touch. "If she is not there, we will marshal our resources to widen the search. You'll contact Lynsley and convince him to use his network to locate her whereabouts, while I'll call on my brothers and my father to muster their military contacts." Whether that would be enough was something he refused to think about.

"Lord James!"

He looked up to see Dwight-Davis strolling toward him, a large package clasped in his arms.

"My, my, how I should like such a military stride." The scholar made a wry face. "Alas, I simply have to toddle along at my own pace."

Jack slowed to a halt.

"Not the nicest weather for a walk," continued Dwight-Davis. "But *Scientia est lux lucis*—knowledge is enlightenment. I just received these new reference books from London and thought I would drop them off at the Antiquities Society for tomorrow's work session. Lady Giamatti always shows up at the crack of dawn, so I wouldn't want to make her wait."

"Do you know where she is now?"

"Well, I had to leave the site around noon..."

Jack started to curse his ill luck when the scholar added, "But Eustace saw her drive off with Orrichetti in his carriage not more than half an hour ago."

Feeling a little foolish, he let his pent-up tension release in a long exhale. A ride with the conte was nothing to worry about...

"Oh, and Bellazoni was with them as well."

The breath caught in Jack's throat.

"I daresay we have been working them so hard, they haven't had a moment to reminisce."

"Did Eustace say which way they went?" asked Jack in a measured voice.

The scholar pursed his lips. "I'm afraid not."

"No matter." Catching Marco's eye, he cocked a nod at the far entrance gate to the square.

"Now, about that essay you suggested I read, Lord James—"

"You had best hurry and get inside." Jack flicked a raindrop from the wrapping paper. "Before the books get wet."

"Indeed, indeed!" Dwight-Davis gave a baleful look at the heavens before rushing off.

"Let's go—and quickly," said Jack, his nerves once again on edge. "I don't trust Bellazoni farther than I can spit."

Gravel crunched beneath their loping strides, the rough, sharp sound scaring a pair of ravens from their perch atop an ornamental fountain.

Jack was suddenly aware of a smaller figure shadowing their steps. He signaled for Marco to stop. "Aye, lad?"

"Ibeenwatchingferye—"

"Slow down. Catch your breath."

The boy drew in several great gulps of air and rubbed a ragged sleeve to his nose. "Sorry, sor," he stammered, still gasping for breath. "I been looking all over fer ye. The lady..." Unclenching a fist, the boy revealed a folded piece of paper. "She passed this te me all secret-like and whispered that I was te give it to you."

Jack snatched it up and quickly smoothed out the creases. He skimmed over the writing, then shoved it in his coat pocket. "You know the lady's house. Run there as fast as you can, and tell the butler—Ferraro is his name—to bar the door and let no one near Isabella until I return. *No one!* Understand?"

"Yes, sor!"

To Marco, he barked, "Come on!"

"But—"

"I'll explain later! We haven't a moment to lose!"

The pungent scent of the sea hung heavy in the damp air as the carriage rolled through the outskirts of Bristol. The sky had cleared for a short while, but now the last vestiges of sunset were barely visible through the encroaching clouds. Alessandra brushed the mist from the glass, watching the harbor loom larger and larger. Against the hazed streaks of burnt orange and dusky mauve, the masts and rigging of the ships looked like a giant web woven by a rum-drunk spider.

She turned away from the window, trying to keep a brave face. Terror knotted her insides, and a tiny trickle of sweat snaked down her spine. Once she set foot aboard the yacht, Alessandra sensed that her fate would be sealed. Never again would she see Isabella.

Oddly enough, that thought gave her strength.

Pietro and Frederico had taken her husband, they had taken her good name, and for over a year they had taken her peace of mind. She wouldn't let them take her daughter or the rest of her life. James Jacquehart Pierson had rekindled a spark of hope. Of joy. *Of love.*

Of all the absurd ironies that a man named 'Black Jack' had brought such light into her heart. She could feel its glow deep inside her, fighting to keep darkness at bay.

Yes, it was time to fight back.

*But how?*

Through the fringe of her lashes, Alessandra looked at the two men sitting across from her. Frederico was too restless to sit still. He kept up a constant fidgeting—crossing and recrossing his legs, gnawing at his thumb, toying with the fittings of his pistol, all the while shooting her dark looks. Was he having second thoughts about the conte's decision to change their plans? Frederico liked to be the one in command, as she well remembered.

Orrichetti, on the other hand, appeared to be napping. His head was resting against the squabs, and his eyes were closed, his face relaxed, his mouth curled in a soft half smile. But she somehow doubted he was sleeping.

Of the two, he frightened her far more than Frederico. *Click. Click.* "We're nearly there." *Click. Click.* As if to punctuate his words, Frederico cocked and uncocked the pistol several times in succession.

"*Si, si.*" Orrichetti patted back a yawn. "Do stop that before you shoot off one of your testicles."

The clicking ceased.

In the uneasy silence, the galloping thud of her heart seemed amplified by the prison of polished wood. In the weak light of the carriage lamp, the shadowed space appeared to be closing in on her. For one wild moment, she contemplated grabbing for Frederico's weapon. It was madness, of course—she would be overpowered in an instant. But if she was going to die anyway, taking one of the miscreants with her was a tempting thought.

If she got her finger on the trigger, she would not waste the bullet on Frederico's balls.

*No.* Knotting her hands in her lap, she stayed still. Her erstwhile friends considered themselves diabolically clever. Well, she must use her brain to figure out a way to outwit them.

"What if the crew refuses to sail us across to France?" demanded Frederico abruptly.

"They won't." Orrichetti finally opened his eyes and gave a feline stretch. "They are *English* to the bone. And the captain will follow their absurd code of honor to the letter. Trust me, they would sail through the gates of hell if a lady's life was at stake."

Frederico finally appeared to relax. "The *Inglieze*. How pitifully easy they are to manipulate," he said with a smirk. In the wavering light, his eyes had a slitted, serpentine look. Flat and utterly devoid of emotion. "Almost as easy as you, Alessa. But then, you have the same blood in your veins."

"Yes," she replied softly. "I have only half of a Machiavellian mind. But don't be so sure that cunning will conquer courage."

"Brains always win out over brawn," said Orrichetti. "Do remember that, Alessa." He slanted a glance through the window. "Ah, we are coming up to the docks. Freddi, you will stay here and keep our lovely companion company, while I make a quick reconnaissance of the area." A self-satisfied smile flitted over his lips as he consulted his pocketwatch. "By my calculations, the crew should all be gathered in the galley for tea." Tucking the gold oval back in his waistcoat, he leaned forward in his seat and rapped a signal for the carriage to stop. "It's yet another weakness of the English. You can set your clock by their little rituals."

Frederico gave a nasty little laugh. "How true. They are so predictable. So regimented in their routines." He cut a mocking flourish through the air. "The English have no imagination. Lord James is a perfect example. For weeks we have been scheming and he had no idea of what was going on right under his nose."

"He might surprise you," replied Alessandra, more to buck up her own spirits than to offer any real threat.

The gun barrel danced close to her face. "You had better pray he does not."

"That's enough, Freddi." Orrichetti laid a finger on the pistol and pushed it away. "There is no need for posturing. And you, Alessa—try not to taunt him."

Muttering darkly, Frederico set his shoulders back against the plush upholstery.

"I'll remind you once again that we all have reason to cooperate. We've come this far without any trouble. Let us keep it that way." The softness of Orrichetti's voice did not belie the note of command. The punishment would be swift and sure for any disobedience.

The carriage door opened just enough to allow the conte to slip out. But as it swung back, Alessandra gave a twitch of her cloak, so that a corner of the hem caught in the molding, just enough to prevent the latch from locking.

Frederico, still talking to himself and checking his reflection in the glass, didn't notice. His contempt for her was obvious. And it was making him careless.

The tiny act of rebellion sparked a small flare of confidence. She no longer had to reach the brass handle. A simple push would open the door. Not that she had any clear plan of how to make use of her trick.

Not yet. But if she was to have any hope of escape, it had to be done quickly, in the short interlude while the conte was absent.

*Think.* Surely she was smarter than Frederico.

Her gaze flitted around the interior of Orrichetti's rented carriage. Neither the lacquered paneling nor the brass fittings offered much in the way of a weapon. Thick velvet fabric made up the cushions and the draperies— hardly a match for flint and steel. Alessandra let her eyes linger a little longingly on the holster where the carriage pistol normally hung. But of course Orrichetti was no fool. It was empty. There was little else to see in the smoky light of the oil lamp...

She stared at the pale flame, flickering inside the glass globe.

After giving a last little primp to his tousled curls, Frederico pulled a flask of brandy from inside his overcoat and took a long swallow.

"M-might I have a sip?" she asked. It wasn't hard to let a quaver creep into her voice.

His mouth slowly curled. "Ask me nicely, *cara*."

"*Prego*," she whispered. "Please."

Frederico laughed, a low, lewd sound that made the hairs on the nape of her neck stand on end. "Oh, I have a feeling you will be saying that quite often during the coming journey to Italy. Remember how you used to beg for my attentions, Alessa?" He leaned close, so close she could feel the heat of the wine on his breath. "Perhaps we shall rekindle that old flame, eh? I always liked your passion."

Alessandra kept her eyes on the flask. "Shall we drink to old times?"

He took another swig before passing over the flask. "There, you see, *cara*, I can be nice, too."

She lifted it to her lips—and then let it slip through her fingers.

A hitch of her hand made sure that it spilled onto the seat right beside her.

"*Diavolo*," snarled Frederico, slapping away her clumsy attempts to pick it up. His face fell as he swirled the remaining contents. "It's almost empty."

"I'm s-o s-sorry," she said, deliberately drawing out her stammer. "But you've no idea how frightened I am." Frederico liked to exert control over his women. The trick was to turn his strength into a weakness. She recalled Jack saying that such a strategy was the key to defeating a powerful enemy.

Looking somewhat mollified, Frederico handed her his handkerchief. "I am sure there will be more spirits aboard the ship."

Brandy fumes wafted up from the wet velvet. Alessandra swallowed hard, knowing she must make her move in the next few seconds. The blood was pounding in her ears, and seemed to be growing louder and louder.

"What's that?" He jerked round, craning his neck to see out the window opposite the door.

*Now or never.* Alessandra leaped to her feet with a choked moan. "Oh, I fear I am going to be sick!" She swayed and threw up her hands to steady her stumble. The swipe knocked the near lamp from its bracket, shattering the glass globe. Oil splashed over the brandy, and as the wick touched the fabric, a flame shot up.

"Sit down!" screamed Frederico, fumbling to find his pistol.

An acrid black smoke billowed up from the seat. She kicked the door open and heard the clatter of boots on the cobblestones.

Orrichetti. *Damn, she had been a fraction too late.*

Still, maybe she could make a run for it.

She scrambled down the iron steps, but just as her feet touched the ground, an arm snaked around her neck and the kiss of cold steel touched her cheek.

"You aren't going anywhere, Alessa," said Frederico.

"Oh, yes. She is." A figure stepped clear of the yawing shadows. "She's coming with me."

# Chapter Twenty-six

$J_{ack!}$"

"Yes, sweetheart. I've come to take you home."

Tightening his choke hold on Alessandra, Frederico stumbled back from the smoking coach. "Oh, what a pretty scene—the hero comes to rescue the damsel in distress," he sneered after clearing his lungs with a cough. "But this isn't going to have a storybook ending. Throw down your pistol, Lord James, or I'll put a bullet through the lady's brain!"

"I don't think you would be that stupid, Bellazoni." Jack kept a calm front, though his innards were clenched tight as a fist. "For in the next instant, your own face would be spattered in gory bits across the cobblestones. And I daresay you value your handsome hide far too much to have that happen."

Frederico's eyes betrayed a flicker of indecision.

"So let us be reasonable and come to terms. There's no reason we both can't get what we want. Let Alessandra go and you are free to walk away."

"Ha! You want me to trust in your word of honor?"

"A foreign concept to you," replied Jack. "But be assured that I am bound by my word."

"Let me think." Frederico slid sideways as he spoke, edging for the head of the carriage. The horses were stomping and snorting, their iron-shod hooves clacking a nervous tattoo on the cobbles as a plume of smoke swirled up from inside the carriage. The echo rattled off the soot-streaked bricks of the surrounding warehouses, all now shuttered tight for the evening.

Jack mirrored the other man's moves, his boot sending a pebble skittering over the uneven stones.

"Orrichetti—," began Alessandra, but Frederico gave a rough jerk to her neck, squeezing off her warning.

"I know, sweetheart," he said. To Frederico he added, "Do that again and you are a dead man."

"You're in no position to make threats." In a rush of backward steps, Frederico splashed through a puddle and pulled even with the coachman's perch. "For all your fancy medals, you are a pathetic soldier, Lord James. You allowed me to maneuver you into certain defeat." His voice now bristling with confidence, Frederico snapped off a volley of Italian to the caped figure on the box above him. "Luigi has orders to shoot if you don't drop your weapon by the count of three. *One.*"

"Take cover, Jack!" cried Alessandra.

"It's all right, sweetheart."

"*Two.*"

Jack raised his pistol.

Wetting his lips, Frederico hesitated and then shouted "*Three!*"

The slap of the sea and the thrum of the wind floated

in from the harbor. Off in the distance, a faint rumble of laughter seeped through the planks of a dockside tavern. Overhead, a sign creaked on rusty hinges.

"Luigi!" Frederico was no longer looking so smug. "Fire, damn you." He added a shrill threat in Italian.

"*Quindi dispiace*—So sorry, Bellazoni, but your coachman is not in any condition to hear you. He'll soon wake with a sore head. As for you, *amico*..." Marco shifted his position on the driver's box, his words punctuated by a metallic click. "Release my cousin. And I suggest that you do it this instant—I'm not nearly as patient as Lord Giacomo."

As Frederico looked up in stunned shock, the other oil-filled lamp inside the carriage exploded with a force that shattered the windows. Glass flew through the air and bright orange flames licked out from the splintered casement. Eyes wild with fright, the horses reared in their traces, hooves slashing at the air. The impact knocked Marco from his seat.

*Bloody hell.*

"Take cover, Alessandra!" shouted Jack as he lunged for the panicked animals to keep them from bolting through the unloading wharves. Stacked high with wooden crates of cargo from the Americas, the area would be like a tinderbox. One spark and the whole place would turn into a raging inferno.

Rolling clear of the lurching wheels, Marco grabbed the collar of the fallen coachman and dragged him to safety. Out of the corner of his eye, Jack saw Frederico slip, his foot tangled in the trailing reins.

An oath slipped through his teeth. Diving into the maelstrom of thrashing horseflesh and whipping shackles,

Jack ducked under the center shaft. Jagged metal scraped across his knuckles and the oozing smell of mud and sweat clogged his nostrils, making it difficult to catch a breath. He could feel the warm wetness of his own blood trickling between his fingers.

"Damn," he swore, trying to see through the murky blur of spinning shapes. A flash of light blinded him for an instant. Lanterns. And voices. The burning carriage had been noticed.

Dodging a kick, Jack dropped to a crouch and spotted Frederico sprawled on the stones, tearing feverishly at the length of leather wrapped around his high-top Hessian.

"Yank off your boot," he called, but his words were drowned in Frederico's scream as the front axle snapped and a flying shard of steel cut a gash across his cheek.

Jack flung himself forward, somehow managing to slip his knife free of its sheath. A quick slash cut the reins, and as he hit the ground, he twisted sideways, pulling the Italian free of the careening wheel.

"*Santa Cielo.*" Frederico collapsed on the cobbles, moaning like a stuck pig. He touched a hand to his face and when it came away dripping with blood, he promptly puked.

"You're a bloody idiot," said Marco, taking hold of Jack's ripped coat and hauling him to his feet.

Jack shook him off. "Where is Alessandra?"

"Safe and sound. I told her to stand there—" Marco pointed to a sheltered spot between two of the buildings. But there was nothing there now, save a stirring of murky black shadows.

"Son of a bitch!" swore Marco.

"Stay here with Bellazoni." Hauling Frederico to his

feet, Jack cocked a fist and hit him as hard as he could. "He won't give you any more trouble," he added as blood spurted from the Italian's broken nose. Then, regripping his knife, he turned and plunged into the alleyway.

"You can't escape—surely you see that," gasped Alessandra.

"Not at all, my dear." Orrichetti sounded unperturbed, as if they were merely taking a pleasant afternoon stroll through the park. "This merely makes my plan even simpler." He veered left as the alley forked into several twisting passageways, quickening his pace through the oozing mud. The path narrowed, forcing them to go single file. She tried to dig in her heels, but the soft leather soles of her shoes kept slipping on the slick of rotted fish scales.

His grip was surprisingly strong, and he still had his pistol. As they hurried past a shuttered window, a gleam of lamplight showed that the snout was pointed at her chest. "While Freddi and your friends create an effective diversion, we will find it even easier to board the yacht and sail out of the harbor unnoticed." He let out a light laugh. "Lord James has actually done me a great favor. Freddi was becoming a nuisance. His hubris was making him far too erratic."

"You're mad. Jack will call out the authorities."

Orrichetti looked back at her, and though they were once again enveloped in darkness, she could just make out the pearly gleam of a smile. "On what charge?"

"Murder," she replied.

"You are quite alive, my dear. And will remain so, unless you do something extremely foolish."

"But your portmanteau is in the carriage. The papers are proof of your guilt."

Their steps slapped through the muck. "We will be long gone before anyone thinks to read through them."

Alessandra decided to hold nothing back. "Jack knows the truth—I passed one of the incriminating letters to the basket lad."

"Did you?" She felt his foot skid. So, finally she had him a bit off-balance. "That wasn't very wise of you, my dear. We had an agreement."

Up ahead, a glimmer of lanternlight showed that the alley was opening onto the cargo wharves. She saw the hulking silhouettes of the stacked crates and barrels—and then the long, lean shape of a familiar figure.

"Alessandra doesn't do deals with the devil."

At the sound of Jack's voice, Orrichetti shot an instinctive look over his shoulder. His attention wavered for only a heartbeat, but Alessandra seized her chance. Lashing out with a stinging blow, she knocked the weapon from his grasp. It hit the brick wall with a thud and exploded with a deafening bang.

In the flash of firegold sparks she saw his expression spasm from disbelief to fury.

"*That* was for Stefano." Wrenching free of his hold, Alessandra darted out of reach and ducked down to pluck the spent pistol from the mud. She was dimly aware of Jack's racing steps and echoing shouts, but all that mattered was the dark, shadowy shape of her erstwhile friend. "And *this* is for me."

She threw the weapon with all her might and heard the satisfying sound of its *thunk* hitting Orrichetti square in the chest.

He slipped to a knee, and swore a vicious oath. But with Jack closing in on him, he had no choice but to abandon his effort to recapture her.

"You may elude me for now," he called as he spun away into one of the side passageways. "But you'll never escape from my power."

"Yes, you will, my love." Jack gathered her in a fierce hug, his hammering heart drumming against the sweet softness of her body. "His hold on you is over."

"Thanks to your heroics." Her lips feathered over his stubbled jaw. "I . . . I—"

Much as he wished to hear what she meant to say, he silenced her with a swift kiss. "Time enough for that later, sweetheart. Words don't always come easy for me, but I have much to say to you. Now, however, I mean to finish this once and for all."

Her lashes fluttered against his cheek. "Let him go. It doesn't matter."

"No, he's gotten away with his crimes for long enough. I mean to see him brought to justice."

"Giacomo! Alessa!" Marco's shout reverberated off the blackened walls.

"Here!" replied Jack. Brushing another kiss to her brow, he broke away. "And if you let her out of your sight again, I'll break every damn bone in your body," he added as her cousin swept her into his arms.

"*Si, si*—and you may slice up my liver for fish bait!" he exclaimed.

"Be careful, Jack," cried Alessandra as he turned to go. "Orrichetti is dangerous."

"So am I," he said grimly.

As he entered the dank passageway, Jack readied his knife. The squelch of his own steps covered any sounds that his quarry might be making, but he decided that speed was more important than stealth. His guess was that Orrichetti would not linger in the warren of alleys. The man was too clever to be trapped like a rat. He would seek open ground and from there look to steal a boat or a horse.

As he edged around a sharp corner, a gust of salt breeze stirred the fetid air. An opening appeared, showing a sliver of the loading area. Two iron lampposts flanked the entrance to the cargo wharves, their oily light softened by the glow of the rising moon. Several merchant ships were still berthed close to the cobbled cart paths, the seawater lapping gently against their wooden hulls.

*Cat and mouse.* The area appeared deserted, though the night watchman had not yet locked the gate. Slipping inside, Jack dropped low and used a row of grain sacks to cover his approach to a better vantage point. Off to his rear, a throng of dockhands was still gathered around the smoldering remains of the carriage. He doubted Orrichetti would risk the chance of backtracking and being spotted.

A more likely route was to circle around to the taverns at the far end of the harbor. From there a man could lose himself among the drunken sailors and winding streets. He ventured a peek over the rough burlap but the wharf was piled high with a dizzying array of merchandise— everything from exotic spices and dried fish to spare sailcloth and raw cotton was crammed along the walkways.

Holding his breath, Jack listened for any sign of movement.

There it was, close by—the brush of wool against wood.

Jack pivoted and then went still.

This time he heard the faint crunch of shells. Just as he suspected, Orrichetti was stealthily creeping toward the sounds of raucous laughter.

Inching around a mountain of coiled hemp, Jack shot to his feet and hurdled a pile of spruce spars.

The conte burst out from between two rows of sugar barrels and began a weaving run through the crates of nutmeg and mace.

The silvery hair was deceptive—he was as fast and agile as a man half his age. But Jack was quickly gaining ground. Orrichetti slanted a look around as he skidded through a turn. Seeing that the distance between them was narrowing, he suddenly cut to his right and disappeared behind a billowing sheet of canvas.

"Damn," muttered Jack, realizing that they must have stumbled upon a sailmaker's workspace. Rack upon rack of ghostly white cloth fluttered in the night air. He slowed his steps and shifted his weight to the balls of his feet.

*Flap, flap, flap.* He didn't need the whispered warnings to stay alert.

At the next gap, he turned to make his way to the perimeter of half-stitched sails. Halfway along the line, the rasp of metal on metal sounded for just an instant. Jack ducked, just as a length of anchor chain tore through the canvas, smashing the wooden frame overhead. Spinning sideways, he pushed through the tangle and lunged for Orrichetti. He caught the conte's wrist but Orrichetti twisted and hammered a hard blow to his hand.

His fingers slipped and the conte darted away.

"Give it up," shouted Jack, kicking aside the wreckage. "I'm not going to let you get away."

*"Va' all' inferno!"*

Jack nearly laughed at the familiar curse. "I'll go to hell and back to see you brought to justice." He caught sight of Orrichetti running past an empty dray cart. His gait was beginning to look a little labored.

Perhaps fear was catching up with the conte.

*Let the dastard feel his heart pound and his pulse race. Let him taste the bitter tang of bile in his throat.*

Spying a shortcut, Jack angled around a stack of broken crates and leaped over a tangle of fishing nets, slicing the distance between them in half.

Sensing the danger, Orrichetti suddenly swerved and bolted for the fence that separated the wharves from the warehouses. Stones skittered as he shoved a water barrel up to the iron stanchions and scrambled over the top. He landed awkwardly, knees scraping the ground. Jack heard a sharp rip, but the conte was on his feet in an instant, making for the nearest building, where a gleam of light was just visible through the half-open door.

Jack hit the ground running.

Orrichetti was no longer looking urbanely elegant. His hair was a wind-snarled tangle of silver, his boots were coated with slime, and somewhere along the line he had thrown off his coat.

"Here, now, we're locking up. You can't come in here!" A watchman tried to block the doorway, but the conte threw an elbow and knocked him down the front steps.

"Stop!" From his hands and knees, the man voiced a groggy protest.

"Summon the magistrates," called Jack as he barreled by.

The inside of the building was unlit, save for the single lantern hanging in the entrance foyer. The smell of wood shavings and pine tar was thick in the air, and through an open set of double doors, Jack saw that the entire first floor was one cavernous space. A bank of windows let in enough moonlight to show rows of workbenches and a vast assortment of woodworking tools hung on the walls. In the middle of the room, the ribs of a dory were taking shape on a scaffolding.

*A boatbuilding establishment.*

Looking around, Jack saw a set of stairs leading up to a loft. For a moment he hesitated, knowing both floors offered a means of escape. The workshop would have a number of sliding doors for the boats, while up top, there would be at least one large hatchway with pulley and ropes for hauling up supplies from the street.

*Damn.* He hadn't come this far to let the dastard slip through his fingers.

Shifting his knife from palm to palm, he suddenly picked up the lantern and peered down at the floor. A coating of sawdust covered planks. Hobnailed work boots left a distinctive pattern—one quite different from the smooth-soled tread of a gentleman's boot. Moving the beam to the foot of the stairs, Jack saw the only mark there was a telltale scuff of fine leather.

Swiftly, silently, he took the steps two at a time.

It was darker than the main workspace. Deep, pooling shadows teased in and out of the tall storage lockers and stacked supplies, leaving the far end of the room black as midnight. Jack paused to let his eyes adjust to the gloom.

Strangely enough, there seemed to be an odd glow in the middle of the floor. After a moment, he saw it was a large opening in the planking, giving access to the main shop below.

The rattle of chains drew his gaze. The hatchway was wide open, the square door swinging back and forth in the breeze. Jack moved cautiously, aware that it could be a ruse. After each step, he held his breath, listening for any sign of life.

A sudden shove toppled a row of nail kegs. One struck his shoulder, knocking him backward, but as Orrichetti charged, swinging a sledgehammer, Jack managed to parry the attack with his blade.

"You'll have to do better than that," he said calmly. "I'm not an elderly scholar or his trusting wife."

Orrichetti was breathing hard, and his movements were jerky as he danced back out of arm's reach. "You are a bloody nuisance, that's what you are." However, the show of bravado rang a little hollow.

"Why don't you put down your weapon before someone gets hurt," suggested Jack.

"So that you can march me to the gallows? I think not."

"The proof is rather sketchy." Jack feinted right and spun to his left. "You'll likely only get life imprisonment."

Orrichetti swung again, hitting only air.

"Reflexes getting a little slow? Fear does that to a man."

The conte retreated a step, and for several moments they circled warily in the slanting shadows of the storage shelves, silent save for the whisper of leather sliding over wood.

"Very well, you win." Orrichetti suddenly straightened and raised his hands in surrender. "Here." He tossed the heavy hammer at Jack's feet.

Experience had taught Jack never to take his eyes off an enemy at close range. So despite the distraction he saw the blur of movement a split second before the conte grabbed a beaker full of lye and hurled it at his head.

Diving to the floor, Jack spun away in a tight roll as the glass shattered against the wall and the blinding liquid splattered harmlessly over the planking.

With a roar of rage, Orrichetti grabbed up a loose barrel stave and came at him, swinging it like a club.

Jack kicked out at the conte's knee, buckling his leg and sending him crashing into a cooper's bench.

Crawling clear of the debris, Orrichetti looked around wildly for another weapon. His shirt was torn and spattered with blood from a cut lip.

Jack was already on his feet, his knife retrieved from the floor. "Enough."

"*No!* Never." In desperation, the conte grabbed one of the fallen nail kegs. Staggering to his feet, he lifted it over his head.

*Hell.* Jack made a lunge, trying to catch hold of Orrichetti's shirttail.

But the weight had thrown the conte off-balance. He teetered for a heartbeat in midair before falling backward through the opening in the floor.

A plummeting scream was followed by a splash.

"*Si vos ago per mucro, vos must exsisto paratus morior per mucro,*" murmured Jack as he stared down into the huge vat of viscous pine tar. With a last sucking slurp, the ripples subsided and the surface smoothed to a flat black calm. "If you live by the sword, you must be prepared to die by the sword," he repeated.

Orrichetti had come full circle in wielding botanical extracts as a lethal substance. Perhaps Minerva, in her infinite wisdom, had meted out a certain poetic justice, he mused. The ancient gods often showed a diabolically dark sense of humor when it came to punishing human hubris.

After one last look, Jack turned away, suddenly aware of every scrape and bruise to his body. From the street below rose shouts and the clatter of running feet. Brushing the tangle of hair from his brow, he slowly started down the stairs.

"Hail the conquering hero!"

Alessandra elbowed Marco in the ribs and then flung herself into Jack's arms. "If you don't murder my cousin, I will," she snuffled through her tears. "Oh, Lud, I was so frightened for you." She touched her fingertips to the scrapes on his chin and the purpling bruise on his cheek. "You're hurt."

"Naught but a few bumps and scratches." Jack gave a lopsided smile. "I may not be much to look at right now, but at least I got the job done."

"You are the most beautiful sight in the world," she whispered, pressing her lips to the corner of his mouth. He tasted faintly of salt, of blood. Of something that defied description in words. Closing her eyes, she made a small, inarticulate sound in her throat.

"*Amore*," said Marco, exaggerating a soulful sigh.

"Ghiradelli..." Curling his fingers in the fall of her hair, Jack drew her closer. "*Va' all' inferno.*"

A bark of laughter rose above the gentle murmur of the waves. "Perhaps I'll just take a stroll to *Purgatorio—purgatorio* for my countryman, that is. The local magistrate has Bellazoni locked up in the harbormaster's office. In the morning I'll arrange for him to be taken to London, and from there he'll soon be sent to hell." Her cousin's sardonic expression softened into a smile. "The danger from him is over, Alessa."

She found herself shivering slightly, despite the enveloping warmth of Jack's arms. "For now."

"Forever," corrected Marco.

"There's no real proof of any serious crime," she replied. "Kidnapping, perhaps. But the threat to kill Isabella is my word against his. As for the plan to steal the artifact, even if we had concrete evidence, a judge won't send him to prison for more than a few years."

"He won't be standing trial before any English court of law. You forget that the Austrians are now King George's allies," said Marco. "Lord Lynsley has already said that he plans to pass over our prisoner to their representative in London. Bellazoni will face their justice—and the Austrians do not take kindly to the murder of their officials." He slanted a questioning look at Jack. "As for his cohort…"

"Orrichetti has already answered for his sins," said Jack, and he added a terse explanation of what had happened. "It's poetic justice, when you think about it," he said after a solemn pause. "I saw by the letter that he killed your husband with hemlock, a botanical poison. Well, pine tar is derived from trees. A brazier beneath the vat kept it heated to a near boil, and you know how thick and viscous it is. By the time the night watchman

returned with help and we were able to fish him out..."
His words trailed off in a slight shrug.

She remained silent for a moment, letting the news
sink in. "I should feel some pity, I suppose, over such a
horrible death. And yet, I confess that my only sentiment
is relief. Relief that he will no longer be able to hurt or
manipulate any other person's life."

"No one will ever hurt you again, Alessandra." Jack
cradled her face in his strong, sure hands. His palms were
cracked and covered with grit. And nothing in all the
world had ever felt so exquisite against her skin.

*Hard and soft.* Somehow in Jack it wasn't a contradiction.

Marco shoved his hands into his coat pockets and started
whistling an aria from Mozart's "The Marriage of Figaro."
"I think I shall take that walk now. And not hurry back."

As he sauntered away, Jack's silent laughter tickled
against her ear. "That rascal is lucky he has some
redeeming qualities. Else he'd be fishing his cods from
the seaweed."

"Men can be so arrogant, so aggravating," she
murmured.

"I trust those adjectives do not apply to me."

"No, for you I would say artistic..." Alessandra
traced the line of his jaw, the chiseling of his chin. "And
altruistic."

"Ah, for a moment I was afraid you were going to say
'arse.'" He teased a kiss to the hollow of her throat. "You
called me some *very* bad names when we first met."

*"Si grande nero diavolo."*

"'Big black devil' was not the worst of them," he
reminded her.

She wrapped her arms around him and held him close, feeling the steady beat of his heart fill her with a pulsing joy. "You frightened me. After fleeing Italy, I was determined to keep my distance from men. But you stirred feelings inside me, feelings I dared not admit, even to myself."

"What feelings, Alessandra?" His dark eyes were inscrutable in the dappling of starlight. "Shall we play another word game?"

She felt her lips quiver. "You wish for me to say it aloud?" It was still frightening—how much she had come to love him.

"Please," he said, his voice oddly tentative. "I would like to know if I have any hope of convincing you to give marriage another try. I know your recent experiences with men have made you wary. But I am different."

"Surely you must know how much I care for you."

"Care?" he repeated. "Somehow that feels damned with faint praise."

Alessandra swallowed hard. "Love," she amended. "*Ti amo*. I love you, Jack. So much that it aches. But I—I doubt your father would approve of me. I am not a dewy-eyed virgin fresh from the schoolroom, but a widow with a child. A foreigner with odd notions on female independence and intellect."

"It's not the Duke of Ledyard who is asking you to marry him. It's me. James Jacquehart Pierson," he replied. "But perhaps it's you who should have practical reservations. I don't have a title, or very much money of my own."

"A title is naught but a string of letters. It has nothing to do with the true worth of a man. And as for money, I am wealthy. Very wealthy."

"Yes, I know. It was, I admit, a compelling consideration."

Her insides gave a little lurch.

"But after thinking long and hard about it, I decided to offer my hand in spite of your fortune." Jack drew in a deep breath. "I am not asking you to marry me on account of money, Alessandra. I am asking you to marry me because I love the way your mind works, daring to challenge and change conventional thinking. I love the way your eyes spark in the sunlight, turning from deep emerald to the color of a spring leaf. I love the way you mother your daughter, caring so deeply that she grow up to be a thoughtful, compassionate woman."

Through the blur of tears, she saw the shimmering shape of his face bathed in the moonglow. "You paint a far too flattering portrait."

"I am blinded by love," he said with a breath of laughter.

She blinked the beads of salt from her lashes. "Then don't ever open your eyes."

He kissed her, a long, lush embrace that left her a little weak in the knees. Twined two as one, they held each other, letting the sounds of the slumbering ships serenade them.

"Does that mean we have a meeting of minds?" he finally asked.

"And a meeting of hearts," she murmured. "Of spirits."

"May I take that as a yes?"

"*Si.*"

His sigh tickled against her cheek. "I think Italian must be the most beautiful language on earth."

# Chapter Twenty-seven

Wrapping a last layer of cotton wool around the gold *imago*, Alessandra placed it in the traveling case and locked the lid.

Jack looked up from sketching a statue of Minerva, his charcoal stick hovering over the grained paper. "It was generous of Haverstick and the Bath contingent to give such a treasure to the Julius Caesar Society in London for permanent display."

"He acknowledged that without our help, it would never have been found," she replied. Her lips quirked as she ran a finger along the brass bands of the box. "And I have a feeling that, given the rout of the ancient Roman army and recent battle, he fears that it may be cursed."

"On the contrary, I consider the *imago* a blessing in disguise. After all, it brought us together." Jack tapped the page. "Though in all fairness, we must give the devil his due. Without Bellazoni and Orrichetti, it may have lain undiscovered for another thousand years."

She carefully rearranged her papers. "It's ironic, isn't it? The last thing they intended was to make a lasting contribution to serious scholarship."

"Divine retribution," he murmured. "Minerva did not take kindly to having her sacred grounds desecrated by evil."

Alessandra heaved a sigh. "Minerva showed her usual wisdom, but what a fool *I* was. I never suspected Pietro was capable of such cold-blooded malice."

Setting aside his charcoal and paper, Jack covered the distance between them in two quick strides. "You must stop blaming yourself for the past, sweetheart," he said, drawing her into his arms. It still was a source of wonder that she was soon to be his wife. "Orrichetti fooled a great many people."

"Yes, but I made such terrible mistakes."

"We all make mistakes."

She looked up with a tremulous smile. "Not you."

"Yes, me. I tied your daughter to a tree..." A chuckle rumbled in his throat. "Though actually, come to think of it, it was one of the smartest things I've ever done. Otherwise, you would likely have ignored me for the entire excavation."

"You are rather hard to ignore," she said, sliding her arms around his waist.

"Especially when my cold, dark hands stray here... and here."

"*Jack!*"

He nibbled at her earlobe. "Er, speaking of the imp, where is Isabella?"

"Marco has taken her for ices in Milsom Street. They should be back shortly," replied Alessandra.

"I trust he is not feeding her any new curses."

"If he does, you have my permission to slice off his tongue."

"I'm not sure I want to cross swords with your cousin," said Jack. "For all his braggadoccio, I have heard he is one of the best blades in all of Europe."

"Oh, I am sure your steel is just as sharp."

"Mmmm." Perching her on the worktable, he edged closer. "I wonder, have we enough time..."

A thump and rattle of the townhouse front door made them both jump.

"I suppose not," he sighed as she hurriedly smoothed out her skirts. He turned as the ancient oak swung open—and blinked. One blond head appeared, followed by another."

"George? Neddy?"

A second pair of fair-haired gentlemen stepped into the entrance hall.

"Wills? Charles?" Good Lord, what next...

Jack immediately regretted asking the question as a leonine mane of silvery hair was suddenly silhouetted against the blackened wood.

"*Father?*"

"We heard there might be a spot of trouble in Bath and thought you might need reinforcements," murmured George as he shook out the capes of his driving coat.

"Thank you," replied Jack evenly. "But I have the situation well in hand."

William cast an appreciative look at Alessandra before answering, "So it would seem."

Both Edward and Charles smothered their chortles in a cough.

Ignoring their levity, the Duke of Ledyard marched to

the front of the ranks. "So, you mean to say that you have vanquished the enemy?" he demanded.

Jack quelled the urge to salute. However much his father might rattle his saber, he was no longer the general in command. From now on, Jack intended to choose his own battles. Clearing his throat, he casually straightened to his full height and folded his arms across his chest.

*Might as well face the fire.*

"Yes, sir," he answered slowly. "Sorry you made the trip down from Town for naught. But since you are here, allow me to present you to my—"

"Ledyard," barked the duke, inclining a brief bow at Alessandra. "Father of this impudent pup. And you are...some sort of foreign name, eh?"

"Yes, Your Grace." She met the duke's gimlet gaze with an unruffled calm. "Marchesa Alessandra della Giamatti."

His father's bushy brows took on a menacing tilt, and a scowl cut across his craggy features. It was, Jack knew, a look that had left many a seasoned soldier quaking in his boots.

His bride-to-be actually smiled, a subtle curl that showed off the lovely Marchesa Mouth to perfection.

It was the duke who blinked first.

Jack relaxed slightly. His father would not find it so easy to intimidate Alessandra.

"You must be extremely proud of Lord James," she continued. "He single-handedly saved a very important cache of ancient art from being plundered."

"Art, you say?" Ledyard peered at the fragments of sculpture and bronzework laid out on the worktable. Pulling a pair of spectacles from his waistcoat pocket, he perched them on his patrician nose and leaned down for a closer look.

"Yes, art. In fact, Lord James has been a great asset to our excavation by employing his drawing skills to record the details of our discoveries."

Jack gave an inward wince as she opened a portfolio of his watercolors.

"As you can see," she went on smoothly, pretending not to see his hand signal. "He is an extraordinarily gifted artist."

"Hmmph." The duke began to thumb through the sketches.

Jack gritted his teeth and remained silent.

"And here are some of his paintings from Rome."

Edward and William craned their necks for a look over the duke's massive shoulders.

"You are a scholar of antiquities in your own right, are you not, Lady Giamatti?" inquired George loudly.

"Yes." Her chin rose a fraction. "My main field of study is the technical analysis of ancient artifacts."

Ledyard looked up.

The winking light made it impossible to decipher the look in his eyes. But Jack could well imagine what his father must be thinking—and 'bluestocking' was likely the kindest word being considered.

*To hell with bland and boring London ladies.* If his father did not approve of females who dared to be different, so be it. He didn't intend to march for the rest of his life under false colors.

Countering the duke's sharp gaze with his own show of steel, Jack explained, "Lady Alessandra is considered one of the foremost experts in ancient archaeology. I have been extremely fortunate to work with her on this project. I have learned quite a lot."

Edward coughed.

Ledyard's brows rose ever so slightly and then he returned to perusing the paintings.

A lengthy silence settled over the room. His brothers exchanged amused looks as Jack shifted his weight from foot to foot, trying to appear at ease. *The damn scamps.* They were heartily enjoying the situation.

Jack shot them a glowering look—one that promised future payment for their perfidy—before making another attempt to broach the subject of his upcoming nuptials with the duke.

"Father, I have some news that I wish—"

"By Jove." Once again, the duke cut him off. Directing his comments to Alessandra, he added, "These are rather good."

"Yes, Your Grace. They are," she replied.

Ledyard pinched the bridge of his nose and looked thoughtful.

She drew out several paintings from the bottom of the pile. "This series from Milan is particularly interesting. It shows Renaissance architecture, rather than Roman ruins, but as you see, the stonework is quite unique. Leonardo da Vinci designed the city's military defenses to withstand enemy cannonfire and siege tactics."

The duke came to stand beside her and braced his big hands on the table. "You don't say?"

"Indeed, as a scientist, Da Vinci was quite conversant with tensile strength of the iron used in gun barrels, which determined the size of a projectile, and at what distance and velocity it could be fired."

"Science and soldiering," he mused. "Hmmm."

"The formula used for gunpowder was also an important factor. The technique of corning had just been discovered in the early fifteenth century, which made the mix thirty percent more powerful. So as you see, the towers had to be shaped at a certain angle and thickness to withstand a direct hit..."

Heads bent low over the painting, the two of them fell into what promised to be a lengthy discussion.

Jack leaned back against the worktable and snapped a mental salute to his bride-to-be. His father was a formidable force to reckon with. But so was she. If anyone could soften the duke's steel, it was this beautiful, brainy lady who had won his heart.

"The marchesa is awfully knowledgeable about military history," murmured William.

"Yes, she is exceedingly smart," said Jack with a touch of pride. "About a great many subjects."

"Marriage must not be one of them," quipped Edward. "Seeing as she said yes to you."

"That is, Father seems to think you have proposed," added George. "Is it true?"

The duke might not be a deity, thought Jack, but somehow he always seemed to know more than any mere mortal. "How the devil did he learn of it?" he demanded.

William shrugged. "God only knows."

His other brothers chuckled.

Easy for them to make light of the subject, thought Jack, suddenly feeling strangely nervous. Not for himself, but for Alessandra. She had no real family of her own. Her English relatives had remained distant, while her ties to Italy had grown tenuous. He wanted very much for the Pierson clan to welcome her into their ranks. His brothers, despite all their rough-edged masculine teasings, would offer their support. But the duke?

Jack shifted his gaze to his father. Encroaching age had done little to diminish Ledyard's air of imposing authority. The bullish shoulders were still firmly muscled, the spine still ramrod straight, the voice still booming as cannonfire. From the tips of his polished Hessian boots to the brush of his thick, silvery hair, he was every inch the autocratic aristocrat.

Seeing as Alessandra did not fit the mold of a traditional wife, his father would likely oppose the match. *A woman should be seen and not heard.* The duke had very regimented ideas on propriety.

And she had just spent the last few minutes blasting them to flinders.

A wry smile tugged at his mouth. The only battle that really mattered had already been won. *Love conquers all.* Though his friend Lucas would tease him unmercifully if he ever voiced the sentiment aloud, he had actually come to believe it. He and Alessandra had each other, and together they could triumph over any adversity.

Jack realized at that moment that he must be a romantic at heart. Whatever the obstacles, he was confident that he would eventually vanquish any of his father's misgivings.

*After all, Rome wasn't won in a day.*

A shuffling of paper announced that the discussion on warfare had come to an end. The duke slowly turned to face his sons. "Speaking of combat, Jack, it seems you have not lost your edge when it comes to a fight. We heard from Mr. Dwight-Davis that you uncovered a dastardly plot and vanquished a ruthless enemy."

"With the help of Lady Alessandra, who showed great courage under fire," said Jack firmly. Determined this time to clear any lingering smoke from the field, he charged ahead. "But—"

"But now, you were planning to outflank me? What is this I hear about a special marriage license?"

Jack stood his ground. "Well, sir, a good soldier should always adapt his strategy to achieve victory with the least amount of bloodshed."

Ledyard's mouth quirked. "Don't throw military tactics in my face, lad. I was a dab hand at maneuvering before you were even a gleam in my eye."

Before Jack could reply, he went on. "So don't think for a moment that I shall allow you to marry in a strange church with none of your family present."

The duke then addressed himself to Alessandra, his voice turning a touch tentative. "Tradition has always called for Pierson men to marry in the family chapel at Ledyard Manor. I hope that you will consider the invitation, Lady Giamatti."

His father making a *request*?

"I think I need smelling salts," murmured Jack.

"I think I need a bottle of brandy," replied his eldest brother. "By the by, you owe me another case for this."

He grinned. "I owe you the whole damn vineyard."

Alessandra studied the duke's imperious face, seeing the chiseling of familiar planes and angles beneath the lines of age. *Strength, character, honor.* Principles that Pierson men had passed on for centuries, from generation to generation.

"It would be a great honor, Your Grace," she replied. "I

know I am not the bride you would choose for your son. A widow, a foreigner, a bluestocking, a—"

"A lady who obviously makes him very happy," said the duke gruffly. He took off his spectacles and took a moment to polish them on his sleeve. "I may be an old battle-ax, but I'm not blind, Lady Giamatti. Jack has always been a little different. Marched to his own drummer, though I daresay he thought I didn't notice."

He cleared his throat but his voice remained a little rough around the edges. "I confess that I cast my eye around, looking for someone who might suit. But just as he has always done, Jack simply followed his own heart. He rarely feels the need to rattle his saber, but anyone who thinks that quiet calmness indicates a lack of backbone is making a grave mistake. The lad has a spine of steel."

She stole a look at Jack and saw that for all his outward show of casual nonchalance, he was deeply touched by his father's oblique praise.

"As an expert in metallurgy, Your Grace, it's obvious to me what forged his character," replied Alessandra.

The duke's dark eyes—so similar in shade to those of his youngest son—lit with a warm spark. "Speaking of steel, I should like to hear more about Renaissance cannons. I have always wondered about—"

His words were interrupted as Isabella burst into the room and flung herself into Jack's arms. "Look, look, I drew a picture of you and Mama," she said proudly. "The two of you are kissing," she added, holding up a smudged sketch that displayed an imaginative tangle of limbs. "Marco said you wouldn't mind."

"It's lovely, imp."

"My daughter, Isabella," explained Alessandra to the duke. "*Tesoro*, remember your manners and make a proper greeting to Jack's father and brothers."

"*Buongiorno*, everyone! Jack is teaching me how to paint, and how to ride a pony, and lots of other things," she announced in a rush. "Including how to behave like a proper young lady."

"Oh?" said George. "Do you misbehave?"

Isabella bit her lip "I sometimes say bad words."

The duke chuckled. "So do I. Soldiers swear like devils."

She looked relieved. "Jack is a great gun!" she announced. "I didn't like him at first because he tied me to a tree."

"A *tree*?" said the duke, shooting Jack a bemused look.

She nodded solemnly. "Yes, but I forgave him because it was the only way he could go rescue my best friend, Perry."

"Isabella." Alessandra intervened with a gentle reminder. "That is a story for some other time." So far, the duke had been remarkably calm in confronting the sudden changes in his youngest son's life. But subjecting him to a chattering child was a little like setting off sparks near a keg of gunpowder.

"On the contrary, I should like to hear the tale of how my son rescued your friend," said Ledyard.

Isabella grinned. "It's a *corking* good story."

The duke offered the little girl his hand. "Well then, let us find a quiet corner, missy, and you can tell me all about it." As he passed Jack, he gave a wink. "I hope you will soon be adding a few more troops to the ranks of my grandchildren. It's a little too quiet at Ledyard Manor these days. During holidays, it would be nice to have a whole regiment of bantlings."

"Yes, sir." Jack grinned.

"Now, about the tree, missy."

"Remember the time we hung Jack by his ankles in the old elm by the fountain?" said Edward as his father was led away by the little girl.

"Ha, ha, ha," chortled Charles. "It took the gardener over an hour to find him and cut him down."

"And then there was the time Wills lashed one of the garden statues to the donkey cart..."

Giving a grimace, George took his two closest brothers by the elbow and made a face at Charles. "I see a tray of decanters on the sideboard. I suggest we reminisce over a glass of port, and leave these two a moment to recover from the shellshock of our sudden appearance."

"I see where you learned your skills with rope," said Alessandra dryly, as Jack's siblings moved off.

Jack smiled, the slow, subtle curving of his lips sending a thrill of tiny shivers down her spine. "The only thing I intend to tie these days is the knot that binds you to me forever." In the spark of silent laughter his eyes were warm as melted chocolate. "Unless you have decided that the rabble of rowdy Pierson males is too daunting a force to join."

"Let me think about it for a moment." As his brows arched, she reached for her reticule and searched through its contents. "Ah." Withdrawing a coil of twine, she pressed it into his palm. "Shall we go find a tree?"

The laughter moved from his eyes to his lips. "As long as it's somewhere secluded," he murmured after a long and lush kiss. "My hands will not be cold as ice against your bare skin, my love, but I cannot promise that they won't be doing something extremely improper."

"*Si grande nero diavolo*—you big, black devil. It's a good thing my favorite color is black." Alessandra kissed the corner of his mouth. "You are painting a *very* naughty picture."

"Mmmm." He gave a wicked grin. "As you know, I am quite skilled with a brush. And at the moment I am imagining some very creative uses for soft sable bristles."

"I have a feeling that I'm going to enjoy learning all about art, and the infinite nuances of style and technique."

Enjoy a sneak peek at

*Cara Elliott's*

sizzling new romance!

Please turn this page
for a preview of

*To Tempt a Rake*

Available in March 2011

# Chapter One

"Ah, a naked lady. How lovely."

Katharine Kylie Woodbridge felt a whisper of breath tease against her neck, its gossamer touch warm and wicked on her bare flesh.

"A naked *statue*," she corrected. Ignoring the sardonic smile reflected in the diamond-paned glass, she carefully turned to the next painting in the portfolio.

The Conte of Como strolled a step closer and perched a hip on the edge of the library table. "It appears that Lord Giacomo has quite a talent for painting the female form," he drawled, leaning his well-tailored shoulder a little closer.

A little *too* close.

As heat speared through the thin layers of silk and wool, like a hot blade melting butter, Kate tried to quell the liquid quickening of her pulse. *Don't*, she warned herself. Oh, don't react. It would be flirting with danger—nay, utter disgrace—to encourage the attentions of Giovanni Marco Musto della Ghiradelli.

Of all the men in London, he was the only one who might recognize the truth...

"Do you not agree?" The conte—who preferred Marco to his more formal string of names—traced a fingertip along the deckled edge of the watercolor.

Perhaps if she were rude enough, she could make him go away.

"Indeed," replied Kate, keeping her voice deliberately cool. "Lord James is a highly accomplished artist." She paused a fraction. "How nice to see a gentleman apply himself to mastering a laudable skill. So many aristocrats idle away their lives in debauched revelries."

"I, too, have devoted a great deal of time to the serious study of feminine shape and proportion," replied Marco, a flutter of amusement shading his gaze.

*No man ought to have such long, luxurious lashes.* Or, for that matter, such exquisite brandy-gold eyes, or such a supremely sensual mouth. Kate quickly looked back at the painting. And it was *most* unfair of the Almighty to bless a rakehell rogue with beautiful bones and hair that tumbled in sin-black curls to kiss the ridge of his shoulders.

No wonder he was said to be the very devil with women.

"And I would say that Lord Giacomo could use a little work on sketching the shape of a lady's breast, *si*?" went on Marco. Lowering his aquiline nose to within inches of the textured paper, he made a show of studying the painting from several angles. "It's not quite perfect. Perhaps he should draw from life instead of inanimate stone." The indecently long lashes gave another silky swoosh. "After all, he now has a lovely model close at hand."

"What a *very* vulgar suggestion, sir," replied Kate, pinching back the urge to laugh with a thin-lipped frown. "Especially as the lady in question is your cousin."

"You don't think Lord Giacomo will be tempted to sketch his new bride in the nude?" asked Marco with a provocative smile. "As a connoisseur of Italian art, he seems to appreciate seeing the principles of symmetry and proportion stripped to their bare essentials."

The mention of body parts, clothed or otherwise, was absolutely forbidden in Polite Society, but as usual the conte seemed to take obscene delight in making a mockery of *English* manners. Which, in truth, was rather refreshing. She, too, found the all complex rituals and rules of the *ton* horribly constricting.

However, as she could never, ever admit that to Marco, Kate snapped the portfolio shut with an exaggerated grimace. "You are outrageously lewd, sir. And crude."

"So is Lord Byron," murmured Marco. "Yet women find him...intriguing, do they not?"

"That's because Lord Byron *is* intriguing. He writes wildly romantic poetry when he's not being naughty. While you—I shudder to think what you do when you're not flirting or drinking."

Marco rose and smoothed a wrinkle from his elegant trousers. "I might surprise you, *bella*."

Her eyes flared in alarm at the whisper of Italian. Dear God, surely he didn't suspect that there was any connection between a long-ago night in Naples and the present...

*No. Impossible.*

But all the more reason to keep him at arm's length.

Quickly masking her reaction with a mocking laugh, Kate hastened to add, "Ha! And pigs may fly."

"Have I made you angry?" His sensual mouth slid into a lazy smile. "Come, let us cry *pax*. I was merely trying to tease a touch of color to your cheeks with my banter."

"Your mere presence is enough to do that," retorted Kate. "Your arrogance is really quite intolerable."

Marco clapped a hand to his heart.

*Assuming that he had one*, thought Kate. The gossip among the ladies of London was that the conte possessed only one sensitive organ—and it was *not* located in the proximity of his chest.

"You wound me, Miss Kate-Katharine."

"Actually, I've only insulted you," she replied. "You are lucky I am wielding only my tongue and not a rapier. Else your voice would be an octave higher."

A casual flick of his wrist set the fobs on his watch chain to dancing against the silk of his waistcoat. "Trust me, Miss Kate-Katharine. If we were to cross blades, you would not come out on top."

To Kate's chagrin, she felt a fresh flush of heat rise to her face.

Marco slid a step closer and flashed a lascivious wink. "I am considered one of the best swordsmen in all of Europe."

Much as she wished to riposte with a clever retort, she found herself momentarily at a loss for words. For all his braggadocio, he wasn't exaggerating his skills with sharpened steel. Even if she hadn't known for a fact that he routinely bested Angelo, the premier fencing master in London, she would have guessed at his physical prowess. In her former life, she had learned to assess a man's strengths and weaknesses in one glance.

*And Marco?* His gestures were deceptively lazy, but

beneath the pose of an indolent idler, the conte moved with a predatory grace. *Like a lean, lithe panther.* A sleek wild animal, all whipcord muscle and coiled quickness.

But that was not the only reason he was dangerous...

Recovering her voice, Kate stepped back and slowly drew on her kidskin gloves. "What a pity we cannot put such a claim to the test." He was not the only one who could employ theatrics.

Marco watched the soft leather slide over her skin. "You could use one of those to slap me across the face and challenge me to a duel." The hint of laughter in his voice—a rumble redolent of aged brandy and smoky boudoirs—sent a tiny shiver prickling down her spine.

"Tempting," she said. "But I mustn't forget that I am a lady."

"There is no danger that such a fact will ever escape *my* mind, *cara*."

*Danger.* The word stirred another whispered warning inside her head. Kate averted her eyes, reminding herself that she mustn't encourage him to look too carefully at her features. The chances were razor-thin, but he just might remember...

"No doubt because you rarely think of anything but sex," she said tartly, trying to deflect his attention. "Do you never tire of the subject?"

At that, Marco laughed aloud. "On rare occasions I do think of other things."

"Now you *have* shocked me, sir."

"Not as much as you interest me, Miss Kate-Katharine—"

"Do stop calling me by that ridiculous moniker," she interrupted.

"Yes. It is." She raised her forefinger and crooked it up and down. "After all, without science, your steel might bend at an inopportune moment."

He was suddenly blocking her way. "I have heard of the phenomenon, but having never experienced it, I am not sure what could cause such a malfunction. Perhaps you would care to explain it to me?"

She gasped as his coat brushed against her breasts, the heat of him singeing through the silk. "*Nemernic.*"

The dark laugh sounded again, far too close for comfort. "I speak enough Romanian to know that I have just been called a *very* bad name." His wide, wicked mouth was now only a hairsbreadth from hers. "I thought you weren't going to forget that you are a lady."

"I—" Her words were cut off as his lips came down on hers. Their touch was shockingly sensual, like sun-warmed velvet stroking over the most sensitive spot of flesh.

The sensation held her in thrall, but only for a heartbeat. Recovering her wits, Kate struck a sharp uppercut to his jaw, her knuckles landing with a good deal more force than his teasing kiss.

Marco fell back a step. His nostrils flared as he drew in a taut breath and then he let it out slowly, looking oddly bemused. "Where did a gently bred female learn to punch like that?"

"Never mind," she muttered, surreptitiously flexing her fist. He had a *very* solid chin.

His nose quivered, like a bird dog on the hunt. "You smell like oranges and...something else."

*Damn.*

Before Marco could go on, a shadow slanted over the alcove.

"Oh, there you are, Kate." Alessandra della Giamatti—now Lady James Jacquehart Pierson, wife of the Duke of Ledyard's youngest son—paused in the oak-framed doorway, her new husband by her side. "Excuse me, are we interrupting a private conversation?"

"*Ciao*, Alessa," answered Marco. "No, your learned friend and I were just having a very stimulating discussion on fencing."

A tiny furrow formed between her brows as Alessandra spotted the lingering red welt on his jaw. "Fencing," she repeated softly.

"*Si*, and had I known science was such a provocative field of study, I would have asked to join your little group ages ago." He moved quickly to kiss her on both cheeks and added a rapid-fire volley of Italian. "You are more beautiful than ever this morning, *cara*. Marriage must agree with you."

"And you are more incorrigible than ever," murmured Alessandra, deflecting the sly innuendos with a wry smile. Turning to Kate, she said, "If my cousin is annoying you, feel free to tell him to *va' all' inferno.*"

*Go to hell.*

Kate made a face. "He's probably been there and back several times over."

"Aye." James Jacquehart Pierson chuckled. With his midnight locks, olive complexion, and muscled military bearing, he was known throughout London as 'Black Jack.' But Alessandra had assured Kate that he had a heart of gold. "I imagine that the Devil booted him back to our world, after finding him far too obnoxious to tolerate for any length of time."

"Izzz wrong?" he asked, greatly exaggerating his accent. "My cousin Alessandra calls you Kate and your maid calls you Katharine. Knowing the English fondness for double names, I assumed—"

"Please spare me the long-winded explanations." As she preferred a more informal name to 'Katharine,' she was called 'Kate' by her close friends. Among whom the Conte of Como did not number. "And please address me properly. To you, I am 'Miss Woodbridge.'"

"Propriety is so boring," he murmured. "I should think that a lady of your intellectual inquisitiveness would agree."

Ignoring the remark, Kate stepped away from the display table. "If you will excuse me, I must find the bride and groom and take my leave."

"Why the rush back to London? Most of the wedding guests are staying until tomorrow."

"Charlotte has a lecture on medieval metallurgy to prepare for the Mayfair Institute of History and Science." The elderly scholar was, like herself, a member of the Circle of Scientific Sibyls, a small group of intellectual females who met each week to share their knowledge. And their friendship.

Given that the *ton* did not approve of serious learning for ladies, the five members had taken to calling themselves by a more informal moniker—the Circle of Sin. Kate felt a small smile twitch at the corners of her mouth. Without the stalwart support of the 'Sinners' over the past year, she wasn't quite sure how she would have navigated through the uncharted waters of Polite Society.

"Sounds fascinating," drawled Marco.

Marco contrived to look hurt. "And here I thought we were *amicos*, Lord Giacomo."

"Friends?" Jack arched a dark brow. "Don't press your luck, Ghiradelli. Your presence here is tolerable. Barely. In fact..."

Leaving the men to their verbal sparring, Kate drew Alessandra into one of the arched alcoves and brushed a kiss to her cheek. "Much as I hate to agree with your cousin on anything, you do look glorious. And happy."

"I am," replied Alessandra. Which for her was a notable display of emotion. Of all the 'Sinners,' she was the most reserved about her feelings and her past, even with her closest friends.

*With good reason*, acknowledged Kate. Alessandra had a dark secret from her past life in Italy that had recently come to light and threatened to destroy both her and her young daughter. But Black Jack Pierson, a highly decorated veteran of the Peninsular campaign, had proved his mettle in love as well as war by vanquishing a cunning enemy and winning her heart.

Glancing at the rows of leatherbound books, Kate felt her lips quirk. *Just like a storybook hero*. What a pity that a noble knight could not transform from ink and paper to flesh and blood.

Not that any mortal man could slay her dragon. Some secrets were worse than others...

Forcing a smile, Kate gave a light laugh. "We are all so delighted for you."

Alessandra squeezed her hand. "Without the Circle of Sin, I don't know how I would have survived the last few months."

"That is what friends are for." She paused, feeling a little pang of regret that she would be leaving Ledyard Manor that afternoon. "Speaking of which, I was just coming to tell you that Charlotte is anxious to return to London, on account of her upcoming lecture."

"Of course." Alessandra slanted a look at Jack and Marco, who were still exchanging barbs. "Come, let us fetch Ciara and Ariel from the conservatory, and visit her room while she finishes her packing."

The idea of circling their little group, if only for a short while, lifted Kate's spirits. "What an excellent suggestion. You don't mind leaving Jack to fend for himself?"

"Oh, once he and Marco stop needling each other, they will actually enjoy conversing on Roman art and antiquities. For all of my cousin's frivolous teasing, he is very knowledgeable on the subject."

"I never would have guessed that the conte had any interest in intellectual subjects," she replied slowly.

"Marco has a number of unexpected facets to his character, which he takes great pains to hide." Alessandra's voice took on a wry note. "But then, who am I to talk?"

Kate hesitated for a moment before answering. "I daresay we all have things that we keep to ourselves."

*Let her go.*

Assuming an expression of bored indifference, Marco slowly looked away from watching the two ladies walk off.

"Set your sights elsewhere," murmured Jack, as if reading his mind. "You may be her cousin, but Alessandra will chop off your *testicolos* and feed them to the Tower ravens if you try to play your usual wicked games with Miss Woodbridge."

Though he was thinking much the same thing, Marco reacted with a cynical smirk. "What makes you think she wouldn't welcome my attentions?"

"The fact that you are a conceited coxcomb and your arrogance is insufferable at times."

"*Si*." Marco widened his mouth to a wolfish grin. "But most females find that intriguing."

"Alessandra's friends are not like most females," pointed out Jack. "Their intellect sets them apart, so you can't expect to charm them with your usual approach." He paused. "I imagine that Miss Woodbridge is smart enough to see that you are an arse."

"Trust me, Lord Giacomo, I don't need advice on flirting from you."

"No? Well, from what I have observed, you don't appear to be making much progress on your own."

Leaning a shoulder to the fluted molding, Marco watched the last little flutter of seagreen silk disappear down the corridor. To be sure, Kate Woodbridge was no ordinary young lady. But it was not just her brains that set her apart. There was an unexpected glint of grittiness shading her lovely aquamarine eyes. As if she had seen the grim realities of the world outside of the gilded confines of Mayfair's mansions.

Which was, of course, highly unlikely. Kate was the granddaughter of the Duke of Cluyne, one of the highest sticklers of Polite Society. She had been born into a life of wealth and privilege, and was surrounded by an army of servants ready to do her bidding.

Such coddled innocence bored him to perdition. *So why did the sway of her shapely hips provoke the urge to follow?*

"Perhaps I haven't tried very hard," drawled Marco, turning his attention to the folds of his cravat. Smoothing a finger over the folds, he added, "It's hardly a fair match of skills. And contrary to what you may think, I do not deliberately toy with an innocent young lady's affections."

Jack gave a mock grimace. "Good God, you mean to say that you have a conscience?"

Marco straightened from his slouch. "You military heroes are not the only ones with a code of honor."

"Well, you need not wage any great moral battle with your self-proclaimed noble scruples. According to Alessandra, her friend can look out for herself."

Marco let out a grunt of laughter. "Miss Woodbridge may be clever and possess a cutting tongue, but that does not mean she is equipped to deal with the darker side of life." He curled a lip. "Rapscallion roués, jaded fortune hunters. Or rakehell rogues like me."

"Don't be so sure of that," countered Jack. "From what I gather, Miss Woodbridge has had a rather eccentric up-bringing. Her mother tossed away title and fortune to elope with an American sea captain. She's spent most of her life sailing around the world."

He felt his sardonic smile thin ever so slightly. His cousin had not talked much with him about her friends. No doubt feeling that he couldn't quite be trusted with the intimate details of their lives.

"The fact is, I think she had a rather rough time of it these last few years," continued Jack. "Her parents died of a fever within days of each other, and only a deathbed promise to them brought Miss Woodbridge here to seek a reconciliation with her grandfather." He shrugged.

"Apparently the waters at Cluyne House are anything but calm. She's fiercely independent, which tends to make waves with the duke."

"That begins to explain her salty language," murmured Marco thoughtfully. Today was not the first time she had let fly with a very unladylike word.

Jack chuckled. "Alessandra says she can swear like a sailor in nearly a dozen different dialects."

"Interesting."

"Yes, but not nearly as interesting as the collection of rare books I have here on classical architecture." For Jack, ancient Rome was a far more fascinating topic of conversation than Katharine Kylie Woodbridge. "Come, there is a seventeenth-century volume of engravings on the Temple of Jupiter that I want to show you..."

Marco reluctantly pushed aside all thoughts about ladies—naked or otherwise—to follow Jack to one of the display tables set by the bank of leaded glass windows. Yet, somehow the tantalizing scent of Sicilian *neroli* and wild thyme stayed with him, teasing at his nostrils.

Strange, it seemed hauntingly familiar, but he just couldn't place it.

*And no wonder*, he thought, dismissing the notion with a sardonic shrug. He had inhaled too many perfumes in his wicked, wanton life to recall them all. In truth, none of the women had been very memorable.

Save for one clever whore in Naples who had dared...

"Pay attention, Ghiradelli. If you drool on that Doric column, I swear, I shall cut off your tongue."

# THE DISH

*Where authors give you the inside scoop!*

♥ ♥ ♥ ♥ ♥ ♥ ♥ ♥ ♥ ♥ ♥ ♥ ♥ ♥ ♥ ♥

*From the desk of Margaret Mallory*

Dear Readers,

Am I unkind? I made Sir James Rayburn wait until the third book in my All the King's Men trilogy to get his own story. First, as a toddler, he watched his mother find love with her KNIGHT OF DESIRE, William FitzAlan. Then, as a young squire, he played a supporting role to his uncle Stephen, the KNIGHT OF PLEASURE, in his quest for true love. And now, when I finally give this brave and honorable knight his own book, I let the girl he loves stomp on his heart in the prologue.

After that unfortunate experience, all Jamie Rayburn wants—or so he says—is a virtuous wife who will keep a quiet, ordered home waiting for him while he is off fighting. Instead, I give him the bold and beautiful Linnet, whose determination to avenge her family is bound to provoke endless tumult and trouble. Worse, this heroine is the very lady who stomped on Jamie's heart in his youth.

Why would I do this to our gallant knight? After he has shown such patience, why not reward him with the sweet, undemanding heroine he requested? Although that heroine might prove to be a trifle dull, she would be content to gaze raptly at our hero as he told tales of his victories by the hearth.

Truly, I meant to give Jamie a softer, easier woman. But when I tried to write Jamie's story, Linnet decided she *had* to be there. And when Linnet sets her mind to something, believe me, it's best not to stand in her way.

Besides, Linnet was right. Who better to save Jamie from a staid and tedious life? No other woman stirs Jamie's passion as she does. And what passion! If our handsome knight must contend with murderous plots, court intrigues, and a few sword-wielding sorcerers before he can win his heart's desire, then so be it.

I am sure Jamie forgives me. Our KNIGHT OF PAS-SION knows a happy ending is worth the wait—and it's all the more satisfying if it doesn't come easy.

I hope you enjoy reading Jamie and Linnet's adventurous love story as much as I enjoyed writing it!

*Margaret Mallory*

www.margaretmallory.com

♥            ♥            ♥

## From the desk of Robyn DeHart

Dear Readers,

Who out there isn't fascinated by the lost continent of Atlantis? The legend is as compelling as Jack the Ripper and El Dorado, those unsolved mysteries that have been perplexing people for hundreds of years. But it was Atlantis that captured my attention for the second book in my Legend Hunters series, DESIRE ME.

With Atlantis, you have a little bit of everything—Greek mythology, hidden treasures, and utopian societies. I couldn't help but add my own flair to the myth and make my Atlantis home to the fabled Fountain of Youth. Add in an ancient prophecy, a lost map, and Sabine Tobias, a heroine who is a living, breathing descendent to the Atlanteans—and you've got a recipe for adventure coupled with plenty of trouble.

But what does any damsel in distress need? A good hero. A sexy-as-hell, smart-mouthed hero who is, shall we say, good with his hands. That is, he's handy to have around when you're stuck in an underground chamber or when you need to slip into an old estate without being seen. Enter Maxwell Barrett, legend hunter extraordinaire and expert on all things Atlantis.

With DESIRE ME, I return to my series about Solomon's, the exclusive gentleman's club of Legend Hunters. This book was, at times, harrowing to write, but not nearly as dangerous for me, the writer, who sat safely at home in my jammies with my faithful kitties to keep me company. Poor Max and Sabine, though, are on a perilous race against time, trying to solve the ancient prophecy before a nasty villain destroys them both. But they find themselves neck deep in trouble about as often as they find themselves wrapped in one another's arms.

Visit my website, www.RobynDeHart.com, for contests, excerpts, and more.

Robyn DeHart